ENRAPTURED

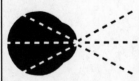

This Large Print Book carries the
Seal of Approval of N.A.V.H.

SECRETS OF THE LOCH

ENRAPTURED

CANDACE CAMP

THORNDIKE PRESS
A part of Gale, Cengage Learning

GALE
CENGAGE Learning®

Farmington Hills, Mich • San Francisco • New York • Waterville, Maine
Meriden, Conn • Mason, Ohio • Chicago

GALE
CENGAGE Learning®

LIBRARY OF CONGRESS CATALOGING-IN-PUBLICATION DATA

Names: Camp, Candace, author.
Title: Enraptured / by Candace Camp.
Description: Large print edition. | Waterville, Maine : Thorndike Press, 2016. |
© 2016 | Series: Secrets of the loch ; #3 | Series: Thorndike Press large print core
Identifiers: LCCN 2015050204 | ISBN 9781410488121 (hardcover) | ISBN 1410488128 (hardcover)
Subjects: LCSH: Large type books. | GSAFD: Love stories.
Classification: LCC PS3553.A4374 E57 2016 | DDC 813/.54—dc23
LC record available at http://lccn.loc.gov/2015050204

Published in 2016 by arrangement with Pocket Books, an imprint of Simon & Schuster, Inc.

Printed in Mexico
1 2 3 4 5 6 7 20 19 18 17 16

For Barbara and Sharon,
the best sisters ever.

ACKNOWLEDGMENTS

Thanks once again to the wonderful team at Pocket, especially my super-editor, Abby, whose patience and advice are invaluable through my periods of indecision. Also, I am in awe of the art department and their beautiful cover for the original publisher's edition. You guys knocked it out of the ballpark.

I couldn't do any of this without Maria Carvainis and her crew at the Maria Carvainis Agency.

Thanks most of all to Pete and Stacy. You're always there for me.

PROLOGUE

"Faye. *Mo cuishle.*"

Faye heard his voice, soft and insistent, and joy leapt in her. "Malcolm?"

Her mother bent over her bedside, her forehead creased in worry. "What? Faye? Did you say aught?"

"Nae. Nothing." Tears shimmered in Faye's golden eyes. She had only imagined his voice. Malcolm was gone. She knew it, had known it deep inside a long time. She would soon be gone as well. "I'm sae tired."

Nan Munro wiped Faye's face with a cool rag. "It was a lang, hard birth."

Birth. "The bairn?"

"Aye, love." Nan smiled, though tears were in her eyes as well. "She's a bonny lass. A guid set of lungs, too. Hear her?" Nan cocked her head at the sound of the baby's cry across the room.

"Aye." Faye stirred. A sharp pain was between her legs, a soreness all through her abdomen. Her breasts were full and aching. It was nothing like the ache she felt when Malcolm touched her, the yearning for his touch. "It hurts."

"You lost a lot of blood, lass." Nan frowned. "The bairn is hungry. You maun feed her. Can you hold her?"

Faye nodded, eagerness and yearning rising in her. "Aye. Gie her to me."

Her mother laid the baby in the crook of Faye's arm. A small, red-faced scrap of a thing, wrapped around with a blanket, howled, her feet and hands flailing. Her eyes were scrunched closed, and her chin wobbled piteously. Her hair was plastered wetly to her head.

"She's beautiful," Faye whispered, and tears slid from her eyes.

"There, there. Dinna cry, Faye love. She *is* beautiful. And you maun feed the wee thing."

Faye bared her breast and lifted the baby to it. The child instinctively nuzzled into her and began to suckle. A wondrous peace and joy twined through Faye. She stroked her finger across the baby's wondrously soft cheek. Her daughter. Their daughter. But Malcolm would never see her.

"I will name her Janet."

When the babe fell asleep, satiated, Faye's

10

mother came to take her. Faye tightened her arms around Janet for an instant, then let her go.

"I've made you some broth."

"Nae, I canna." Faye turned her head away.

Nan grimaced. "That boy David's outside, asking to see you."

"He's not the one, Ma. Dinna blame Davey."

"Och, I know that." Nan stroked a hand over her daughter's. "Is there anyone you want to see? Is *he* . . ."

"Nae. He is no' here; he never will be. Let Davey in."

Her mother sighed. "He canna stay lang, you ken. You maun rest."

David came to the side of the bed. His face was drawn, his eyes swimming with tears. He knows, she thought, that I am not here for long.

"Davey."

"Faye." His smile was almost as wobbly as the bairn's chin. "How are you?"

"No' good."

"Nae, dinna say that. You'll be fine. A few days. You'll see."

"Will you do something for me?"

"Anything. You know that."

"Reach here." She patted the edge of the

11

bed. "Beneath the mattress."

He looked puzzled but bent down and reached tentatively under the mattress. His face changed. "I found something." He pulled it out and stared at it. "A book."

"Aye, it's for my bairn. What she needs to know. Take it and gie it tae her when she's auld enough. Will you do that for me, Davey? Will you keep it safe for me?"

"Aye, of course." Tears shone in his eyes. "But you willna die. I'll gie it back when you're well again."

"Thank you. I knew I could count on you."

"Always, Faye."

After Davey left, she dreamed of Malcolm. He was with her, his big hand wrapped around hers, telling her to be patient. "Soon," he said. She heard the rumble of his voice in his chest, as she used to when she lay with him. She felt his warmth encircling her.

Then her mother was at the bed again, pulling back the covers to change the folded pad beneath Faye. "You maun stop," she heard Nan say, her voice shaking. "You canna lose more blood."

Faye wanted to open her eyes and tell her mother not to cry. It was hard to leave the bairn, but she welcomed the peace.

12

Later still, her mother put the baby in her arms again, and Janet began to suckle. Faye opened her eyes at the sweet sensation and gazed down at her daughter. The wee thing had red hair. Not her own black nor Malcolm's blond. No one would guess, and that was good. Her mother took away the bairn, and Faye's arms were empty without her.

She had no sense of time any longer. Malcolm was there in front of her, smiling. The edges of her vision were growing dark; only he was in the light. Faye wanted to tell him that she had done as he asked. She had hidden what he'd entrusted to her where none could find it save her child, the one who would carry their legacy, their duty.

But of course he already knew. He was waiting for her. Soon the pain would be gone. She would rest in his arms again.

"Malcolm." Her lips moved, the sound that floated out on her last breath too soft to hear. *Mo cuishle.*

1

October 20, 1807

The coach lurched through another rut. Violet grabbed the leather strap above her head, hanging on grimly. She was beginning to think this journey through Scotland would never end. She tucked her hands back inside her fur muff, deciding that sliding about on the seat was preferable to frozen fingers.

Thank heavens for the muff, a remnant of her life in her father's house. After all these years, it was a mite bedraggled, but it still kept her hands toasty. Her practical flannel petticoats and woolen carriage dress were warm as well. She wished she could say the same for her ice-cold feet. It was not that she was unused to difficult weather or rough travel; she had accompanied Lionel to other sites throughout Britain, subjecting herself to every extreme of cold, heat, and rain. But she had not been prepared for how cold it was in late October in the Highlands of Scotland.

Still, she had been right to come early, instead of waiting for spring as Uncle Lionel would have done if he were still alive. Her situation was entirely different now. Violet swallowed hard at the thought of her mentor. She would *not* cry. Lionel himself would have pointed out that it was ineffective and unnecessary. Her tears would not bring him back, and she must not arrive at her future patron's home looking woebegone and red-eyed. She had to be firm, strong, and professional if she hoped to convince the earl that she was the person most fit to take her uncle's place.

It was vital that she seize this opportunity before other antiquarians heard of it. Before the Earl of Mardoun learned of her uncle's death and offered the ruins to someone he deemed more worthy — in short, to a man.

Violet suppressed a sigh. It was no use thinking of the inequities of life. She was accustomed to the ways of the world. She had long since learned that she must struggle for everything she accomplished. Only Lionel had accepted her abilities.

At a muffled shout, the carriage halted abruptly, sending Violet sliding from her seat and onto the floor of the post chaise.

She sat up, a trifle stunned, hearing more voices, followed by a loud crack. Was that a gun? Violet jumped to her feet and flung open the door.

"What in the —" She stopped, her mouth dropping open at the scene before her.

It was dark, for evening fell early here, and the scene was illuminated by only the lantern in the postboy's trembling hand. The lad was huddled on the lead horse, bundled up against the cold till only his reddened nose and wide, frightened eyes were visible above the woolen scarf. Two men blocked the narrow roadway, facing the post chaise, four others to the side of the road. They were attired in similar bulky clothing, hats pulled low on their heads and thick woolen scarves wrapped around their necks and lower faces, making it almost impossible to discern their features in the poor light. It was easy to see, however, that one of them held a musket trained on the postboy, and two more carried pistols.

Anger surged in Violet. "What do you think you're doing? Stand aside and let us pass."

"Och! A wee Sassenach," one of the men cried gleefully, his words muffled by the scarf.

Between his thick accent and the cloth

covering his mouth, Violet could make little sense of what he said, but she understood the word *wee* well enough, and it added fuel to the fire of her anger.

"Get out of my way." Violet's eyes flashed. "I do not think the Earl of Mardoun will be pleased that you detained his guest." *Guest,* of course, was stretching the truth since Mardoun had no idea she was coming, but the principle was the same.

"Oooh, the Earl of Mardoun, is it? Noo I'm shaking in my boots." He laughed, and the men around him joined in. "Throw doon your jewels, lassie, and your purse, too. Then we'll let you gae on your way . . . if you ask nicely."

"I haven't any jewels." Her chin jutted stubbornly. She had precious little money in her reticule either after paying the expenses of this journey. If she gave it up, she would be utterly penniless.

"What's those bobs in your ears, then!" He gestured at her with his pistol.

Violet's hands flew up to her ears, knocking her bonnet back. "My grandmother's drops! No! Absolutely not."

The man's jaw dropped in surprise at her defiance and so did his pistol hand, so that for an instant Violet thought she might have won the day, but then he scowled and started toward her. "Maybe you're wanting to pay me some ither way."

Violet knew that her fury and, yes, fear had carried her too far, but though her stomach clenched with dread, she reached back inside the carriage and grabbed her umbrella, turning to face her opponent. Again the man halted in astonishment. One of the men let out a hoot, and everyone laughed.

Her enemy's face darkened, and he rushed forward. Violet swung with all her might, and the umbrella whacked into the side of his head. He let out a screech and stumbled back. But her umbrella had snapped beneath the blow. Violet had no idea what she would do now. She braced herself.

Suddenly, with a shout, a large man hurtled out of the darkness into the circle of light cast by the postboy's lantern. He charged straight toward Violet.

Startled, Violet swept down the umbrella as hard as she could, though its being broken rendered the blow feeble. In the next instant, she realized that the newcomer had grabbed not her, but the fellow who had accosted her.

Her apparent rescuer turned to her in astonishment, still holding the front of her attacker's jacket with one hand, and reached up with the other to yank the umbrella from her hand. "What is the matter with you? I'm trying to help you!" He tossed the umbrella onto the carriage floor behind her and turned back to the man he still held in place with one huge fist. Digging his hands into her attacker's jacket, he lifted him up so that only his toes touched the ground. "What the bloody hell are you doing, Will?"

For once bereft of words, Violet could only stare at her rescuer. He was a behemoth, towering over everyone else. His wide shoulders owed little to the heavy jacket he wore, and his broad, long-fingered hands held the other man up as if he weighed no more than a child. Seemingly impervious to the elements, he wore no muffler or cap, and his jacket hung open down the front. His thick, tousled hair glowed golden in the light of the lantern.

He shoved the man he called Will to the other side of the road, saying disgustedly, "Is this what you've come to?" He moved his scornful gaze over the row of men. "Preying on travelers like a band of reivers! Robbing innocent women! I'm ashamed to call you Highlanders. Look at her." He swung his hand toward Violet. "She's just a wee lassie! Hardly bigger than a child."

"Wee!" Violet bristled at his description of her.

He swung around and glared. "Aye, wee. And apparently mad as a hatter as well. Canna you see I'm trying to *help* you? What the devil is your husband thinking, letting you jaunt about the countryside alone at night? The man should have better sense."

"Let me? Let me?" Violet stiffened. "Fortunately, I am not married, so I need no man's permission to go where I please and do what I want. I make my own decisions about my life. And I may be 'wee,' but I am no child. Just because I'm not . . . a . . . a *giant* doesn't mean I'm not capable of taking care of myself."

He swept his eyes down her in one swift, encompassing glance. At some other time, Violet might have found his strong features handsome, but at the moment, she saw nothing except the scorn in his eyes. His mouth quirked up on one side. "Oh, aye, I can see that you are doing splendidly. No doubt your broken umbrella would hold off any number of men."

"I don't need you." Violet knew her words were untrue, even silly, but she was too angry to be reasonable. Primed as she was for battle and with a lifetime of male belittling to fuel her wrath, this huge, supremely confident man's dismissal of her sparked her fury. Her hands clenched. She had a strong desire to hit him.

"Do you not?" His eyes widened, something between heat and challenge flashing in them before he drew his brows together in a scowl. "I dinna ken whether you're blind or silly, but there is only one of you — one small one — and you wouldna have won this fight."

"I did not ask for your help."

One of the men chuckled, spurring her aggravation.

"Nae, you dinna," her rescuer shot back. "And I am beginning to regret offering it. Now would you cease this jabbering and get back in your carriage and let me handle this?" He swung around, effectively dismissing her, and addressed the other men again. "Give up this idiocy before the lot of you wind up with your necks in a noose." He gestured toward the men blocking the carriage's way, and they dropped their gazes, shuffling over to the side of the road. "Rob Grant, what would your gran say if she knew you were out frightening young lassies like this?" One of the robbers turned his head away, easing back behind the others. "And Dennis MacLeod. You should be ashamed of yourself. You've a wife and bairns at home."

The man lifted his chin. "Aye, and I hae to provide for them."

"Then you best be tending to your croft, hadn't you? Stealing from travelers won't mend the thatch on your roof. And May and the bairn will be hard-pressed to raise the crops alone next spring while you're sitting in gaol."

"That's all easy for you to say, Coll, now that you're one of *them,*" Will said.

One of *whom,* Violet wondered — and was Coll her rescuer's name? It seemed odd, but then, there was nothing about this situation that was not odd.

"Sitting all snug and bonny, aren't you?" Will went on bitterly. "Carrying out his lordship's orders. You used to be one of us."

"I am not one of *them,*" Coll retorted in a goaded voice. "I'm of this glen, same as I've always been. I dinna take on this job for him. I did it for the crofters. There willna be any more families tossed out of their homes."

The other man let out a snort of disbelief. "For how long?"

"For as long as I've breath in this body. Dinna try me, Will. I have no hope for you any longer; you're on your way to the gallows as fast and straight as you can go. But

I willna let you take the others with you." Coll took a long step forward. "Is that clear?"

"Aye." Will set his jaw, not meeting Coll's gaze.

"Then be off." He swept them all with an encompassing gaze, then crossed his arms and waited. The other men began to melt back into the trees. In moments, they were gone.

Violet watched with a jaundiced eye. It must be handy to be able to shake others into submission. Authority came easily to such a man. He had saved her and she must be grateful for that. But she had too often been shoved into the background by men who were louder, larger, and stronger than she to like this bully who had come to her rescue. His obvious contempt for her rankled. Like all men, he did not see her as a person in her own right, but only a possession of a husband or father.

He swung back to her. Disconcertingly, even though she stood on the step of the carriage, his face was level with hers.

"Are you going to issue orders to me now?" Violet arched a brow, her hands on her hips.

He took in her pugnacious stance and, irritatingly, smiled. "You are a bonny bruiser, are you not? Nae, I have no orders for you, though someone should have taken better care of you."

"*I* take care of myself. I am a grown woman."

"Aye, I can see that for myself." Casually he planted one hand on the carriage, leaning against it. "Still, you're a stranger to the Highlands. And these roads."

"I have become quite well acquainted with these roads, believe me."

His mouth twitched, but he said only, "You shouldna be out here at night. It's dangerous."

"Are you threatening me now?"

"What?" He stared. "You think I would harm you? I'm the one who just came to your rescue, if you'll recall."

"You chased off one set of thieves. But how am I to know you were not simply eliminating the competition?"

"Och, but you've a bitter tongue on you. Most people would have been grateful for my aid."

"I'm sorry. No doubt I should have fainted. Or perhaps you expect payment?"

"A simple 'thank you' would have sufficed. But I can see there's little likelihood of that. So I'll choose payment." One large hand clamped around her nape, holding her still, and he leaned in to kiss her.

The touch of his lips was brief and soft, and it sent a shiver through her. Violet's lips parted in surprise. He raised his head, and his eyes roamed her face, settling on her lips. "I think perhaps my price has gone up."

His mouth came down on hers again. He tasted her, the kiss slow and lingering. His tongue teased along the parting of her lips, then slipped inside to caress and explore. Heat surged in Violet, every sense suddenly wildly alive. She had never felt anything like this before, and the onslaught of heat and pleasure stunned her.

He made a low, satisfied sound deep in his throat, and his arm came down to curl around her waist. "Sweet," he murmured against her lips.

The word shot through her, waking her from her daze. Sweet. Wee. Melting in his strong, masculine arms.

Violet jerked out of his grasp and jumped back into the carriage, calling to the postboy to drive on. The vehicle rumbled away, leaving Coll staring after it in surprise. Violet did not look back.

She crossed her arms, unsure if her trembling was the result of the cold or delayed fright or the strange, delicious sensations that had flooded through her. The man was impertinent. Forward. Overbearing. Rude. Crude. Obviously the sort who was accustomed to shouldering his way through life, expecting men to stand aside and women to fall into his arms. And why not? That was exactly what had happened.

Shame washed over Violet. How could she have reacted like that? She had spent all her life fighting men's opinion of women as weak, emotional, and incompetent, yet in an instant she had thrown it all away. She had been scared and in need of rescue, and when he kissed her, she had not even had the fortitude to push him away. No, she had just stood there, helpless, betrayed by her own body, while he held her still and took what he wanted.

No, he had not taken; she had been happy to give it to him. Indeed, she had been on the verge of throwing her arms around him and asking for more. Violet closed her eyes, remembering the feel of his mouth on hers, the velvet softness, the way his lips had moved over hers, the touch of his tongue. She let out a soft noise that was as much pleasure as anger. She barely paid attention to the village as the post chaise rolled through it and turned off onto a smaller road. She was too busy trying to calm her racing pulse and banish the heat that pooled low in her abdomen. It would be disastrous to face her new employer in this shaken, frayed, tender state.

Violet took a calming breath and then another. That was a little better. At least she had, in the end, come to her senses and pulled away from him. She recalled the look of astonishment on his face as she jumped back into the carriage, and she felt a certain grim satisfaction. No doubt he was unused to being rejected by any woman. He was far too handsome for that.

She closed her eyes, picturing the glint of his hair in the low light — too long and untidy to be fashionable. What color were his eyes? It had been too dark to tell. But she had seen that firm chin well enough . . . the square jaw . . . the broad shoulders. Unconsciously she let out a sigh.

He was massive, his hands huge. Yet the fingers that had curled around her nape had held her gently. His lips had been unbearably soft, his mouth seeking, not demanding. Pleasure curled in her abdomen all over again at the memory. Long ago she had been kissed by the man she had almost been foolish enough to marry, but it had felt nothing like that.

How delicious Coll had tasted. If she had let herself throw her arms around him, she knew his muscles would have been thick and hard beneath her touch. She imagined sinking her fingers into his arms. His shoulders. His back. She thought of his deep, rumbling voice, softened by a Scottish burr. It had rolled through her like warm honey.

The voice had fit the man — outsize and solid, reassuring. She wondered who he was. His clothes had not been those of a gentleman. They had been rougher, plainer, like a worker's garments. Yet something about his speech had set him apart from the other men.

It was not just that his accent was less thick; something in his words, in his turn of phrase, spoke of . . . gentility? No, that was not quite right; he had clearly called himself one of them. Education, perhaps? Violet smiled to herself. No, there was nothing of the narrow, hunched academic in that man's broad shoulders.

The carriage turned, and she pulled herself from her wayward thoughts, lifting the curtain to look out. They were approaching a pair of tall, ornate gates, opened wide. She straightened and peered in front of her as the vehicle rumbled down a long drive. Trees grew close to the road on either side, but finally they emerged onto a wide lawn. An enormous mansion loomed before her. Violet craned her neck to look up at the ornate towers atop the castle — there was no other word for it, with its crenellations and turrets. The post chaise pulled to a stop in front of a set of massive double doors.

For a moment, Violet feared her courage might fail her. But she squared her shoulders, wrapped her cloak around her, and stepped down from the carriage. There was more wind up here than there had been in the valley below, and it sliced through her, tugging at her cloak and hat as she mounted the steps to the front doors. The house was utterly dark; no lights shone in the myriad of windows, not even a glow through the drapes or around the edges.

Violet raised the ornate knocker and banged it firmly against its plate. After a long moment with no response, she gave it several more sharp raps. At last one of the heavy doors opened, revealing a young man holding a lamp in one hand.

"I am Lady Violet Thornhill," she said briskly. She had learned long ago that one could not show any sign of hesitation or lack of confidence if one hoped to be taken seriously. "I am here to see Lord Mardoun."

The young man gaped at her. A woman's voice sounded faintly somewhere in the house behind the man, and with a look of relief he turned away. "Mrs. Ferguson! Some lass is here tae sae the earl."

"What nonsense is this?" He stepped back as an older woman appeared at the door. Mrs. Ferguson was a square, substantial woman wrapped in a heavy flannel dressing gown. Her hair, liberally sprinkled with iron gray, hung braided in one thick plait over her shoulder. She regarded Violet suspiciously. "What do you think you're doing, pounding on people's doors at all hours of the night?"

"It is barely eight o'clock." Violet returned an equally steely gaze. "I am here to see Lord Mardoun."

"Well, you have nae chance of that. Go on with you now." Mrs. Ferguson made as if to close the door, but Violet hastily slipped inside.

"I am here at the express invitation of Lord Mardoun." That was stretching it, but the man *had* invited Lionel, and Lionel would have brought Violet with him if he had been able to come.

Mrs. Ferguson crossed her arms, blocking Violet's entry farther into the foyer. "That's a puzzle, then, since his lordship is not here."

"Not here!" Violet's stomach sank. "What do you mean? Will he be gone long?"

31

"Aye. He's in Italy on his honeymoon. As you would know if you were a friend of Lord Mardoun's." With a triumphant expression, Mrs. Ferguson began to close the door.

"No, wait." Violet dug in her reticule and pulled out her silver, chased card case, extracting one of her calling cards. "I did not say I was a friend of Lord Mardoun. But he is acquainted with me. I am Lady Violet Thornhill."

The mention of her title had the intended effect. Mrs. Ferguson paused, took the card, and perused it, frowning. Violet dug in her reticule again and found the earl's letter.

"This is Lord Mardoun's invitation to my mentor, Mr. Lionel Overton, to visit and examine the ancient ruins on his estate. You can see it is written in his hand. Here, read it."

Mrs. Ferguson drew herself up and said frostily, "It is not my place to read his lordship's letters."

"Then surely it is not your place to turn away Lord Mardoun's guests, either." Violet was pleased to see uncertainty flicker across Mrs. Ferguson's face. She pressed her advantage. "If his lordship is not in residence, who is in charge of Duncally?"

"I am the housekeeper here."

"Does that leave you responsible for deciding whether or not you will refuse Lord Mardoun's hospitality? He delegated such authority to you?" Violet felt a twinge of remorse at adopting her father's aristocratic, contemptuous tone. But she could not fail after she had come so far.

The housekeeper turned to the footman, still hovering in the background. "Jamie, fetch Munro."

The young man beat a hasty retreat. Mrs. Ferguson regarded Violet stonily. Violet, affecting an air of unconcern, sat down on the hall bench. Minutes dragged by. There was no sound but that of a large clock striking the hour. Finally, she heard a door closing somewhere in the back recesses of the house, and heavy footsteps came toward them.

Violet turned toward the sound and saw a tall blond man stride into the room. Her stomach sank.

He came to an abrupt halt, his brows drawing together thunderously. "You!"

2

Coll stared at the woman by the front door. He had thought the night could not get any worse, but clearly it had.

He had set out this evening just to have a wee dram at the tavern, but before he reached the village, a lad came running to tell him what that idiot Will Ross was up to. Coll had had to clean up the messy situation first — and that strange, infuriating woman had berated him for rescuing her! Then he had acted completely unlike himself, grabbing her and kissing her even though it was abundantly clear that she wanted nothing to do with him.

It wasn't like him. Lord knows she was a tempting, shapely morsel of a woman, and Coll enjoyed the touch of a woman's lips as well as any man. But he did not grab a woman and kiss her without even a by-your-leave, especially not a lady he'd never before met — and if he had been in the habit of doing so, his sister would long ago have had his head for it.

But somehow, standing there looking at the bad-tempered, sweet-featured English-woman, he was unable to resist. He'd meant only a teasing peck, a joking challenge. Then he tasted her — sweet and tart mingled in a velvety, alluring softness. And he had had to know her mouth — to inveigle and entice and explore. She responded, initial surprise giving way to her own tentative exploration, and that sent desire humming through him.

Until she pulled away and took off like the hounds of hell were after her. Clearly one of them was insane, but Coll was not sure which. Maybe both.

When he had finally trudged back to the tavern, it was impossible to have a drink in peace, what with everyone wanting to know what Will Ross had done, and Cuddy Hamilton pointing out that it would never have happened if only Coll had stayed with the lads, and Dot's father hinting that Coll had not come to visit in an age. Coll was usually patient, but he didn't have it in him to deal with them all tonight. So finally, when Kenneth MacLeod started whining about the sorry state of his finances (which everyone knew would not be so dire if only he didn't spend every evening drinking at the tavern), Coll gave up and left.

He returned to his cottage inside the gates of Duncally, knowing he would doubtless sink into a solitary brood about that woman — and strangely looking forward to it. But even that dubious pleasure was denied him when he found Jamie lurking on his door-step, summoning him to solve yet another problem.

The problem, of course, turned out to be the dainty beauty now perched on the stone bench across from him. Her back was perfectly straight, hands crossed in her lap, a cloak folded neatly on the seat beside her, and a black bonnet atop it. Everything about her was trim and plain, from the top of her thick, chocolate-colored hair, braided and wrapped into a serviceable bun, to the toes of her black, leather half boots. Para-doxically, the severity of hairstyle and dress only made the alluring femininity of her face and figure more obvious. Her dark doe eyes were the sort that could melt a man right down to his soul — if they had not been fixed on him in a furious glare.

"You." Coll was pleased that his voice held only irritation and none of the irrational fizzing pleasure that blossomed in his chest. "I should have known."

She rose to face him. It did not surprise

him that she offered no greeting or explanation or acknowledgment of his prior help, but immediately assumed a battle face. "I cannot imagine why you would have."

"Because wherever you go, there's trouble."

"No doubt you fancy yourself witty, but I have had quite enough Scottish humor for the day."

"Aye, I can see that. Why don't you tell me what the problem is?"

"Precisely who are you?" She lifted her chin.

"I might ask you the same thing."

"I am Lady Violet Thornhill, but I can't see why this is any of your concern. First you are out patrolling the roads and now you are taking care of the earl's business? Are you in charge of everything that takes place in this village?"

"No, but I *am* in charge of Mardoun's business." He felt a little lick of pleasure at seeing that he had managed to shake her, at least a little. "My name is Coll Munro; I manage Duncally. And one might think you would be grateful that I was 'patrolling the roads.' Oh, but I forget — you dinna need my help, did you?"

A flush rose in her cheeks at his words. "It's no surprise you throw that up to me.

Of course you have my thanks for coming to my aid — though I believe you already took that."

Coll could not hold back a slow, knowing smile. "Indeed, you repaid me most . . . satisfactorily. Still, 'tis pleasing to hear you say it. Now, it seems, I can assist you again. What is the problem?"

Mrs. Ferguson jumped in before Lady Violet could respond. "The problem is that she came here without a word of warning, expecting us to put her up for the night."

"I did not just drop in, looking for a place to sleep."

"She *claims* she's a lady." Mrs. Ferguson's voice was laced with suspicion. "She *says* she's a friend of his lordship. But why would she come visiting while he is gone?"

"I said that I am an acquaintance of Lord Mardoun," Violet countered. "And I did not come here for a 'visit.' I am here to study the ruins Lord Mardoun discovered. I am an antiquarian."

"An antiquarian!" Coll blurted. "But you are a woman."

Violet's dark eyes iced over. "Despite that grievous liability, I have studied antiquities and ancient sites under the tutelage of one of the foremost authorities of our age, Dr. Lionel Overton. Lord Mardoun invited Dr.

Overton to study the ruins on his estate."

"Aye, Mardoun mentioned it." Coll glanced around. "Where is Dr. Overton? He wasn't in the post chaise."

"No. He — Uncle Lionel —" Violet suppressed the quiver in her voice. "Dr. Overton passed on a month ago."

"My condolences. But . . . well . . . why are you here?"

"Exactly what I said." Mrs. Ferguson gave a triumphant nod of her head. "What's she doing gallivanting about the countryside by herself?"

"I am hardly 'gallivanting.' I am here in Dr. Overton's stead. I told you: I intend to study the ruins. Here." She stepped forward, proffering the folded paper in her hand. "Lord Mardoun's letter to Dr. Overton. You will see that I'm telling the truth. The earl invited Uncle Lionel to dig at the site he'd discovered." Her voice lifted a little with excitement. "Lord Mardoun thinks it could be ancient, given that no one in recent times seems to have known of its existence."

"It was a surprise, true enough." Coll took the note from her hand. The broken red seal of wax was his brother-in-law's, and Coll was unsurprised to see Damon's handwriting on the inside. He glanced over the letter. "This says nothing about you."

Coll intended to let Violet remain; there was no way he would allow Mrs. Ferguson to turn out any woman into the cold night, much less this one. But he could not resist pretending that the matter was in doubt. He supposed he should feel guilty about teasing her, but the truth was, it was too enjoyable watching her attack all obstacles in her way. He only wished he could get rid of the housekeeper.

"My uncle would have brought me with him had he not been stricken ill," Violet argued. "I assisted him, not only with his research and writing, but also at the sites. He would have wished me to come here and continue his work." Emotion clogged her voice as she went on, "Dr. Overton would have been so excited at the prospect, so happy."

"No doubt." Her obvious grief touched Coll, but he knew she would not welcome any show of sympathy from him. His voice, however, was gentle as he went on, "Mardoun intended for Dr. Overton to come next spring. It is cold already and will be worse in winter."

"I'm eager to get started and quite able to work in the cold. I am not a fragile female, I assure you."

"Clearly." Coll handed the letter back to

her. "Mrs. Ferguson, please have a room prepared for Lady Thornhill."

The housekeeper swelled up like a pouter pigeon. "Coll Munro! Dinna say that you intend to put her up here! That you believe her story?"

"I canna think why anyone would lie about wanting to visit those ruins, can you? And it's far too cold to send her away even if it is a lie."

"Hmph." The housekeeper sent a suspicious glance toward their visitor but turned to issue terse orders to the other servants.

"I will write Mardoun," Coll told Violet. He did not add that Mardoun's reply scarcely mattered; Coll intended to let her remain. He was, however, too honest not to warn her, "But the weather is harsh. Most of the earl's servants returned to London with them. The rooms are shut off and laid with dustcovers. The food is plain. You'd do better to come back in the spring."

"Mr. Munro, on excavations I have slept on the ground in a tent and eaten my food cooked over an open fire. I believe I can endure sleeping in an empty mansion and eating 'plain' fare."

Coll's lips wanted to twitch up into a smile. He wasn't sure why he was so intrigued with this combative, irritating

41

woman who looked like a soft, sweet armful but was as prickly as a thistle. It would take a brave man indeed to touch her. But he found that he itched to discover what sweetness lay beneath the armor of nettles.

"Welcome to Duncally, my lady."

3

Violet awoke at dawn, as the first tentative glow crept between the draperies. She lay for a moment, blinking at the unfamiliar tester above her head, before she remembered where she was. The events of the night before came flooding back, and she grinned, shoving back the covers and going over to push apart the curtains. Duncally!

The sun was just creeping above the horizon, lightening the dark blue sky. She could make out the darker lumps of hills, and in the foreground, vague shapes of the outbuildings. She was here. She had reached Duncally and won the right to stay, at least for the moment. Now she would have to prove herself — but she was confident she could.

Last night, after the obstructive Mr. Munro had left and the dour housekeeper had led her to her room at the remotest end of the dark hall on the second floor, she had felt a stab of loneliness and uncertainty. Those sort of emotions she worked to keep at bay and was usually quite successful. But last night, once she'd achieved her goal, she had let down her guard, and the aching loss of her uncle and mentor had crept back into her heart. When she was safely alone in her room, she had given way to tears.

Fortunately, a good night's sleep had banished her gloom. She refused to allow sorrow or fear to rule her. Her uncle's memory was best served by proving how well he had trained her, by accomplishing what he would have done with this opportunity. Excitement thrummed through her at the prospect.

She wanted to see the ruins — breakfast could wait. Quickly she ran through her morning's toilette, dressing in one of her serviceable, dark woolen gowns, flannel petticoats beneath to ward off the chill, and braiding her hair and coiling it into a tidy bun at the crown of her head. Picking up her cloak, gloves, and bonnet, she left the room. The hallway was dark, even forbidding, none of the walls' sconces lit and all the doors closed. Of more concern to her was the sudden realization that she did not know how to find the ruins.

No servants were about in the large, silent

floor below. She didn't want to waste time roaming through the empty house to find them. Better, really, to ask Coll Munro. As estate manager, he would know the location, and she had heard Mrs. Ferguson say he lived in the gatehouse, which would be easy to find.

Outside, the sky was lighter, the horizon washed with pink and gold. The air was chilly, but she scarcely noticed it. She dismissed, as well, the odd feeling buzzing along her nerves and knotting in her chest. It was dread, no doubt, at encountering that man again.

She could not help but remember the feel of his lips against hers, the treacherous yearning that his kiss had aroused in her. It was embarrassing that it had taken her so long to pull away from him — and maddening that he, like other men, saw a woman only in that way. Still, she had faced him down last night despite her embarrassment, so the worst was over. And perhaps today, he would see past the dainty feminine appearance that was the bane of her existence and notice the competence, the intelligence, the *person* beneath the curvaceous form.

Not, of course, that there was any reason he should be different. And certainly no reason that she should care. Coll Munro had no place in her life. Her career, her work, was what was important, and a man, however pleasing to look at, however charming, had no part in that.

Violet grinned to herself at the thought of calling Munro charming. He had been anything but that — blunt and unwelcoming, scowling at her and throwing up every obstacle he could think of to dissuade her from staying. No doubt he would be equally obstructive this morning. But somehow the prospect of verbally jousting with him raised her spirits even more.

The house just inside the massive gates was tidy and small. Violet was glad to see that light glowed in one of the windows. She rapped sharply upon the door. When there was no response, she knocked again and was rewarded by a low, grumbling voice within.

"Aye, aye, I heard you." The door swung open and Coll Munro loomed in the doorway, frowning. "I told you I would —" He stopped abruptly when his gaze fell on her.

Here in the light of dawn, she could see that his eyes were sky blue, sleepy and heavy lidded beneath eyebrows of cinnamon brown, darker than the deep gold of his hair. Clearly he was as handsome as he'd seemed in the darkness, his jaw sharply cut, his chin

46

square, his lips full and well shaped. He had not shaved yet, for his lower face was covered with stubble, which, like his brows, was darker than his hair and intriguingly tinged with red.

Violet's stomach dropped as if she had missed a step on the stairs or stood at the edge of a precipice. She glanced away hastily, and her gaze fell upon his chest, where his unbuttoned shirt hung open, revealing a wide swath of skin. A center line of curling, red-brown hair led downward, disappearing into the waistband of his trousers. Thoroughly flustered, Violet tore her eyes from the sight of his firm, ridged chest and dropped her gaze to the floor. His feet were bare, and the sight seemed far too intimate.

She struggled to come up with something to say to end the awkward moment, but her mind was perfectly blank — well, no, not blank, but filled with images that it was better not to think about.

"Oh — ah — Miss — I mean, my lady." Coll fumbled at the buttons of his shirt, taking a step back. "I didn't realize — I wasn't expecting you. I —"

"I need directions to the ruins." Violet realized that in her rush to cover her awkwardness, her words had come out abrupt and graceless. She added in explanation, "I'm afraid I don't know how to get there."

Munro stared at her. "Now? You're going to the ruins at this hour?"

"That *is* why I came here, after all. It is my vocation, not a pastime. I'm eager to get started."

"Yes. I can see." He took another step back. "Come in, then; it's cold. Give me a minute, and I'll take you."

Violet's insides fluttered. She thought of walking with him to the ruins and how awkward it would be, with nothing to say and her mind filled with the image of Coll when he opened the door. His sleep-tousled hair and the wide swath of skin between his shirt, the curling hair that she wanted, most peculiarly, to glide her fingers through. She forced a bright smile. "No need to go to such trouble. I am sure I can find the way if you give me directions."

"It's no trouble. Easier than trying to explain since you don't know the country-side. I just need to finish dressing." Color tinged his cheeks, and he glanced toward a door in the far wall. No doubt it led into his bedroom.

Violet felt her own face heating as well. It was foolish to feel embarrassed — after all, he was the one who had answered his door half-dressed. She had done nothing wrong, and she had learned long ago not to worry about propriety or appearances. They were unimportant and usually acted as barricades to a woman's career. Yet somehow Coll Munro seemed to be able to turn her blushing and tongue-tied at every turn.

"Please come in." Coll stepped back farther. "I'll just, um . . ." He glanced around, then nodded to her without finishing the sentence and hurried into the other room. He appeared, Violet thought, as relieved to escape as she was to be left by herself.

Violet relaxed when the door closed behind him. The room seemed too confined with him in it, as if he took up all the air. She drew a deep breath and composed herself. She must not allow herself to become flustered again. From bitter experience Violet knew that men expected to command in any situation, and that in the face of even the slightest hesitation or uncertainty, they would rush to fill the void. She had to maintain firm control, not only of the situation but of her own reactions, as well.

She did her best to ignore any sounds from the other room, whether it was thuds or rustling or a low, muttered curse. Better not to think about Coll Munro dressing a few feet from her — his fingers working their way down the line of buttons, grazing the skin of his chest and stomach as they moved, tucking the shirt inside his breeches. Even imagining him shaving sent the oddest sensation through her.

She wondered exactly what a man did as he shaved, an intimate sort of activity to which an unmarried woman was not privy. She was aware of the instruments involved, of course, but how long did it take and where did one start and how did he shave the narrow space between his lip and nostrils, especially the dip in the middle? What would it feel like to stroke her finger down that little valley?

Violet shook her head, dispelling the thoughts, and strolled around the room. Coll Munro was neat, and the furniture, though plain, was sturdy and well made, the wood sanded and polished to a gleaming smooth surface. The peat smoldering in the fireplace gave out the odd odor Violet was becoming accustomed to in Scotland, but another pleasant, woodsy smell mingled with it. It was, she discovered, the scent of wood shavings discarded in a pail, along with some blocks of wood, beside a set of shelves. Several carved objects lay on the shelves, one of them a statue of an elf peering out from around a tree, so charmingly done she had to smile.

There were woodworking tools, as well, and pieces of paper weighed down by another small block of wood. She could see the edges of a sketch emerging from beneath the paperweight. Her fingers itched to pull the papers out and look at them, but even Violet's rapacious curiosity could not make her breach the laws of polite behavior to that extent.

Coll Munro had an artistic streak. She imagined his large, capable fingers working on a piece of wood, pulling forth the delicate traceries and whorls. Turning away, her eye fell on the opposite wall, where a sketch hung in a simple frame. The portrait, done in charcoal, was of a woman so lovely it took one's breath away. Laughter shone in the subject's large bright eyes, and her mouth was quirked up at one corner in the beginnings of a smile. Her hair was a mass of tumbling tresses, held back on one side by her hand as if to shield her curls from the wind. In the static drawing, Violet could see the motion, the almost tangible energy and vivacity that radiated from her.

Was this the woman Coll loved? Affection and familiarity permeated every line of the drawing. A fiancée? A lost love? Violet took a step closer. The woman's beauty was such that Violet could not help but admire it, yet she felt an unfamiliar twinge of envy. Violet had never wished she were more pleasing to the eye; indeed, Violet had found her looks more a detriment than a source of pride. But in this moment she knew a sharp, brief twist of longing. What must it be like to be a woman whom men cherished?

The door opened behind her, and Violet whirled almost guiltily. Coll once more filled the room with his presence. He was fully dressed now and clean shaven as well — though bearing a thin, red line across his jaw that she suspected might have been the cause for the curses she had heard earlier.

"I — um — was looking at the portrait." Violet gestured vaguely toward it. "Did you draw it?"

"Aye. That's Meg."

"She's beautiful." The name tickled in Violet's brain. She stared. "Meg? You mean — isn't that the name in the earl's letter? His new wife?"

"Aye." Coll grimaced. "She's Lady Mardoun now."

Violet swung back to study the drawing again. She had been surprised to read in Mardoun's letter that he had married again. From her admittedly limited knowledge of the earl, he had not seemed a man who embraced the role of husband. That he had married a woman he'd met here — and after only a few weeks — made it even more curious. But now she understood. A woman as beautiful as this could turn the head of even the worldly Earl of Mardoun.

Was Coll in love with the earl's wife? Violet cast a speculative glance at him. He had gone to the fire to retrieve a kettle and was busy pouring water into it from a pitcher. The twist of his mouth when he said "Lady Mardoun" had indicated a certain displeasure, but he did not fit Violet's picture of a heartbroken man.

"Would you like a cup of tea? I have some of Sally McEwan's scones here, too."

"No, thank you," Violet said automatically, though her stomach rumbled in protest. She had been too eager this morning to wait for breakfast.

"You haven't tasted Sally's scones." He set a basket on the table, folding back the cloth to reveal a pile of golden-brown cakes. "They're a bit of heaven." He smiled, and a long dimple popped into one cheek, his blue eyes warm and vivid.

Violet smiled back, taking an unconscious step toward him before she pulled herself up short. Sitting down to a companionable breakfast with the man was not the way to establish her authority and professionalism.

"I prefer to get to the ruins as soon as possible," she said stiffly. "I must make my plans for excavation."

Despite her refusal, Coll continued about his tasks, pouring two cups of tea and setting other small containers on the table. "Those ruins have been there for hundreds of years. I imagine they could wait another ten minutes." He sat down, pushing the basket toward her. "Eat. Better to work on a full stomach."

Violet clenched her teeth. Munro was clearly not going anywhere until he'd eaten. It was irritating, but it would be useless to argue with him. She could not force him to go, and losing the argument would only make her appear weak. Besides, what he had said was perfectly reasonable. And the scones looked delicious.

She perched on the chair across the table from him, pouring a bit of milk into her tea. The drink was hot and strong, and a pot of honey provided sweetness. Violet could not quite suppress a sigh of satisfaction after it slid down her throat.

Coll's eyes danced. "Wait till you've tasted the scones."

Violet suspected uneasily that he was

laughing at her, and she had no idea how to respond. She had never been good at making conversation. Her mother could chat for ten minutes without ever really saying anything, but she had been unable to instill that ability in her daughter.

There were no plates, no utensils, so she followed Coll's lead and simply plucked one of the scones from the basket, breaking off a piece and putting it in her mouth. The bread was a delightful combination of tastes, at once buttery and dry, sweet but with a twinge of tartness. It was, in short, as close to perfection as a bread could be. Violet couldn't hold back a smile.

"Dinna I tell you?" Coll asked with a chuckle.

Such good humor was in his tone that Violet's smile turned into a laugh as well. "Yes, you were right. Miss — McEwan, was it? — makes delicious scones. You are lucky to have such a generous friend." She was blatantly fishing for information, but Violet was too curious to be polite. There seemed to be a number of women in Munro's life.

"You're lucky, too. Sally is the cook at Duncally. You'll eat her food every day. As do I — she takes pity on me, poor bachelor that I am, and lets me sup with them up at the house."

"Oh. I will see you at supper tonight then." Violet suppressed the fizz of anticipation in her chest.

"Nae. Mrs. Ferguson will serve you in the dining room. She's a stickler for propriety, that one. She wouldna put a lady at the table in the servants' hall."

"Why? I work for Lord Mardoun, the same as you."

"Ah, but your name has a *Lady* before it, and that makes all the difference."

"It shouldn't."

"Aye?" His brows rose lazily. "Then why did you use it last night?"

Violet grimaced. "You are right, of course. It was expedient. I did not want to lose the opportunity to explore the ruins."

"Now dinna turn to starch again. I dinna mean to insult you."

"I'm sorry. I was unaware I had 'turned to starch.' It sounds a most uncomfortable state. But I am reminded of my purpose here, which is not to sit about having tea and scones. I should be at the site."

"We'll go, then." Coll downed the rest of his tea in one swallow. But at that moment, a knock came at the door, and with a sigh Coll went to answer it.

A young man stood on the porch. "Coll, I came to ask —" He glanced past Coll into the house and saw Violet. His eyes widened comically. "Oh! I dinna ken — I'm sorry, miss, uh, ma'am, um . . ." His face flooded with red, and he whipped off his cap, bobbing his head toward Violet.

Following the young man's gaze, Coll stiffened, his expression suddenly so guilty that Violet was sure he had merely confirmed the other man's suspicions. Coll cleared his throat. "It's not what —"

A torrent of words rushed out of his visitor's mouth, cutting him off. "I'm sorry, Coll, I never thought. I mean, I wouldn't hae come if — it was just —" He twisted his cap between his hands.

Violet covered her mouth to hide a smile as Coll said something short and sharp under his breath and stepped out the door, pulling it almost closed behind him. "What is it, Dougal? The sun's barely up, man. Could you not wait?"

Violet gave way to giggles as the two men talked on the porch. She did her best to pull her face back into sober lines when Coll stepped back into the room, but her effort clearly failed, given the scowl Coll directed at her.

"You're laughing?"

She pressed her lips together, but somehow it only made her want to giggle more.

"You looked — you looked so guilty!"

"I dinna," he grumbled. "I thought *you* would be embarrassed. But clearly I dinna need to worry about that."

"I can't control what other people think about me, Mr. Munro. I gave up worrying about it long ago."

"But your reputation —"

"Is abysmal. I think we have already established that I don't act as a lady should. I am pushy and sharp-tongued and stubborn. What does it matter if people decide I'm a hussy as well? 'Tis you who should worry about blackening your reputation by associating with one such as I," she said lightly, standing up. "Now, I think we really should be on our way, shouldn't we?"

He looked at her for a moment, and then, surprising her, he laughed. "Aye, I suppose we should." Coll grabbed a coat from a hook on the wall and pulled it on as he ushered Violet out the door. "Easiest way to get there is to take the road." He gestured through the tall gates. "There's also a path from the gardens behind the house. It's shorter, but a rougher walk. If you like, we can return that way."

He set out with a long, easy stride that ate up the distance. Violet had to hurry to keep up with him, but she was accustomed to doing whatever was necessary to put her on an equal footing with the men her uncle taught.

"Do people often come to your door at dawn?" she asked, a little breathless but determined not to show it.

"I suppose they must since I had two of them this morning." Coll cast her a teasing glance, then slowed his pace.

"There's no reason to go at a snail's pace for me," Violet assured him, marching on at the same rate. Coll, looking amused, returned to his usual speed.

"To answer your question, no, they are not always so early. But it comes with running Duncally." He sighed. "Dougal's wanting work for the winter while the croft's idle. His wife's going to have a bairn in April, he says, and they need the money. His da's croft can't support them all as it is."

"I would think they might have considered that before."

"Aye, of course." The corner of his mouth quirked up. "But reason isna what's driving one at the time." He stopped, looking chagrined. "I'm sorry. That's not fit talk for a lady's ears."

"I think we've established I'm a lady only by birth," she retorted. "I'm not easily shocked."

The road leveled out, and Coll turned to the right. There before them were a group of long, weathered stones standing improbably on end.

"Oh!" Violet stopped abruptly, her breath catching. "A ring!" She turned to Coll, her face radiant. "I didn't realize! There is a circle of standing stones here as well!"

She hurried toward the ancient rocks as if drawn by some unseen force, her steps quickening until she was almost running.

4

Violet stopped as she reached the first stone and took a long look around. "It's magnificent!"

The circle was almost intact, the stones placed at regular intervals with only one or two gaps. The long rocks were weathered and pitted, of some indeterminate color between white and gray, their arrangement slightly elliptical rather than perfectly round.

"Lord Mardoun did not mention a ring. I had no idea." She glanced at Coll, who stood watching her. Violet suspected that he found her enthusiasm over the stones peculiar; people outside Lionel's scholarly circle usually did.

"You are interested in the ring as well as the ruins?"

"Oh, yes." She nodded. "The circles were already standing here before the Romans reached Britain. So little is known about them. These antiquities interest me far more than the remains of the civilization the Romans left behind them. Such sites are uniquely *ours.* It is my hope that the ruins Lord Mardoun found will turn out to be that, as well."

"Have you visited other circles?"

"Indeed. Stonehenge, of course, and some others. Ignorant and uncaring people have torn many stones down, and time and weather have taken their toll. But this ring is marvelous." She swept her gaze over the area again. "I have never seen one with this configuration — these two stones outside the circle. Yet they are clearly set in a line with each other and with the ring. This one is most unique."

Violet went closer to the odd stone. Standing several feet from the edge of the circle, it was little more than half as tall as the other towering rocks. In the center was a round hole larger than a person's fist.

"It goes all the way through." She bent to peer into the opening.

"They call it the Troth Stone," Munro offered, coming up beside her. "People would come here in the old days to handfast. That's a sort of marriage ceremony from before there were churches." He glanced down at her with a faintly inquiring look.

"Yes, I've heard of handfasting."

"Some still come here to plight their troth. They stand on either side of the stone and clasp hands through the middle as they pledge to marry each other."

"Fascinating." Violet regarded him with interest. "You seem very familiar with the customs and traditions."

He shrugged. "I've lived here all my life."

"Many people are unaware of that sort of history. Oral traditions are easily lost as one generation succeeds another."

Munro smiled faintly. "Not if you're a Munro. My mother knew a lot, and she passed it on. But if you really want to know about this area, you canna do better than to talk to Aunt Elizabeth."

"Your aunt? Would she speak with me?"

"Nothing she would like better. She knows every tale, every legend, true and fanciful alike. But she is not my aunt; we were just in the way of calling her that. She's Lady Elizabeth Rose, and she lives at Baillannan." He gestured in a southerly direction. "The great, gray house on the other side of the loch."

"I should very much like to meet her."

"I will ask her, then, if you'd like."

"I would appreciate it. It is . . . good of you to help." Violet hesitated. "I must apologize, Mr. Munro."

"You must?"

"Yes. I — it was rude of me last night not to thank you for helping me."

"You're welcome." He paused. "I was . . . rude, as well."

His eyes glinted at her, the faintest notion of a smile touching his lips. Violet glanced away quickly, making a vague, dismissive noise. It was better not to think about the "rude" payment Coll had demanded of her. She pretended not to notice that Coll continued to study her.

"It comes hard to you, I think, thanking me," he went on after a moment. "There's naught wrong, you know, with needing help now and then."

"Easy to say when one is like you."

"*A giant,* you mean?" His eyes twinkled.

He was making fun of her again. "It makes life considerably easier to be able to lift things and reach the highest shelf and look down at people instead of up." She sighed, annoyed with herself for letting him goad her. "But that is not the point. I'm trying to apologize."

"And so you have." He started walking again. "The ruins are this way."

"I must thank you, too, for letting me stay at Duncally."

"Och, you are full of obligations this

64

morning. Swallowing all your medicine at once, eh?"

"Yes." Violet let her shoulders relax. "But I do appreciate it. Mrs. Ferguson was bent on turning me out."

"Mrs. Ferguson does not like bumps in her road."

"And I am a bump?"

"Aye." Amusement crinkled the corners of his bright blue eyes. "She wasn't expecting you. It was her bedtime, so there she was in her dressing gown and nightcap, without the armor of her keys and watch and starched clothes. You did not quail before her. Worse, she was unsure where you fit. She found you bumptious, but you had the voice of a lady, and an English one at that. She feared offending a friend of the earl. So, little as she likes me, she decided the safest thing would be to let me make the decision and suffer the embarrassment if I was wrong."

"Why does she not like you? I'm sorry; that was rude again. Curiosity is my besetting sin."

"If curiosity is your worst fault, I would say you're doing well. I dinna mind. I'd rather straight speech than dancing about uttering platitudes."

Violet relaxed even more. Coll's size and

masculinity were a bit overwhelming, and the laughter in his eyes did odd things to her insides, but it was a relief to feel she did not have to search for something acceptable to say. "We should get along famously, then."

"I hope so."

Violet looked up and met his eyes, and her momentary comfort fled.

"As for Mrs. Ferguson's dislike . . . well, she is not fond of many people. She considers my family especially improper. The Munros are an unruly lot. The women have never, um, conformed to the common rules of behavior, especially marriage."

Violet looked at him in surprise. Plain speech, indeed. She had no idea what to say in response to his statement. Was he implying that his birth was illegitimate?

Coll's face remained as emotionless as his voice. He shrugged. "No reason to hide it. You will hear the same from someone soon — most likely Mrs. Ferguson herself. She is of the opinion that Meg and I have gotten above our station."

That statement brought Violet to a halt. She stared at him. "Meg!"

"My sister, Meg."

"You mean . . . the woman in that drawing?"

"Aye. Meg married Mardoun." The tone of his voice, the tilt of his chin, carried a challenge.

Oddly, Violet's initial response was not amazement that the earl had married not just a local lady, but a woman who was the sister of his estate manager — and born on the wrong side of the blanket as well. Rather, what swept her was a strangely giddying realization that the lovely woman in Coll's drawing was not some beauty for whom Coll pined, but his sister. Violet let out a breathy laugh. "I thought . . ."

"What?"

"It doesn't matter." Violet started walking again. "Then you are Lord Mardoun's brother-in-law? No wonder Mrs. Ferguson deferred to your decision."

Coll gave a dismissive grunt. "Not from respect, I assure you. Like most, she thinks that is why he gave me the position."

"You were not the estate manager before?"

"Nae." He let out a short, humorless laugh. "I was not. I've always been a Baillannan man. It's the Roses gave my ancestors their freehold. They ruled here for centuries; the Englishman's lot are newcomers."

"I see."

"I doubt it." He scowled.

"I can see that you don't like managing the estate."

"I don't like people thinking that it's because I'm Meg's brother. I don't like people saying I've gone over to the enemy."

"As that highwayman said last night."

"Who — oh, Will. I suppose that is what he's become, the daft lad." Coll shook his head. "*His* opinion is of no importance. But the truth is, Mardoun trapped me. He knew I wouldn't refuse. Could not, for it meant I could end his clearances."

"Clearances?"

"His manager was throwing crofters from their plots so he could turn the land to sheep. It was legal, for it was Mardoun's property, but heartless. The way he did it was worse — burning them out of their homes, without a thought for what they would do after that. Bairns and old ones alike, didn't matter if they were sick or dying."

"Lord Mardoun countenanced this?"

"Not after he realized what MacRae was doing. I'll give him that. Damon sent the man packing. But he needed a new manager, so he maneuvered me into doing it. Mardoun's a canny one." Coll sighed. "And I canna even continue to dislike the man, as he makes Meg happy, it seems."

"Ah. You *are* trapped." Violet let out a little laugh.

He gave her a rueful smile. "Foolish to rail against it when so many others would be ecstatic to have a roof over their head and work to do."

"That isn't always enough." Violet heard the revealing emotion in her own voice and pulled back. She gave him a brief, perfunctory smile. "We should press on to the site. No doubt you are eager to get back to your own work."

"Yes, of course." He, too, reverted to formality.

A silence fell on them as they walked across the meadow beyond the circle of stones. Violet regretted ending the temporary easiness between them. She invariably made a misstep in conversation. She was too blunt; she was too serious; the things she brought up were considered odd. It did not bother her usually, but she had been enjoying her conversation with Coll Munro.

"There they are." Coll's voice brought Violet out of her thoughts, and she raised her head.

In front of her, before the edge of the cliff, a series of low, flat stones jutted out of the sandy ground. Violet's pulse quickened. She hurried forward and squatted down, heedless of her skirts, to examine the rocks stacked on one another. "A wall, not mortared. The stones are not cut, but of course that does not mean they are of ancient origin. No one knew of them before?"

"Nae. Damon and Meg found them after a great storm blew the sand away and left the stones exposed. Before then, it was just an ordinary hillock that people have walked past — and over — for years. You can see there is a path down to the shore just ahead. It's a common way to walk. No one's heard of a house here, even the older folks. There aren't even legends of anyone living here."

Violet began to brush away the dirt at the base of the stones, her movements small and deft, heedless of dirtying her gloves. "The wall goes farther down. It's buried in the sand."

"There are more."

Violet lifted her head, looking in the direction he pointed, where more stones peeked above the ground. Rising, she walked over to them. "Perhaps this was an outer wall. A sort of fortress? It is at the most accessible path up from the ocean, where invaders would be likely to come."

"It's at the mouth of the loch, too." Coll nodded toward their right, where the land rose sharply to another cliff edge. "Loch

Baille's a sea loch, and that is the channel into it from the sea."

"A very strategic place."

"That would have had to be very long ago," Coll surmised. "For the last few hundred years, the old castle was the guardian against sea raiders."

"Really? Is the castle close?"

"I'll show you."

He led her across the gradually rising land to where it ended in a dramatic, straight drop to the sea. He pointed to the loch opening out from the narrow inlet between cliffs.

"There, on the other side of the loch, you can see some of the castle ruins. The original Baillannan. It stood for as long back as anyone remembers. They built the new house almost two centuries ago. That's it, farther along."

Violet lifted her hand, shading her eyes. "Yes, I see it. Built when they no longer needed to be protected from marauding Viking bands."

"Aye, or other lairds." Again that elusive glint of amusement lit his eyes. "Or reivers."

"Reivers?"

"Thieves. Robbers."

"Ah. So the original castle would have been built during the time of Viking raids?

Those stopped when — ninth century?"

He nodded. "By then the Norsemen were intermarrying with the clans. I suppose the earliest parts of the castle were built before then. It was a rambling place, built up and added on to many times. There were enormous cellars that connected to caves, they said, for easy escape if the walls were breached."

"But would that not have also given invaders easy access?" Violet's brow wrinkled.

"You have not seen the caves." Coll grinned. "More like, strangers coming in through the caves would have wound up hopelessly lost and starved to death, unless, of course, they fell down a pit first."

"They sound a fearsome place."

He cast a suspicious glance down at her and said sternly, "Dinna try exploring them on your own. If you want to see the caves, I'll take you. They're no place for a — for a person who does not know them."

Violet narrowed her eyes. She was certain he had been about to say "for a woman" and had changed it at the last moment. Or perhaps he had meant for a "wee" person. Turning sharply, she started back toward the ruins. "You'll need to provide some workers. Two or three men should be enough to start with."

"Will it then? It's good of you to inform me. I take it you're in charge of Duncally now."

She turned to face him, crossing her arms. "I realize you have difficulty dealing with a woman, but I am the one in charge of the project, and I have a far better idea than you of what is necessary."

"I dinna have difficulty with you because you're a woman. It's your assumption that everyone else has to jump to your orders."

"I did not order you. I simply asked —"

"Asking is precisely what you did not do."

"I see. I must ask you at every turn what I may or may not do? Am I to beg you to give me enough workers to do my task properly?"

"I have no need to see you beg, which I doubt very seriously you know how to do, anyway. But I'll point out that if you want a person to do something for you, you might try requesting it instead of telling him what he must do. That's true whether you're a woman or a man or a three-legged dog."

"It is not a *favor* I'm asking. It is a necessity if I hope to finish the project within the foreseeable future."

"Still, as you're wanting me to put two of my workers to some task other than their job, I'd like to hear an explanation."

Violet narrowed her eyes. "I assure you, I am not trying to be difficult. Or demanding."

"Och, you needn't try. It comes to you naturally."

"It seems little enough to me to assign a couple of your workers to the dig, given that it is winter and there is less work to be done. You just told me that young man came to you this morning looking for work. I fail to understand why you are being so obstructive. Other than, of course, your male need to always be in charge."

"I dinna always need —"

She plowed on over his words. "But you are right: they are your workers, and it is your decision. Fortunately, I am capable of doing the work myself. At least I will be assured of it being done correctly." She spun and started toward the farthest rock wall.

Behind her, she heard him emit a low growl. "I did not say I would not send you workers."

"Do as you please. It is immaterial to me. Now, if you will excuse me, I have work to do, and I am sure you do as well." She did not look back at him until she reached the row of stones at the far end and knelt beside them to begin digging. When she cast a glance over her shoulder, she saw that he was gone.

Violet sighed and looked all around her. The place was empty, even desolate. But it was hers. And that was all she really needed. Digging a trowel from one of her capacious pockets, she started to work.

5

He should not have let her provoke him like that. Coll wasn't sure why the woman was so easily able to get under his skin. She had been right; it was obvious she would need workers to dig out the stones. He didn't begrudge her the help. It was the peremptory way she had told him what he should do — *must* do — that had galled him. It wasn't because she was a woman. Was it?

No, that was nonsense. It was the arrogance of it, the certainty of the English aristocracy that everyone else was put on earth to serve them. A moment earlier they had been talking easily, no assumption of inequality between them, so that one could almost forget there was a gulf of social class between them. But then, in an instant, Violet was back on her high perch, ordering him about like a servant. It would have been the same if it had been a man issuing the orders. That the words came from those eminently kissable lips made no difference, any more than it mattered that ice had formed in her warm brown eyes or that he had a moment earlier been imagining the softness of her skin beneath his fingers.

Well . . . perhaps it did matter that she was a woman.

And even though she was supremely irritating, it had been wrong of him to just walk away from her like that. She was new here and all alone on the cliff. Perhaps he should turn around and go back, make sure she remembered the way back to Duncally.

Fortunately, he came to his senses before he could act on his thoughts. He would look a fool. And Lady Violet would doubtless blister his ears if he intimated she might be unable to manage the site alone or to find her way home by herself. He would return at the end of the day and show her the shorter, quicker path up the hill to the gardens. He could mend his fences with her then.

The day seemed to wear on forever; Coll kept glancing out the window to see if the sun was low enough in the sky that he could count the day over. Then, just when the afternoon was drawing to a close, John Grant and Dan Fraser came in. He struggled to quell his impatience as the two men started on a long explanation of their sides over the meadow between their crofts.

Finally Coll snapped, "Good Lord, you're grown men. Canna you reason it out yourselves? Just share the bloody bit of land." He scowled at Grant. "You're not even one of the earl's crofters."

The two men looked taken aback, but Grant went doggedly on, "Aye, weel, that's the thing, isn't it? The meadow lies between Mardoun land and Baillannan."

"It's Mardoun's," Fraser put in.

"Share it. That's Mardoun's answer, and I dinna doubt Isobel will agree." He sighed, feeling a trifle guilty over his short words, and added, "I'll talk to Isobel about it."

That seemed to satisfy the men, though they left still grumbling in a way that seemed more habitual than heated. Coll wasted no time in grabbing his jacket and starting out the door. He groaned under his breath when he saw Dermid Boyd walking purposefully toward him. Coll stepped out and closed the office door behind him. At least he could walk as Boyd laid out his problem.

"Boyd." Coll nodded. "What brings you up here?"

Dermid nodded back and fell in alongside

Coll. "I tried tae tell you last night at the tavern, but I couldna before you left."

"Aye? What's amiss?"

"Not really my concern, but I thought you'd want tae know: Donald MacRae is here."

"What?" Coll stopped and turned to Dermid. "Are you certain?"

"Aye. I saw him myself in Kinclannoch."

"What does that bastard want?" Coll started forward again.

"I dinna ask. But he was staying at auld Mrs. Stewart's; she takes in boarders, you ken." Boyd paused. "Will you be gang to see him then?"

"I will." Coll's steps quickened as he strode down the hill. He glanced toward the standing stones as he passed. He had to take care of this first. With any luck, he'd be through with MacRae in time to catch Violet at the ruins.

He loped down the last stretch to the village, leaving Boyd behind him. Auld Mrs. Stewart answered the door, and between the old woman's deafness and the greetings and inquiries about family that courtesy demanded, it took several minutes to find out if Mardoun's former estate manager was in fact residing there.

"Aye," she said finally, nodding. "First

room on the richt, top of the stairs. But I dinna want you brawling in my house, mind."

"I won't hurt him," Coll assured her as he bounded up the steps, adding beneath his breath, "This time."

His knock was thunderous, and he did not wait to open the door. MacRae whirled as Coll strode in. He held a candlestick in his raised hand.

"Dinna even think about it." Coll cast a contemptuous glance at the weapon. "You couldna reach my head."

"It'd do little enough damage to your hard head, anyway," MacRae agreed sourly.

"What are you doing here, MacRae?"

"I dinna answer to you." The man held Coll's gaze for a moment, then glanced away. "I have debts to collect. I've a right to get my money."

"Whatever money's owed you, I'm sure you dinna earn it any decent way."

"That's not your business."

"No? I'll warrant it's the earl's."

"Oh, yes, I heard you're the earl's man now. There's a change." MacRae gave Coll a sly look. "It's a wonder how fast you turned your coat — and what you can get from a sister sleeping —" He broke off and took a hasty step backward as Coll moved forward, his fist clenching.

"If you value your miserable life, you'll not mention my sister. Now pack your things and leave Kinclannoch. I'll do you a favor and not tell Mardoun you came back."

"Mardoun's an earl, not God. He canna stop me from going and coming as I please."

"Well, I can. I will."

"You're threatening to kill me now?"

"Nae. I'd not kill you, MacRae." Coll gave him a chilling grin. "But I can make you wish I had. Get out."

"Now? You canna toss me out on the road this late. It's almost dark."

"I never noticed that stopping you when you threw folks off their own crofts. But, no, I'll give you the night to get your things together and collect these debts of yours. But you'd best not be here when I come back tomorrow. Understand?"

"Yes," the other man said grudgingly. "I understand. I'm leaving."

Coll nodded and left. A faint smile touched his lips as behind him he heard MacRae slam his erstwhile weapon to the floor, cursing. Coll took the shortcut from the bridge to the ruins, but when he reached the cliffs, he was not surprised to find the place vacant. As that worm MacRae had pointed out, night was falling fast.

Violet would be fine, Coll told himself as he climbed up to Duncally. She would remember the way they'd come this morning, and she'd have no qualms about setting out on her own. Surely she would not have tried to find the shorter trail through the woods on her own. Still, the knot in his chest loosened when he reached the kitchen at Duncally and learned that Lady Violet had already returned to the house.

"She had her tea and went up to her room," Sally McEwan told him. "Are you wanting to see her? I could send Rose up to fetch her."

"No. No. No need to bother her. I just wanted to make sure she'd had no trouble."

"I ken that one can handle most any trouble," the plump, gregarious cook told him, grinning.

"No doubt you're right."

"I warrant you could use a wee bite." Sally steered him toward a stool at the kitchen table. "Sit yourself down, and I'll fetch you something to eat." She paused, tilting her head. "Unless maybe you're coming back tonight to eat with her ladyship."

"Now, why would I be doing that? I've no interest in dining at the grand table."

"And no interest in sitting down with a bonny lass?" She quirked an eyebrow.

82

"Och, Sally, you know I've got no eye for bonny lasses. How can I when my heart belongs to you?"

"More like your stomach, you mean." She snorted, smiling as she bustled off.

"Sally, can you make a poultice for lumbago?" he asked as she set down a filled plate in front of him. "Graeme MacLeod came by this afternoon, wanting one for his grandda. Meg makes him something for it. She made up a few tinctures and such for me to give people, but not that."

"Aye, I could do it if I knew what Meg uses. Do you have her recipe?"

He shook his head. "I could look in her books. I'll come back to look in the library tonight." Later, after he'd had a chance to go home and clean up. Look a bit more civilized in case he ran into Lady Violet. Not, of course, that that was likely. Not that it mattered.

As it turned out, Coll waited too long. He could see as he approached Duncally that all the windows were dark. Doubtless Violet — and everyone else — had gone to bed. She had arisen with the birds, after all, and worked at the site all day. She'd be tired.

He was quiet as he slipped in the side door and made his way to the library. He lit the oil lamps on the table, an imposing expanse of mahogany that would have dwarfed any room besides the cavernous library. The bookshelves lining the walls remained in shadow, the lamps providing only twin pools of light in the darkness.

Coll didn't mind. He preferred Duncally at night when its palatial proportions and ornamentation were decreased and softened by darkness. He felt at home in the library, where he often spent an evening. Though grander by far than the one he was used to at Baillannan, it carried the same comforting scents of old books, leather chairs, and burning lamps and offered the same alluring possibilities of hundreds of volumes.

He strode to the glass-doored cabinet where Meg kept their grandmother's journal and took it to the table to read, opening and turning its yellowed pages with care. It was all he and his sister had of their grandmother — indeed, of their grandfather as well, since he had given it to her. Reflexively Coll touched the sgian-dubh he carried at the back of his belt, wondering if it, too, was indeed Malcolm's.

It was easy for Coll to get lost in a book, especially one such as this that held old secrets, but tonight he had difficulty concentrating. His thoughts kept turning to Violet, somewhere in the rooms above him. He wondered which bedchamber was hers. Was she curled up in a chair by the fire, reading as he was? She was sure to be a bookish woman. Or was she asleep, tucked up in one of the great monstrosities of a bed that Duncally offered, sheltered by looming headboards and canopies and heavy draperies? He shifted restlessly in his chair, thinking of her nestled among the pillows, dark lashes casting shadows on her cheeks, a doubtlessly chaste white nightgown covering the soft swell of her breasts.

Sharp, rapid footsteps in the hall roused him from his wandering thoughts. Coll lifted his head, pulse quickening, as Violet Thornhill strode through the door. She stopped abruptly when she saw him, letting out a little gasp, but recovered her composure quickly.

"Mr. Munro."

"Lady Violet." He rose to his feet, his blood pumping through him in a hot, hard rhythm.

She was dressed for bed, soft slippers on her feet and a brocade dressing gown belted around her. The heavy robe concealed her body more than any frock would, but something about the knowledge that she was dressed for bed was inherently arousing.

Between the lapels of her robe, he could see a small V of that white cotton gown he had imagined a moment earlier. And her hair — ah, her hair, thick and dark and lustrous, spilling over her shoulders and down her back — was enough to make him weak in the knees.

"I'm sorry." Her voice was quick and a trifle breathless. "I did not expect to see you here."

"Amazingly, I am able to read, despite my low birth."

"I didn't mean that!" Color rose in her cheeks. "I just — I was unaware you were in the house. You are uncommonly quick to take offense."

"Mm. You should know about that."

She lifted her chin, but then, surprising him, she dropped her pugnacious pose, looking faintly embarrassed. "I know I can appear somewhat, um, prickly."

"Can you now?" He widened his eyes dramatically.

Violet gave him a dark look. "Yes; I am well aware what people think of me. However, I do not mean to give offense."

"Then I shall strive not to take it." Coll smiled. "As long as you will promise to do the same for me."

"I will." She extended her hand.

He had no choice but to take it. In truth, though he suspected it was not wise, he *wanted* to take it. Her hand in his was small and soft and feminine despite the firmness of her handshake. He would have liked to slide his fingers up onto her wrist, discovering the steady beat of her pulse, the tenderness of her skin. And higher, under the full, loose sleeve of her dressing gown.

Coll dropped her hand and stepped back. "I trust you found everything at the ruins to your satisfaction." He cleared his throat. "I told two of the gardening staff to report to you tomorrow morning. I sent a message to Dougal as well."

"Thank you." She gazed at him in her disconcertingly level, candid manner.

"You're welcome. I was rude earlier, and I apologize."

Violet smiled, her face lighting in a way that made his chest tighten. She had, he saw, a most alluring dimple in her cheek. "No, do not apologize. We have agreed upon a general truce, have we not?"

"Yes." He smiled back at her. "That we have."

He cast about for something else to say, something that would keep her here and talking with him in this easy way. It turned out he did not need to.

"I went by the barrow when I started home," Violet told him. "By the circle of standing stones."

"Aye? Are you interested in it as well?"

"Oh, yes. Its entrance — the narrow end, where there is that great jumble of large rocks — lies in a direct line to the two stones standing beyond either end of the ring. That had to be purposeful; it is too exact to be happenstance."

"That is unusual?"

She nodded. "In my experience, it is. Barrows vary in size, some large, some small, some oval, some rectangular. But I have not seen this alignment with the standing stones before. I should very much like to study it."

"Instead of the ruins?"

"Oh, no! I meant, in addition to the ruins, I want to open the barrow. Does it belong to the earl as well?"

"The ring and barrow do not 'belong' to anyone, to my way of thinking, but to everyone."

"Yes, of course. It is our common history; it's important to everyone. But the land must be owned by somebody."

"It's on Duncally lands. But Damon gave that part, where the stones and barrow lie, to his wife as a wedding gift. He knew Meg holds it dear."

"What a wonderful thing to do! The earl must be a very forward-thinking man." Coll thought somewhat sourly that this woman, too, was probably enamored of the handsome earl. Mardoun was the sort a lady would swoon over — for that matter, women of all sorts tended to fall at the man's feet. Violet went on, "How — I mean, when she married Mardoun, the land would have become his property again."

Coll nodded. "Aye. So Damon gave it to the Munros — to the trust that he set up, that is. Meg and I are the ones who direct the trust."

"Then it is to you that I must make my appeal."

Coll looked at her a little warily. "I suppose it is."

"This could be a very important site. The arrangement is unusual, and in a remote area such as this, it may have been little disturbed over the centuries."

"But it is sacred ground. It doesn't seem right."

"Knowledge is sacred." Violet looked at him intently. "We could learn so much from an untouched site."

"But surely the dead deserve some respect."

"I don't mean any disrespect."

"Opening up their graves? Poking about among their bones and such?" He frowned. "How could it not be?"

"I would exercise the utmost care, I assure you."

"I do not doubt that. Still . . ."

"I shall not give up," she warned him.

He smiled ruefully. "I am sure of that." He shrugged. "I'll write Meg and ask her opinion. 'Tis the Munro women who are the keepers of the old ones."

"The 'old ones'? Who are they?"

"It's just the name some give to the stones — and to the ones who built them as well."

Violet fell silent. Coll studied her. She was clearly lost in thought; he could almost see the ideas chasing one another across her face. He would like to draw her — a study in charcoal, with her looking into the distance, the breeze catching a strand of hair and tossing it across her face, as it had this morning. He remembered how he had wanted to reach out and move the stray curl back, his fingertips gliding across the smooth skin of her cheek.

He turned away abruptly. "Well, I must not keep you from finding a book to read. There's enough here, whatever subject interests you." He gestured vaguely toward the multitude of shelves and went back to his seat at the table.

"What is that you are reading?" Violet nodded toward the book open before him. "It looks quite old." She craned her head. "Is it handwritten?"

"Aye. It's not one of Duncally's books. 'Tis Meg's. It was our grandmother's journal."

"Really?" He supposed he should not have been surprised that Violet's eyes lit up with scholarly fervor. She came around the table, leaning in to read the yellowed pages.

Her hair fell forward, brushing his hand on the table, and Coll jerked reflexively. He curled his fingers into his palm, resisting the urge to take the silky strand between his fingers. Her scent teased at him, faint and surprisingly feminine and flowery. His tongue had welded to the top of his mouth.

"This looks like a recipe." Violet looked at him.

Coll knew he should say something. Had to say something. But all he could think of was how soft and rosy and inviting her lips were and what it would feel like to sink his mouth into hers.

"I . . . um . . ." He shifted, tearing his eyes from her face and focusing on the journal. "Yes. Faye wrote down remedies in there as well. It's a mix of things, really —

what she did, what she thought, recipes for some of the cures that had been handed down for generations through the Munro women. I was looking for a salve for one of Meg's patients. Since she's not here, he came to me."

"Your sister is a healer?" Violet stared at him. "The countess?"

"Aye." Coll stiffened. Now, he thought, she would pull back; after the surprise would come the condescension that had been amazingly missing this morning when he'd revealed his low birth. He had been prepared for it then, but now he dreaded it.

"Your ancestors were healers as well? It has been handed down from mother to daughter for years? This is wonderful."

"It is?"

"Yes, of course. I told you how interested I am in the customs and traditions of a people. Knowledge that has been passed through generations like that is remarkable." Violet dropped into the chair beside him. "There are so few written records of folk remedies."

"My grandmother was the first of her family to read and write."

"Not surprising. When was this written?"

"Seventeen forty-seven."

"Sixty years ago! It is more astonishing,

really, that she was literate." Violet ran a finger lightly along the edge of the cover. Coll watched her, his nerves tightening. It was far too easy to imagine her finger trailing over his skin. "This is very precious. May I?" She glanced inquiringly at him, her hand poised over the book.

"What? Oh, yes, of course."

She began to turn the pages slowly, even reverently. She commented and asked questions, and Coll answered as best he could. It was difficult to concentrate with her only inches away. It was too easy, too pleasurable, to watch the way her eyes lit or to notice the shadow her lashes made upon her cheeks, to gaze at the movement of her lips, the velvety softness of her skin. He could not help but imagine how her skin would feel beneath his fingers, how her lips would taste.

He realized that Violet was watching him expectantly, and he knew that she must have asked him a question. He swallowed, his mind a blank. Her eyes were locked on his, dark and fathomless, pools a man could fall into, he thought, and never again surface. Her lips parted, but she said nothing. It would take so little to kiss her, to lean in and take her mouth . . .

Coll pulled back abruptly. "I . . . um, I'm

sorry. I was not . . . I did not hear what you said."

A flush rose in Violet's cheeks. "I asked — I hoped I could look at this journal again."

"Yes, of course. Whenever you'd like . . ." He was sliding into far too dangerous a territory here. It had been one thing to kiss her the other night on the road. Then it had been merely flirtation and she a woman whom he would not see again. But now . . . now he knew she was a lady, and if that did not place her far enough beyond his reach, she was a guest of the earl's, which put her under his care.

He made himself stand up. "I am sorry. I am keeping you from your bed." That was foolish. The mere mention of her bed was enough to send fire shooting through him. "I should go." Feeling inordinately clumsy, he pushed back his chair and closed the journal. "Good night, my lady."

He walked out, doing his best to keep his pace slow, as if he were not running away.

Three men waited for Violet at the site the next morning, just as Coll had promised. One of them was the young man, Dougal, who had seen her at Coll's table the morning before. He watched her with a combination of embarrassment and curiosity. They

94

leaned on the handles of their shovels, picks lying on the ground around them.

"You won't need your tools," Violet told them, and began to pull implements from a sack. "I brought the things you will use to excavate."

The men frowned down at the trowels, gardening forks, and brushes of varying sizes spread out on the ground. "We hae our shovels. We dinna need those wee things."

"This is a different sort of digging. You must be careful how you go about it." She knelt and began to show them the proper way to excavate. "Here around the stones, you must be especially precise."

The men watched her. "I dinna see why we maun gae sae slow," one of the gardeners said. "They're already auld and in pieces."

It took her a moment to figure out what he had said. "No." Violet shook her head emphatically. "That is exactly why you must be cautious. We cannot cause these stones any more damage. They are fragile."

"Fragile! But they're rocks."

"Very *old* rocks," Violet countered.

They continued to stare at her doubtfully. "But I dinna ken —"

"I realize that you do not." Violet fixed a

firm gaze on them. "However, that is the way you must do it."

With a shrug, the men picked up the trowels and began to dig where Violet directed. Her own work went slowly, for she repeatedly had to stop one or the other of the men to correct his work. Still, she was pleased with the progress they had made by the time they stopped at noon. The men tromped off, presumably going back to Duncally to eat, but Violet had brought a cold lunch for herself in a basket, and she ate in solitude, sitting on a rock at the top of the cliff and watching the ceaseless roll of the ocean.

Her mind went, as it had several times today, to Coll Munro. Last night, for a moment, she had thought he was about to kiss her. Obviously she had been wrong. He had not even been listening to her, and at the first opportunity he had bolted. Thank goodness she had done nothing to embarrass herself. At least, she hoped he had not sensed that she was leaning toward him, ready to give her lips to him.

Her cheeks flooded with heat. What if he had been aware of her reaction and that was the reason he left? Had he guessed that her eyes had been drawn to the sight of his bare arms, sleeves rolled up? That while she talked, she had been studying the golden hairs curling on his arm, the bony outcroppings of his wrist, the wide, capable hands? Had he guessed she'd wanted to trace the lines of bone and sinew with her fingers?

Violet prayed she had not been so transparent. Otherwise, she did not know how she could ever face the man again. She could only hope that he had merely been bored or that he thought her distinctly odd. She was accustomed to both reactions.

Shoving aside these humiliating thoughts, she plunged back into her work. She was soon so absorbed in it that it was almost midafternoon before she realized that her workers had not returned to the job. Violet let out a sigh. She was not surprised. Over the years, she had found that few men were willing to take orders from a woman. It was one reason why her uncle had always dealt with the workers.

It would take a long time to do all the work herself, but she had little expectation that Coll would give her more workers, given how little time she had been able to hold on to these. At least working alone would assure her of many months, even years, of activity . . . provided that the earl did not take the project away from her and give it to someone else when he returned.

It was all a very lowering prospect. The best thing was to get back to work and not think about it. As she picked up her trowel again, she spotted a man walking toward her. Coll Munro. An increasingly familiar flutter began in her stomach, and she rose to her feet, watching him.

His stride was long and confident, and despite the gray sky, his hair shone golden, stirred by a stray breeze. Coll glanced up and saw her, and she was surprised to see him smile. She had assumed he would be stern, even frowning. She had little doubt that he had come to take her to task for frightening off her workers.

"Mr. Munro." She went to meet him. "I know what brings you here."

"Do you now?" His eyes twinkled.

"I assume your men have refused to work for me any longer."

"That happens to you often, does it?" His voice was genial, his blue eyes twinkling. Violet wondered why the crinkling at the corner of his eyes was so appealing. "Nae, they dinna refuse to work for you."

"You surprise me."

"I can be very persuasive."

"Oh." She regarded him suspiciously. "Then why are you here?"

"Could it not be that I thought to keep

you company?"

"You left your work to keep me company? I find that hard to believe."

"Och, you are far too young to be so cynical."

"I am old enough to prefer plain speaking to flummery."

"You leave a man little choice." He thrust his hands into the pockets of his jacket and regarded her. "The McKenna brothers and young Dougal complained, that's true. They felt you did not appreciate their work."

"They didn't know how to dig properly. I had to instruct them. They cannot attack a site like this with picks and shovels. Far too much damage is done by enthusiasts, even antiquarians. Artifacts can be broken. It can make dating objects difficult, almost impossible."

"I understand."

"They simply did not like taking orders from a woman."

"You do them an injustice. Like any good Highlander, they do not like taking orders from anyone."

His words surprised a laugh out of Violet. "How did you convince them to return to work?"

"I told them that you are a trifle mad, as all English are, but since you are a friend of the earl's, they must put up with your eccentricities. It may have helped that I told them they dinna have a choice in the matter if they wanted to keep working for the earl."

Violet stared at him. "Truly?" Warmth spread through her at the thought that he had taken her side.

"Well, I canna have workers who do what they want instead of what I tell them."

"Oh." The warmth fled. "Of course not. Then I suppose you're here to tell me that though you ruled in my favor this time, you want me to change."

"Nae, I wouldna try to change you." He cast her a sideways smile. "But it might help you with the men if you dinna take everything so seriously. Life is grim enough; there is no need to make it more so."

"I appreciate your talking to the workmen, Mr. Munro, but you cannot understand my situation."

"Can I not?"

"You have a position of authority. You are an imposing figure." Violet began to tick the points off on her fingers. "You have a voice that impels obedience. Most of all, you are a man. I, as you have pointed out yourself, possess none of those assets. I *must* be forceful. Otherwise I am immediately dismissed, my words ignored. I cannot afford to be good-natured or mild or charming."

Coll studied her for a moment. "Come. Let's walk a bit." He turned, strolling back in the direction from which he had come, and Violet fell in beside him. "You are right. I am large and a man, and that makes it easier to get people's attention. But I was not always big, and my position of authority, as you call it, is a new thing. People do not obey every man they meet. Isobel Kensington is a lady, but her people do as she orders. There are other aspects to it."

"There may be, but I do not have them. I know I am considered difficult. I am not charming nor adept in conversation." Violet stared steadfastly ahead of her.

"Och, we both know that is not true. You are a dab hand at talking."

She gave him a rueful smile. "I am referring to the quality of what I say, not the quantity. I do not have 'winning ways.' Even if I did, I cannot allow myself to appear weak."

"Only a fool would consider you weak. I'll admit that men are not apt to look past a woman's beauty."

Violet glanced at him and quickly away, heat rising in her cheeks. Did he think she was beautiful? No, surely he had been speaking in generalities. Anyway, that was precisely what she despised — that women were considered worthwhile only for their looks — yet here she was, flattered that Coll might find her attractive.

Coll continued, "But that does not mean we are blind to a woman's character. How you conduct yourself tells me more than the way you look."

"And you think I should conduct myself differently." She crossed her arms.

He shrugged. "What you choose to do is up to you. But I know the people here. I can give you a bit of advice." His eyes twinkled. "My sister would tell you I always have a bit of advice."

"Very well. What would you advise?"

"It would help if you let everyone know you better."

"I don't understand."

"People listen to me because they know who I am, what I've done, how I act. When I tell someone how to build something, they believe I know what I'm talking about."

"But that is just it. I do know what I'm talking about."

"Yes, but they do not know *you*. To them, digging is digging, and who are you, after all, to tell them how to do it? They would not like me telling them the same thing, but they would admit I was apt to be right."

"I cannot change the fact that I am a stranger here."

"Aye, well, it will not happen immediately, but you could try to acquaint yourself with the people of the glen. Let them meet you and hear you. When you talk about the things you love, there is power in you. Perhaps you do not realize it."

Violet studied him. His words pleased her more than she wanted to consider. "But how am I to do that? I cannot go about introducing myself to everyone."

"There is a dance this Saturday. 'Tis a good place to meet people."

"A dance! Oh, no, I am not good at parties."

"How is one good or not good at a party? They are just there to enjoy."

Violet could not remember any party that she had enjoyed. They were invariably filled with stilted conversation — either she was tongue-tied or bored people to tears — and her watching other people dance, as all the while she wished she were someplace else. "I'm not even invited. How would I —"

"Ah, but I am. I'll take you."

"Oh. Well." Violet didn't know where to look. "That is kind of you, but I —"

"It won't be all common folk, if that is what worries you. There will be others like

103

you. It is at Baillannan."

"Others like me? What do you mean?"

"The gentry. Isobel, the woman giving it, is the old laird's daughter."

"You think I am too proud to visit with 'common folk'?" Violet faced him, fisting her hands on her hips. "That I am too high in the instep?"

"Nae, I dinna mean that. Only that you will have people there to whom you are more accustomed. Well-read, educated sorts. Isobel's husband is English. Her aunt is the one I told you about who knows all the local lore."

Somewhat mollified, Violet admitted, "I would like to talk to her."

"There will be music," he went on in the way of one offering enticements. "Dancing. Singing."

"But I — you mean Scottish dancing?"

"The sort of thing you said interested you. Customs. Traditions. Old stories. Old songs."

"It would be interesting to see."

"More fun to do. I'll teach you."

"Oh. Well." Just the thought of dancing with Coll made her heart pound. She glanced up and found him watching her. His eyes were the color of the sky on a sunny day, and a light was in them that made the blood sing in her veins. "That would be . . . but I do not . . . that is . . ."

"The whiskey will flow, the music will be fine; I can guarantee that, as my own father is playing. You might even get to see me make a fool of myself with a song or two, if the lads have gotten enough drams in me."

"You sing?"

He shrugged. "I've been known to."

Perhaps that was the reason his voice was so compelling, why the sound of it warmed her like brandy.

"Well, I could not pass up a chance to see that, could I?" She smiled up at him. "Very well. I will go to the dance with you."

6

Violet was ready for the party far too early, of course, another habit her mother regarded with disapproval. But Violet simply could not see the benefit in being late or in making a gentleman hang about waiting for her. Especially tonight. She pressed her hand against her stomach, unsure whether the fluttering there came from eagerness or trepidation.

She took a final slow twirl in front of the mirror. Her gown was plain, its only ornamentation an edging of black lace along the neckline, but at least it was not dowdy. Fashionably high-waisted and low-cut, the brown satin had a lustrous, almost coppery sheen. She had swept her hair up in a less severe style than usual, allowing a few soft curls to fall from the knot atop her head, and she had even fastened an ivory cameo around her throat.

She wondered what Coll would think

when he saw her. She had always considered it a great waste of time and thought to try to make her image into one a man would find pleasing, and she had been scornful of her mother and sisters for doing so. But now, thinking about the light that flashed in Coll's eyes sometimes when he looked at her, she could not keep from wishing she could bring about that look again.

Coll was already waiting when she went down the stairs. He turned and looked up at the sound of her footsteps. His eyes widened, moving slowly down her, and his mouth softened in a way that was disturbingly gratifying. Violet was glad she had her hand on the banister, for her legs seemed suddenly not to work.

"Ah, lass, you look bonny."

"I, um . . ." Violet hesitated on the stairs. "Thank you."

He smiled. "That was not so hard, was it?"

"I am not entirely devoid of manners." She went down the last few steps to join him. "And it is *not* that I am snobbish."

His brows sailed upward. "Is it not then? I fear you have lost me — what are we discussing?"

"My woeful way of making people dislike me."

"I am certain I dinna say that." He stepped back and took her cloak from the hands of the waiting maid. "And I have no desire to argue with you this night." He settled the cloak around her. His hands rested on her shoulders for an instant before he turned away. "Bundle up. We're going across the loch, and it can be chilly on the water."

"You mean, in a boat?"

"Unless you'd rather not. 'Tis the quickest way."

"No, I have no objection." Violet stuck her hands in her well-worn fur muff and followed him into the garden behind the house. He led her down the multiple levels to the stone balustrade overlooking the loch, where yet another set of stairs led down to a small wooden dock on the loch itself.

Coll climbed into one of the boats tied there, and to Violet's surprise, he turned and grasped her waist, lifting her down into it. Violet gasped in surprise, instinctively putting her hands on his arms to steady herself. His fingers dug into her, his large hands engulfing her waist, and for a moment they stood, as still and silent as if they were statues. Even through the layers of clothing, she could feel the warmth of his hands, the solidity of his arms. They were almost as close as if in an embrace, and

Violet felt a sudden, rushing urge to move those last few inches. It was so startling a thought that she stepped back, setting the boat to rocking beneath her feet.

"Careful." Coll released her waist but took her arms in a steadying grasp. "Sit down easy, or you'll have us both in the loch." He guided her onto the wooden plank seat.

Violet braced herself on the bench, somewhat uneasy at the gentle rocking of the boat. Coll reached up to untie the boat from the dock, then settled onto the seat across from her and took up the oars.

"Is this your first time on the water?"

"Yes." She frowned. "How, um, deep is the loch?"

"Deep enough." He peered at her. "Dinna tell me you are frightened?"

"Of course not. Only . . . I do not know how to swim."

"I'll have to teach you when it's warmer. Dinna worry." His grin flashed white in the darkness. "I won't let you drown."

Violet pulled up the hood of her cloak and thrust her hands into the warm muff. A peaceful hush hung over the dark water, broken only by the rhythmic splash of the oars. Moonlight glimmered on the surface of the water. Violet's nerves subsided. Watching the steady strength of Coll's arms as he pulled on the oars, it was easy to feel secure.

As Coll had said, it was not far across the loch, and they soon docked the boat and walked up the path to Baillannan, a far less steep and taxing climb than the sheer cliff of Duncally. The house before them had none of the whimsical towers and crenellations of Duncally. It was a simple, massive gray-stone block. Violet suspected it would be termed bleak by many who saw it, but its solidity had a certain sturdy appeal, heightened by the warm glow of its lit windows.

A number of buildings made of the same gray stone were grouped around the house, and Coll made his way to the largest of these. The wide double doors stood open, light and noise spilling out. Inside, lanterns hung from the rafters, casting a warm glow over the crowd. Wooden trestle tables had been placed against one wall of the vast room, and across from them stood another table topped with a large keg, around which a number of men had gathered. At the far end was a raised platform where some musicians were tuning their instruments.

How different it was from the ornate ballrooms where she had attended dances before. Violet had little time to take it all in before Coll guided her toward a group of people. One was a striking dark-haired man, elegant in formal black and white, and beside him stood a tall, willowy woman, equally fashionably dressed in a sky-blue gown. Pearls gleamed at her neck and throat. She glanced up and broke into a wide smile.

"Coll!" She held out both her hands to him, and Coll went to her, beaming.

Coll loved this woman; it was clear to see. Jealousy shot through Violet, startling in its intensity.

"Isobel." Coll took the woman's hands and placed a chaste kiss on the cheek she offered. This, then, was the woman Coll had mentioned, the descendant of the lairds of Baillannan. The man beside her, presumably, was her husband, Jack Kensington.

"We have not seen you since Meg's wedding," Isobel scolded playfully. "I think you have forgotten us."

"Nae. How could I do that?" Coll squeezed her hands and released them, turning to extend his hand to the man beside her. "Jack."

"Coll." The other man shook Coll's hand, seemingly unperturbed by the woman's fond greeting. Jack's gaze slid over to Violet, standing a few feet away. She had the sense that little escaped this man's attention.

"I'm sorry. I've forgotten my manners." Coll turned and came back to Violet. "Come meet Jack and Isobel. You needn't be shy. They are easy to talk to."

"I'm not shy," Violet said repressively. "I did not wish to intrude."

"Intrude?" He gave her an odd look. " 'Tis why we came here, is it not?"

Coll introduced her to the couple, explaining, "Lady Violet is here to study the ruins."

"Oh! Indeed?" Isobel looked surprised. "How wonderful! We are so interested in finding out about that place. Auntie . . ." She tugged at the elbow of a gray-haired woman. "Did you hear? Lady Violet is here to excavate the ruins. Lady Violet, allow me to introduce you to my aunt, Lady Elizabeth Rose."

To Violet's astonishment, the older woman's eyes lit up. "My dear . . ." She reached out to take Violet's hand. "This is wonderful! I am so eager to hear about the ruins. I was quite astonished when Meg and that nice young man — what was his name?" She glanced toward her niece.

"Lord Mardoun?"

"Yes. Mardoun." Her eyes crinkled. "Such a handsome young man. Well, when he and Meg stumbled across the place, we were all amazed. No one had any idea there had ever been a building there."

"That is what Mr. Munro told me."

"Was it a house, you think? Or just a wall? Isobel and I looked at the stones, but we could not tell much."

"I have only started, so I do not know how extensive it is or from what time it dates. But I think it is possible it may have been more than one dwelling."

"How exciting! That was once part of the Baillannan lands, but even the oldest of our records have no mention of any dwellings there."

"You have records?"

"Yes, hundreds of years of records. Not continuously, of course. There have been fires and sieges and such. And many a Rose was not as careful as they should have been." Elizabeth compressed her mouth in disapproval. "You know how men were in the Middle Ages — uninterested in knowledge or history, spending all their time drinking and fighting." She paused, reflecting. "Many still are, I suppose."

"You have record books from the medieval period?" Violet's voice was awed.

"Yes, perhaps you would like to look them over sometime?"

"I would love to."

"You must come for tea one day." Elizabeth tucked her hand in Violet's arm and steered her away. "Now tell me, what do you think happened there . . ."

"Well, that's the last we'll see of them," Coll said, and laughed.

Violet ignored him, engrossed in conversation. Elizabeth led her to a bench tucked away in a quiet corner of the room, and they settled down happily for a lengthy discussion of the ruins. Elizabeth, Violet discovered, was much more informative and dramatic regarding the discovery than either Coll or Lord Mardoun's letter had been.

"It happened after that storm, you see," Elizabeth said, settling into the cadence of a born storyteller. "The storm of the century, people are calling it — though I would not think that would be so great a distinction, as this century is only seven years old. Oh, but the wind howled around Baillannan that night! I can only imagine what it must have been like for poor Meg and her sweetheart, trapped in the caves."

Violet smiled at the description of the supremely sophisticated Earl of Mardoun as "Meg's sweetheart," but said only, "Mr. Munro showed me the cliff."

"Yes, they are riddled with caves. Meg knows her way about in them, but she had

114

not expected to get caught by the storm. Their boat was destroyed, so they had to climb out over the cliff. When they got to safe ground, they found that the winds had blown away so much sand that the tops of the rocks were exposed. So their ordeal was worth it. They found the treasure, too — not the whole treasure, of course, but at least the evidence."

"The treasure!"

"Yes. The gold that my father brought back from France for the Prince."

"The Prince?" Violet eyed Isobel's aunt uncertainly.

Elizabeth caught her glance and chuckled. "I have not lost all my wits, I promise you. There really was a treasure, no matter how much skeptics like my cousin like to scoff. It was during the Uprising, and my father, Malcolm Rose, brought back money from the French king to aid Bonnie Prince Charlie."

"Oh." Violet nodded, relieved. "I see."

"Most people believed Papa never came home. There were other tales that he had returned and that he had brought gold from the French king and hidden it. But no one ever found it."

"But Lord Mardoun and Coll's sister came upon it in the caves?"

"Not the entire treasure. They found only a few coins and the remains of a money bag with the Rose insignia on it. Still, it proved that the treasure was real and not just another of the old legends."

"Mr. Munro said that you are the expert on the old legends."

"I'm hardly an expert," Elizabeth said self-deprecatingly. "But I do know a great many of them. Are you interested in the old stories?"

"Indeed I am. In all the traditions and customs of the area. I hope you will tell me about them."

"I would be delighted." The older woman's cheeks pinked with pleasure, and she began to talk.

They were soon so lost in the tales that neither of them noticed Coll's approach until he cleared his throat. "Ladies?"

"Oh!" Violet's head flew up. "Mr. Munro. I did not realize —" She glanced around vaguely.

"I noticed." He smiled.

"Oh, dear." Elizabeth looked contrite. "I have been monopolizing our guest, haven't I? I am sorry."

"It has been delightful talking to you," Violet assured her. "I would love to chat with you again."

"So would I. But now . . ." Elizabeth's eyes twinkled up at Coll. "I believe that Coll wants to sweep you off to the dance floor." She rose, patting the man's arm.

"The dance floor?" Violet's eyes widened in alarm. "No, indeed, I don't know how —" She turned toward Elizabeth, but the older woman was already walking away.

"Dinna worry. I'm not here to force you to dance. I brought you a taste of the local nectar." He held out a glass.

"Whiskey?" Violet eyed the golden-brown liquid with interest. No one, not even her uncle, had ever offered her whiskey. It was considered scandalous for a lady to drink anything stronger than a glass of sherry.

"You canna know the Highlands if you dinna have a wee dram. Think of it as a remedy to make meeting the natives more pleasant." A challenge was in his smile.

Violet smiled back in much the same way, taking the glass and sampling the golden-brown liquid. It hit her tongue like liquid fire. "That is — that is —"

"Nae, lass, you must not sip at it like a bird. You have to embrace the whiskey. Toss it down." He demonstrated with his own drink. "That's the way."

Violet gulped the rest of it down in one swallow. For an instant, she thought she had lost her breath entirely. Her insides joined in the conflagration of her mouth.

"You tricked me!" she accused when at last she recovered her voice. A long shudder ran through her.

"I wouldna trick you." His dancing eyes belied his words. " 'Tis the way to do it. And now you will understand Highlanders better."

"I understand that you are all mad to drink such a thing."

He laughed. "But your nerves have disappeared, have they not?"

To her surprise, Violet joined in his laughter. She did, actually, feel rather . . . pleasant.

"What do you say to meeting a few people?"

"I say yes."

To her surprise, Violet found herself enjoying meeting the other partygoers. It was easy to start a conversation with Coll by her side. He knew everyone and, even more astonishing to Violet, could find something to say to each person. Coll introduced her to Sally McEwan, the cook at Duncally, whom Violet had not yet met. Sally's greeting was polite but guarded. However, at Violet's heartfelt praise of her meals, the woman warmed up, and when Coll mentioned

Violet's interest in the "old ways," Sally happily launched into a description of the various winter traditions around the loch.

"Now, if you want to know about the past," Sally said, breaking off from the story she was telling and nodding toward someone behind Coll and Violet, "it's Auld Angus you should ask."

Violet glanced over her shoulder and saw a small, wizened man approaching them. His face was lined and leathery, and his bushy, white eyebrows gave him the illusion of scowling. Or, Violet thought, looking at the set of his mouth, perhaps it was no illusion. Coll muttered something beneath his breath.

"Weel, Munro," the old man said with grim satisfaction, "so you've joined the tyrant."

"Hello, Angus. Always a pleasure to see you."

Angus snorted and turned his gaze on Violet. "Another Sassenach, I see."

The old man's expression was so filled with gloom, his voice so ripe with resignation and disapproval, it made Violet want to laugh. She crossed her arms and raised her chin in a manner that mirrored his. "Yes, I am. And you are another Scot."

Something twinkled in his dark eyes. "Ah,

weel . . ." Angus heaved a sigh. "I knew how it would be once Red Meg bewitched that devil."

At Violet's blank look, Coll supplied, "He means my sister and the Earl of Mardoun."

"Ah. And why is the earl the devil, Mr. . . . um . . ."

"McKay." Coll sighed. "This is Angus McKay. Angus, allow me to introduce you to the woman you are offending — Lady Violet Thornhill."

"Aye, I ken who she is." The old man cast Coll a look of contempt. "All the glen knows the mad Englishwoman whae's digging up the rocks." Ignoring Coll's smothered groan, Angus turned back to Violet. "The English canna let anything be."

"And you, I take it, have no curiosity?" Violet countered. "You would pass by a wall of rocks suddenly poking out of the ground and not wonder why they were there? Or when they were laid? And how they came to be covered up?"

The old man let out a strangled noise that Violet thought might be a laugh. "Aye, I micht wonder a wee bit."

"As did I." Violet smiled. "Perhaps you would like to take a closer look at the dig, Mr. McKay. If you want to come by some afternoon, I would be happy to show you around."

"Hmmph." McKay regarded her for a moment. "And sae I micht."

Sally distracted Old Angus by asking him about the state of his ailing back. He responded with a fierce admonition that it was none of her business, followed by a lengthy description of each and every twinge of pain he had suffered.

As the others chatted around them, Coll bent his head toward Violet's. "Now you've let yourself in for it. Old Angus will be there to visit tomorrow, I'll wager."

"I look forward to it."

"I believe you do." Coll grinned. "I might have known. The two of you will squabble the whole afternoon and doubtless enjoy every minute of it."

Violet laughed. "Are you comparing me to a crotchety old man?"

"Nae, I'm not fool enough to step into that quagmire." Coll's blue eyes danced, and Violet's heart lifted in response. It was almost impossible not to glow under the warmth of his smile. His eyes darkened, the warmth turning into another sort of heat.

Violet felt herself blushing, and she looked away, her gaze falling on a young blond woman on the other side of the room. The girl had a fresh, pretty face, but it was

121

marred by the scowl that creased her forehead. She stared at Violet as if contemplating where to plunge the knife.

Startled, Violet glanced away quickly. Before she could ask Coll the girl's name, the girl herself swept up to them, her face now beaming.

"Coll Munro!" The blonde reached out to give his arm a playful tap. "It's been ages since I hae seen you. Pa was saying yesterday that you maun hae got too grand for us." She did not glance toward Violet or the others, her eyes fixed on Coll.

"Nae, now, Dot, you know I'm not too grand." Coll shifted from one foot to the other. "There's a deal of work to be done and, um . . ." He glanced at Violet. "Have you met Lady Thornhill? My lady, allow me to introduce you to Miss Cromartie."

"Ooh, a lady." Dot's eyes widened dramatically and she bobbed a curtsy. " 'Tis an honor. I hope you dinna find it too quiet and simple for you here, my lady."

Violet suspected the girl meant the opposite. She also suspected that Miss Cromartie had her sights firmly set on Coll. She wondered if Coll reciprocated her feelings. He appeared a trifle stiff and uncomfortable, but Violet was not sure how to interpret that.

"Your da's been playing for half an hour now," Dot went on, gazing up at Coll with limpid eyes. "And you hae no' asked me to take the floor with you even once."

"Um, well, I've been talking."

"But you maun dance!" Dot aimed a dazzling smile at him, leaning in. "I heard him say a reel's next. Will you no' come and dance with me?" She held out her hands.

"Well, um . . ." Coll glanced toward Violet, then Sally, and finally said, "Yes, of course. If you will excuse me . . ." He nodded toward the others and started with Dot toward the dance floor. Violet noticed he did not take the girl's hand.

"Och, that Dot, she's been chasing Coll for two months now." Sally shook her head.

"They are courting?" Violet asked casually.

"*She* is," Angus McKay snorted. "Not Coll."

"She's not one who could hold his interest for long," Sally agreed.

"The lass is thick as a plank of wood," Angus added.

"There's many a man dinna mind a foolish wife, but not our Coll." Sally gave an approving nod.

"I am surprised Mr. Munro is not spoken for," Violet said. "He seems a very eligible bachelor."

"Aye, that he is. But particular." Sally gave Violet an assessing glance. "It's the way he was brought up. Here at Baillannan with all the Roses."

"Och, the Munros hae ayeways been choosy." Angus shook his head.

"Coll seems very fond of Mrs. Kensington," Violet ventured, glancing over at Isobel. She was a beautiful woman, blond and tall and slender as a sylph. Just the opposite of Violet herself.

"Oh, aye, he's nigh as much a brother to her as he is to Meg," Sally said.

Violet was not as certain that Coll's feelings for Isobel Kensington were those of a brother. She watched Isobel as she smiled and nodded to a departing guest, then turned back to her husband. Jack bent his head toward his wife's, his eyes as soft on her as a caress. Isobel gazed back up at him, smiling, and though they did not touch, intimacy and love radiated from them with such clarity that it took Violet's breath away.

What must it be like to love like that and be loved in return? To feel the closeness, the warmth, the magical exclusion of all else in the world? A pang pierced Violet's chest. She herself would never know the feeling, the oneness; she had given up hope of that long ago. Yet for an aching instant she could not help but wish that she could know the sweet taste of love.

Resolutely Violet turned away. She was certain now that Isobel did not love Coll beyond the sisterly affection Sally had described. But that did not mean he felt the same way about Isobel. Perhaps he loved her even though her heart was given to another.

Violet's gaze went to the dance floor, where it was easy to find Coll, taller than anyone else. She watched him, flushed and smiling, as he circled the floor, the lantern light catching the gold of his hair. He did not look like a man suffering from unrequited love.

Violet realized suddenly that her companions had fallen silent, and she turned to find them watching her. "I — I beg your pardon. My mind had drifted."

"Och, no matter." Sally waved it away. " 'Tis a lively song they're playing. What lass wouldn't rather be out on the floor than talking to old folks?"

"Oh, no — I'm not going to dance."

"What? A lass who does not like to dance? I canna believe that."

"No. I mean, I do not know these dances."

"Then you must learn! Coll!"

Violet saw that the music had stopped and Coll was strolling back, thankfully without Dot Cromartie. "Oh, no, Sally, do not make Coll —"

Beside Violet, Angus shook his head, saying with some sympathy, "Nae, you micht as weel try to stop the sea as Sally McEwan when she's got the bit between her teeth."

"Coll Munro, hae you no' taught this girl our dances?" Sally clucked her tongue in disapproval.

"Dinna scold, Sally." Coll grinned. "I promised I would show her tonight."

"You just want to see me look foolish stumbling about among all these nimble-footed people," Violet teased Coll, amazed by how fiercely she wanted to dance with him.

"Never," he denied, holding out his hand to her.

"Very well, then. Teach me." Violet took his hand.

"Here you go, lass." Angus pulled a flask from inside his jacket. "Take a wee sip; it'll gie you courage."

Violet took a gulp from his flask. Her eyes began to water as her insides burst into flames. However fiery the drink Coll had coaxed her into taking earlier had been, it was the sweetest of wine compared to this.

Indeed, she thought perhaps the old man had mistakenly filled his flask with kerosene.

Angus beamed with pride. "Angus McKay's whiskey cures all."

"I daresay." It would, she thought, kill any number of pestilences.

Coll leaned in, chuckling. "I dinna think to warn you: never take whiskey from Old Angus."

"My mouth is numb." Violet licked her lips. "And I think the top of my head is about to explode. I cannot possibly dance now."

Coll's laughter increased. "Ah, nae, lass. Many a Scot will tell you, a dram makes the dancing easier."

He showed her the steps, then led her through them, with Sally and Angus offering their encouragement and conflicting advice. Amazingly, with Coll's hands at her waist, guiding her through the steps, Violet did not feel clumsy or ignorant, and her mistakes only made her laugh along with him. When he pulled her out onto the floor, she went easily, not caring whether she appeared clumsy or could think of nothing to say. Indeed, with the music and the sound of feet stamping and people clapping or laughing or calling out, there was no need to speak at all. Here, with Coll, dancing was not methodical, stiff, and boring. With Coll, it was . . . delightful.

The rest of the evening whirled by for Violet, both literally and figuratively. She danced not only with Coll, but with Jack and Isobel's cousin Gregory and several of the Baillannan crofters whose names she did not know. She spent a half hour chatting with Elizabeth and Isobel. Isobel introduced her to Coll's father, a handsome man with twinkling blue eyes and a ready charm. It was easy to see where Coll had gotten both his looks and his smile.

When Coll and Violet left the party, she was in a soaring mood. As they walked to the boat, she broke away to dance a few of the steps she had just learned. The trip across the loch held no fear for her this time. Violet, humming beneath her breath, pushed back her hood and let the air cool her flushed cheeks. Coll began to sing the words to the tune, and Violet wrapped her arms around her knees and leaned forward, losing herself in the sound. It was a sad, haunting song, but Violet did not care. All that mattered was the moonlight on his hair, the hush of the night, and the way his voice wound through her. Listening to Coll, she thought, she could not be cold.

When they reached Duncally's dock, Coll

climbed out to tie up the dory, then reached down to help her up the wooden ladder to the platform. His hand engulfed hers. She had forgotten her muff when they left the party, and now she was glad, for his hands were strong and warm and the roughness of his skin against hers added to the thrumming energy inside her. When she reached the dock, Violet swung around, arms upraised and face lifted to the sky.

"It was a wonderful evening!"

"Careful." Coll reached out to steady her. "We canna have you tumbling into the loch." He did not take his hands away.

"I shan't." Violet smiled up at him, resting her hands on his arms.

"I'm glad you enjoyed the party."

"It was perfect. I learned dances; I heard stories; I met wonderful people."

"So you did." He smiled. "You also sampled the whiskey. Perhaps too much."

"Nonsense." She paused, tilting her head consideringly. "Though I do fear that after Old Angus's 'wee sip,' my tongue may be forever singed."

Coll laughed, his fingers flexing on her waist. His thumbs began to circle slowly. "You are a beautiful woman."

Violet's lips curved, and she swayed toward him. Taking his lapels in her hands, she gave a little tug. "I think *you* are the one who drank too much whiskey."

"Nonsense." He tossed back her answer as he bent toward her, his fingers spread wide, urging her gently toward him.

"I am 'wee' and dictatorial."

"You are perfect."

He lowered his head, and Violet stretched up to meet him. Then his mouth was on hers and his arms were around her, lifting her up into him. She wrapped her arms around his neck, every nerve in her body igniting. She clung to him as her world tilted, then narrowed to just this man, only this moment.

The wool of his jacket was scratchy beneath her fingertips, his heat all around her, his lips like velvet and tasting faintly of whiskey. The night air caressed her cheeks, and the smell of the loch mingled with the scent of peat fires; the water lapped hypnotically against the dock. It all twined and twisted in her, part of the surging hunger, the pleasure and excitement that rushed in her so hard and fast she trembled.

Coll pressed her into him, his mouth consuming hers with the same fiery urgency that burned in her. His hands slid beneath her cloak, roaming over the soft curves and dips of her body. Violet shuddered, astonished and aroused. She ached with a yearning to know more, feel more, taste more.

With a groan, Coll pulled his mouth from hers. "Violet . . ." His chest rose and fell in rapid breaths. He closed his eyes and leaned his forehead against hers, his hands resting loosely on her hips. "I canna do this."

"Oh." Violet stiffened. She pulled back, embarrassment burning through her. "I beg your pardon."

"No . . . wait." He followed her, reaching for her arm, but she sidestepped his touch. "You've been drinking. I canna —"

"Of course. You are right." Violet's voice was brittle. "Clearly I am not in full possession of my senses." She fairly ran up the stairs to the garden. Her cheeks flamed, not with passion now but shame. She had been drunk, he was saying. She had fallen into his arms like a drunken hussy.

Violet thought back with horror. Perhaps she had been drunk the whole evening. What if all the bonhomie, the fun, the conviviality, had merely been the product of her inebriation! It occurred to her now that everyone had been humoring her because she was Coll's guest. She had been an embarrassment to him.

She heard him coming after her. "Violet . . . please. I am sorry. I dinna mean to

— I should not have kissed you, but I was — you were so . . ."

"Bosky? Besotted?" Violet whirled to face him, shame fueling her anger. "Yes. I realize. The whiskey went to my head. I acted like a fool. I wish I had not gone. I wish you had not asked me." She caught her breath, dangerously near tears.

He stiffened, his hand falling to his side. "I apologize."

"You need not accompany me any farther. I can find my way through the garden. Good night, Mr. Munro."

"My lady."

She did not pause until she had reached the upper gardens, and when she looked back, Coll was no longer there.

7

Violet awoke the next morning with a violent headache and the bitter taste of regret in her mouth. She had made a proper fool of herself, and she didn't know how she could face Coll again. But then, she would probably not have to — he would make sure to avoid her. The thought did little to lighten her spirits.

Since it was Sunday, she did not have even the distraction of working at the ruins to keep her from brooding over the humiliating way she had thrown herself at Coll last night. She had told Coll that she did not care what others thought of her, but she realized now that she did indeed care — very much — what Coll thought of her.

She had been so sure he felt the same desire she did. His mouth had been so hungry, his embrace so tight. But then he had pulled away, saying he could not do it, as if he had forced himself to respond to

133

her advances but finally gave up. Clearly, she knew nothing about men.

It was a relief a day later to be able to throw herself back into work. The discovery of a small pierced, carved piece of bone also raised her spirits — though she wished, with a fierce pang of sorrow, that Uncle Lionel were here to share in the excitement.

Later in the day, she glanced up from her sketch of the site and the artifact's position in it and was surprised to see a man walking toward them. He was small and wore a bright red, knitted cap, beneath which a fringe of white hair peeked out. In one hand, he gripped a gnarled, dark wooden staff, but from the spryness of his walk, he scarcely needed it. Violet recognized him at once.

"Mr. McKay." She smiled. Behind her Dougal let out a groan, but she ignored him. "I am glad you took me up on my invitation."

"Aye. I'd a mind to see what you were up to." The old man surveyed the ruins. "Doesna look like much tae me." He turned his gaze on the McKenna brothers and Dougal. "I would hae thought young Munro would gie you better workers."

Bruce McKenna rolled his eyes, and his brother said, "Whisht, now, Angus, hae you naught better tae do than tae watch men work?"

"Is that what you're doing?" Angus retorted. "Hae you found aught but sand?"

"As a matter of fact, we did." Proudly, Violet unwrapped her handkerchief to reveal the small article inside.

Angus leaned in to peer at the piece of bone. "A bit wee, isn't it?"

Violet laughed. "Mr. McKay, do you ever say anything nice?"

"Course I do." He ignored the snort from the men. "When I see something that warrants it."

The old man settled down on a nearby rock and spent the rest of the afternoon watching them work, now and then tossing in a comment about their efforts and the results (or lack thereof). He returned the next day, so apparently he had enjoyed his visit, though Violet was not sure why.

Violet saw nothing of Coll the next two days. That was precisely what she wanted, of course; she was careful not to walk past the gatehouse — indeed she was careful not to even look in that direction. She avoided the library in the evening. It was somewhat lowering that Coll just as assiduously avoided coming to the main house.

When she did see Coll again, she was

completely unprepared. She was kneeling at the excavation site when she felt an intangible change in the atmosphere and looked up. Coll Munro was walking toward the site. He moved with his usual easy grace, and she was reminded all over again of how wide his shoulders were, how long his legs. He wore no cap, and the wind teased the strands of his hair.

Her throat closed, her chest tightened, and for a moment she could not move. Then she popped to her feet, stepping on her skirt and stumbling. Already she looked a fool.

Violet lifted her chin. "Mr. Munro." Her voice sounded tinny in her ears. "To what do we owe this pleasure?"

"My lady." He stopped several feet away. The sun was behind him, making it difficult to read his expression. "I, um — Isobel would like to visit your site."

Isobel had asked him. Of course that would bring him. Violet kept her voice steady. "Mrs. Kensington and her aunt have an open invitation."

"Yes, well. She sent a note saying they planned to visit this afternoon. I thought you might like to know." He shifted. "So you could expect them."

"No doubt they would find us doing the same thing, expected or not. But thank you

136

for the warning."

Coll nodded and glanced toward the men, who ostentatiously turned and went back to work. He came closer, and Violet moved to the side.

"Vio— I mean, my lady." Coll followed her. "I wanted to speak with you."

"Indeed?" She could see his expression clearly now. He was frowning.

"Yes. About the other night . . ."

"It was an enjoyable party." She smiled brightly. "Thank you for suggesting it to me."

"I am glad you enjoyed it, but that wasn't what I meant. I was talking about afterward, at the dock." He shoved his hands into the pockets of his jacket. "I wanted to apologize."

"There is no need. 'Twas I who was at fault."

"You!" He stared.

"Yes. My actions were inappropriate. As you said, I had been drinking, and —"

"Inappropriate?"

"Yes. I am aware my actions were unwelcome and . . . and forward."

"Forward!"

"Really, Mr. Munro, are you going to parrot everything I say?"

"But you — I was not saying that *you*

were —"

"There is no need to soften the blow." Was he being purposely difficult? "Clearly you cannot make yourself want to — well, engage in, um . . ."

"Are you daft? What are you saying?"

Violet bristled. "I am saying that I acted out of character. I assure you, it will not happen again. And it is time this conversation ended. Good day, sir."

"Wait. Why are you the one to decide if this conversation is over?"

"Mr. Munro! Lower your voice!" Violet hissed, glancing toward the workers.

Coll clenched his teeth, casting a glance over his shoulder at the three men, who had given up all pretense of work and stood watching them. "The devil!" His eyes moved past the men. "Bloody hell. They would show up now." Violet followed his gaze. Isobel and her aunt were walking toward the ruins. Coll swung back, scowling. "This conversation is *not* over."

"Indeed?" Violet raised her eyebrows and swept past him. "Lady Elizabeth, Mrs. Kensington, I am so glad to see you."

Despite the way it began, Violet enjoyed the afternoon. Coll took his leave almost immediately. Violet guided the two women around the site, explaining where she and

the men were digging and why, and show-
ing them the pieces of pierced bone they
had found. It was gratifying to share the
discovery and even more so to see the real
interest in their faces.

"You think these were part of some jewelry?" Isobel asked, turning the larger piece
of bone over in her fingers.

"Yes, I believe the holes drilled in them
would indicate so. We found these other two
small pieces yesterday, very near the location of the larger piece."

"They must be very old." The awe in Isobel's voice was so similar to Violet's own
feelings that she warmed to the other
woman.

After all, Isobel could not help being the
ideal of beauty that Violet could never hope
to attain. Nor was it Isobel's fault that Coll's
face had lit up when he saw her at the dance
— which was an absurd reason to resent a
person, anyway. If Coll nursed an unrequited love for Mrs. Kensington, it was no
business of Violet's.

They chatted at length about the possible
origins of the site and how Violet planned
to proceed. Rarely was she able to converse
with another female who had the same
eagerness to learn as her, and Violet enjoyed
the conversation so much that she per-

suaded Isobel and Elizabeth to have tea with her at Duncally after they finished at the site.

For the first time since the dance at Baillannan, Violet went to bed that evening in a happy mood — which made it even odder when she awoke in the middle of the night, heart pounding, filled with a vague sense of unease. She pushed back the bed curtains and looked out over the room. The coals in the fireplace lent a dim reddish glow to the darkness of the chamber, against which the furniture made even blacker shapes. Just as she was about to close the heavy draperies and go back to sleep, a low metallic clank was followed by a muffled exclamation. Someone was in the house.

It had to be Coll, visiting the library again. Violet slipped out of bed and tiptoed to the clock on the mantel. Two o'clock. Coll would not be in Duncally looking for a book in the middle of the night. Perhaps one of the servants. But the servants' hall and bedrooms were on the floor below. There was no reason for any of them to be in this wing now.

Violet opened the door into the hall and peered out. The corridor was not completely dark; a sconce or two high on the walls burned dimly, leaving pools of shadows up and down the way. The house loomed around her, dark and silent, the long stretch of corridor with its closed doors on either side whispering of hidden things.

She watched, nerves stretching. Suddenly a shape moved out of a door down the hallway, dark and silent, heading toward the stairs. Violet jumped, her nerves zinging through her. Without thinking, she flung her door wide. "Stop! Who is that!"

The figure took off at a run. Violet pelted after him, grabbing up a heavy candlestick from one of the tables as she ran. As she reached the top of the staircase, she saw the figure turn the corner of the landing and race downward. Violet followed, gripping the empty candleholder like a club.

A dim light was on the floor below, and it moved away as footsteps clattered across the marble floor. When Violet reached the bottom of the stairs, she turned toward the light and saw a dark figure carrying a lantern slip through the front door. Violet ran after him, bursting out into the night. Something crashed down on the back of her head, and she pitched forward onto the steps.

The blow stunned Violet, but it did not knock her out, and instinctively she broke the fall with her hands. For a moment she lay there, stunned, then lifted her head. It was drizzling, she realized, and cold. Patches of fog drifted across the drive, but she caught sight of the lantern light, diffused by the fog. A figure ran down the driveway and into the mist, the lantern bobbing at the level of his knees.

Violet pushed herself up and ran after him. She was vaguely aware of the sting of her palms and the throbbing in her head, but they did not slow her as she tore along the driveway. The moving light drew farther and farther away until at last it disappeared altogether, swallowed up by the night. She slowed and finally stopped, her chest heaving. She shivered, realizing all at once how cold and wet she was.

Ahead of her was the dark bulk of a cottage. The gatehouse. "Coll!"

She ran forward. A light appeared in the window as she reached the house. Violet pounded her fist against the door. "Coll!"

She braced one hand against the doorframe, her head whirling, gasping for air. The door jerked open, and Coll stood in the doorway. He had obviously been pulled from his bed by her cries, for he was barefoot and shirtless and his hair fell messily around his face. Behind him a candle flickered on the table.

"Violet! Good Lord!" He reached out to take her arm. Violet tried to take a step, but her limbs seemed strangely disconnected from her. Her stomach pitched. She saw Coll's lips moving, but she could not hear his words. Her knees began to buckle.

Coll caught her as she crumpled to the floor.

8

Coll swept Violet up in his arms and carried
her across the room to the fireplace. She
leaned her head against him, closing her
eyes on the suddenly tilting room. His chest
was warm and solid, reassuring, and it was
tempting to let go, to slide into the darkness, held by him. Safe.

He knelt, setting Violet on the floor before
the fire, his arms still around her, and laid a
hand against her cheek. "What happened?
You're shaking like a leaf."

She realized that she was, indeed, shiver-
ing, and she clenched her jaw to keep her
teeth from chattering.

"It's all right." Coll's voice was low and
soothing. "You're safe now." He shifted so
that he was sitting on the floor, and he
cradled her against his chest.

In the back of her mind, Violet knew she
should pull away, not allow herself to be
weak and dependent, but she could not

move. It was too nice here, enveloped in his warmth. The sensation of his bare skin against her cheek was odd, but pleasurable as well, smooth skin and the prickle of hair. She thought of the way he'd looked standing in the doorway — the wide expanse of bare chest with the overlying V of curling, red-brown hair, the hard, straight line of his collarbone and broad shoulders, the curve of muscle beneath the skin.

Her cheeks warmed. "I'm sorry. I'm getting you all wet."

"Dinna fret about that."

With her cheek against his chest, she felt the rumble of his voice as well as heard it, and it turned her soft and achy inside. The surge of feeling alarmed her, giving her the strength to pull away. Coll leaned back, his eyes dropping from her face to her chest. Red flared along his cheekbones, and his eyes went dark. Violet realized that the rain had soaked her nightgown. The wet material clung to her body, almost transparent, her full breasts and darker nipples, prickling from the cold, clearly visible.

She could not move. In the silence, she could hear the breath in Coll's throat turn harsh and fast. His face softened, eyelids drooping down over the sudden heat in his eyes. Finally, by force of will, Violet turned

145

her face away, wrapping her arms around herself. As if her movement had released him, too, Coll surged to his feet. "I'll, um, get you a . . ."

He grabbed a colorful, knitted afghan from the back of the armchair beside the fireplace. Violet rose and took it, wrapping it tightly around her. She felt stronger, less vulnerable now, but she was aware of an odd twinge of loss as well.

Coll picked up a poker and prodded the fire into life, tossing in another brick of peat. The flare of light tinged his skin red and gold. Violet watched the movement of muscles across his back, the sharp outthrust of shoulder blades. He was a powerful man; it was even more obvious without the covering of his clothes. She should, she thought, be intimidated by his size and strength. Instead she was . . . excited.

Coll turned back to her, and Violet glanced away, embarrassed at being caught staring. He set the poker in its stand with a clang and strode from the room. When he returned, he had donned a shirt and carried a folded blanket. Draping the blanket around Violet's shoulders, he went to pour water into a kettle and hang it over the fire.

"What happened? Why did you come running out without anything — um, I mean, dressed in —" He did not look at her as he pulled out cups and the tea tin.

"Someone broke into the house." Violet avoided the subject of her attire.

"What?" Coll whipped around. "Into Duncally? Who? Why?"

"I don't know. I didn't get a good look at him — though I doubt I would have recognized him anyway."

"A thief. Bold, to steal from Mardoun." His eyes narrowed, and he stiffened. "Or was he — did he come into your room? Did he hurt you?"

"No — I mean, he did hit me, but that was later."

"He *hit* you?"

"Yes. Don't shout. I ran after him out of the house, and he must have hidden behind the door. He popped out and knocked me on the head." Her hand went up, searching for the soreness.

"Where?" Coll grasped her shoulders and dragged her closer to the candle on the table, his eyes running over her face and hair.

"On the back of my head." Violet gingerly laid her fingers on the spot.

Coll let out a low curse and planted her on a chair beside the table. "Why didn't you tell me?"

"I just did."

Coll made a disgusted noise and strode off, returning with a bottle and a cloth, as well as a kerosene lamp, which he set down beside her on the table. Turning up the wick, he examined her. "Aye, you'll have a bump, all right. 'Tis fortunate your head is so hard." He poured a dark liquid from the bottle onto the cloth and began to dab at the wound.

"Ow!" Violet shot him a dark look.

Coll slanted back an amused glance and continued to treat her. "I dinna see any blood." His big hands were surprisingly gentle. When he finished working, he slid one hand down over her hair before pulling it away. The touch sent a shiver through her that had nothing to do with either the cold or the pain in her head. "I don't think there's a cut, but just in case, that will help heal it."

He turned away to pour hot water over the tea leaves. "Now." He set the pot on the table beside Violet, then put a stool directly in front of her and sat down on it, staring into her face. "Tell me exactly what happened. Why were you chasing this fellow about the house?"

"I woke up. I must have heard a noise. Then I heard a clang. He must have dropped something or knocked it over."

"In your bedchamber?" Coll kept his voice level but his face was hard as stone.

"No, no. It was nothing to do with me. The noise was down the hall. I got up and looked out. At first I didn't see anything, but then a man came out of one of the rooms closer to the stairs." She shivered involuntarily at the memory of that shadow slipping silently along the hall. "It scared me."

"Scared you so much you gave chase to him."

"I couldn't just let him get away, could I?"

"Aye, you could. A sensible woman would have. He could have hurt you — worse than he did."

"I didn't have time to think. I yelled at him and he ran, so I went after him. He ran down the stairs and out the front door."

"So you took off into the night after an intruder? Unarmed? Wearing naught but your night rail?"

"I told you, I didn't stop to think about it! Would you have sat there twiddling your thumbs and let him get away?"

"No, of course not, but —"

"I know, I know, you're twice the size I am and you're a man, so it's all right for you to want to thwart a thief, but not a weak woman like me."

"I would never call you weak."

"Anyway, I wasn't unarmed. I grabbed a candlestick from one of the tables."

A short bark of laughter escaped Coll. "A candlestick!" He sat back, crossing his arms, and regarded her with a blend of amusement and exasperation. "All right, so you ran after the fellow, wielding your fearsome candlestick . . ."

"And when I stepped out the door, he hit me from behind." Violet sighed. "I should have thought of that."

"Ah, but your blood was up."

"I realize that you derive a great deal of amusement from my mistakes," Violet began tartly. "But I fail to —"

"Nae, not that!" Coll took her hands. "I have no joy at seeing you injured. You must know that. It is your spirit I enjoy." He glanced down as if surprised to see her hands in his. He frowned. "You dinna tell me he hurt your hands as well."

"Oh, that. I fell down when he knocked me on the head, and the stone scraped my palms."

Frowning, he poured more of the brown liquid on the cloth and began to wash her palms. His head was bent over his task, and

Violet was free to watch him. His hair glistened in the glow of the lamp, a mingling of gold and silver that fell carelessly across his forehead. She wondered what it would feel like beneath her fingers. The medicine stung, but she scarcely noticed, too aware of Coll's nearness and his warm, work-roughened palm beneath her hand.

He set the rag aside, his hands sliding slowly from hers, and as he leaned back, his eyes dropped down her. He drew in a sharp breath. "Dinna tell me you ran all that way in your bare feet."

Self-consciously Violet tucked her unshod feet beneath her chair. "Well . . . yes."

"You're a madwoman." Coll dropped to one knee and shocked her by taking her heel in his hand to examine the sole of her foot.

"I doubt the intruder would have waited for me to put on my stockings and shoes." Violet jerked her foot away, feeling at once foolish and jittery and surging with heat. "I'm fine."

"Naturally." Coll walked away.

Violet contemplated her feet. They looked obscenely naked. She had never really thought about her feet before, but she realized now that they were too bony and white. Altogether unpleasing. Not only were they ugly, they were *dirty*. And scratched.

And Coll had touched them. No other man had ever touched her feet. Indeed, no other man had ever *seen* her feet. He must think her an awful heathen. What sort of woman would go running out as she had, clad in only her nightgown, pursuing a thief, paying no attention that it was raining and she wore no shoes? A madwoman, as he had said.

The feel of his fingers had set everything inside her churning, just as it had the other night. Violet closed her eyes. She could not let him see how he affected her. She must not embarrass herself again. She heard Coll returning and cut her eyes toward him. He placed a large bowl on the table and poured water into it. Picking up the brown bottle, he added a dollop of medicine to the water.

"What are you doing?"

"Someone has to tend to you." He poured the remainder of the water from the teakettle into the bowl. "Since clearly you dinna have any care for yourself."

He knelt, setting the large bowl on the floor in front of her, then lifted her feet and put them in it, astonishing Violet so much that she could not get out even a squeak of protest. The water was blissfully warm on her feet, and unconsciously Violet sighed with satisfaction. Coll cast an amused glance up at her, but said nothing as he picked up a cloth, wet it, and, holding her heel in his hand, began to wipe the cloth gently across the sole of one of her feet.

A sizzle of shock ran through Violet, and her foot jerked in his hand. Her heart began to hammer. "What are you doing?"

"Shh. Dinna fret, lass. I'm only cleaning your cuts and scrapes. You must have been a sore trial to your nurse."

"I was not. I was a perfectly proper child." When Coll cocked one eyebrow in disbelief, Violet laughed. "Oh, very well. You are right; I was utterly horrid and messy and always sticking my nose into everything. My aprons were dirty and my ribbons untied, and I did not possess a pair of stockings without ladders."

He chuckled. "Just as I thought." Coll's hand was gentle as he worked, and though the cuts stung, his touch was soothing. "Och, your poor feet. You'll have more than a few bruises tomorrow. Hold still." He gripped her heel tightly and plucked out a thorn.

"Ow!"

"That's the worst of it. You were lucky not to slice them to ribbons. The pine needles cushioned the path, though I'll warrant you met a few pebbles."

"I did once or twice." Violet shifted in her seat. She was having trouble focusing on his words. His actions were simple and impersonal, and she knew she should not interpret them as anything but kindness. But each stroke of the cloth sent tendrils of heat through her, and the curve of his palm around her heel made her nerves dance.

She should object. Tell him that she would do this task herself. But she could not force out the words. However wrong it was, however unknown and startling to her, she did not want to stop the sensations coursing through her. The tenderness and strength of his fingers, the focus in his face as he worked over her skin, the caress of the cloth, and the heat of his hand — all stirred her beyond measure.

Violet wanted him to continue. Indeed, in some dark, secret place, she wanted him to go farther, to slide his hand up her ankle to her calf. She wanted him to rise onto his knees, positioning his large body between her legs as he glided his hands up under her gown. Her skin tingled at the imagined touch, anticipating his fingers awakening flesh that had never known a man's touch.

She would not have guessed she could feel as she did now, the heat pooling low in her abdomen, the ache blossoming between her legs. Heat flooded her face; it was all she could do to keep her breathing steady. She could not let him see what he did to her. If he realized the wanton direction of her thoughts, it would be even more humiliating than his rejection of her the other night. At least then she had had the excuse of being inebriated.

Coll had gone as silent as she. Wordlessly he moved his attentions to her other foot. Did she imagine that his fingers trembled slightly on her skin? Could it be that he felt the same thing she did? Perhaps he, too, imagined caressing her, moving his hand under her skirts and discovering the texture of her skin.

She swallowed, looking at him. His eyes were turned down, watching his fingers with an intense concentration. The light of the lamp gave a golden glow to his skin; his lashes cast shadows on his cheeks, and his mouth . . . ah, but his mouth was tempting, his lips darkly colored and full. He would taste intoxicating.

The memory of their kiss filled her head, swamping her senses with the remembered scent and taste and feel of him. The smooth pressure of his lips, the warmth of his mouth, his hands sliding beneath her cloak and spreading out over her body. She remembered the blazing heat of his arms encircling her, his body pressing into hers, fiery even amidst the chill of the autumn night. She remembered, too, the wild, exultant feeling rising up in her, threatening to sweep her away from all reason and sense.

Coll lifted his head and the full force of his gaze pierced her. His hands tightened on her foot. She was certain he was about to surge up and take her in his arms, envelop her with his heat and power. She leaned toward him.

He turned away and rose lithely to his feet.

9

Violet's stomach dropped in bitter disappointment. Whatever she might feel, Coll did not feel the same. Not looking at her, he emptied the water bowl, then busied himself with washing and tidying up his supplies. Violet clasped her hands in her lap and studied them as she tried to shove her wayward thoughts back under control. When he returned, she had managed to school the turmoil from her face. She could only hope that he had not seen the desperate desire in her eyes earlier.

They sipped their tea, silence stretching between them awkwardly. Coll shifted in his seat. He cleared his throat. "I wonder who would break into Duncally. What was he after?"

Violet was relieved to have something innocuous to discuss. "I would think it is an ideal place to rob. Almost deserted. Full of expensive things."

"True. But it's an enormous risk to take, stealing from the earl. He'd be facing transportation — if he was lucky."

"You said there were a number of people dispossessed around here. No doubt that makes people desperate."

"True. But Mardoun stopped the clearances. He has compensated several of those who lost their homes. I have given jobs to as many men as I could."

"It didn't keep Will Ross from taking to highway robbery."

"Aye." Coll nodded. "That was where my first thought went. But there were others with Will that night. Dennis MacLeod has bairns to feed, and that can make a man desperate. Rob Grant was there as well. I dinna see Dougal, but he has run with them in the past. I was sure he had settled down with the baby on the way, but . . ." Coll stiffened. "Or perhaps — I told him to leave, and I thought he had. But what if he did not?"

"Who? Dougal? Did not leave where? What are you talking about?" Given the look on Coll's face, Violet would not have wanted to be whomever Coll was considering.

"Donald MacRae."

She looked at him blankly for a moment before she recalled the name. "The former estate manager? The man you told me about?"

"Aye," Coll agreed grimly. "He would know Duncally better than the others. And he has a powerful grudge against Mardoun. And against me, as well."

"Breaking into houses doesn't seem the sort of thing estate managers would do, even angry ones."

"You don't know MacRae. He has the soul of a criminal. I'd believe far worse than that of him. He was in the village recently. I warned him off, and I thought he had gone. But I'll have to check more thoroughly. What size was the intruder? Tall? Thin? Medium? Heavy?"

Violet shook her head regretfully. "I'm not sure. I saw him so briefly, and there was little light. He was in the shadows." She closed her eyes, thinking back. "He was not tall. Nor thin — though that is hard to tell, for he wore a jacket. And there was something odd about his head — I think perhaps he had on a soft cap. Oh!" She sat up straight. "He wore one of those mufflers, like the highwaymen did the night they stopped my carriage. I watched him running away into the fog, and it was floating behind him." She sighed. "But I suppose that description could fit any number of men around here."

Coll nodded, setting aside his cup and rising to his feet. "I'd better look over the house, see if I can tell what he might have taken." He eyed her doubtfully. "Do you feel up to walking back? You could stay here by the fire if you like. Or go to sleep." He gestured toward the other room.

Violet went still, blood rushing up into her face.

Coll stopped, looking disconcerted. "I mean — that is — 'twould be no problem — I'll be gone and . . ."

He had meant nothing by his words, but now all Violet could think of was the image of his bed, softly rumpled, and of her slipping beneath the covers that had so recently wrapped around him.

She tried to speak, but nothing came out. Violet cleared her throat and began again. "No. It is kind of you, but I would rather return to the house. I'm fine; it is no distance, really."

"Of course. I'll, um —" He swung away, then back. "I'll get you a jacket. Or perhaps you'd rather keep the blanket." His voice was rushed, distracted.

Coll did not wait for a response, but headed for his bedroom. When he returned, he carried a heavy, dark plaid cloth.

"Here. 'Tis a tartan; it'll be easier than a coat." He began to unfold it.

Violet looked at the length of material doubtfully. "There's a great deal of it."

"Aye, but, unlike a coat, it can be wrapped snug around you, and there are no sleeves to swallow your arms." A smile tugged at the corner of his mouth. "I dinna think my coat would fit you."

She would have looked absurd in it, but she was not about to give him the satisfaction of smiling at the picture he'd called up. Violet slipped off her blanket, embarrassingly aware that her nightgown was still damp and far too revealing. She reached for the tartan.

"Nae, just stand there. I'll do it for you." He laid one end of the cloth against her side. "Put your hand there, now, to hold it." He brought the cloth behind her back and around her once more, winding up by pulling the remainder up from her back and over her shoulder. His scent clung to the cloth, teasing her nostrils. "Rightly, I should have had you lie down and wrap yourself up in it, but this is easier. There now."

He smoothed the tartan over her shoulder, his hand perilously close to her breast. Violet hoped he could not feel the tremor that ran through her at his touch. She dared

161

not look into his eyes. His hand fell away.

"It's still against the law to wear it, I suppose, but as you're a Sassenach, it doesna matter." His words were light, but a thick underlying tone to his voice twined like warm honey through her abdomen.

"I feel like an Egyptian mummy." Violet kept her voice tart. "Or perhaps a sausage. I don't know how I shall walk in this."

"It falls more loosely around your legs, but it doesna matter since you are not going to walk."

She stared at him.

"I will carry you. You canna walk with your feet like that."

"I managed it coming here."

"And you'll regret it tomorrow." He shrugged into his heavy jacket and reached for her.

Violet took a quick step back. "Don't be absurd. You cannot mean to carry me all the way to Duncally."

"I do."

" 'Tis too far. I'm too heavy."

He laughed. "You? You're just a wee thing."

Violet gave him the glare she reserved for anyone who referred to her diminutive size. "I'll not be carried like a baby. I am not a child."

"Aye. I know." His eyes glinted.

"Perhaps I could borrow something of yours."

He sent her a wry look. "You mean to wear my boots?"

"Of course not, but . . . oh, I don't know; I could wrap something around my feet."

He heaved a sigh. "Do you think you could deign to be carried if I dinna hold you like a baby? You could ride pickaback instead."

She stared at him blankly.

"You know, as you did when you were a child and your father would carry you on his back."

Violet's jaw dropped. "Clearly you don't know my father."

"You mean to say you don't remember being carried like that?"

"I am certain I was not."

"Och, well . . . we'll have to rectify that, then, won't we?" He grinned and led her to a stool. "Stand on this." He lifted her onto the stool, then turned his back to her. Taking her hands and pulling them over his shoulders, he said, "Go ahead. Climb on."

It was ludicrous. Ridiculous. Violet leaned forward, and her arms went so easily around his neck that she could not resist. Coll reached back, hooking his arms beneath her legs and pulling her forward. She went with him instinctively, her grip tightening around his neck and her legs wrapping around his waist. She was flush against his back, her breasts pressing into him, her cheek against his hair. It was thoroughly indecent and terribly exciting. Violet clung to him like a limpet as he blew out the light and started forward.

"Now duck," he warned as he bent and went through the doorway. He started off, not taking the driveway but cutting through the trees. Now and then he reached up to hold back a low branch so it did not hit her. "How do you like the view from there?"

"It's wonderful!" To see the world from this perspective, to not feel the ground beneath her feet, was heady, altogether silly and childish and amazingly freeing. Violet could not hold back a giggle any more than she could cease clinging to Coll. Yet as young and giddy as she felt, the contact also aroused something strong and sensual. It was impossible not to be aware of his muscles moving beneath his clothes, of the breadth of his chest, the strength that carried her so effortlessly. She delighted at the feel of Coll's body beneath her, his thick hair tickling her face. She yearned to rub her cheek against his hair and feel it glide, smooth and silken, across her skin.

As they neared the house, Coll pretended to sag, exclaiming, "Och, lass, you've broken my back. I shall never be the same."

"I like that!" Violet playfully slapped his shoulder. " 'Twas you who insisted" — she lowered her voice and infused it with as much Scots burr as she could — " 'Och, you're just a wee thing.' "

He laughed. "That isna how I sound." Coll dipped his shoulder, as if to toss her off, and Violet let out a shriek and clutched his jacket. He opened the door and went inside. There was no danger here of her knocking her head as they passed through.

Reluctantly Violet slid from his back, and he turned as she did so, his hands going to her waist to steady her. His eyes were dark and unreadable. His hands slid slowly down to rest on her hips. He leaned forward, his voice low. "Violet —"

"Coll Munro!" They both jumped as if struck and whirled around to see Mrs. Ferguson crossing the entry hall, a candle flickering in her hand. "What is the meaning of this? First all that shouting and now this. What is going on?" Her disapproving gaze fell on Violet, and her jaw dropped. "My lady! What are you — is that a tartan?"

Violet lifted her chin. With this woman, it

was best to brazen it out. "Yes, it is. His Highness the Prince, you know, was quite taken with Highland dress when he visited Scotland. 'Tis all the rage in London." Coll's eyes widened almost comically, but Violet ignored him. "And it is quite warm."

Seemingly unable to respond to this, the housekeeper swung back to Coll.

"There has been an intruder," Coll told her. "Lady Violet came to apprise me of the situation."

"An intruder!" Mrs. Ferguson was successfully diverted from the subject of Violet's attire. "Are you certain?"

"Yes. He struck Lady Violet."

"Struck her!" another voice joined in, and they looked over to see the cook bustling in. Sally's head was covered in a puffy nightcap that resembled a giant mushroom, and her sturdy figure was wrapped in a red flannel dressing gown. In one hand she carried a small kerosene lamp and in the other a rolling pin. "Who? A robber? I knew it. Dinna I tell you, Mrs. Ferguson, someone's been in here?"

"You had no way of knowing that," the housekeeper replied stiffly. "Just because there were a few papers lying on the floor —"

166

"It wasna a clumsy maid," Sally interrupted.

"Wait. Stop." Coll raised his hands, and the two women fell quiet. "What are you talking about, Sally? What papers? Where? When?"

"In his lordship's study, that's where. Just now."

"We were awakened by noises." Mrs. Ferguson hastened to take command of the narrative.

"We heard shouting and doors slamming," Sally amplified.

"We came to see what had happened. All we could find were a few papers strewn about the floor of Lord Mardoun's study. They could have easily been knocked off by a careless maid." The housekeeper turned to Violet. "But if he tried to harm you . . ."

"I do not think he particularly meant to hurt me, just to stop my pursuing him. However, I did not see him near the study. He was upstairs."

"Let's look there first." Coll took Sally's lamp from her and started up the staircase, the others following. By now, two maids and a footman had joined them, all wide-eyed and whispering among themselves.

"Which room did you see him leaving?"

Coll asked Violet, and she pointed down the hallway.

"That one."

"His lordship's chamber!" gasped one of the maids.

Coll strode down the corridor and opened the door, lighting the interior of the room. The furniture inside was covered with dust sheets, but the one covering the dresser was pushed awry, and several of the drawers were open. The door of the wardrobe stood ajar, and two paintings had been removed from the wall and stood leaning against it.

"Obviously someone has been here." Coll looked toward Mrs. Ferguson. "I presume those paintings were not taken down by the staff."

"No, of course not."

"Was he looking for a wall safe?" Violet asked.

"It seems likely. Is there a safe in here, Mrs. Ferguson?"

The housekeeper drew herself up primly. "I am not privy to where his lordship keeps his valuables."

Coll looked over at Violet. "Where would it be?"

"How would I know? I've never been inside this room before."

"Because you come from the same kind

of people. The same kind of home."

"Believe me, there are few homes like Duncally," Violet retorted. It annoyed her that he insisted on setting her among the aristocracy, separating her as if she were a different sort of person from normal people. "However, my father had a safe in his dressing room."

Coll entered the small anteroom. It smelled of cedar and was filled with neat shelves and drawers, boots and shoes lined up beneath them. Behind the footwear, flush with the wall, was a small, square metal door, locked. Coll squatted down to inspect the door.

"It's still locked, so I presume he either did not find it or was unable to open it." Coll returned to the bedroom and glanced around. "I don't know how we could tell if something was missing. Would you know?" He turned to Mrs. Ferguson. "Or the maids?"

"Of course not!" Mrs. Ferguson replied, shocked. "No one pokes about in here. Only Lord Mardoun's valet handles his things."

Coll suppressed a sigh and stepped out into the hall. "Where were you when you saw him?" He looked toward Violet.

"My bedroom is down there." She strode along the corridor, the others on her heels, and stopped in the doorway, suddenly self-conscious. Her gaze went to her bed, rumpled, the covers thrown back, her dressing gown flung across the chair beside it. It seemed too intimate to be standing here with Coll, even with everyone else there as well. She stepped back and came up against Coll. He jerked away. Violet hastily shifted forward and cleared her throat. "As I said, he didn't come in here."

"Let's look downstairs." Coll turned away. They went first to the study, where Coll picked up a few of the papers that had been scattered across the floor. "This looks like a deed. A will."

"The sort of important papers one might keep in a safe." Violet glanced around the room. A squat safe stood against one wall. Its door was closed, but it opened easily at Coll's touch. He muttered a curse as he stared into the empty interior.

"Do you know what was in here?" Coll looked at Mrs. Ferguson.

She shook her head. "I've no idea."

"What about the estate money?" Violet asked. "The rents and such?"

"That's in the safe down at the gatehouse. Nobody's tried to break in there. I think Damon kept some jewelry in here, but they might have taken that with them to London."

"The silver! The butler's pantry!" Mrs. Ferguson whirled and headed toward the servants' hall almost at a run. Opening a door, she hurried through a narrow room to the door on the opposite end. She sagged with relief. "It's not been opened."

"Let's check it in any case," Coll decided. "You can tell if aught's missing here, can't you?"

"Oh, aye." Mrs. Ferguson's voice was grim. "Let me get the key."

As they waited for the housekeeper to return, Sally turned to Violet. "You look fair knackered, lass. You shouldna be standing aboot. Bed's the place for you."

"I'm not sure I could sleep."

"Weel, hot chocolate will take care of your nerves. I'll whip you up a cup." Sally bustled off toward the kitchen, harrying the maids and the footman before her.

"She's right. You should sleep." Coll steered Violet along the hall to a bench. "Dinna worry. No one will get into Duncally again. I'll be here till dawn; I intend to look through every room in the house. I'll make sure all the windows and doors are locked as well."

When Sally returned bearing two cups of

171

steaming chocolate, Coll took the tray, saying, "Ah, Sally, you brought a cup for me as well? You are the woman of my dreams."

"Aye, weel, you maun remember that the next time I want more money for the kitchen."

Coll sat down next to Violet, taking a sip of the rich, hot liquid. Violet let out a sigh and leaned against the wall, stretching her feet out in front of her. When Mrs. Ferguson returned with the key, Coll went with her to inspect the butler's safe, but it seemed too much effort to Violet. She stayed on the bench, nursing her drink and letting her mind drift. Why would a thief break in and not take any of the expensive things lying about the house? Why . . .

"Och, lass, you're about to spill chocolate all over you."

Violet's eyes flew open as Coll plucked the cup from her hands. "Oh! I'm sorry. I didn't realize." She shook her head. "Was anything missing from the butler's pantry?"

"Nary a spoon." He set the half-empty cup down on the bench and pulled her to her feet. "Now, let's get you to bed."

"I am a bit sleepy." She covered an enormous yawn.

"Is that what you call it? Dead on your feet is more like it."

"Coll!" she shrieked as he swept her up and started for the stairs. "There's no need to carry me. I am perfectly capable of walking on my own."

"Aye, I ken you are indomitable." He started up the stairs. "But this once you dinna need to prove it."

Violet sighed. She should argue with him, but instead she leaned her head against his shoulder. It was wonderfully warm and pleasant here in his arms. She could hear the steady thump of his heartbeat, and her own pulse seemed to fall into rhythm with his. It was so easy, so right, to let her eyes close and her mind relax.

Her eyes opened again when he laid her down on her bed. Coll leaned over her, bracing his hands against the mattress. She could not read his expression in the darkness.

"Violet . . ."

She smiled sleepily, putting her hands on his forearms. "Thank you."

He remained still for a moment longer, then straightened. "Good night."

He pulled the covers over her, and Violet turned onto her side, snuggling into the down mattress. As she sank into sleep, she thought she felt his hand glide over her hair.

10

Bloody hell! What was he doing? Coll strode down the hall to the stairs. He paused at the top, aching to turn around and go back to Violet. He thought of the way her mouth curved up when she opened her eyes and saw him, of how warm and soft and inviting she looked lying there, her hair spilling across the pillow. It was the sort of image that could torment a man.

He forced himself to continue down the stairs. A woman like Violet Thornhill was not for him. *Lady* Violet. He could not forget that she was titled and he was so many things that would repel an aristocrat that it hardly bore counting.

It did not matter how soft and sweet she had felt in his arms or how the sight of her in that almost transparent nightgown had set his blood pounding. It did not matter that she had run to him. Most of all, it did not matter that when he'd kissed her the other night, she had turned to flame in his hands. She had been drinking; it meant nothing. Ever since then she had been like ice to him.

Violet had avoided him so assiduously — never coming down to the library no matter how many evenings he'd loitered there, leaving Duncally at dawn's light — that he had finally been reduced to visiting her at the ruins. That scene had been as awkward as he'd feared, with her workers watching, and he had felt a proper fool. It had been impossible to thrash the thing out with her. Could she really believe that he did not want her? She had sounded not just angry but hurt.

Maybe she had felt the same roaring burst of passion he did. Maybe tonight when he was tending to her, she had felt the same lick of desire. He remembered the glide of the cloth over her, the feel of her satiny skin. That something so mundane as washing her feet should light every nerve in his body was absurd, but it had. And when he'd raised his head, the soft, dreamy-eyed look on Violet's face had tempted him almost beyond bearing. He had wanted in that moment to pull her to the floor and sink into her, his need so fierce, so fiery, that it had taken all his strength to turn away.

Coll realized that he had again come to a

dead halt and was standing at the door to the terrace, hardly aware of anything along the way. He let out a low growl of frustration and twisted the bolt on the door. Unlocked, of course. Probably half the doors in the house were. No one would dare to break into Duncally.

Except someone had. That was what he should be thinking about, not wandering around brooding over a lass. Could it have been MacRae? The man had left auld widow Stewart's, but he could have gone somewhere else — though Coll could not imagine who would have taken MacRae in, even for money, and the idea of MacRae setting up camp outdoors was ludicrous even if it hadn't been cold. More likely the intruder had been a local. Still, Coll rather hoped it was MacRae. He'd pound the bloody bastard into dust if he had hit Violet. Hell, he'd want to thrash any man who'd struck her.

Here he was, thinking about Violet again. He was behaving like a fool. He was concocting hunger in her out of his own pounding desire. Even if by chance Violet did feel as he did, he could not act upon it. He had been raised around Isobel and her brother Andrew; he knew how much a lady of quality was sheltered from the cruder facts of life.

She was a guest here. He was supposed to protect her, not ravage her. And if those things were not enough to restrain him, Violet Thornhill was also the most contrary woman who ever lived. Every day with her would be a battle. That was all very well for the excitement of the moment, but a man could not live like that.

He continued his inspection of the house, cursing each unlocked window and door. By the time he had finished, the sun was up and the kitchen staff was bustling about. He cadged a plate of breakfast and a cup of tea from Sally. After that, he sat down to wait for Violet to come downstairs, leaning his head back against the wall and closing his eyes.

"Coll?"

His eyes flew open and he jumped to his feet. Violet stood at the bottom of the stairs, as tidy and contained as always. Nothing like the wild, flushed woman with the unbound hair who had come running to him last night. "Lady Violet."

"Did you find that anything else was stolen? Or where he broke into the house?"

He shook his head. "There was nothing obvious missing. If a knickknack here or there is gone, I wouldna know. The place is full of them. He would not have had to break in. Only one of the doors was locked. There are too many windows to count, and many of them were also unlocked. I locked them, and I can make the rounds of the house each night to make sure they stay that way. But even then, it would be easy enough to get in. So I intend to move in here."

She blinked, momentarily silenced.

"If there is another intruder, I'll be here to stop him. I can make sure everything is locked up, patrol the house before I go to sleep."

"It, um, sounds like a very sensible plan."

He drew a breath. "You must return to England."

Her brows sailed upward. "I beg your pardon? I told you when I got here that I had no intention of leaving."

"Things are different now. I cannot guarantee your safety."

"I have not asked you to."

"That does not change the fact that I am responsible for your welfare as well as for this house."

"No, you are not."

"If anything happened to you, I would be the one who did not stop it."

"Oh, twaddle! I am responsible for my welfare. Besides, I thought your purpose in staying here was to protect Duncally."

"Yes, of course, but . . ."

"Then I won't come to harm."

The simple trust in her voice warmed him as much as it astonished him. "I appreciate your confidence. But there are more ways to be harmed than just physically. What about your reputation? I will be living in the same house with you."

She cocked one eyebrow. "Do you intend to ravish me?"

Coll felt the heat rush into his cheeks. He wasn't sure if it was anger, embarrassment, or arousal. "Devil take it! You know I would never —"

"Yes, yes, I am aware of how unlikely that is. So there is no need to be alarmed for my virtue."

"We will be alone. I will sleep right down the corridor." And *that* was a thing that was better not to consider.

"Mrs. Ferguson is here. The other servants."

"Tucked away in the servants' hall. That's no chaperonage. Your reputation would be in tatters if people knew you spent weeks under the same roof alone with a man. Particularly a man such as me."

"A man such as you? Hardheaded, you mean? Autocratic?"

"Not of your class," he growled. "A bastard, to boot."

"I don't see what your parentage has to do with anything," she said coolly. "But if that's so, it is a good thing I don't care about my reputation."

"Easy to say, but reality is a different matter altogether."

"The *reality* of it is that I do not care. I am already an embarrassment to my family. They do their best not to acknowledge my existence. I have no intention of marrying, so I needn't worry about losing a future husband."

He snorted. "That is what Meg used to say. Then she met Damon. You may think you dinna care now, but what about when you meet a man whom you want to . . . to be with?"

"I do not have to marry a man to 'be with him.' "

Every nerve in Coll's body sprang into fierce, sizzling life. He could not speak — or indeed even think — for the lust suddenly choking him.

"I am a modern woman," Violet went on calmly. "I do not believe in the shackles of marriage. I intend to pursue my career, not become someone's shadow, without even a name of my own. People find it acceptable for a man to live without a wife. Nor do they expect him to be celibate because he does not marry. Why should it be any different for a woman? Now, if you will excuse me, I must get started with my day." With a cool smile, she turned and walked away.

Coll stood, watching the sway of her hips, struggling not to run after her and kiss her until that cool challenge on her face gave way to heat and desire. Somewhat shakily he swiped his hands over his face and through his hair. Good Lord. For the sake of his own sanity, he'd better find this intruder quickly.

It should have been a terrible day. The sky was gloomy, hanging low and gray, mist hovering in the air. Violet had slept only a few hours; her head was sore; her scraped palms hurt, and her home was no longer safe. Yet her mood was strangely lighthearted.

Unsurprisingly, the workmen at the site had already heard about the intruder. It was somewhat more surprising, however, to hear that Angus McKay also knew what had happened. He arrived early in the afternoon, dark eyes bright with interest.

"Sae you've been brawling at Duncally, lassie," he said, looking considerably heartened by the idea.

"I was not brawling. It's hardly my fault if one of your countrymen broke into Duncally."

"What did the reiver steal?"

"No one seems to know what's missing."

"It was the French gold they was after," one of the workers said with assurance. "Red Meg and Mardoun found it and locked it up in Duncally."

Angus turned a scornful gaze on him. "Don't be daft. Meg and that Englishman dinna find any treasure."

"Or sae they said," the man replied portentously.

"Och, you're as mush-headed as the lads at the tavern."

"Treasure?" Violet asked. "Do you mean the money Lady Elizabeth's father supposedly brought home after the Battle of Culloden?"

"Aye, that's it. A great chest of gold pieces. The casket itself was chased in gold, with a great emerald on top, and —"

"Poppycock!" Angus slammed the end of his walking stick into the ground. "Adam McKenna, you're as great a nodkin as you've ayeways been. As if the Baillannan was walking aboot wagging a chest like that. He micht as well hae said, 'Rob me.' "

"But I thought they didn't find the trea-

182

sure, only a few coins," Violet said.

"Sae they said," Adam repeated.

"They dinna want anyone to know they'd found it all," his brother, Bruce, explained. "Too dangerous, you ken. Someone micht try to steal it. And sae they did, last night." He shot Angus a triumphant glance.

Angus rolled his eyes. "Are ye saying Meg would lie to us all?"

"Weel, she's one o' them now, isn't she?"

"It was her own granfaither!"

"Her grandfather?" Violet wrinkled her brow. "I don't understand. Are you talking about Lady Elizabeth's father?"

"Aye. Turns oot the old laird was Meg's mither's da as well."

"Nae surprise," Adam offered. "The Munros hae ayeways been thick as thieves with the lairds of Baillannan."

"Oh." Violet blinked and returned to her digging, losing track of the others' conversation as she considered the ramifications of Angus's words. Locals thought a hoard of gold was somewhere in the house. And if Malcolm Rose was Meg's grandfather, then he was Coll's as well. Little wonder, she supposed, that he had such an obsession with his illegitimate birth.

Lost in her thoughts, it was some time before she was aware of an itchy feeling in

183

her upper back, a subtle awareness of being watched. She glanced over at Angus, expecting to find him staring critically at her work. He was still in a heated discussion with Adam McKenna, paying no attention to her. The odd tingling along her spine remained, so strong that Violet turned to look behind her. No one was there. She swiveled full circle, scanning the horizon, but saw no sign of anyone.

Her nerves were getting the best of her. Last night had shaken her, making her start at shadows. Determinedly she went back to work. However, she returned to the castle that evening when her workers left instead of staying on as she usually did. Tonight she preferred not to be alone.

She wondered if Coll would be at supper or whether he planned merely to sleep at Duncally. It would be nice to have company at the meal, even if Coll had looked as if he were swallowing a bitter draft this morning when she insisted on remaining.

Doubtless he would also take it badly when she informed him that she intended to help him thwart the intruder. However, he would get over it soon enough; he did not hold on to his anger for long, one of the most appealing things about him. Like his smile. Or the way his hair fell forward onto his forehead so that he impatiently brushed it back. Or his long fingers and callused palms, moving with gentle care over her cuts and bruises.

No. She was not going to dwell on those things. She was determined to be cool and casual around Coll. She was not going to sit around mooning over him. She felt things for him that he did not feel for her; she could accept that. She would be unemotional. She would treat him as she would Mrs. Ferguson or one of Uncle Lionel's colleagues.

And if she took a little extra time over her appearance tonight, he would not know about it — and where was the harm, anyway, in wearing a bit of jewelry or arranging her hair in a softer style? It was not as if she were trying to seduce him. She would not know how to even go about such a thing.

Coll was pacing the corridor outside the dining room when she went down to supper. Violet hid the little fillip of pleasure inside her. His eyes ran swiftly down her before he pulled them back to her face.

"Are you joining me for supper?" She kept her voice cool and polite.

"I hope you do not mind. Mrs. Ferguson insisted."

"I see." He had not sought out her company. Violet ignored the lump that settled in her throat. "That is kind of her. It gets somewhat boring by myself. Though I must say I am surprised she would be concerned about it." Violet walked past him into the dining room.

"Nae." Coll snorted. "It was not that; it's the impropriety of Meg's brother eating with the servants. I stay in one of the family rooms, so I must have supper where the family does."

"I am sorry she imposed on you. I can explain to her that you would prefer not to dine with —"

His eyes widened. "Nae! I did not mean that. It's not that I dinna wish to eat with you. I thought you might not want — that you would think it inappropriate. I'm just —" He stopped and sighed. "Och . . . the truth is, all this" — he swept his hand out — "I am not used to eating in grand style."

Violet smiled at his pained expression. "I am forced to endure it every meal, so I see no reason why you should escape it."

He relaxed, giving her a sheepish grin as he took his place in the chair across from her.

"At least she did not force you to sit at the head of the table." Violet's eyes twinkled.

"Thank goodness for that. No doubt she

feels only the earl is worthy of that spot." He leaned back in his chair, watching uneasily as the footman dished food onto his plate.

Violet turned to the servant. "We would prefer to serve ourselves, Jamie."

The footman regarded her with trepidation. "But Mrs. Ferguson said I was to wait on you."

"I am sure Mrs. Ferguson will not blame you if I tell you that you may leave."

"Uh . . . yes, miss." He shifted uncertainly, cast a glance toward Coll, then hastily set the food down and left the room.

"You've put young Jamie in a quake. He canna decide whether it's worse to disobey you or Mrs. Ferguson."

"I feel sure Mrs. Ferguson will add it to the list of my sins and punish me accordingly. I suspect her serving my meals in this mausoleum is retribution for disturbing her order of things." Violet cast a look of disfavor down the long table with its intimidating array of silver epergnes and candelabras.

"I would have thought you were accustomed to dining in a room like this."

"Our house had nothing this grand. We ate in the informal dining room usually, and even the formal dining table was half this size. In any case, I have not eaten there these many years. I am much more used to my uncle and aunt's cozy little table."

"You do not live at home?"

"I do not live at my parents' house. But Uncle Lionel's is my home — *was* my home." Her eyes glimmered with moisture, and she looked away. "My father and I do not . . . see eye to eye on a number of things, I'm afraid. 'Tis easier to live apart."

"I can understand that." Looking more relaxed now, Coll began to eat.

Violet glanced at him in surprise, thinking of the fiddler at the dance, with his quick grin and easy charm. "You do not get on with your father?"

Coll scowled. "Dinna tell me — you found him most agreeable. Women do." Grudgingly he added, " 'Tis hard to argue with the man."

"Yet you found a way to do so, I take it."

"Nae. We dinna argue." Coll shrugged one shoulder. "The man is as slippery as wet soap. A will-o'-the-wisp. Here today and gone tomorrow. You canna depend on Alan McGee."

"I see." It was easy to glimpse the roots of Coll's rocklike reliability.

"I know," he went on as if she had argued. "I should not blame him for what is only his nature. Meg takes him as he is. So did

188

our mother. But I find it hard to forgive him for leaving Ma to handle everything on her own. He would come back, and it would be all singing and laughing and telling tall tales. He'd go on about how much he missed us, how beautiful Ma was, and how sweet it was living in the glen. Then after a time, he'd grow restless. You'd see it in his eyes, hear it in his music. And he would leave again."

"It must have been hard."

"It was hard for Ma."

"For you as well," Violet said mildly. "I imagine a boy needs his father."

"I managed well enough. The Roses were good to her. To us. And by the time Andrew no longer needed a nurse, I was old enough to help her."

"No doubt you did." Violet could imagine the sturdy lad he must have been, big for his age and doggedly taking on jobs that should have been handled by a man. "I am sure your mother appreciated it."

"She used to say I was her rock." Coll gave Violet a self-deprecating smile. "I think she mostly meant my head."

Violet chuckled. "Maybe only a little."

"Why did you and your father not see eye to eye?"

"You can guess. I was not the daughter he wanted. Not like my sisters. I harassed my brother's tutors for answers to my questions and often did my brother's schoolwork for him. Father thought I was too interested in reading and too little inclined to be pleasant and compliant."

"You? Not compliant? I would never have guessed."

Violet rolled her eyes. "I wanted to learn interesting things, not how to walk and dress and play the piano."

"You argued?"

"Endlessly. When I was fourteen, he sent me to live awhile with my mother's sister and her husband." Violet smiled, remembering. "Aunt Caroline and Uncle Lionel. I think his intent was to show me what happened to a woman who did not land a suitable husband — living in a small house and worrying about money, having only one servant to clean and cook, wearing old dresses and not going to fashionable parties. But I was in heaven. My uncle let me read his books, and he answered my questions. I helped him and went to digs and listened to conversations with his colleagues. I lived with them for eight months before I had to go back home."

"I take it your father found you not improved."

"No. We had terrible rows. He would cut

off my correspondence with Uncle Lionel or confine me to my room or take away my books. It made my mother miserable, and finally Father sent me away to school."

"Ah."

"Not a real school." Violet scowled. "It was a 'young ladies academy,' which meant we were taught piano and sketching and deportment. How to pour tea and carry on a meaningless conversation and speak enough French to buy gowns in Paris."

"They sent you home?" Coll guessed.

Violet laughed. "No. They were too fond of my father's money to give up on me. It was better than being immured at home. There was a small library. A tutor came in to teach us literature, and he would lend me books. We went to museums every now and again, and best of all, I was able to correspond with Uncle Lionel. I was able to slip out and go to some interesting lectures. Of course, I had to pretend to be a boy to get into them, but . . ."

"You pretended to be a boy?" Coll's brows shot up.

Violet nodded. "Sometimes I was turned away because they thought I was too young." She sighed. "It is difficult to pretend to be a man when one is no taller than I."

"There must have been . . . other difficulties." His eyes dropped to her breasts, then hastily away.

"I managed."

"Your father must have relented. Obviously you pursued your studies further."

"Clearly you don't know my father. After school I had to make my come-out. I did not 'take,' as you might imagine. Eventually I reached the age of twenty-one, and I was free to pursue the life I wanted rather than the one Father chose for me. I went to live with my aunt and uncle again and studied with Uncle Lionel. I have not seen my father since."

"Your father disowned you?" Coll gaped at her.

"No. That would have been a scandal in itself. But I am not exactly welcome at my father's table. He does not speak of me, so of course neither do my mother or sisters. I have gone home once or twice when he was away, but it made my mother uncomfortable."

"What about your brother? Your sisters?" Coll leaned forward, his forehead creased in concern.

"I am something of an embarrassment to them as well." She smiled at him. "What do you say here — dinna fash yourself? We are all happier this way."

"Your father sounds a hard man."

She shrugged. "From what I have seen, most men are like my father."

"Not all men. There are fathers who are not dictatorial."

"No doubt. My uncle was different." A smile quirked her mouth. "And there are fathers who are agreeable will-o'-the-wisps."

"Och, lass, surely there must be some who are in between the two."

"Mm. Perhaps." She toyed with her fork, not looking at him. "There was a man I thought was different. A scholar studying with my uncle. We talked of books and sites and methods. I thought he was a man like Uncle Lionel, and I daydreamed about a life with him. Loving each other. Working together. He asked me to marry him. I said yes. I thought it was all very romantic."

"What happened?"

She looked up to see Coll watching her with his calm, steady gaze. "One day he favored me with his vision of our married life. It would be wonderful to have a wife who understood his scholarly world. I would not mind when he spent his time at ancient sites or in libraries while I took care of children, hearth, and home. I would respect him for his mind and his accomplishments rather than the pedestrian things most women wanted, such as money and fine clothes. He would enjoy sharing his knowledge with a woman of intelligence. I could even help him by taking notes or copying out his papers or listening to him rehearse his lectures." Violet smiled wryly. "He was surprised that I broke off our engagement."

"I'm sorry."

Violet shrugged. "It was a long time ago and best forgotten. It was a fortunate thing, really. I can see now that I would have been miserable if I had married John. I couldn't have gone to excavations with Uncle Lionel as I did or spent my time studying what I wanted. I cannot marry and still have the life I want."

"You could not marry *him.* But another man —"

Violet snorted. "What husband would be happy to let his wife go off on her own for weeks or months? What man would not mind that she stayed up till all hours reading because she found something interesting? Or not be bothered that she spent many evenings in discussions with male scholars?"

He shrugged. "I dinna know. I never thought about it."

"Of course you didn't. A man does not have to face such decisions. But a woman really has only two choices: she can have marriage or freedom. If you choose marriage, every other option in your life belongs to your husband. Where you live, what you may or may not do, what happens to your children. A wife gives her very self into a man's hands and can only hope that he will treat her well."

"Nae, it's not like that." Coll stared at her, aghast. "What a bitter view you have of men! Not all husbands are tyrants."

"I suppose not."

"There are men who love their wives." He leaned forward earnestly. "Who treat them with tenderness and care, not trample them beneath their feet."

"Kind men." Violet thought of the gentle way Coll had cleaned her wounds last night, and warmth stirred in her chest, but she pushed that thought aside. "But kindness is not liberty. Whatever a wife may have or be or do, it is only on her husband's sufferance. There are a great many degrees of control that are milder than tyranny, but they are still control. And that is why I shall never marry."

Coll frowned, and she could see him gathering his arguments. Violet made a dismissive gesture. "But I suspect that neither of us is likely to change the other's mind on the issue. And that is not what I wished to speak with you about."

He looked at her warily. "You wished to speak with me?"

"Yes. I think we should discuss what we should do about the intruder."

"*We?*" His brows drew together. "There is no '*we*' to the matter. I will —"

"You are very much mistaken if you think you will handle this alone. I intend to deal with the problem — the question is whether I do it with you or alone."

11

Coll let out a short, sharp word in a language she did not recognize. Violet suspected it was not complimentary. "It's not your concern," he said at last. "It is my responsibility, and I will deal with it."

"Since I am the one who was struck on the head last night, I would say that it is very much my concern."

"That's exactly why I told you to leave. So you would not be in danger."

"We can squabble about this as long as you wish." She fixed him with a grim stare. "In the end, do you think I will slink off and leave it to you?"

"You are the most infuriating female I —"

"Yes, I know, I am well aware of how you feel about me."

"I doubt that."

"Unless you intend to lock me in my room as my father did, you cannot keep me from looking into the matter. Since you are familiar with the area, the house, the people, it would be of great benefit if you participated, but if you do not care to . . ."

"It is no surprise that someone hit you over the head."

"No doubt. But if you will remember, that did not stop me."

Coll planted his elbows on the table, dropping his head into his hands. "You will be the death of me."

"That seems unlikely. Have you thought of how you are going to catch him?"

"Of course I've thought of it. If he breaks in again, I will grab him."

"That seems a trifle . . . uncertain. What if he does not break in again?"

"Then there is no problem."

"What if he breaks in and you don't hear it? Do you plan to sit up every night, waiting for him?"

"I am a light sleeper. I woke up when you came to my door the other night, didn't I?"

"I was screaming."

"Then you tell me how I should capture him," he challenged. "Should I set up traps about the house?"

"That doesn't seem workable."

"I agree. I walked through the house last night and all around it this morning, but I could find nothing to give me a hint of who your attacker was." He added with a grin, "I did discover your weapon."

"My weapon?"

"The candlestick. It had rolled under one of the shrubs in front. You must have dropped it when he struck you down."

"It was not very useful." Violet frowned. "But you saw no trace of the man?"

"No handy scrap of material torn off on a thornbush. No muddy footprints through the hall. There were tracks around the house, but nothing I could distinguish as belonging to him rather than some gardener or servant. I've questioned everyone who works here. The maids say that small objects have been vanishing over the past few weeks, but they dinna know who is taking them. They were afraid Mrs. Ferguson would blame them if they brought it to her attention."

"As she no doubt would have."

"True, but it doesna help me to find the thief. I went to the village this afternoon, but I had no luck there either." He sighed. "Some no longer regard me as a man in whom it's safe to confide. Those who do are less likely to have the information I want."

"I suspect your highwayman might be a good place to start."

"Will's was the first place I went, but he

claims to have been home all night, and his ma swears he was. She would lie for him to the bitter end, but I have no proof. Indeed, I dinna know he's guilty. There are other larcenous souls about."

"What about that other man? The manager."

"He left Kinclannoch almost a fortnight ago. Mrs. Stewart thinks he was headed back to the Lowlands, and Ron Fraser passed him on the road out of town." Coll sighed. "I asked all over the village and no one said they'd seen him since or heard of him staying with anyone. He's no friends here to hide him or cover his tracks, so I suppose I must rule him out."

"Then your only hope is to catch the thief in the deed?"

"I fear so. I told no one today that I planned to spend the nights here, but after tonight, word will spread. The next night or two are the only ones I can hope to catch them in the act, and I dinna know if he will come again so soon." Coll shrugged. "I canna understand why he's come more than once yet taken so little. A silver saltcellar. A wee lion with a mane of gold and topaz eyes."

"Perhaps he takes pieces that he can sell for enough to live on, hoping that because they are small, no one will notice or that the servants will keep quiet, as they did."

"I suppose. But where does he sell them? There's no one hereabouts who could afford to buy them, and anyone would suspect where they came from. He'd have to go to Inverness, which is a long walk. Even there, I would not think there's much market for them."

"Maybe he holds them until he has several things, then takes them together."

Coll's eyes lit. "It would be a fine thing if we could find them all in his possession."

"Perhaps we will get lucky. Do you intend to sit up tonight waiting for him?"

"I thought to go to bed early and sleep a couple of hours, then get up around midnight and keep watch."

"We should divide the hours. I will take the first watch and wake you halfway through the night."

"I will counter your offer and take the first watch, then hand it over to you."

"Hah! I am not that gullible, sir. If you are on duty first, you will 'forget' to wake me."

"Lord, but you are a suspicious woman." He shook his head sorrowfully.

"I am a woman of experience." Suddenly the air was thick with undertones of meaning. Violet's tongue stuck to the roof of her mouth.

Coll shifted. "Do you propose to go after the man with a candlestick again?"

"Not unless I have to. If I hear anyone entering the house, I will wake you. I shall not take him on by myself. Though, of course, I must have something to hit him with if necessary." Violet looked thoughtful. "A walking stick like Old Angus carries would be handy."

"Heaven help me."

"Since the intruder arrived so late last time, it's clear I have given you the more dangerous assignment. That should soothe your masculine pride."

" 'Tis not a matter of pride."

"Of course not." Violet made her tone extravagantly soothing.

"You are the most ag—"

"—gravating female," Violet finished with him, and they both laughed. "Now . . . do we have a bargain?"

"You know we do. You knew from the start that you would talk me into it."

"Which makes it particularly gratifying." Violet rose to her feet. "Now, if you will excuse me, I must change into my sleuthing attire." She turned away, then pivoted back. "I have — it has been very . . . nice, dining with you. Thank you."

She whipped around and left the room before he could speak.

Violet felt her eyes drifting closed, and she pulled herself awake, rubbing her hands over her face. Keeping watch was proving to be boring. One could do only so much thinking about scholarly topics without beginning to drift off. All other thoughts invariably led to Coll and the way he had looked the night before when he answered the door. His bare chest, the firm swell of muscle in his arms, the strength of his fingers as he gripped her arms.

She had never before come face-to-face with a half-naked man. Heat stirred low in her abdomen at the memory. She shifted, trying to find a comfortable position on the hard wood floor, and reached into her pocket to look at her watch. It was just past two. She pondered awakening Coll. It would be kinder to let him sleep longer. On the other hand, it would be disastrous if she fell asleep and missed the intruder.

She stood up, stretching her stiff muscles. It occurred to her how improper it would be to enter a man's bedchamber. How strange. How titillating. She slipped up the stairs and paused at Coll's door, then eased it open. The room was dark, the only light the glow of the sconce in the hall behind her, but she could see the looming bulk of the bed. Her breath was suddenly uneven as she started toward it.

Despite the chill of the night air, Coll must be warm, for his bed curtains were drawn back and tied. As she neared the bed, she could see that the covers were pulled up only to his waist, his bare chest exposed to the cool air. Violet stopped, her eyes fastening on his chest. She wondered if he slept entirely naked beneath the sheets and blankets. Heat gathered insidiously between her legs.

Coll stirred as she watched him, his head moving restlessly on the pillow. He let out a soft groan, turning onto his side, his hand spreading out across the sheet. He rubbed his cheek against the pillow, a whisper issuing from his lips. With another low sound, his fingers dug into the mattress beneath him. Violet realized that he was flushed. Was he feverish? Ill? She laid her hand gently on his arm, whispering, "Coll? Coll, wake up."

His eyes flew open. "Violet!"

One hand shot out and grasped her arm, and he rolled onto his back, gazing up at her with hot, dreamy eyes. His mouth curved in a slow smile, and his other hand went to her hip, spreading his fingers out in a caress. "It *is* you."

His skin was searing hot where he touched her, and the soft movement of his fingers made warmth blossom between her legs.

"Of course it is I." She fought her jangling nerves. "Who else would it be? Are you sick? You feel hot."

Coll's eyes widened. He jerked his hands back as if he had laid them upon a hot stove and shot up to a sitting position, grabbing the covers as they slid farther down his body. "Violet. What are you doing here?"

"I came to wake you up, remember? Really, Coll, are you feverish?" Violet put her palm against his forehead, and he skittered back, clutching the covers.

"No! I'm fine!" His voice rang in the silence. He lowered his tone. "I am not feverish. I — um — I was dreaming."

"Oh. A nightmare." Violet nodded. "That was why you were twitching."

"Twitching? What was I — did I say anything?" Alarm mingled with the dazed expression on his face.

"Nothing I could understand."

"Thank God." He pulled up his knees beneath the covers and crossed his arms on them, muttering to himself as he dropped his head to his arms.

"It's most annoying when you mumble like that. I can't understand what you're saying."

"It's better you don't know."

"No doubt." Violet's eyes strayed down his back, bared by his position. Her fingers itched to glide along the bony ridge of his spine, and she curled them into her palms. She noticed that the covers had slipped more when he moved, falling away at his side so that a slice of his bare hip was exposed. He *was* naked beneath the sheets.

Her mouth went dry as dust. She had to wrench her eyes away. "Well . . . then, um, I shall go. If you are, uh, sufficiently awake."

"I am wide-awake," he snapped, then sighed. "I am sorry. I'm a bear when I awaken. Anyone will tell you."

"That many have been with you when you wake up?"

"What? No. I mean — I dinna mean . . . Meg and Ma and um . . ."

"And a few other women." Violet watched the color flare along his cheekbones. She wasn't sure why the sight made the nerves dance beneath her skin or why she enjoyed the tumult. Or why she felt such a compelling urge to provoke him. It was almost as if she wanted to see him explode.

That was such an odd, disturbing thought

that she turned away abruptly. "Well. I shall go to bed then. Good night."

Coll stared after Violet as she strode into the dark hall and out of sight. Letting out a low noise, half groan, half growl, he flopped back onto the bed. He rolled onto his side and buried his face in his pillow, muttering oaths, none of them adequate to express what burned through him. What if she had understood his mutterings? Had she realized the state he was in?

He had been dreaming of her. It had been summer in his dream and they'd been swimming at the loch. She had worn only a shift, and the wet cotton clung to her body, revealing every delectable inch. She lay back on the ground beside the loch, holding up her arms to him, and he went to her, burying his mouth in hers, his hands sliding under her shift and over her slick skin.

Then she had said his name, and he had opened his eyes to see her standing before him. For an instant, still lost in passion and sleep, he had reached for her. He was fortunate he had come to full consciousness before he dragged her into his bed.

He grunted. Aye, fortunate. So much better to be lying here sweating and shaken, still hard as a rock and no chance of release, at least not in the way he ached for. Why did he let the woman torment him so? Yes, she had those doe-soft eyes, lambent and huge, and her breasts were full and soft and would cup so sweetly in his palms. Her lips were luscious, eminently kissable. But other women were beautiful, other women were softer, sweeter, more pliant.

Yet none of them beckoned him as she did. That tartness in her made it all the more tantalizing to taste her sweetness. The possibility of watching the warmth and pleasure unfold in her lured him. He yearned for the powerful, primal satisfaction of awakening that most hidden part of her — as if she had locked inside her some deep, shimmering secret that only he had the key to open.

Coll sat up. He must get up and dress; he must turn his mind to other things, forcing the roiling, pulsing hunger inside him to ease. If he did not learn to do so, it would be an exquisite torture living in the same house with her. Perversely, it seemed that he ached to race straight toward that torment.

Sighing, he lay back, crooking his arm across his eyes, and, for just a few more moments, gave himself up to thoughts of her.

■ ■ ■ ■

Violet sailed into the dining room the next morning. Despite the fewer hours of sleep the previous night, she felt strangely invigorated. Coll was already seated at the table, nursing a cup of tea.

"Good morning," she said cheerfully, going to the sideboard.

Coll's response was more a low grunt than a greeting. Violet cast a glance at him over her shoulder. His eyes were clouded and his hair tousled, drifting every which way. A long, thin, red line ran down one side of his face where he had obviously slept against something ridged. He hunched over his cup of tea, one hand cradling it, as if it were his only comfort, looking rumpled and sleepy and disagreeable. Somehow the sight of him lightened her chest.

"It's a lovely morning, isn't it?" She piled food onto her plate.

"It's raining."

"Ah, but rain can be lovely, can it not? I suppose it's all in how one looks at it." She sat down across from him with a smile.

Coll cast her a jaundiced look. "Are you always this . . . bubbly in the mornings?"

"You, I take it, do not greet the morning

209

with pleasure. I would have thought you were accustomed to rising early, growing up in the country."

"I am accustomed to it. Doesn't mean I enjoy it." He took another swallow of tea.

"Perhaps I should be the one taking the last watch. I appear to be more alert." Violet decided not to mention that she had struggled to keep her eyes open on her own watch. "Though I admit I would be less useful at subduing the intruder."

"Mm. Perhaps you could talk him into insensibility." Coll looked up at her from beneath his lashes, eyes glinting.

Violet struggled to suppress a smile, but could not. "Ah, I see your brain has awakened."

Reaching over to snag a slice of bacon from Violet's plate, Coll leaned back in his chair, chewing thoughtfully as he studied her face. "And I can see that you've some mad new scheme on your mind. Go ahead. Out with it."

She lifted her brows haughtily. "Just for that I should not tell you."

He simply waited.

"Oh, very well. I did a good deal of thinking last night as I waited for our culprit."

"Lord help us."

"Returning to the house multiple times

would increase the thief's chances of getting caught. It seems very foolish."

"Which would be unsurprising if it's Will Ross."

"That may be true, but I wondered if the small items taken were merely incidental to the main purpose. An impulsive grab, thinking it would not be noticed and reasoning that he deserved some bit of payment for failing in his main objective."

"Which was?" Coll lifted his brows.

"What if he was searching for something larger? More valuable. So valuable that it is worth returning time and again to search for it." Violet leaned forward, her eyes intent on Coll's face.

"And what might this valuable object be?"

"Well, Mr. McKay suggested —"

"Auld Angus! What the devil does he have to do with it?"

"Nothing, except to offer his opinion, as he is wont to do." Violet's lips curved up in amusement.

"I might have known. When did he favor you with this opinion?"

"He's come to the site twice now. The first day it was to critique our work. Yesterday he seemed more interested in the intruder."

"I'd like to know how he learns everything that happens in the glen when he lives like a hermit." Coll glowered. "I suppose he pointed out I'd bungled the thing."

"No. So far he has not had to go further afield than my workers to find ample things to criticize. He and the workers discussed the possibility that the intruder was seeking treasure."

"Treasure! Oh, bloody hell . . ."

"Adam seemed to think your sister and the earl discovered the French gold brought home by Malcolm Rose. Angus declared that to be nonsense."

"Angus has the right of it — much as I hate to agree with the man. All Meg found was a bit of leather and a couple of coins. Hardly a treasure. Those coins could have been the laird's traveling money."

Violet frowned. "I can see that you are determined to take the most prosaic view possible."

"I'm a prosaic man," Coll retorted. "Simple explanations tend to be the likeliest."

"Be that as it may, the existence of the treasure is not the point."

"No? Then what is?"

"The fact that people *believe* it exists. And that some believe it is hidden in this house. *That* could be what the intruder is looking for."

Coll set his jaw stubbornly, but after a moment he let out a sigh and relaxed. "You may very well be right. But there's nothing I can do about it if people are determined to believe it's here."

"Well, there is *one* thing we could do."

"Aye, and what's that, then?"

"We can find it first."

12

"A treasure hunt? That is your solution?" Coll stared at her.

"No, my solution is *finding* the treasure. Until it is discovered, people will persist in thinking it is here and will look for it. But if we found the treasure and secured it in a bank, they will know hunting for it here is useless."

"But I have no idea where it is."

"That is why we have to discover what happened to it."

He narrowed his eyes at her. "You just want to look for buried treasure."

Violet laughed. "I do in fact enjoy a good puzzle. That does not make finding it any less necessary. Besides, it will give us something to enliven the evenings."

"I think my evenings have been lively enough since you arrived." Coll sighed. "Very well. But exactly how do you propose to find it? The one place I am certain we would not find it is here in Duncally. Damon's family was on the opposite side of the war. They would never have been entrusted with money meant to save Prince Charlie's cause."

"Might they not have stolen it from the laird? Do you know anything about what happened to it?"

"We know that Lord Mardoun was in England at the time, not here. We know that Sir Malcolm returned because Isobel and Jack found his body. And we know he was murdered by his wife and brother."

Violet stared. "His wife and brother killed him? Why?"

"Jealousy. His younger brother resented him for getting the title and estate. And Sir Malcolm's lady had ample reason for her jealousy. Sir Malcolm loved another woman. But it seems clear that neither of them took the money. Until Meg and Damon found those coins, we assumed it had been stolen or else he had not brought it back with him. Now Meg believes the laird entrusted it to Faye Munro. Our grandmother."

"She was the woman he loved?"

Coll shrugged. "No one knew who our grandfather was; Faye dinna reveal it, and she died giving birth to our mother. Meg had a bee in her bonnet, wanting to find

215

out who the man was, and when she managed to track down the location where they exchanged messages, she found two French louis d'or and a scrap of leather with the Roses' emblem. Whether that proves that the treasure existed or not, I dinna know. But I suspect it does mean Sir Malcolm was Faye's mysterious lover."

"So you and your sister are related to the Roses then. And you so despising the aristocracy!"

"On the wrong side of the blanket. I've little delight in discovering my grandfather was a philandering aristocrat, another man who went about taking his pleasure when and where he liked, betraying his lawful wife and also abandoning the woman he professed to love. It certainly does not make me any more than I was before."

"No, you would not be a man whom that would change." Violet smiled faintly. "But it does make you cousins with Mrs. Kensington."

"That is a good aspect of it, I suppose."

"How did your sister track down the meeting place? Why did she think Sir Malcolm had entrusted the treasure to your grandmother?"

"It came from Faye's journal."

"The book you were reading that night in

the library?"

He nodded. "Sir Malcolm gave it to Faye. He taught her to read and write."

Violet's face softened. "Truly?"

Coll laughed. "Trust you to find that romantic. Meg did, too."

"Of course. It shows he really knew her. That he truly cared for her. A man might toss any woman a trinket, but to take the time and trouble to do that indicates something more than mere desire."

"Apparently he knew her well enough that he entrusted her with the treasure."

"She wrote that he gave her the gold, but she didn't say where she hid it?"

"She was very cryptic about the whole matter. She never wrote his name, only called him 'my love' or 'he.' She referred to his leaving her something and talked about wondering what to do with it. She says she moved the thing he left her. There are some pages torn from the book as well."

"A mystery indeed." Violet's eyes sparkled. "The journal is where we will start."

"We will?"

"Yes. Don't be stubborn, Coll. There isn't a reason in the world why we shouldn't hunt for this treasure except for the fact that you like to aggravate me."

"I like to aggravate you? 'Tis you who

delight in driving me mad."

"What nonsense." Violet grinned and popped a final piece of bacon in her mouth as she rose from her chair. "Then this evening, after supper? In the library?"

"Yes. We will begin your treasure hunt."

Violet was waiting for Coll when he walked into the library. Paper and pencils were laid out neatly on the table before her. He was prepared to see her — indeed, he had spent far too much of his day thinking about it — but still it gave him a little jolt of excitement.

It was absurd. He was becoming a stranger to himself, prone to bouts of nerves and frustration, churning with anticipation over even the most mundane of things. All through supper, he'd found himself contemplating the edging of lace along the neckline of Violet's gown or the way the fringe of her shawl brushed over her bare arms, separating softly over her skin. He wanted to draw her, to catch the shadowed cleft between her breasts, the fragility of the lace upon her milky skin. No, it would be better in wood; nothing flat could capture her allure, her grace.

He had lost track of their conversation so often that Violet doubtlessly wondered if he was a fool. Coll was certain he was. Being with her, watching what he wanted and could not have, made him ache. Yet here he was, condemning himself to an evening with her. And eager to do so.

Violet looked up as he walked in, and she smiled. Jumping up, she pulled out the chair beside her. "I'm glad to see you. I need your help."

Coll was unsure whether it would be worse to sit across from her and look at her all evening or beside her, only inches away. Either sounded like a bad idea. He took the chair she indicated, and she resumed her seat, sliding a piece of paper in front of him. She leaned in to point at what she had drawn.

His question was answered — it was infinitely worse to be beside her, her scent in his nostrils, hearing every breath she took, every rustle of her dress as she moved, his gaze locked on the swell of her breasts above the row of lace. He forced himself to focus on the drawing before him.

"You drew a map of the loch?"

"I always sketch the sites we're exploring. It's rough, of course. I've marked where the ruins are and Duncally, the road into the village, the circle of stones, et cetera. Is this location right for Baillannan? The cave where they found the coins? Where did your grandmother live?"

Concentrate. "You're very close with Bail-lannan." He took the pencil from her and sketched in a few shapes. "This is the cave. Here are the castle ruins."

"The one you pointed out the first day? The old Baillannan? Didn't you say its cellars connected to the caves?"

"So they say. But not to the cave where they found the coins," he added quickly. "The only entrance to it is in the cliff."

"Still, doesn't it seem a likely place to hide a treasure?"

"Aye. There are cellars and subcellars and tunnels. I've never found one that led to a cave. One led to the new house, but it caved in along the way. I've gone through one or two, but they had caved in, as well, so I'm not sure if they led to the caves or not. It stands to reason the Roses would have had a tunnel to the caves or at least beyond the outer wall, in case they needed to escape."

"They seem to have been a secretive lot."

"The Roses were . . . suspicious. No doubt that is one reason why they prospered. If Sir Malcolm had been the one to hide the gold, it might well be in the ruins. But Faye would not have been as knowledgeable about them, and according to her letter, it

220

was she who hid the treasure."

"What letter? I thought you had only her journal."

"There was a note in the cave where Meg found the coins. It was from Faye to Sir Malcolm; it was their habit to leave messages there."

"Do you have it? May I see it?"

"Of course." He went to one of the glass-fronted shelves and pulled out the old leather-bound volume Violet had seen him reading before. Opening it, he took out a piece of yellowed, torn paper, which he unfolded carefully and laid on the table before Violet.

She bent over the creased note, squinting to read the faded lines.

My love, I pray you find this, well and happy. What you left me is safe; I have hidden it, and you will know where and when to find it. If you have gone on, as my heavy heart fears, it will be there for our child. My time is coming, and I do not fear it, for I pray I will find you waiting for me. I love you with all my heart.

Faye

"How sad. 'My time is coming.' She sensed her death?"

"Perhaps. Or she meant that she was about to give birth. Maybe both, for she died soon after the bairn came into the world."

"She does not say the man's name or what he left her."

"No. We made that leap because of the gold coins and the Rose emblem. It could be nonsense. But it does fit. Faye was accounted a rare beauty — enough to tempt a laird, even a married one. He was a married man and of high stature, which would explain why Faye kept the secret of his identity so assiduously. He was educated, so he would have been able to teach her to read and write. He had wealth, so he could buy her a pair of hair ornaments, which Damon assures us would have been beyond the financial means of an ordinary man. He gave her this dirk, as well." Coll reached around to his back and pulled a short, black-handled dagger from his belt. It was obviously old and worn, plain except for an odd symbol engraved on its hilt.

"Do you always go about thus armed inside?"

He shrugged. " 'Tis sometimes handy to have a knife."

"Was this Sir Malcolm's, too? I see no rosette."

"I don't know. It, too, is of good quality, but that does not necessarily mean it was the laird's. It is a sgian-dubh. Many a Scot carries one at the top of his sock."

"What is this emblem on it?"

"I dinna know."

"It looks like some sort of rune. I shall have to check my books." She handed it back to him. Her fingers brushed Coll's, sending a frisson up his arm. His fingers clenched around the hilt and he took his time putting the dirk back into his scabbard.

"Why did he leave the treasure with Faye instead of hiding it himself? Or taking it to his house?"

"He might have felt he could not trust his wife or his brother; it would not be surprising, given the end he met at their hands. Perhaps he trusted Faye above all others. She had, after all, kept the secret of his identity. The Roses' history is entwined with that of the Munro wisewomen. Long ago the Baillannan gave them their cottage in freehold. In many a place, my ancestors would have been scorned as witches, even killed; certainly the . . . unusual ways of the Munro women flouted tradition. But they were considered under the protection of the laird."

"Why?"

"I dinna ken why. Most of the legends are fantastical, so it's hard to tell where the truth lies. More mundanely, Sir Malcolm may have considered the cave where they left their messages the safest spot to store the money. But clearly she moved the gold elsewhere."

"Why did your sister search that cave? How did she know where they left messages?"

"In one of her entries, Faye refers to it as the place where she gathered Irish moss. Meg knew which cave she meant. That particular moss grows only in a tidal cave — one that's submerged by ocean water in high tide — and Meg, of course, knew where the Munro healers gather their Irish moss."

"That would seem rather public for a secret hiding place. And if it is underwater at high tide, how could their messages remain safe?"

"The hiding place wasn't in the tidal cave but in a higher cave behind. They had to crawl through a tunnel to get to it. Even the outer cave is difficult to reach; you have to go by boat and at low tide. And there is no reason for most people to go there."

"Yet Faye seems certain that not only Sir

Malcolm, but her child, too, would know where she concealed the gold."

"My mother knew about the outer cave, but if she knew aught about the secret one beyond it, she didn't pass that information on to either of us. Ma was not old when she died — I was but twenty and Meg only seventeen. She collapsed one day and was gone . . . almost immediately." Coll stopped, remembering that moment when he returned from cutting peat and found Meg on her knees beside their mother, weeping.

To his surprise Violet reached out and touched his hand. "I am sorry. That must have been very hard for you."

"Aye. She had been fine when I left that morning. She'd had a headache a few times in the days before. But she took a draft and looked better. Meg said she let out a cry and sank to the floor, and she was just . . . gone. If I hadn't left to cut the peat that day, if I'd been there —"

"You could not have kept it from happening." Violet squeezed his hand gently. "You must not feel guilty."

Coll realized with a start that he had taken her hand in his. It felt so right there, so warm and natural, that it was a struggle to release it. He stood up, putting some distance between them, and shoved his hands in his pocket, beginning to pace. "It is good of you to say so. You're right, of course. Meg would have been better equipped to help her than I, and she could do nothing. But what I meant to say — given the suddenness of Ma's passing, there might have been some Munro lore that she had not yet told Meg or me, thinking to wait till we were older."

"If that is the case, it is lost forever." Violet thought for a moment. "Let's approach this from a different direction. Faye says her 'time is coming.' She has just finished moving the gold."

"So you're wondering how a woman who is large with child moved a chest of gold?"

"Exactly." Violet beamed at his understanding. "She was young and presumably healthy, and given the scrap of leather that was left, I'll assume the gold was in bags, which would have made it easier to carry than a trunk. However, it would still require a good deal of effort to move the gold. She had to row a boat to the cave."

"And crawl to the inner cave where it was hidden," Coll added. "She would have had to go on hands and knees several yards through a tunnel, dragging the gold with her."

"It would have been lighter to carry if it

was in several bags, but then she would have had to make several trips. In either case, it seems unlikely that she would have moved the treasure far from the cave."

"I agree. She would also have had to be careful not to be seen. There were British soldiers around and men returning to their homes. She could not trust anyone, even people she knew, not with gold or the name of her lover. She probably did it in the night or at dawn."

"Which makes proximity even more of a necessity." Violet turned to her map, putting her finger on the spot marking the cave. "Where was her home?"

Coll leaned over, bracing one hand on the table, and drew on the map. He was intensely aware of Violet, only inches from him. He hoped she did not notice the unsteadiness in his fingers as he sketched in the house. His eyes went to the curve of her neck as she bent over the map. Tiny wisps had escaped from her upswept hair and curled at her nape. He imagined twining a silken strand around his finger. Or bending down to press his lips at the juncture of her neck and shoulders. Coll thrust his hands into his pockets and stepped back. Violet looked up at him, her brows raised, and he realized that he'd missed whatever she had just said.

"I'm sorry. I was, um — what did you say?"

"I asked what the actual distances are. How long would it take to go from Faye's home to the cave?"

"Oh. Well." He sat down, scooting the chair back and turning so that he was facing her. "Our cottage is very close to the loch. She would have rowed the dory to the cave. It would take me a bit more time than it did to row to Baillannan the other night. It would take her longer than me, but I'm not sure how much, given her condition. Thirty minutes, perhaps?"

"Then she would have loaded the bag or bags in the boat and — what? — returned to her home?"

"Probably. Of course, she could have rowed along the shore to the village or on around the promontory."

"Or to the other side of the loch, the Baillannan side."

Coll nodded. "Yes. But she would not be as familiar with the village as she would be the land around our cottage. And she dinna grow up at Baillannan as Meg and I did. I think she would be likeliest to row back to our dock."

"She would be tired after all that rowing

228

and hauling. It would make more sense to take it home than make another trip from home to the new hiding place the next day."

He nodded. "She could have found a safe enough spot in or around the house to leave it for a day."

"So it is probably hidden not far from her house." Violet tapped her forefinger on the block representing Faye's home.

Coll leaned forward, steeling himself against the lure of Violet's nearness, and drew his finger in a large, misshapen circle around the cottage. "She would have been very familiar with the area on this side of the loch through the woods rising up to Duncally and back to the cliffs above the sea. The land around the circle is open, not much place to hide anything there. It's much the same on the promontory where the ruins are located. But the rest of it, the trees and burns and paths, that's where the Munro women have always gathered their plants. I've even heard people call it the Spaewife Woods."

"Spaewife?"

"A seer, one who has 'the sight.' Some people have named our home the Spaewife's Cottage. The Munro to whom the laird gave the land was said to see the future, and the Laird of Baillannan relied on her to warn

229

him or to help him lay his plans."

"Handy."

"It was indeed." He turned an amused glance to Violet. She was leaning, chin on hand, watching him, her mouth curved up in a smile. His good intentions crumbled in an instant. Suddenly he could think of nothing but kissing her . . . and more than kissing her. Lust flared deep in his belly, and he pictured himself pulling her up from her chair and into his arms, bending her back over the table. He imagined her hair spilling across the polished mahogany, her body yielding beneath his. Maps, theories, questions, were swept away, along with morals and manners, crushed beneath the tide of his surging desire.

"Coll? Are you all right?"

He pulled his mind back from the brink. "What? Yes. Yes, of course."

Violet stared at him, and he wondered what she had seen in his eyes, if she had glimpsed his thoughts. She was perched straight as an arrow on the edge of her chair, her hands folded in her lap.

"I was — just thinking." Coll wished like the devil he *could* think. He turned, focusing on the map. "It's still a large area to search. Faye could have dug a hole and buried the bags anywhere."

"Yes, but she said in the letter that he would be able to find it. That their child could find it. So she wouldn't have put it in some random place. She must have marked it or left something that would enable her daughter to find it. A clue. A note." Violet gestured toward the old book. "Her journal seems the likeliest place. She meant for that book to be passed down; you said it was filled with her remedies."

"Yes. She did it for her child, but Janet, my mother, didn't know it existed. It was only recently that Meg found the book."

"Have you read it?"

"No. I looked through it a bit the other night, trying to find a remedy, but that's all. I dinna think even Meg has read it carefully. Her main interest was finding references to the man whom our grandmother loved."

"I think that's where we should start — the journal. If we read it carefully, maybe we'll find that clue."

"Yes. Of course." It was a terrible idea. Coll thought of sitting beside Violet every evening, heads together over the book, his senses bombarded by her nearness, his flesh quivering with the urge to touch her. It would be the most exquisite torment. There was nothing he wanted more.

13

Violet hummed under her breath as she walked into the library. She and Coll had been reading Faye Munro's journal for three nights now, and though they had not yet found a word about the treasure, she was looking forward to the evening. She found the journey of discovery as fascinating as the goal itself.

Something about taking that journey with Coll was also intensely exciting. Just her sitting next to him, their shoulders almost touching, was enough to raise her pulse, and the soft rumble of his voice both soothed and stirred her. She found herself daydreaming about spending all her evenings this way, talking over their day's activities and unraveling knotty problems. Every night she was more reluctant to leave the library and retire to her room, which seemed increasingly lonely, dark, and cold.

She feared, however, that Coll was tiring

of the whole thing. Though he participated willingly enough in their search of the journal, he was clearly becoming restless and tense. His body was taut beside her, as though he were coiled and about to spring up at any moment. Indeed, he frequently did jump up to pace around the room.

They had given up keeping watch for an intruder, for by now everyone in the glen was aware that Coll was staying in Duncally, and no one would likely want to confront him. Yet Coll often stayed up late, prowling around the house after Violet had gone off to bed. Once Violet had awakened, heart pounding, sure that she had heard a noise. Dawn was breaking, and when Violet peeked out through her drapes, she saw Coll walking about, wearing no coat despite the cold, his head down as if deep in thought.

Violet suspected that he was troubled. She was tempted to ask him about it, wanting to help him, but the remoteness in him lately discouraged her questions. So she did her best to focus solely on the task before them.

They had given the first part of the journal only a cursory examination, reasoning that the issue of the treasure did not arise until after Malcolm Rose returned from France. Most of the beginning consisted of remedies and Faye's joy in being able to record them, with only a few vague references to the man who had given her the journal.

When they reached the section after Malcolm sailed for France, Violet found it difficult not to get caught up in the girl's wistful musings. Faye did her best to remain circumspect about her unknown lover, but she spoke frequently of her "empty heart" and her impatience for her lover's return. Then joy burst forth upon the pages, making it clear that Sir Malcolm had returned. That had been followed by worry, as well as elation when she discovered she was pregnant. Soon, Violet thought, there must be some mention of the treasure and hiding it.

Coll was seated at the table when Violet came into the library. He stood up, and for an instant a look that she had seen in his eyes often in the last few days appeared, then vanished . . . as it always did before she could identify it.

She gave him a searching glance as she took her seat. "You look tired. You should rest more." The words slipped out before she could stop them.

"I've had a bit of trouble sleeping." He shrugged and gave her a tight smile. "No doubt the beds are too fine for me."

Clearly he had no interest in discussing the matter — at least not with her. She turned toward the book open on the table. "Where did we end last night?"

"This part's all about comfrey and some other herb, then a remedy." He carefully turned the page.

Violet was distracted by the sight of his hands on the book — so large and strong, roughened by calluses and marked with scars here and there, yet his fingers moved with delicacy on the fragile paper, supple and gentle. Violet pulled her thoughts back from their wayward path. "She mentions the cave. Look, she says she gathered Irish moss today, but then says, 'Naught there. I fear he is lost forever.' She must mean she searched for a message in their cave."

"Aye."

"And this — something about — the dory, perhaps? Can you read this word? You are better than I at deciphering her hand."

"I've had some practice the past two months, reading Mardoun's chicken scratches. Clearly handwriting is not an attribute valued in earls. Nae, I think that word is *Davey,* not *dory.*" His voice sounded odd, distracted.

Was he leaning closer to her? "I see. 'Davey is very good to me.'" He *was* closer; she was certain she felt the touch of his breath on her hair. She lost her place on the page. "I, um . . ."

"What are you wearing?" Coll blurted out.
"What?"

Color flared along Coll's cheekbones, and he pulled back. "You smell different."

"I *smell* different?"

Now the red washed over the rest of his face. "Not that you smell, well, I mean you do, of course, you smell wond— quite nice. But tonight you — it's something different. Your perfume. A different perfume, that's what I . . ."

He looked so flustered and furtive that Violet began to chuckle. "Sally McEwan made a cream for my hands. They were chapped from the cold. It has attar of roses in it. See?" She stretched out her arm toward him.

His hand clamped around her wrist, and he pulled in a breath, his eyes closing. "You smell like summer." Coll released her arm, almost shoving it away, and jumped to his feet. He began to pace, his hands jammed into his pockets. "I'm sorry. I wasn't thinking."

Violet watched him, uncertain. Her insides were a tumult of sensations. The touch of his hand around her wrist, the look on his face as he breathed in her scent, the husky quality of his voice — all vibrated through her, turning her warm and shaky and eager. "Coll, are you all right?"

"Yes. Yes, I'm fine." His tone was sharp and impatient. "I'm sorry. I'm — it's just a problem . . . with one of the crofters. I've been distracted; I apologize. Let's go on."

"All right." Violet was sure he was lying, but it would serve nothing to say so. Her instinct was to pursue it, to wring a better answer from him, but she held her tongue, afraid to speak lest the answer cut her.

He slid the book closer to Violet. "Why don't you read aloud, and I'll listen? I think better on my feet."

"Of course." Violet returned to the journal. "That's all she says about that. There's another recipe." Violet read each snippet, which ranged from comments on the weather to the pain in her back to the black feelings that plagued her in the middle of the night. "Poor woman. It's clear she's close to despair. 'The bairn is my hope.' Now it's 'wet November.' Wait, now she says, 'I watched the sun rise this morn, all gold and pink glory. It made me think of him and how we watched it.' " Violet swallowed against the unexpected tears rising in her throat. "There's a space, and she says, 'My burden should rest with those who went before.' Coll . . ." She turned toward him.

He stared back at her. "Her burden? The bairn? Didn't she say the baby was her burden?"

"We thought that was what she was talking about. But, Coll, what if she meant something else?" She flipped back through the pages. "Here. She wrote, 'He has given me my burden and my blessing.' "

"Aye. The bairn."

"Yes, we assumed that the baby was both a burden and a blessing. But every other time she mentions the baby, it's happy, hopeful. What if the burden and the blessing are two different things? After all, Sir Malcolm gave her both the baby and the gold. The gold would have been a burden — a great deal of responsibility for a young woman, what with him disappearing and her having to find a place where no one would discover it."

"You're right. It was a heavy thing for her to deal with." Coll strode back to the table and leaned down, hand braced on the tabletop. He leafed through the pages.

"Stop." Violet laid her hand on his, and Coll went still. His skin was searing hot beneath her fingers. "I thought I saw something on the page before."

He straightened up, folded his hands together behind his back. He nodded toward the book. "Where? What did you see?"

"Maybe nothing." Violet turned the page. "Here, where it says December sixth. Beneath the date, it reads, 'May our ancestors guard it, as we have guarded them.' Ancestors could be referred to as 'those who have gone before,' couldn't they?"

"Certainly. So if she is talking about the treasure, then she put it in a —"

"Cemetery!" Violet said the word with Coll. She jumped to her feet, her face glowing. "She buried it in a cemetery. Among the Munros; that's where we'll find it! Oh, Coll!"

She reached out impulsively, laying her hands on his arms. Coll's face changed, mouth softening and a light flaring in his eyes. Suddenly heat and hunger pulsed from him. He dropped his gaze to her mouth. She knew in that moment that he was going to kiss her. His hands went to her waist, and he leaned down. Violet's eyes fluttered closed and she turned her face up to his.

"Bloody hell!" The words were barely above a whisper but charged with anger. Coll jerked his hands away and whirled around, charging out of the room.

■ ■ ■ ■

Violet lingered in her bedroom the next morning until almost nine o'clock, knowing that Coll always ate breakfast early and left the house immediately thereafter. It was cowardly of her, she supposed, but she could not face him this morning after making such an idiot of herself last night. Why was she always so wrong about Coll?

Violet was realistic about her looks. Her mother and sisters had told her time and again that she would be pretty if only she would make an effort. However, men were not drawn to her like bees to honey. They found her unladylike, unseemly, and lacking in femininity. She knew she was not a woman to arouse grand passion in a man. She had never before mistakenly thought a man desired her, and her behavior with them had always been decorous. Even during her brief courtship, she had been cool and contained.

But now, with Coll, she found herself surging with eager yearnings. Clearly these strange new feelings were coloring her judgment, making her see desire in him that was not there. He had been forced — twice — to reject her. It was no wonder he had been so tense the past few evenings. He was worried Violet would plague him with unwanted advances.

When she was finally sure that Coll would be gone, she made her way downstairs to grab a quick, cold breakfast. Hurrying along, head down, she did not realize her mistake until she stepped into the dining room.

"Oh!" Violet pulled up short as she saw Coll standing by the window.

He turned. His face was taut and stamped with signs of sleeplessness. Violet's heart sank. He was about to tell her he did not wish to look for the treasure any longer. Maybe even that he had decided to move out of the main house. It was alarming how much she dreaded that possibility.

"I thought you would not be here." Realizing how ungracious her words sounded, she hurried on, "I mean, I assumed you would have gone to work." That was just as bad. "I am rather late this morning." She went over to the sideboard and began to pour a cup of tea. Sally's tea was strong enough to wake the dead; perhaps it would improve her thinking. "I must hurry. No doubt the men are wondering why I haven't arrived."

"They won't be there. It's Sunday."

"Oh." She turned to face him. "You are right. I forgot."

There would be no work to occupy her today. Indeed, just yesterday morning she had been looking forward to today, thinking that she and Coll would spend the afternoon poring over Faye's journal. Little chance of that now. Picking up a scone, she took it and her tea to the table.

"Well," she began brightly, not looking at him, "I suppose I shall spend the day working on my notes from the excavation. We have dug down, I believe, to the bottom stratum, exposing one entire wall, and in doing so, we exposed two more walls at either end, both at right angles to the original. That would indicate, I believe, a structure much more likely to be a building of some sort rather than an outer fortification."

"Ah. I see. You will be working on your notes, then, all day?"

The inquisitive tone of his voice made Violet pause in the midst of buttering her scone and look up at him. "No, it shouldn't take that long. Did you have something else for me to do?"

"I thought . . . if you would like . . . we might go to the Munro graveyard this morning." Coll's voice was as stiff as his posture.

"I mean, unless, of course, you have something else to do. Perhaps you intended to go to the kirk. Though the service has already started; Mrs. Ferguson and the servants are all gone." He rambled to a stop.

"Oh, yes!" Violet sprang to her feet, then sat back down, remembering that she was going to be cool and collected. "That would be most pleasant. I mean, useful. Hopefully we shall find something."

"At least it will be a chance to get outside."

Outside where they could maintain a decorous distance from each other. "Yes, no doubt."

Violet hurried through her breakfast. It was difficult to get the food down, and after a moment, she set the remainder of the scone aside and stood up. Awkward as it might be to go anywhere with Coll, it could not be any worse than sitting here, trying to eat and maintain an equable attitude, while he watched her in silence.

She was surprised when Coll took her out through the gardens in back. "Are we not going into the village?"

He shook his head. "We are not buried there. The Munros have never been fully accepted by the kirk. There have always been those who were suspicious of their ability to heal people."

"Mm. Knowledge has often been equated with evil, I fear."

"The Munro graves are behind Meg's cottage."

He led her down the tiers of the garden to the stairs at the very end. Violet thought they were going to the docks, but Coll turned in the opposite direction, taking a path that led to a breathtaking view of Loch Baille and the gray-stone eminence of Baillannan on the other side. From there the path dropped down through the woods.

On this tranquil, inviting walk, the air held a hint of mist and was rich with the scent of earth and pines. Violet would have enjoyed it at another time, when she wasn't walking in awkward silence with Coll. Violet was achingly aware of him beside her. She could not keep her eyes from going to his pale hair, where tiny droplets of mist clung, or to his long fingers, remembering them on the journal, gentle and careful — or on her waist, their heat searing through her dress. Nor could she forget his fingers digging in convulsively and practically pushing her away.

A pebble rolled beneath her foot, and she slipped. Coll's hand lashed out and seized her arm, fingers digging into her flesh to hold her upright. As Violet straightened, he

244

released her, and the back of his hand inadvertently brushed her breast. Heat blossomed where he had touched her, and Violet saw again the look that had been on his face last night, taut and intense. For a moment, the air seemed to hum between them. Violet stared at him, eyes wide, waiting. Coll jammed his hands in the pockets of his coat and strode down the hill.

14

Violet followed, her thoughts tumbling in confusion. What did that look mean? Was what she read as passion in reality anger? Dislike? She *was* certain that the emotion was not mild. And why did it stir her so? She was grateful that he was not watching her; whatever Coll's expression meant, she knew that hers held only desire.

The path widened as it leveled out, ending in a fork. Coll took the trail to the right, and they had not walked long before a cottage came into view. Made of brown stone with a thatched roof, it sat huddled among a cluster of trees. The leafless remains of plants and shrubs lined the front and sides. No smoke came from the chimney, and though it was tidy, an air of emptiness lay about it.

"Meg's cottage." Coll nodded toward the house. "The graves are this way." He left the trail, curving around a small garden and starting up into the trees behind it.

"Why do you call it Meg's cottage? Was it not where you lived, as well?"

"As a lad, aye. But when I grew up, I moved to Baillannan to work as the game-keeper. It's a wee place." He shot her a humorous glance, seeming more like himself now. "I take up too much room."

"That's true enough." Violet was happy to fall into the familiar teasing tone. Maybe they could be at ease again.

"The cottage has always gone from mother to daughter, just as the healing arts do. I never had the interest in it Meg did. It dinna seem my lot in life. The Munros run to small families, and in truth, there are not many men among them." He lifted a branch for her to pass under.

"What is your lot in life?"

He shrugged. "There's a tradition, a bond our family has with the loch, the glen. 'Tis hard to describe in words. A duty as well as belonging. A need to help, to protect."

"You feel you must protect this place?"

"Perhaps more to help it. Meg feels it more than I, the bond. She is connected here and I think she would never be happy for long anywhere else."

"But you could."

"I think I would be much the same wherever I am. That makes me, I guess, a very dull man."

"No." Her words were quick and sure. "Inconstant is not the same as interesting."

"I envy Meg a little, being sure of who she is and what she should do. There is no questioning for her. She wants to heal, to help the people who come to her. She would not be happy without doing so."

"But you help the people around here. Not healing, but it's always you they come to with problems. I've seen them. Not just the tenants or the servants; it's the people in the village, fishermen, other crofters. It's you who gives them advice, who helps them repair their roof or build a new pen."

He shrugged. "Well, I'm handy with wood."

"You are kind and generous."

He slowed, turning to regard her for a long moment. "Is that what you think?"

"Yes, of course."

His mouth curved up slightly. "Some would say I'm meddling."

Violet smiled. "Perhaps some. But most people in the glen rely on you. Respect you. Why else would they come to you for help?"

"Sometimes I wish they would respect me a bit less."

"I can see that it would be tiring."

"It's not that; it's just — there are times when I feel so . . . so weighed down." He shook his head, smiling in an embarrassed way. "That probably makes no sense."

"No. I think I understand. Responsibility drains one's freedom, too."

His eyes drifted over Violet's face. "Yes, I suppose it does." He turned away, stepping over a low stone wall and reaching a hand back to Violet to help her. She put her hand in his, very aware of his touch even through her gloves. Determinedly she kept her eyes on her feet as she stepped over the stones. His hand remained on hers an instant longer, then fell away. He was turned away from her, gazing at the markers in front of him.

"Here we are. This is where the Munros lie."

The small, simple plot was shaded by two trees, one a dark, twisting yew that reminded Violet of the tree that spread over Meg's cottage. Huge and gnarled, it stood in place of the fourth wall of the little cemetery. The other three sides were built of stones, rustic chunks of gray, spotted with green, dark yellow, and black lichen. A wild rosebush grew just outside the wall, low and scrubby and devoid of leaves, leaving only its sharp thorns. A dead tree, far smaller than the yew, stood a few feet beyond another of the walls. Ivy wrapped around its trunk and into the lower branches, dripping down over a few of the graves like a green waterfall. Some of the graves had wooden boards at their heads, weather-beaten, the inscriptions long worn away. A few were adorned with cairns, and those toward the farthest edge had headstones, simply but carefully engraved.

"How many are there? How far back do they go?" Violet's voice was hushed and a little awed even though she was used to age and burials. Something about this spot, hidden away among the trees, guarded by the yew, was timeless and compelling.

"We dinna know. The dates are nearly all gone. The oldest ones I can read go back over a hundred years. Some, I think, had only marks, not words. I've no idea how many there are without markers. Or how many more lie on the other side of the tree."

Violet gazed at the giant yew. A hole near the bottom of the trunk opened up into the nearly hollowed-out interior. Yet still the tree lived. "The tree of eternity."

"My grandmother used to call it the goddess tree."

"I've heard that as well. It figures in a good deal of the ancient lore." Violet strolled among the markers, looking at the names and inscriptions. She felt, as she often did at excavations, as if she were standing in history. But here, the progression and continuity, the age-old tree, seemed to place her in the flow of time itself. Violet thought of the bond of the Munro women with the land. She would like to meet Coll's sister. She wished she could have met his mother.

Violet glanced over at Coll. He was standing in front of the newest marker, gazing down at it. His mother, she thought, a clutch in her chest. She wanted to go to him and take his hand, though she was too sensible to do it. Violet had always considered herself a woman of intellect, not heart. But with Coll her emotions were always near the surface. She didn't understand what she felt for him. Indeed, she did not want to reason it out; she had no desire to dwell in that part of herself for long.

Coll raised his head and smiled when his eyes fell on her. Her heart lifted within her. Danger was here, she knew, and the worst of it was that she yearned for it. Violet turned away.

"I don't know how we can find anything here." She sent an encompassing look around. " 'Tis not a large area, but we can't just start digging."

She wound her way between the graves to the rough, twisted tree and bent down to look inside the large hole.

Coll followed her. "I thought the same. Is there anything in the hollow?"

"No." Violet sighed and pulled back. "It seemed a fitting place, but, even secluded as it is, it's too exposed." She cast a frustrated look around the small graveyard. "I have no idea where to start."

"I canna imagine Faye digging into one of these graves to bury the gold."

Violet nodded. It was a macabre image. A cold wind tugged at her cloak, and Violet shivered, reaching up to pull her hood forward. Coll glanced at the sky.

"Rain's coming. We'd best go back."

Violet nodded, and they started down the hill. The wind off the loch grew stronger, the dark clouds massing above them, casting a deeper gray over the landscape. Violet wrapped her cloak around her, but she could not keep the wind from blowing the hood back from her face and whipping at her hair. They had not yet reached the path to Duncally when the first fat drops of rain plopped on their heads.

Coll grabbed her wrist and broke into a trot. Surprised, Violet ran with him as he cut through the cottage garden and flung open the low wooden door of Meg's cottage. She hurried through the door and Coll shoved it closed behind them. Violet shivered as she glanced around her.

The place was dark and small, but wonderfully aromatic. Tall cabinets covered most of the walls. An open doorway on the right led off into an even smaller room. A low rocking chair was beside the fireplace, and a table and two chairs were near the door. Directly across the room from them, only partly concealed by a folding wooden screen, stood a high, soft bed covered in a homey quilt.

Violet went still, her mouth dry. It was absurd, but suddenly it seemed as if the bed were the only thing in the house. She glanced up at Coll and saw that he, too, was staring at the bed.

He turned aside abruptly. "I'll just, um, light the fire." He strode away, his movements jerky, and knelt at the hearth, laying out bricks of peat and kindling.

Violet turned to examine the rest of the room. Pots, jars, and boxes filled the cabinets, and the variety of scents issued from them, mingling in an indistinguishable but compelling way. It smelled somehow comforting. Her hair was straggling down all about her head, torn from its moorings by the wind. With no hope of tucking it back into place, she pulled the rest of the hairpins from it.

The fire caught at last, licking up and consuming the twigs. Coll rose to his feet in a smooth motion and lit the oil lamp on the mantel. Drawn by the light and warmth, Violet walked toward the hearth, combing her fingers through her tangled hair. Coll turned and went still. His eyes remained fastened on her as she joined him in front of the fire.

"Your hair . . ."

Embarrassed, Violet separated the thick mass into three strands and began to weave them into a single, fat braid. "I know, 'tis a frightful mess, but I'll —"

"No." He reached out to stay her hand. "Leave it." His fingers drifted from her hand to her hair. He pulled back sharply. "That is, I mean, no need to worry about it." He cleared his throat.

Violet moved closer to the hearth, and Coll took a quick step back, his leg coming up sharply against the rocking chair.

"Oh, for heaven's sake, Coll!" Violet snapped, goaded beyond politeness. "I'm not going to ravish you!"

"What?" He stared at her blankly.

"I realize how you regard me."

"You do?"

"It's obvious. You pulled your hand back from me last night as if I'd laid a hot poker on it. You cannot bear to be near me. I understand; I'm not an idiot. You are afraid I will push myself upon you, maneuver you into a romantic entanglement. But I assure you I won't. I have never flung myself at a man, and I would not dream of placing you in such an uncomfortable position."

"*That* is what you think?" Color flared in his cheeks and he loomed over her, his body taut as a bowstring. "That I stay away from you because I dinna want you?"

"Of course! What else am I —"

"Good God, Violet!" He grabbed her arms. "For an intelligent woman, you are remarkably hen-witted." His eyes blazed. "You fill my mind. You plague my dreams. I canna sleep or eat. All I can think about is you." Heat poured from him, more searing than the flames that danced in the fireplace. "Your scent. Your hair. Your skin. Could you not see? I pulled away from you because when you touched me, I thought I would die from wanting you."

Fingers digging into her arms, Coll jerked her to him, and his mouth came down to seize hers.

15

Coll's arms went around her, crushing
Violet to him as his mouth consumed hers,
fierce with longing. She could scarcely
breathe, and she did not care. All that mattered was the feel of his hard male body
pressing into her. His lips, his tongue, his
heat. Violet trembled, digging her fingers
into his jacket. The days of confusion and
uncertainty fell away, leaving only the passion that throbbed in her.

She wanted him. She was not experienced
enough to even be sure what she desired,
but she knew it pulsed through her, seeking
Coll and the matching storm inside him.
She had not been mistaken. What she had
seen in his eyes was this — a need and
ferocity that drowned out all else.

Violet curled her fingers into his jacket
and clung to him as he kissed her again and
again. A primitive hunger was in him, a
barely leashed wildness that stirred her, and

she moaned softly as his hands swept down her body and over her buttocks, fingers digging in as he pressed her hips hard against him. She could feel the hard length of him pushing against her.

Coll let out a low groan that could have been torment or pleasure and pulled her down to the floor with him. Laying her back against the rug, he covered her with his body, supporting his weight on his elbows, one leg thrown across hers. He sank his fingers into her hair, holding her head still as he ravaged her with kisses. Violet moved her hips against him instinctively, and he shuddered.

His mouth moved down her neck as his hand roamed over her body, caressing her breasts and stomach. Impatiently he fumbled at the buttons that fastened her dress, opening it to his questing hand. Slipping his fingers beneath the edge of her chemise, he caressed her naked breast. The feel of his touch on her sensitive skin excited her almost past bearing, and Violet twisted beneath him, hooking one leg around his.

Coll shoved down the top of her chemise and his mouth followed the path his fingers had taken, kissing the soft, quivering flesh. His tongue moved inward in delicate circles that brought a gasp of pleasure from her, until it centered on the hard point of her nipple. He took her into his mouth, pulling with a soft, insistent suction that drew hot, liquid pleasure from her depths.

Violet tangled her fingers in his hair, the silken feel of the strands mingling with the myriad other sensations tumbling through her. Coll mumbled something incoherent against her skin as his mouth worked its way across her chest. Anticipation of what was to come coiled inside her, building to the final little fillip of satisfaction as his lips closed on her other nipple. She could not hold back a soft moan, and at the sound, his skin flared with heat.

Roughly he shoved up the skirts of her gown, and his hand slipped beneath them, traveling up her leg until his fingers found her hot, damp center. Violet jerked in surprise at the intimate touch. She realized, embarrassed, that she was flooded with moisture. She had a moment's worry about what he would think, but Coll only made a noise deep in his throat, almost a purr, and his fingers stroked over her, making her forget all else.

Passion swirled and coiled, and Violet ached for more. She wished the obstructions of their clothes were gone. She wanted to see him, touch his naked skin, but the thick fabric of his jacket thwarted her. Shoving her hand beneath the jacket, she caressed his chest, but still his shirt lay between her fingers and what she desired. Finding the top tie of his shirt, she tugged it open, and then at last her fingertips were on his smooth, bare skin, searingly hot.

Coll went up on his knees, yanking his jacket off and flinging it aside. He pulled the ends of his shirt from his trousers and started to whip it off over his head, but his gaze went to Violet lying there before him, and he stopped abruptly. The only sound was his breath pumping in and out of his lungs as he gazed at her.

"Christ!" He released the ends of his shirt with a groan and sat back on his heels. "What am I doing?" Coll shoved his hands into his hair, pressing his fingertips hard against his scalp.

"Coll?" Violet stared at him blankly, her mind befogged with passion, her body thrumming.

"Get dressed." His voice grated like iron. "I will *not* do this to you."

She was too astounded to move or think. Then anger flooded up, and she shot to her feet. She tugged her bodice back into place, fingers shaking as she fastened the buttons.

"Again? Now I am abhorrent to you once

more?" Humiliation and frustration churned in her, and she had to fight to hold back tears. She would not let him see her cry.

"Abhorrent! Don't be a fool. Of course not! Surely you realize that I want you." He, too, surged to his feet and faced her, every line of his body taut with frustration and anger. "You could not have thought I would pull you down and . . . and all but *consume* you if I did not desire you?"

"Then why!" She clenched her fists, her arms tight at her sides. "Why do you keep kissing me, then pushing me away?"

"Do you think I am the sort of man to treat a woman lightly? To take you without a thought to your honor?"

"My honor?" She gaped at him. "That is what's important? What about *me*? Did you give any thought to that?"

"Of course! Who the devil else would I be thinking of? If all I had thought about was me, I'd be buried so deep ins—" He broke off and swung away, drawing a deep breath. "Well, I wouldn't be standing here talking with you."

"I don't suppose it occurred to you to ask *me* if I wanted you to protect my honor. After all, it's scarcely any concern of mine, is it? No doubt you know far better what I should or should not do."

"It was not about you."

"What?" Her brows soared up. "Now my virtue is naught to do with me?"

He made a noise very much like a growl. "Dinna try me, Violet. I am not talking about your virtue or deciding anything for you. I am talking about what I do. I am not the sort of man to treat a woman that way."

Violet's jaw dropped. "Do you mean — then you have never, um, been with a woman?"

He stared at her. "What? No! Of course I've lain with a woman. But not one like you. A lady. A lass who's untouched. Whose reputation would be harmed."

"You lie only with trollops? With women you pay?"

"I would not take a maiden. I would not seduce a young lass and ruin her reputation."

"I told you!" She ground out the words. "I don't care about my reputation."

" 'Tis easy enough to say, but you dinna know what it's like."

"Oh!" She narrowed her eyes, her hands again tightening into fists on her hips. "I suppose you know better than I what it is like for a woman to be an outcast? To have her family turn away from her or to be treated with scorn?"

261

"People think you are a bluestocking. Perhaps even eccentric. It's hardly the same as being deemed a jade. You have no idea what it's like to be looked upon with contempt, to be whispered about. I know how people regarded my mother. I know the sort of gossip that followed Meg all her life, though she had never done aught to warrant it. I will not have people treat you like that."

"*You* will not have it! Of course. That is what matters. What *you* will have. What you decide. What you want. I have nothing to say in the matter. No doubt I cannot be trusted to make decisions about the course of my life. I am only a weak female and must have a man tell me what to do."

"I never said that." His jaw jutted mulishly.

"You did not have to. I understand the message quite well. I have heard it all my life!" She whirled and grabbed her cloak. "I will not bother you any longer with my shameful behavior."

"Violet! Stop. You canna go out there — the weather."

"I don't care about the weather. I'd rather be out in the rain and the cold than stuck in here with a sanctimonious, overbearing prig!" She strode for the door, tying her cloak around her.

"Wait." He picked up his coat and began to pull it on. "Let me put out the fire, and I'll go with you. You should not be out in this by yourself."

She spun back, fixing him with an icy gaze. "No. I will do what I want. There is no 'should' about it. I am sure we will both be happier if you stay here and take your pleasure by yourself, as you prefer it."

Violet marched out, slamming the door behind her.

The foul weather suited her mood. Her anger took her down the path to where it split off to the castle before she realized that, in fact, the weather was no longer so foul. Though the gray sky still drizzled, it was not pouring down rain, and the wind had also died down, making it possible to keep her hood covering her head and her cloak wrapped around her.

She climbed the sloping path to Duncally at a good pace, her mind in a stew. Of all the insufferable men! To decide what was best for her! As if she were a child who did not realize the consequences of her actions!

Gradually her steps began to slow — and her mind as well. She remembered him sitting with his back to her, his fingers gripping his bowed head, his whole body taut. However frustrating and aggravating his rejection had been to her, it had not been easy for him. A faint smile touched her lips. He was not disinterested in her. His desire had not been illusory nor had it been fleeting.

She walked on, recalling Coll's actions the last few days. Viewed in this new light, they did not speak of indifference. Had he really thought of her so often? Wanted her? Was it unfulfilled hunger that had brought the shadows beneath his eyes, the tension in his face? She thought again of that moment in front of the fireplace when his face had flamed with desire. The faint trembling of his hand when he slid it along her skin.

Violet paused, thinking of that hand, those supple fingers as they moved beneath her gown, the delicious texture of his skin as he touched her sensitive nipples. It was not a terrible trait to have concern for her reputation. She could not revile him for treating her with honor. He would not be a man she could respect if he callously dismissed such things. But, blast it, she should be the one to make the decisions about her life.

A snap came in the trees behind her. Violet tensed. Had Coll followed her? She turned, her eyes scanning the woods. She could see nothing on the path, and the shadows beneath the trees revealed little. It was not Coll; he would not hide.

She started forward again. Her back prickled between her shoulder blades; she could not dismiss the idea that she was being watched. The leaves rustled, and she was not sure if it was the wind that had sent them skittering on the ground or a person's feet. More likely some small animal, running off at the sight of a human.

She spun around. The scene was the same, empty but for trees and shrubs and shadows. She was being fanciful. It was simply the gray afternoon and her own jumbled feelings that plucked her nerves, merely the unaccustomed aloneness after spending the day with Coll.

Holding her head high, she strode forward with purpose. With a sigh of relief she saw the stone steps of Duncally ahead of her. She took the flight of stairs to the lowest garden, then turned and watched the trail she had just traversed. There was no sign of anyone.

She felt foolish. There was no reason for her uneasy feeling. Yet she could not help but think of the time last week when she had had the same itchy sense that she was being watched. She had seen nothing to indicate that the idea was warranted either time; she knew it was illogical. It had been born out of her being generally on edge the last few days, that was all.

Once she was back in her room, her first instinct was to spend the rest of the day there. She could have her supper brought to her on a tray and not have to face Coll. But that would be cowardly. Violet refused to run away. She had dealt with exclusion and rejection all her life; she could deal with this. It would be awkward at first, but they would move past it. Coll had certain beliefs, and she had others. They would accept that and remain colleagues.

She went down to the evening meal at the usual time, both relieved and disappointed to see that Coll was not there. Footsteps sounded in the hall. They checked for an instant at the door, then came closer.

Glad that she had had a moment to prepare herself, Violet turned with a carefully polite expression. "Good evening, Coll." She quelled the small pang of regret. That, too, would pass.

"Violet. I was not certain I would see you here tonight."

"Really? I hope I am not so petty as to fault a man for adhering to his principles. Indeed, I commend you for holding yourself to the same standard of conduct you expect of women. So many men believe that what is loose behavior in a woman is acceptable for a man."

His brows drew together. "I dinna say that your behav—"

"Please." She raised her hand with a cool smile. "Let us not quarrel. I hope that we can put what happened this afternoon behind us and move forward without ani-mosity."

"Of course." His tone was less certain than his words.

"Good. Then you agree that we should continue to work together on deciphering the clues to the treasure?"

"Yes. I dinna want to stop."

"I am glad." Violet ignored the fluttering in her stomach. If she applied herself to the task, soon she would be able to look at Coll without thinking of his hands sliding over her. She would converse with him without focusing on his mouth. Someday she would mean it when she praised him for holding to his morals, without wondering if he would have broken his rules if only she were more desirable.

She picked up her fork. "There must be some sort of marker wherever Faye buried the sacks. Or a further clue."

Coll fiddled with his cutlery. "I agree. We aren't even sure that the Munro graves are what she meant. She said 'our ancestors.' Perhaps she meant Sir Malcolm's ancestors as well or a general group. The graveyard in the village."

"There's also that statement about 'guarding it as we have guarded them.' That could be a hint about a specific area."

"Perhaps the tombs that lie inside the kirk?" Coll ventured.

"That would narrow it down. Do you know how many there are there?"

He shrugged. "No. Several. Some beneath the floor. Stone vaults along the walls."

"That seems a bit difficult, though. She couldn't have pried up the paving stones or the stone lids."

"The Roses have a grand tomb or two in the side yard of the kirk. Then there's the castle."

"They have graves there, too?" Violet asked in exasperation.

"Aye. The lairds of Baillannan liked to be remembered. The old castle had a chapel and small cemetery."

"We can't search all over the glen. Surely she would not have intended for her children to have to. There must be something we have missed."

"It would have been more helpful if she'd just said, 'I'm burying it half a foot deep between Annie's grave and the wall.' "

"Perhaps a little too obvious to anyone who might happen to pick up the book." Violet smiled.

"Let's go back to the journal tomorrow."

"Very well." She was glad he had not suggested that they start tonight. Her nerves were too much at a jangle now, her body still too alive with passion.

This would give her time to steady herself. And she would manage it. She would. If not, she could not remain around Coll — and she could not bear to think of that.

16

Violet threw herself back into her routine the following morning. The days were easy enough. Away from Coll, surrounded by the work she loved, she could forget for whole stretches of time that her body defiantly ached for him. It helped that she was often distracted by Angus McKay, who had apparently decided to oversee the excavation. Every few days, he would pop in for an hour or two to needle the workers and cross verbal swords with Violet. He was there when their careful digging revealed a fourth wall, confirming Violet's conjecture that the walls were likely the remains of a room or a shed.

"It could even be a house," she told Coll over supper that evening. "Of course, that means that the rest of the rock walls in the area are probably other buildings, which is even more exciting."

Coll nodded and asked a polite question.

The progress of her dig was one of the mainstays of their stilted conversations at the dining table. It was impossible to go back to the easy relationship they had had before that afternoon in the Munro cottage. They had to pick their way carefully through whatever they said, avoiding any topic that might bring up the memory of that encounter — as if she needed anything to remind her! Just looking at Coll made it difficult to think of anything else.

It was easier, in a way, to be with him later in the evening when they sat at the huge library table, going through Faye's journal. At least then she did not have to wrack her brain for safe subjects. Yet it was even more difficult because of their enforced closeness — Coll's arm only inches from hers on the table, his leg accidentally brushing hers when he shifted in his chair. His scent. His heat.

She had trouble concentrating on the journal. She found herself listening to the sound of Coll's voice instead of the words. Her gaze was drawn to Coll's long fingers as he turned the pages or to the shadow of his eyelashes on his cheek as he read. It was all too much. Violet felt as if she were constantly vibrating on some low level, a smothered fire not quite extinguished. The only sensible thing to do was to stay away from Coll. Yet each evening she rushed eagerly into the torment.

They went through the journal again, this time starting at the end and working backward. When they reached the first entry that mentioned the burden and the blessing her love had given her, Coll shut the book with a sigh, leaning back in his chair and rubbing his hands over his face.

Violet sneaked a glance at him. He looked weary, his eyes shadowed. Did thoughts of her disturb his nights? She turned away. Better not to think of that.

She opened the journal. "I think this is the most important page." She tapped the entry.

"You think this is the day she hid it."

"Yes. December sixth. It's the only dated entry." Violet went back through the pages. "I cannot find even one other date. And it sounds final, as if she has already placed it there: 'May our ancestors guard it . . .' "

"I agree. So this would be the likeliest part of the journal for her to reveal the location."

"Yes. Why make Malcolm or their child search the whole book? If they were the only ones who could understand the message, there's little point in making it difficult to find."

"Just difficult to comprehend." He grimaced. "Very well. Let's go over this page again." Coll leaned back. "Read it aloud."

"Beginning at the top, there is a remedy — a 'protection,' she calls it. She lists yew and something else — no, I think that's a blot."

"Yew?" Coll frowned and leaned forward to peer at the words. "That's a strange remedy. Yews are poisonous."

"Really?" Violet turned to him.

"Yes. Ma drummed the poisonous plants and mushrooms into me from the time I could walk. Almost everything on the yew is poisonous — seeds, foliage. I think you're right; that next thing isn't a word or is struck out. So she lists only one ingredient." He drummed his fingers on the table. "I never paid attention to the ingredients before. It does not say what it protects one from."

"Perhaps that isn't *protection,* perhaps it's another long word that begins with a *p.* Like *poisonous.* Or . . ." Violet paused, looking thoughtful. "You know, if you guard something, that's protecting it."

"Aye." He looked at her. "The ancestors are *guarding* the 'burden.' So the yew is another hint?"

"It could be a reference to the Munro

graveyard."

"But that would still indicate the entire cemetery. Even if you narrow it to the graves shaded by the tree, that would be near half of them. You looked inside the tree itself, and there was nothing."

"Yes. You're right. There must be something more." She propped her chin on her hand and studied the page. "Coll . . . what if it's the date?"

"What if what's the date?"

"The clue. I assumed she hid the treasure on this date, but why would it be important what date she buries it? Maybe the date is the identifying mark."

"So she hid it in a tomb or a grave of an ancestor who died on that day. Or December sixth of any year, I suppose. She doesn't even put the year on it."

"It could be the date someone was born. But the death date seems more important, and the death date's more likely to be on all of them."

"Except the Munro graves."

"What do you mean? They don't date them?"

"They may have, but you saw what most of those markers are like — wooden and weathered till nothing remains, even the names. Only the last few are legible, and none of them are December sixth."

"Then she couldn't have meant the grave site with the yew tree."

He shrugged. "It's been almost sixty years. The date could have been worn away since."

"In that case, we shall never be able to find it." Violet sighed.

"Aye, but we dinna know that. It's more likely that she left it somewhere else. She thinks Sir Malcolm will know it, and how familiar would he have been with the Munro graves? Maybe the yew isn't important. Or maybe it's some other yew. Graveyards often have a yew tree, do they not?"

Violet nodded. "Yews have long been associated with religion. Eternity. In pagan practices, they were regarded as symbols of death and rebirth. They live for a remarkably long time, so they would be perfect for —" Violet stopped. Coll was regarding her with a smile hovering on his lips. "I'm sorry. I am lecturing again."

"Nae." He curled a hand around her wrist. "Dinna apologize. I like to listen to you." His eyes dropped to his hand, and he released her. "Well, then, perhaps we have our clue. We should try the kirk in town."

"Yes." Violet nodded, trying to forget the feel of his long fingers encircling her wrist. It was difficult when her flesh still tingled

275

from the touch.

"Tomorrow? You could take a day off digging."

"Yes. Of course." Violet's spirits rose. "I am sure the men would welcome a respite."

"Good. Then I'll tell the McKennas to return to the gardens tomorrow. Maybe the head gardener will stop complaining."

They set out early the next morning. Violet was surprised to see that Coll had ordered the carriage. At her questioning glance, he pointed to the leaden sky. "It looks like rain. I dinna think you'd like another drenching."

His words took her back to their escape from the rain the other day and the passion that had flared between them. From the look that flitted across Coll's face, she knew his thoughts went down the same path. He pivoted away to open the door, and Violet climbed in before he could offer his hand to help her up.

They sat facing each other, the silence in the vehicle stifling. It was easier when they reached the small kirk, and they put several feet between them as they walked through the graveyard. Two yew trees were near the church, though neither was as large and imposing as the one that graced the Munro graves. They began their search at the rear, where the yews grew.

No graves close to the two trees bore the date they sought, so Coll turned to a large tomb with a winged angel atop it that, unsurprisingly, held several sepulchres of the lairds of Baillannan. Around them were a jumble of more markers and monuments, many bearing the name Rose.

By the end of the morning, Violet's back ached from the tiring, tedious work of bending down to examine the headstones. Many markers were worn and spotted with lichen, making them difficult to read. Some were cracked or broken; a few showed nothing but the name. None bore the date they sought.

"Perhaps that date is important because no one ever dies here on December sixth," Violet grumbled. She straightened, her hand going to the small of her back, and twisted to look over at Coll.

He was squatting down beside a stone a few feet from her, his eyes fastened on her — more specifically, on the unmentionable part of her anatomy so prominent in her former bent-over posture. Coll glanced away immediately, a flush rising in his face. Violet felt her own cheeks warming as she moved to the next grave, this time squatting to read the marker. She stared at it sightlessly, wait-

277

ing for the sensations tumbling in her to subside. It was absurd that just catching him watching her could bring such a rush of heat and confusion.

But, no, it wasn't his study of her that set off the explosion inside her. The expression on his face — the primitive, undisguised hunger — had been as potent as if he'd run his hand down her body.

Behind her, she heard Coll yanking up weeds and tossing twigs and pebbles, tidying one of the graves. A loud crack made her jump and she sneaked a glance. He snapped a downed branch into small pieces as he walked away, then hurled them with unnecessary force into a pile of leaves and twigs.

He returned to the plot where Violet worked. "We've finished the Roses. And the area near the yews." He glanced around the remainder of the cemetery. "It will take us a while to search this whole place."

"Mm. We'll need more than one day." Violet stood up with a sigh. "I keep thinking that we have missed something important."

"She was damnably cryptic."

Violet put her hands on her lower back and leaned backward, stretching her spine.

"Perhaps we should stop for the day," Coll

suggested. She turned toward him, surprised. His face was shuttered, his voice toneless. "Start afresh another time."

"No doubt you are right." Violet, too, was growing tired of the unproductive work, but she could not quell a pang of disappointment at cutting short her day with Coll.

They walked to the waiting carriage. Coll opened the door for Violet but did not follow her inside. "You go ahead. I have, um, some business in Kinclannoch. Supplies and . . ." He made a vague gesture. "I'll walk."

"But the weather —" She glanced toward the sky. "It may rain. We can wait for you."

He shook his head. "No need. I'm accustomed to it."

"Very well." Clearly that was a dismissal. Violet sat down, turning her attention to straightening her skirts. She did not raise her head until she heard the click of the door closing.

The carriage turned and rumbled down the street. Violet leaned her head against the plush back of the seat and contemplated the empty afternoon ahead of her. She could go to the site. But the men had been assigned elsewhere today, and as Coll had said, it would probably rain. She could catch up on her notes for the site or her letter writing; she had been neglecting them both while treasure hunting with Coll. There was the journal, of course, but she was reluctant to examine it on her own.

She decided to look at the books she had brought with her. The symbol etched in the small knife Coll had shown her intrigued her. The mark reminded her of the Norse runes, and she had been meaning to research it. Though she doubted it would shed any light on their quest, it seemed a good way to spend a rainy afternoon.

Violet found two books on Nordic history as well as a scholarly paper on the Viking invasions of Scotland, and she settled down on the floor to look through them. She was elated to discover that one book contained drawings and explanations of the runes, but unfortunately, the symbol on Coll's knife was not among them.

Violet pulled out the drawing she had made of the knife to study it again. Part of the symbol on the hilt resembled one of the runes. Perhaps the original mark had been changed over time or two different runes had been used together. However, she could not find a rune that resembled the top part of the emblem, which was simply a straight line with five shorter lines crossing it.

She could write one of her uncle's colleagues to inquire about the mark. Unfortunately, most of the antiquarians she knew focused on Roman and Greek times, with only a small smattering of scholars interested in ancient British history. She could not think of any who had studied the Vikings.

Perhaps she would have better luck with a history professor. That Oxford don, O'Neil. His interest was Celtic history, but something about him made her think of runes. Were there Celtic runes as well?

Intrigued, she pawed through the trunk again. Finally, near the bottom, she found O'Neil's history of Ireland and the Celts. She flipped through the pages. Yes, here it was: Ogham. Why hadn't she thought of this earlier?

Running her finger down the page, she stopped short at one of the symbols. She read the words below it, her pulse beginning to pound. She jumped to her feet, sending the book tumbling to the ground. "Coll! Coll, I found it!"

17

Coll prowled through his cottage, unable to settle to anything. He had hoped the walk home would calm down the riot within him, but it had been a futile effort. He could not settle down to draw, and trying to tally the account books or decipher Damon's latest letter was beyond question. He could think of nothing but Violet and the pounding need inside him to be sheathed in her, her body clamped hot and tight around him.

He let out a low growl and picked up the iron poker to jab viciously at the smoldering peat. Sparks shot up from the dark bricks, mirroring the leaping sensation in his belly. He sighed, dropping the poker onto the hearth with a clatter, and roamed over to the window to stare out at the dreary afternoon. He turned to the table and picked up the sketch there, incomplete because he simply could not get her eyes quite right. He moved on to the wooden

282

carving beside it. That, he thought with a new spurt of frustration, looked nothing like her. Coll was tempted to hurl the head across the room. He would like nothing better right now than to break something. But of course he could not, for it also looked too much like her. Coll smoothed his thumb along the cheekbone.

What was the matter with him? Cursing softly, he resumed his pacing. He had never before been so tied up in knots over a woman. Even as a green lad, he had not been led around by his basest hungers. But now, it seemed, he was permanently poised on the knife edge of lust. He spent his sleepless nights — and, truth be known, far too many of his days — imagining taking Violet everywhere and in every way imaginable. It alarmed him how the blood pumped hot in his veins when he thought of sweeping her up and carrying her off to his room, of grasping her gown and ripping it open, of shoving up her skirts and thrusting himself deep inside her. Never before in his life had he ached so to possess a woman, to bend her to his will.

The devil of it was that she had offered herself to him on Sunday. She had been soft and willing, even eager, pressing her body into his and returning his kisses. More than that, Violet had been furious with him for his holding back. He had had to struggle against her as well as himself.

Every day he became more certain that he had been mad to do so. Any other man would have taken what Violet offered without a moment's thought. Indeed, some other man would surely do so in the future, an idea that sent anger like a red-hot spear through Coll.

It was one thing to respect a woman, to not stain her reputation or take her virginity without a thought to the consequences. But, blast it, if she wanted him, wasn't he an utter clunch not to take her to his bed? Especially a woman such as Violet, so independent and sure of herself, so decided in her opinions.

That she did not know the reality of a shredded reputation, that she was innocent and untouched — which, God help him, turned him rock hard as much as it weighed on his conscience — even the intense need he felt to shield her from harm, did not give him the right to make the decision for her. And why, he wondered, did he feel so strong an urge to shelter a woman who had as little interest in being protected as Violet Thornhill? That, he supposed, made him just as contrary as she.

He gripped the mantel, staring down into the low flames, thinking of the way Violet looked this morning as she made her way through the churchyard. The thrust of her breasts when she stretched to ease her cramped muscles. Her firm, ripe bottom as she bent to peer at a marker. He thought of curving his hand over that luscious roundness.

A rap on his door made him start. He turned, irritated. However jangled and jumbled his thoughts were, he preferred to wallow in them alone. The door flew open before he even spoke, and Violet sailed in. Her cheeks were flushed, her eyes sparkling. She glowed with excitement. A bolt of desire struck Coll, so fierce and hot it stunned him into speechlessness.

"Coll! I think I found it." Violet pushed back her hood, smiling.

Coll scarcely heard what she said. He strode across the floor to her and clamped his hands on her shoulders. He stared down into her face for a long, charged moment, the blood pounding in him. When at last he spoke, his voice was thick and grating, as if the words were torn from him. "Take down your hair."

Violet's eyes widened, but she said nothing, simply gazed into his eyes as she reached up and began to remove the pins from her hair, her movements slow and deliberate. Coll watched as her hair loosened and tumbled down, bit by bit. His heart pounded so hard it was all he could hear; everything in him was focused on her fingers moving through her hair.

Stretching out his hand, he took one end of the tie securing her cloak and pulled it. The bow opened, and he pushed the garment back off her shoulders, sending it crumpling to the floor. Hooking his fingers into the neckline of her dress, he glided them slowly back and forth, watching the warmth and softness bloom in her face.

"I dinna want to hurt you." His voice was low, throbbing with the last vestige of his control. "In any way."

A smile curved her lips, slow and delicious. "You will not. I am stronger than I look."

"Violet . . ." He spread his hand across her collarbone, sliding his fingers up her neck, halting as he reached her jaw.

"Yes?"

But he had nothing to say; he spoke her name only to feel it on his tongue. Bending down, he kissed her. His lips were slow and sweet on hers, the rush of his desire tightly clamped down as he opened her mouth to him with tantalizing care. Violet stretched on tiptoe, her arms going up to encircle his neck. His arms went around her, pulling her flush against him as he deepened the kiss, employed tongue and teeth and lips to arouse her.

Finally he pulled his mouth from hers and buried his face in her hair, his breath rasping in and out of his throat, his body trembling from the restraint he forced on himself.

"No," Violet whispered, her hands stroking his neck and shoulders. "Do not stop."

Coll let out a low groan, and he sank slowly to his knees, sliding down her body, his arms encircling her, his cheek flush against her body. His flesh ached with the sweet pleasure of moving over her, and he buried his face in her stomach. He was lost. And he did not care.

He felt her fingers tangle in his hair, and that, too, brought a rush of mingled delight and hunger. He wanted to take her as hard and fast as he could, but even greater was the need to linger, to arouse and awaken her, drawing every last measure of sweetness.

He lifted his head to look at her. Slowly his hands glided down over her back and hips, then moved back up to curve around her breasts. "You are so beautiful."

Violet smiled, her eyes dreamy, and shook her head as if amused by his foolishness.

"I will show you." Coll put his hands on her hips and turned her so he could open the lacings up the back of her simple dress. As he spread the ties apart, the gown loosened and sagged. Violet swung back to him, her hands going up to catch the falling dress and hold it against her chest. He smiled at her sudden shyness and reached up to take her hands. "Nae, dinna hide. Let me look at you."

She let go and the gown floated down her body to pool on the floor. Desire leaped in him. He tugged at the ribbon fastening her chemise, maneuvering it down until her breasts came free. "Ah, lass . . ." He took her breasts in his hands, luxuriating in their weight and fullness. "You are lovely. Creamy smooth and soft, perfect." He eased his thumbs over her nipples, watching them harden. "I've imagined your breasts a million times over — dreamed what it would be like to caress them, kiss them. But naught can match the reality. Like silk. Like honey."

He slid his hands down her sides, watching the movement of his spread fingers over her curving flesh. Desire clawed at him like a beast, but he kept his movements slow, almost lazy, his hands drifting up her body again to tease at her taut nipples. He watched desire darken Violet's eyes and passion slacken her face. The signs of her hunger sent his own soaring. With fingers that trembled a little, he untied the ribbons of her undergarments and shoved them down, his hands lingering on her legs. Wordlessly, her hands on his shoulders for balance, she stepped out of the remaining garments and stood naked before him.

His eyes drank her in. "Come," he murmured. "Let me show you how beautiful you are." Putting his hands on her waist, he pulled her down to him.

Laying her back upon her crumpled clothes, Coll took her mouth in a long kiss, tasting her slowly as his hands explored her body. She was all softness and warmth, her skin trembling beneath his touch. When his fingers slipped between her legs, he found her slick and moist, ready for him, her response so innocently eager that hunger speared him.

Leaving her lips, he traveled down her neck and on to the pillowy softness of her breasts. He was hard and aching, holding on to his control by his fingertips. She opened the ties of his shirt, fingers slipping inside to caress his naked skin, and it was all he could do not to shove her legs apart and thrust into her with all the force of his need. He reared up, wrenching the shirt off over his head and tossing it aside.

Her hands moved down to the buttons of his trousers, and he went still, his breath rasping in and out, poised on the blade-sharp edge of pleasure as her fingers' delicate movements made the sensitive flesh beneath the cloth throb and strain against it. Her eyes flew up to his face, and he saw the surprise and question in her eyes, along with a smoky stirring of delight. A smile curved her lips, secret and filled with feminine power, and she ran her hands under his waistband, shoving down his breeches.

The gesture shook him. He found that the limits of his desire could be pushed further than he had ever known. He rose, shucking off the remainder of his clothes. She watched him with wide eyes, and for an instant Coll worried that she would pull back, frightened by her first sight of a naked male body. But her eyes moved over him, soft and arousing as a touch, and when she held up her arms to him, he went to her like a starved man.

He intended to woo her with tender kisses and soft touches, but he found he could not keep his hunger from slipping its leash. She was too soft, too inviting, too delectable. His mouth roamed her breasts, fingertips digging into the lush mounds of her buttocks. Violet seemed to welcome his hunger, her own hands tangling in his hair as soft whimpers of delight came from her throat, and her reaction spurred his passion.

Sweat dampened their skin, so that his body slid over hers slickly. He heard her breath coming fast and saw the pulse throbbing in the delicate hollow of her throat. His fingers sought out her deepest secrets, and her arousal flooded him, the musky scent teasing at his nostrils. His desire was desperate and aching, and he shuddered under his restraint. When she arched up against him, her hips circling beneath his hand, he could hold back no longer. He slid between her legs, his hands going under her hips and lifting her as he moved slowly into her.

Violet did not flinch, did not retreat, only shifted a little to take him into her, and that small giving of herself tested his control more than anything else. He thrust into her, unable to stop even at the brief tug of resistance. She was tight and hot around him, every stroke a shattering pleasure. Violet clung to him, and the moans that issued from her lips set him afire. She dug her fingernails into his back, the small, sharp pain intensifying the cataclysm building within him.

His world, his life, narrowed to this moment. He was filled with heat, with ache and arousal, ecstasy burgeoning to the point of agony. Then life burst in him and poured out into her. Coll shuddered, crushing Violet to him.

Slowly he relaxed, nuzzling into the crook of Violet's neck, then rolled over onto his back, carrying her with him. Sated and drained, he cradled Violet, his nostrils filled with her scent, her hair flowing over him like a cloud. He pressed his lips to her skin, his hand stroking her head and down her back. He whispered her name, the word a breath upon her skin.

And he slid gently into sleep.

Violet felt him drift into sleep, his arms relaxing their grip, his breath easing, the thunder of his heart slowing beneath her ear. She smiled to herself, content to lie here with him, her head resting on his chest, and listen to him breathe. She was, in fact, too dazed to do much of anything else. The past few minutes had been wild, overwhelming, and her whole being hummed with pleasure.

Everything was different — outwardly the same but fundamentally changed. She felt faintly sore and used but in a most delightful way, her body still thrumming and her insides molten, her skin so sensitive she could feel the very air upon it. It was much too tame to say she was happy. Or satisfied. Or vibrating with sensation. She was all those things, in a way that made her want to giggle, but she was far, far more.

She had run half the way here from the house, eager to reveal her discovery to Coll. Then she had stepped inside, and he had . . . *looked* at her. She could not convey the way his gaze had ripped through her, the hunger in his eyes so stark and raw that it had stolen her breath. And what she had come here to tell him had lost its importance.

Violet closed her eyes, remembering Coll's kiss. The way he had *oozed* down her body to kneel before her, all power and supplication. His face against her, his hands roaming over her, his voice thick with desire. He had made her his, claiming her with his mouth and hands and body. He had kissed and caressed her as if worshipping at her altar. And at the same time he had owned her.

She suspected she should be embarrassed by her quivering response to his touch and the helpless, hungry moans and whimpers he had pulled from her. But what she felt was bliss . . . along with an overwhelming desire to have him do those things to her all over again. Violet pressed her lips softly to his chest, then propped herself on her elbow and studied Coll. He looked utterly relaxed and at peace, the tautness vanished from his face, the sharp lines fallen into softness. That, too, filled her with a fizzing happiness.

She sat up, pulling her knees to her chest and wrapping her arms around them, and watched him sleep. She was too accustomed to analysis not to poke and pry at her feelings. It was odd for her to be so awash in emotion. She was filled with satisfaction, even a sort of pride, in the knowledge that she had been the cause of such passion in him, that he had been so teased and tormented by desire for her that it had at last cracked his control. Conversely, she was equally warmed by the knowledge that she had been the cause of his pleasure, his relief and release, that she had given him with happiness. Peace.

Violet was not accustomed to being connected like this to anyone else. Nothing could match that moment when he had pushed into her, that first sharp pain obliterated by a glorious sense of fulfillment. It was as if, for a time, he was part of her. Somehow, she knew, he would always be a part of her. The idea was exhilarating. And a little frightening.

A shiver ran through her, pulling her for the first time back into the world around her. The fire kept the room from being frigid, but it was not quite warm enough for naked flesh. Coll was lying on her clothes, and she hadn't the heart to wake him. She picked up his discarded shirt and slipped it on. It occurred to her that the door was unlocked, that anyone could come in on them, and she hastened over to lock it.

Walking back, she grabbed the knitted afghan from the chair by the fire and draped it over Coll to keep him warm. Then she settled down beside him and watched him sleep. He looked peaceful, even boyish, all strain absent from his face. Her eyes roamed over his features, taking in the broad brow, the fine blond hair that spilled across his forehead, the sweep of his cheekbones and the firm line of his jaw. She smoothed his hair back, and her fingers lingered to trace the curving lines of his eyebrows. She was tempted to draw her finger along his cheekbones, as well, but she refrained. Her eyes dropped to his lips, firm and well defined.

She remembered them on her neck. Her breasts. The air came a little faster in her throat.

Her gaze moved down, taking in the soft hollow of his throat, the hard, high shelf of his collarbone. How could such a thing be so enticing? Just bone and flesh and yet . . . She could not resist; she traced her forefinger along the ridge of his collarbone and down the centerline of his chest. The curling hairs prickled her fingers, and they drifted across his chest, circling the small, flat buds of his nipples. She slid her palm over the high plateau of his chest, tracing each rib and exploring the muscles that padded them, dropping down onto the soft valley of his stomach. Her fingers crept beneath the edge of the soft blanket and paused.

She should not. It was an invasion of his privacy to gaze at him while he slept, unknowing. She would be indignant if he did the same to her. But heat flooded up her throat at the thought, and excitement stirred in her, not resentment or shame. Her fingers slipped lower, dragging down the knitted blanket an inch at a time. She touched the dip of his navel, her forefinger circling the rim. She ran her hand down him slowly, stirred by the sight of her fingers on his body. The cloth jerked suddenly, and she sucked in a breath. She remembered how he had swelled and pushed against his trousers as she unbuttoned them, how strong and thick his member had been as it sprang free of the restraint. He was responding to her touch now, even in his sleep. Violet itched to see him, to explore him, to discover the texture and strength and heat of his maleness. Her fingers hesitated at the edge of the cover.

"Dinna stop now." Coll's voice was low and husky.

"Oh!" Violet started, surprised, and turned guiltily. Coll was watching her, one arm crooked behind his head, his eyes hazy with sleep, lips soft and sensual, and the expression on his face started up a fierce throbbing deep in her abdomen. She blushed. "I am sorry. I shouldn't; that was . . . rude of me."

His lips curled into a lazy smile. "I think I like it when you're rude." Coll reached out, giving a tug to the shirt she had thrown over herself. "And what's this? It doesna seem fair, me as naked as the day I was born and you all covered up." He slid his hand under the shirt, unerringly seeking out her breasts. Violet melted at his touch, and the masculine smugness in Coll's expression told her he knew that fact well.

"Stop it," she protested feebly, and Coll's smile broadened. He gathered up the loose material in his hand and pulled her to him, lifting his head to take her mouth in a slow, deliberate kiss. By the time he released her, Violet was breathless, the blood pounding in her veins.

"Come. Do what you will with me." He flipped back the cover, exposing the very long, very naked length of his body. "I'll not protest."

"Coll . . ." She could not keep her eyes from straying to the lower half of him.

"What?" He twined a strand of her hair around his hand. She could hear the smile in his voice, but along with it a low vibration of desire. "You know I could deny you nothing."

Violet spread her hand on his stomach. He twitched, hissing in a sharp breath. She cast a glance at him, but nothing was in his face but hunger. He wrapped his fingers around her wrist, guiding her lower.

"Dinna stop, lass."

She drifted over his body in slow discovery, learning the soft skin of his stomach, the sharp outcropping of his hip bones, the tight prickling of his nipples. She twined her fingers through his hair and curled them around his staff, glided down between his legs and cupped him in her palm. With each stroke, each touch, he stiffened and pulsed. That, too, sent need coiling through her gut. She bent to touch her lips to his nipple, which brought a soft groan from him. Violet stole a glance at him. His eyes were closed, his lips parted.

She circled the flat bud with her tongue, mimicking what he had done to her, then settled her mouth on him to suckle, her hand roaming over his flesh. His skin flamed, his breath rasped. She reveled in each tiny demonstration of his pleasure. Leaving the tight bud, she kissed her way across his chest and down the hard line of his sternum, then dropped to the soft skin of his stomach.

He went taut, thrusting his hands into her hair, and grated out something in a language she did not recognize. Violet raised her head; his eyes were intense, so fiery and fierce she thought they should have inspired fear in her, but all she felt was a rush of hunger. She slid up his body and sealed his mouth with hers.

With an inarticulate noise deep in his throat, Coll wrapped his arms around her and rolled over, pinning her beneath him and kissing her as though he would never stop. She arched against him, aching to take him into her again.

At last he pulled back, bracing his hands on either side of her head. She looked up at him dazedly, reaching up to pull him down to her. "Coll, no . . . please . . ."

He rolled to his feet, reaching down to pull her up with him. His grin was tight and feral. "Oh, I will please. I swear that to you. But I intend to do it somewhere far more comfortable than this."

Bending, he swept her up in his arms and started toward the bedroom.

18

Coll carried her to the bed and set her down on her feet. "First, let's get rid of this." He pulled his shirt from her and tossed it aside. His eyes drifted down her. "You are so beautiful it stops my heart." Cupping her face in his hands, he placed a kiss on her forehead, her cheeks, her lips. "I did not take enough time with you before. I was too . . . driven . . . to use the care I should have." He trailed his fingers down her arms. "But this time I will. This time you will have it all."

"I don't know what you mean." Violet's voice hitched as his fingers skimmed over her buttocks and back up her sides.

"I know you don't." He took her earlobe gently between his teeth. "But you will."

His mouth came back to hers, his lips soft and gentle, coaxing every sensation possible from her. His hands moved over her slowly, fingers featherlight on her skin, until her knees were trembling, and she thought her legs might give way beneath her. As if he'd guessed, Coll lifted her, settling her onto the bed with as much care as if she were glass. Then he stretched out beside her and, as he had promised, set out to please her.

With hands and lips and tongue and teeth, he aroused her, tantalized her, traveling every inch of her skin, stoking the fires of her hunger until she thought she could not bear it but must explode with pleasure. She felt as if she were racing toward something, need coiling deep within her. Though it came ever closer, each time when she thought that she was going to snap, Coll pulled back, finding some new place to touch or kiss, some new way to send her spiraling upward again.

He feasted on her breasts until they were heavy and full, her nipples hard and dark rising from the hot pull of his mouth, and all the while his agile fingers played between her legs, opening and teasing her until she was blazing. Then he moved behind her and started his slow way down her back, his mouth traveling along her spine while his hand slid down her side, lingering over the curve of her hip and drifting over to spread across her stomach.

She let out a gasp when his hand stole

between her legs from behind, finding the same slick, throbbing folds. He nipped at the fleshy mound of her buttocks, and Violet writhed beneath his ministrations. She ached for him, yearning to feel again the supreme satisfaction as he filled her, wanting something that she did not know, aware only of her desperate need.

"Please," she murmured, turning to Coll, her eyes huge and lambent, her hands moving restlessly over his arms and shoulders. "I want you. I want to feel you inside me."

His skin, slick with sweat and already blazing, flared even hotter at her words, and his breath came out in a shudder. He rolled over her, positioning himself between her legs, and shoved into her inch by inch. Violet could not hold back a groan as he filled her with piercing sweetness. She shifted to fully take him into her, and he went still, his fingers digging into the sheets beneath her. Then, slowly, he began to move, pulling back and thrusting deep.

Violet wrapped her arms around him, burying her face in his shoulder, as she moved with him. Now the desire that built in her was unstoppable, clawing and tightening with each movement he made. She gripped him tightly, holding on as if she might fly apart. Suddenly, violently, the need inside her exploded. Violet clamped her teeth into his shoulder to muffle the cry that was torn from her, and he let out an answering roar as he jerked wildly, the cataclysm storming through them, sweeping everything before it. Waves of pleasure washed out through her, stunning her and leaving her replete and limp.

Coll collapsed onto his side and pulled her into the shelter of his arms. Violet clung, too astounded, too enervated, to move. She pressed her lips against his flesh, so attuned to his heartbeat, his breath, she scarcely knew where he left off and she began. His skin quivered at the touch of her mouth, and he curved his hand over her hair.

"So *that* is what you meant," she murmured.

"That is what I meant." She felt Coll's smile against her hair, and his voice was laced with masculine satisfaction. He pulled the covers up over them, tucking them in around her shoulders.

"You are right. 'Tis much more comfortable here." Violet snuggled into the curve of Coll's arm.

"Mm." He kissed the top of her head. "I am sorry I spoiled your news."

"What? Oh." She smiled. "It doesn't matter. I much preferred what happened."

"I feared you might regret it."

"No." She lifted her head to look into his eyes, frowning. "Do you?"

"Me? Regret this?" The astonishment in his face was enough to soothe her pride. "Nae. How could I regret making love with you? You are . . . beautiful. Perfect." Coll bent to kiss her lips, then lay back with a sigh. "But I broke my vow. I find that I am weak where you are concerned."

"I did not ask for your vow."

"I know. 'Tis fortunate, since clearly I canna keep it."

She looked into his eyes. "I do as I choose."

"I know." He smiled, his hand coming up to cup her cheek. "And I am glad you chose me."

Violet felt awash in happiness. Coll had accepted how she felt, what she wanted. No doubt he understood her position better than most men, having grown up with such independent women as his mother and sister. Even more amazing, he knew her better than anyone else ever had and yet still he wanted to be with her.

She stretched up to kiss his lips, and his hand went to her nape, holding her there for a longer, deeper kiss. When at last she pulled back, he said huskily, "You'd best go ahead and tell me now before I lose track again. What was it you found?"

"Well, I didn't find it exactly." Violet sat up, heedless of the covers sliding down to provide him with an enticing view of her bare breasts. "It's more that I found what it meant."

"Did you now?" His eyes drifted downward, and he reached up to brush his knuckles across one rosy nipple.

"Coll . . . you're not paying attention."

"Oh, but I am." He cupped his hand around the heavy orb.

"Not to my words." She could not keep from smiling even as she pushed his hand away. "Where is that shirt?" She twisted around to look for it.

"No, no. Don't put it on. I'll be good. I promise." He linked his hands behind his head. "Now tell me."

"I think I figured out the mark on that little knife of yours."

"The sgian-dubh?" His gaze sharpened.

"Yes. It reminded me of a Nordic rune. So today I went through my books."

"Why would there be a Nordic rune on my knife?"

"I don't know. I presumed it had something to do with the Vikings who invaded Scotland hundreds of years ago. According

306

to my book, they often left their runes carved on things — as a message to their compatriots, I suppose, or maybe a sort of signpost for other Norsemen who came afterward."

"But why on a knife? And why would Sir Malcolm have a sgian-dubh with anything Norse on it?"

"I have no idea. That's why I was intrigued."

"Was it a rune?"

"Not exactly. There was one quite similar — a sort of Y with a pole in the center." She drew the mark with her fingertip on his chest.

"Ah, the part that looks like a bird's footprint."

"Yes, I suppose it does. But that is only the bottom part of the mark. The top section is a line with the five crosshatches." Again she sketched the pattern on his chest with her fingertip.

"You keep doing that, and I shall lose track of the conversation again."

Violet rolled her eyes. "Hush. So I was at a loss."

"Not for long, I'll warrant."

"Actually, I think I was very slow. But then it struck me. The Irish used symbols, too."

"The Irish?"

"Yes. They came here, too. Everyone wants Scotland. You're both Celts, so it isn't a great leap that Scots used the same or similar symbols. An alphabet rather than runes. Different marks stood for various sounds, like letters."

"So it spells a word? Let me guess: Rose."

Violet laughed. "No. A symbol can also represent a certain tree. A line with five lines crossing it is . . ."

His eyes lit up with understanding. "A yew tree."

"Yes. I think the insignia is two different marks that have been put together."

"Why would someone do that?"

"I don't know. Maybe someone saw them both carved somewhere and thought they were one mark. Or maybe there is a message in it. The top is a yew tree, and the rune on the bottom means 'protection.' "

Coll sat up, too, his face suddenly much more serious. "As in guarding?"

"That was my thought. The word above *yew* on that page of Faye's journal is *protection*. I thought that was the name of the remedy. But maybe she meant the symbol on his knife — and that is why she thought it would be so easy for him to recognize. Perhaps the knife was the real key. Maybe the mark identifies where the treasure is hidden."

"So we should look for a grave with that mark on it?"

"We don't know that it's necessarily a grave, but I think it must indicate something of the Rose family's — ancestors, the symbol, and so on. It could be something larger and more noticeable. Perhaps a location that Sir Malcolm would have known instantly."

"Like the old castle."

"You said the Roses had built tunnels beneath the castle running to various places. Or there might be a secret room where it was safe to hide."

"Och . . . not another hidden room."

"You said they were a secretive family."

"That they were." He let out a long breath, thinking. "It makes sense. He and Faye used to meet, we think, in the room Jack and Isobel discovered last summer. She had some familiarity with the ruins. I don't know why their child would recognize it, though, if the laird never returned."

"It's been many years now, much longer than she expected. Perhaps it was something more well-known back then."

"Aye. Perhaps knowledge of it was lost when the English banned the Highland traditions. She couldn't have known that the English would do that, that the knowledge might be suppressed and die out."

"We could try the castle next."

He nodded. "I canna go tomorrow." He cast a faint smile at her. "I got little enough done here today."

"I thought you were working in the village."

"My work was staying out of the carriage with you."

Her brows shot up. "Well, I like that!"

"I knew I could not keep my hands off you in that little space." Coll's eyes darkened. "It was all I could do not to touch you in the churchyard." He reached out, taking her arm and pulling her down onto the bed with him. His eyes traveled over her body, following the path of his hand as he caressed her. "I'm surprised I wasn't struck by lightning for my thoughts at the kirk."

"Oh, really?" Violet stretched languorously beneath his searching hand. "What were you thinking?"

His gaze heated and he bent to trace his tongue around her nipple. "I was thinking of doing this." His hand slipped beneath her to squeeze her buttocks. "And this." He nuzzled her neck, his breath hot upon her. "I wanted to pull you to the ground and make love to you right there."

"That might have shocked the vicar."

"It might." Coll trailed kisses down her.

"But I would have liked it."

Coll let out a throaty chuckle. "Then perhaps I should do it now." He rolled between her legs.

"Yes," Violet agreed, linking her hands behind his neck. "Perhaps you should."

And with that, talk ceased.

It was long past supper when they returned to Duncally. Violet was sure they were both in Mrs. Ferguson's black books now — worse, they were probably in Sally's as well. But Violet had not wanted to face any of the servants tonight. Anyone who saw her would doubtless guess what she had been doing this afternoon. It was not so much her disheveled state as the glow that lit her face.

They made do with a supper of cheese, bread, and tart apples, eaten before Coll's fireplace, and afterward they sat in sweet lassitude, Violet leaning back against Coll's chest, and watched the flames flicker. Violet wished they could stay here all night, locked in their own little world.

But they could not. It would first cause unwarranted worry among the staff at Duncally, followed no doubt by tremendous scandal. At first Coll said Violet should return to the house alone, with him following later, thinking, unsurprisingly, of Violet's reputation. But by the time she started out the door, he had changed his mind.

"I dinna like you walking by yourself." He looked past her into the night, his fingers intertwined with hers.

"I came here by myself."

"Yes, but it was day." Idly his thumb rubbed over the back of her hand as he considered.

"You think something will happen to me between here and the main house?" She cast an amused glance at him.

"It's possible." He moved a step closer, his other hand slipping around her waist. "It's dark. There was an intruder in the house."

"Weeks ago."

"Little more than a week." His hand caressed her back. "Trust me. I have counted every day I've been in that house with you."

"Indeed?" Violet's eyes lit provocatively and she swayed toward him.

"Every day. Every hour." His mouth softened, his eyes turning darker. "I should walk with you."

"I'd like that."

He brushed his lips over her forehead. "We'll go together till we can see the house. Then you continue and I'll wait to follow."

"Lurking in the trees?" She grinned and went up on tiptoe to press her lips softly to his. "That seems a bit silly, doesn't it?"

"Maybe." His mouth followed hers as she went back down on her heels. "But I'd be sure you're safe."

"I am sure it would have nothing to do with stopping now and then." She spread her hands out on his chest. "To do this." She stretched up to kiss him again, her lips lingering.

"Not at all." He nuzzled her neck. "But maybe — a little — to look at you in the moonlight." His teeth worried her earlobe. "To watch you walk."

"To watch me walk?"

"You have a particular way of walking. I have discovered it's a very . . . pleasant view."

"You stand around watching me walk?" She quirked an eyebrow at him.

"I stand around watching you do a number of things." He pulled her hips flush against him. "To be fair, sometimes I *sit* to watch you."

She could feel him hardening against her, and her lips curved in a knowing, gratified way. "Coll Munro, I do believe you are positively lecherous."

"And I believe you are positively seductive."

"I am?" A laugh bubbled out of her. "I have never been accused of that."

"I'm glad." Coll kissed her with slow deliberation, then released her with a sigh. "Come. We'd better leave, or I'll wind up dragging you back to my bed."

"We could arrive a little later."

"No." He assumed a stern expression and shrugged on his jacket as he followed her out the door. Hands stuck in his pockets, he walked a careful foot away from her side.

Violet glanced at Coll as they walked. Though she would not have told him so, she found his concern over her reputation endearing. Or perhaps, she reflected, in her present mood she found anything he did endearing. There was, for instance, the way his fair skin showed, immediately and vividly, his embarrassment — or his passion. Or the way mischief sparked in his eyes, belying the serious set of his jaw.

That was in addition to all the more obviously appealing things about him — the long, supple fingers, the breadth of his shoulders, the length of his legs. She enjoyed watching him walk, as well. It was too bad, she thought, her eyes sliding over to him, that his loose-fitting workman's breeches did not adhere as tightly as a gentleman's garb did. She had enjoyed very much the sight of his naked buttocks and thighs as he moved across the floor today without any concealing garments.

Violet realized that she was now close beside him, and their steps had slowed. He curled an arm around her shoulders, fitting her to his side, his stride slowing to an amble. It took them far more time than it would normally have to reach the clearing where the great house lay. When they came to the edge of Duncally's wide lawn, they stopped, still in the concealment of the trees.

"We should go in separately." Coll kept his arm around her shoulders for a long moment, not moving. He kissed her, his mouth hot and hard. "Now go."

He released her, jamming his hands back into his pockets, and Violet started forward alone. It felt strangely empty not to have Coll beside her, and she was tempted to turn around and look back at him. But she knew he would fuss, and besides, it seemed a weak way to act.

Violet stepped into the house and paused, taking stock of herself in the wall mirror. Her hair was knotted insecurely, strands straggling down her neck; she had not been able to find all her hairpins. Her lips were soft and faintly swollen, a deep rose. She touched her mouth. Could someone tell that she had been kissed? Kissed many, many times? Her eyes turned lambent and dreamy. She twined a loose lock of hair around her finger, her mind drifting.

"My lady."

Violet jumped, letting out a squeak, and turned. Mrs. Ferguson stood on the other side of the wide, square entrance hall, her hands folded primly in front of her. Violet felt a flush rising up her cheeks. She knew how she must appear to the other woman. Her mussed hair and her face dreamy with remembered passion gave away what she had been doing before she returned to Duncally. It had been easy to say she did not care what other people thought of her, but now, under Mrs. Ferguson's basilisk stare, Violet could not help but quail a little. If everyone learned that she had spent the afternoon in Coll's bed, she would see this disapproval from others, too. What if Sally looked at her this way? Or Isobel and her aunt? Violet swallowed. It was harder to be indifferent than she had thought.

But that was not going to stop her. She refused to let others rule her life, least of all

Mrs. Ferguson. Violet lifted her chin and said coolly, "Good evening, Mrs. Ferguson." It occurred to Violet that she should already have prepared a story to explain her absence this evening. "I apologize for not returning for supper. I was working, and I fear time slipped away from me." Firmly she repressed the urge to babble on in explanation.

After a long moment of silence, the housekeeper inclined her head. "Of course, my lady. I believe Cook kept some food warm for you in the kitchen."

"Oh. Thank you. I mean, please thank Cook for me, but I, um . . ." Violet wanted only to escape to her room, but it would be strange indeed to turn down food since her excuse had not included a meal. "Of course. That is very kind of her. Of you."

They started down the corridor to the kitchen, but Mrs. Ferguson stopped at the sound of footsteps coming from the rear of the house. Coll strolled in from a side hall. He stopped abruptly.

"Mrs. Ferguson. My lady." He nodded, his hand raking through his hair. "I was, ah, taking a last look around the house before I turned in." He kept his eyes on the housekeeper.

"I was about to give Lady Violet the supper Cook held back for her. Perhaps you would like some as well?"

"Oh. No. No, thank you. I was at one of the crofters', and they, um, offered me supper. I am sorry I missed the meal. My apologies." His gaze slid to Violet, then quickly away. "You did not dine here either, my lady?"

"No. I was at the ruins."

He stared at her. "Of course. Well, um, if you will excuse me, I must, um . . .." He made a vague gesture toward the stairs. "Good night."

Coll strode off without looking back. Mrs. Ferguson stared after Coll, frowning.

"I'll just get my food," Violet said quickly, to distract the woman's attention from Coll. The man was a terrible liar. Of course, she had not done particularly well in that regard either. She would have to be more careful in the future.

Her intent was to take the plate up to her room. With luck, perhaps she would be able to slip out the back door and dump its contents under one of the bushes. But that plan was foiled when she found Cook still in the kitchen, and the woman happily sat down at the big wooden table to keep Violet company.

At least she had had time to work on her

story, and she spun what she felt was a credible explanation of examining the ruins at night, throwing in a number of scientific words and impressive-sounding phrases. Sally seemed to accept it easily enough, though Mrs. Ferguson continued to stand over her like a warden as Violet forced down a few bites of roast and potatoes.

Finally the housekeeper left. Sally heaved a gusty sigh and turned her bright gaze on Violet. "She's a suspicious one, that woman. Next time, best leave a note."

"Yes, of course. I am dreadfully sorry to put you to so much trouble. I hope you did not worry."

"Nae. I saw you go running off, so I knew." Violet looked at her. Did the woman suspect? Sally's eyes had a decided twinkle in them. "That you had something important to do, I mean."

"Yes. Well. Thank you." Violet could feel color flooding her face.

"Weel, I'll let you finish on your ain now." Sally rose from her seat. "If it's too much food, just toss it in the dog's dish. Nae doubt you took a wee bit of bread or something with you to eat."

Gratefully Violet dumped the remaining food into the bowl by the rear door and hurried out of the kitchen. The hallway upstairs was disappointingly empty. She told herself it had been foolish to think Coll was up here waiting for her. She started toward her room, and as she passed Coll's door, it swung open, and a hand reached out to grab her arm.

"Coll." She turned to him with a smile. "You startled me."

"Aye, I can see how alarmed you are." He stuck his head out his door and glanced up and down the hall. "I was afraid she would escort you up to your room."

"No, she went to bed. Sally and I talked a bit."

"Sally? She was there, too? Lord." He closed his eyes.

"She was very nice. I think she is fond of you."

"Yes, but . . ." He released her arm. "We must be circumspect, Violet."

"I understand."

"You should go on." He nodded toward her room. "Someone might see us talking."

"We frequently talk."

"Violet . . ."

"Perhaps you could walk me to my room." She smiled. " 'Twould be the gentlemanly thing to do."

He quirked an eyebrow, but fell into step beside her. "I am serious, Violet. You dinna know how talk travels here. It's like lightning. If a servant saw me take your hand or . . . or look at you a certain way, it would be all over the glen in a matter of hours." He grimaced. "Dinna give me that look. I know Loch Baille."

"I realize that you have a certain reputation to maintain."

He made a noise deep in his throat. "It is not me I'm thinking of. It is your reputation that will suffer. I will not set them to whispering about you. I will not let men look at you like —" He broke off. "It is for the best. Trust me."

"All right." Violet opened the door to her room and turned to him. "Then I suppose you will not be coming in with me."

"Violet . . ." Coll grasped the doorframe on either side of her. "It canna be as it was in the gatehouse today."

"Very well."

He narrowed his eyes. "You are being very agreeable."

She laughed. "Now you are objecting to my being agreeable?"

"Not objecting, no. But it seems . . . too easy."

"I am not always difficult." She reached out a hand, toying idly with a tie of his shirt. "And tonight I don't feel difficult at all."

She went up on her toes, leaning in conspiratorially, and whispered, "I think you have found the way to turn me sweet."

She walked into the bedroom, hands going to the buttons at the neck of her dress. She looked back at him over her shoulder. Coll still stood in the doorway, his eyes on her, jaw set, his fingers in a death grip on the frame. He let out an oath and stepped inside. "You are death to my good intentions."

He closed the door and strode toward her.

19

Violet woke up the next morning alone in her bed, but Coll's scent lingered on the pillowcase beside her. She buried her face in the pillow, letting herself drift on warm waves of contentment. Her body ached a little, carrying the reminder of what they had done the day before, and her skin was supremely sensitive to the touch of the sheets against her naked skin. She smiled to herself and stretched like a cat, reveling in this new awareness of her body.

By the time she washed and dressed and went downstairs, Coll had already eaten breakfast and left the house. It was just as well, she thought, for she wasn't sure how she could look at him without giving everything away.

For the first time she could remember, Violet's work could not hold her interest. Her thoughts kept turning to Coll and the night before. The night ahead. In the end, she called a halt to their work a good hour before the usual time and followed the workers to Duncally.

With the extra time, she took the opportunity to soak in a bath liberally scented with attar of roses. Remembering the way Coll had run his fingers through her hair as he lay beside her, watching the strands fall to spread featherlight across his chest, she washed her hair with the perfumed water and brushed it dry in front of the fireplace. She was not sure why he found her hair so fascinating — it seemed unremarkably brown to her and irritatingly thick as well — but she could not pass up the lure of pleasing him.

Afterward, she searched her wardrobe for a dress that might bring that light of desire to his eyes. The choices were, she found, depressingly slim. Did she have nothing that would show off her bosom instead of concealing it? She finally settled on a dark blue velvet gown. At least the material was sensual to the touch, and once she removed the lace fichu, the neckline skimmed across the tops of her breasts.

Satisfied with the results, she wound her hair in a softer style than usual — one more easily taken down. Surprised to discover that she was fifteen minutes late for supper, she hurried down the stairs and into the dining room, arriving a trifle out of breath and flushed. Coll, who had been sitting at the table, sprang to his feet as if he'd been stabbed with a pin.

"Violet." He took two long, quick steps around the table toward her, then halted, glancing over at the footman. Continuing at a slower pace, he cut off the footman to pull out her chair for her. "Good evening."

A shiver ran through Violet as his fingers brushed over her shoulder. She hoped the tremor did not sound in her voice as she replied, "Good evening. I apologize for being late."

Coll sat down across from her. "I was afraid that you did not want —" He cast another glance at the footman, now hastening to their table to serve them. "That you would miss supper."

"I lost track of time." As the footman left the room, she went on, "It takes a while to dry my hair."

His hands stilled on his utensils. He cleared his throat. "You washed your hair."

"Yes. And took a long soak in the tub."

His eyes flashed. He began to determinedly spoon up his soup.

"I thought after we ate, I might show you the books I looked through yesterday," she said after a time.

"What? Oh. The symbols. Yes, of course." He set down his spoon with a clatter. Not looking at her, he said in a low voice, "I don't know how to do this."

"To do what?"

"Act as if everything was the same. As if nothing had happened."

"Must you act the same?" Violet set down her spoon as well.

"We canna do anything, say anything, that would give us away."

"The footman is gone."

"Yes, but who knows when he'll pop back in," Coll growled. "Damnation. All I can think about is kissing you. You needn't grin like that. I've been useless all day. When you didn't come to supper, I thought you were afraid to face me."

"I am not afraid."

The corner of his mouth twitched. "I meant, I thought you might regret it." He leaned forward. "Do you? Regret it?"

Her gaze was unwavering. "Not a moment of it."

His eyes darkened, and he started to rise. The footman reentered the room, and Coll sat back down, turning his attention to the food.

"We have uncovered a good deal more

since you were at the ruins last," Violet told him.

"Indeed?"

"Yes. We found a pit behind one wall."

"Interesting."

Violet looked at him in annoyance. Coll was hardly making the conversation easy. He was idly toying with the knife beside his plate, his gaze fixed on her chest. She cleared her throat ostentatiously, and he pulled his eyes back to her face.

"I'm . . . uh, that's good," he added.

"It may have been a refuse pit. With shells and such."

"Really? Well . . . that's good."

Jamie laid out the second course and left once more.

"Will you come to my room tonight?" Violet asked.

Coll choked on his food. He took a gulp of wine. "Are you trying to kill me?"

"No. Merely asking for information."

"It's madness." He cut up the fish on his plate with vicious swipes. "What if one of the servants sees me?"

"The servants live in the hall below. There are a small number of them. And they are never on the family floor that late."

"The maid comes in the morning to light the fire."

"You left before that time this morning."

"And what if I fall asleep and I'm still there when she comes in?"

"I shall lock the door."

He groaned, rubbing a hand across his face. "You will be found out. Your reputation would be in shreds. You could have a child. Don't you understand? For me to take you to bed with no thought to the consequences would be reprehensible."

"Mm. And I am glad you are the sort of man who would care. Still, that does not answer my question. Will you come to me tonight?"

His eyes glittered. "You must know I will."

In the days that followed, Violet spent each evening with Coll, carefully avoiding an accidental touch or heated glance or any other indication that more was between them than mere acquaintanceship. All the while, desire thrummed in her, her senses alive to even the faintest stimulation, thoughts of making love occupying her mind, making it hard to concentrate on anything else. As the evening drew to a close, anticipation built until she could wait no longer and retired to her room. There she waited, pacing, sitting, then jumping up to pace again. Then, at last, Coll came to her. And she could finally go into his arms to seize her hours of joy.

Often she would change into her night-gown and brush out her hair before he came. Sometimes she left it to him to help her undress. Once, in a bold mood, she undressed and slipped naked between the sheets to wait for him. Another time Coll followed almost on her heels, whisking her inside as soon as she reached her room, his kisses and caresses feverish with desire. One long, aching night he did not come and she finally went to bed, feeling empty. But in the middle of the night, he climbed into her bed, making love to her with a desperate hunger.

Every night ended the same way, with Violet falling asleep in Coll's arms. Every morning she awoke alone.

When Coll suggested that Violet abandon her work at the ruins for a day and spend it with him exploring the old castle, she was quick to agree. Even more than the chance to explore the castle ruins, she was filled with excitement at the prospect of spending an entire day with Coll away from the prying eyes at Duncally. Coll wheedled a cold lunch from Cook to take with them so that they would not have to return to eat.

As Coll rowed across the loch, Violet luxuriated in the freedom of watching him without fearing she would reveal what she felt for him. He took off his jacket to wield the oars, and Violet studied the flex of his muscles beneath his shirt as he rowed. She wished that it were warm enough that he had rolled up his sleeves.

"If you dinna stop looking at me like that, lass, I'll forget what I'm about and we'll both wind up in the loch," Coll growled.

Violet laughed. "I wouldn't want that." She leaned forward in a confiding manner. "But I do want you."

The rhythm of the oars stuttered and stopped. He rested on them, regarding her. "Do you just say anything that comes into your head?"

"No. I've thought a great deal more than I have said." She quirked an eyebrow at him. "Would you like to hear what else has been on my mind? I could tell you about the way the sun glints on your hair."

"Och, now, Violet . . ." Coll started rowing again.

Delighted by Coll's boyish look of embarrassment, Violet continued, "Or I could tell you I was contemplating how long your fingers are and how strong on that oar, but how gentle they feel on my skin." The oars bit through the water with increasing swiftness. "Then there's the length of your legs

and how I'm tempted to slide right up them
—"

"Enough!" He flashed her a searing glance. "You'll be the death of me."

"I wouldn't want that. I'll be good." Violet propped her elbow on her knee and her chin on her hand and simply watched him, savoring the rise and fall of his chest, the blazing blueness of his eyes.

When they reached the dock, Coll jumped out and tied the boat, not saying a thing, then reached down to lift Violet out. He set her down on the dock with a thump, and his fingers dug into her waist, jerking her forward as he bent to kiss her. His mouth was hard and hungry, and his hands slid down to her hips, pushing her pelvis into him. Violet wriggled. He groaned deep in his throat and tore his mouth from hers. He dug his fingers into her hips and rested his forehead on hers.

"God, but you tempt me. I'd like to pull you down right here on the docks, and the devil with who might see us."

"I might like that."

"I think you would." His mouth returned to hers just as the merry sound of a whistled tune came through the air. Coll's head jerked up, and he bit out a short, sharp oath. "Angus McKay. I might have known."

Coll released Violet and took a step back, watching the old man stroll down the path toward them. A fishing pole rested on his shoulder, and his gaze was fixed on the path in front of him. He raised his head, and his steps checked.

"Weel, Coll, not working today, eh?" Angus said in greeting and continued to the dock. "You grow more like your faither every day."

A dull flush rose in Coll's face, and he started to retort, but Violet spoke before he could. "Mr. Munro has agreed to help me today, Angus."

"Has he noo? You are not mucking about by the sea this afternoon?"

"No. I have a mind to see the ruins of the castle."

"Ah, so that's what you're doing then?" He snorted. "Looking at the castle?"

Coll sent him a sharp glance, but Violet merely smiled. "Yes. You, I see, have come to fish in the loch?"

"I hae a standing invite frae himself."

Coll grunted. "Jack is generous with his friendship."

"Aye. He's not one to begrudge a puir auld man a fish noo and again."

"No doubt that stretches to cover rabbits, too."

Angus's eyes danced. "Mayhap it does."

Coll grimaced and reached down to the dory to retrieve the bag containing lunch. Slinging the sack over his shoulder, he wrapped his hand around Violet's arm and started up the path, his face grim. Violet gave McKay a parting wave over her shoulder.

"Meddling old fool," Coll muttered.

"Coll . . . I'm not your prisoner."

"What?"

Violet looked down pointedly at his grip on her arm. "You're hauling me off as if you think I'm about to bolt."

"Oh. Sorry." He dropped her arm, and sticking his hands in his pockets, he strode on. "I think he saw us."

"Yes, of course, he saw us."

"Before, I mean."

"When we were kissing?"

"Yes." Coll shot her a flashing glance. "And it wasna only a kiss. I had my hands all over you."

"I remember."

"Well, I think Old Angus saw it. He just pretended to glance up and act surprised to see us there."

"Then he was unexpectedly tactful."

Coll snorted. "Oh, he let me know. That's

what his barb was about — that I'm like my father."

"I thought he was teasing you about not working today."

"That as well. Nothing makes him as happy as being able to slide in two knives at once."

Violet chuckled. "He would not tease you if you were not such an easy target."

"Trust you to take his side." Coll gave her a fulminating look.

"Now, Coll . . ." She looped both arms around his arm, her tone that of one speaking to a cranky toddler. "You know that it's your side I favor."

He gave her a sideways look, but he looped his arm around her shoulders, pulling her up against him. "Even though I'm a man steeped in sin?"

"No." She slipped her arm beneath his jacket and around his waist, leaning into him and laying her other hand on his chest. " 'Tis not your sins that make Angus love to poke at you. It's that you take them so to heart." She moved her hand in a soothing circle over his chest.

Coll brought his other hand up to cover hers, his steps slowing. "It is wrong of me to do this with you." His voice was low and he did not look at her. "But I canna stay away. I tried the other night not to come to your room, but I could not do it."

"I'm glad. I want you to come to me." She glanced up at him. "I cannot help but wonder why you want to stay away."

"I don't *want* to! If I did only what I wanted, I fear I'd never leave your bed. But I am compromising you."

"I don't mind."

"You should. You should have more care for yourself." He paused. "I should take more care of you."

"I am able to take care of myself. There is no reason for you to do so. I'm aware of what I am doing; I accepted the consequences when I made the decision not to marry. I refuse to foreswear any pleasure in my life simply because I choose not to have a husband." Violet pulled to a stop and turned to him, her eyes searching his face. "Coll . . . I am beginning to think that you regard me as a fallen woman. Is that true? Have I lowered myself in your eyes by coming to your bed?"

20

"What?" Coll's brows shot up, the shock on his face gratifying. "No! How can you — I dinna say that."

"No? You seem so concerned that others will think less of me that I can only wonder if *you* think less of me."

"No. Never." He took both her hands and brought them to his lips. "I think you are a woman of great honesty and worth. I am amazed . . . honored . . . that you have given yourself to me." He paused. "It's me I think less of for taking what you have given."

"*I* do not think less of you." She copied him, bringing his hands up to press her lips to them, one by one. She could see the shudder run through him. "I do not find you lacking in any way, be it honor or intelligence or looks." She grinned. "And if I am so worthy and honest, then you should value my opinion."

A smile broke across his face, and he

kissed her, hard and fast. "You have an argument for everything."

"I do." She stepped into him, her arms sliding up his back beneath his jacket, as she went on tiptoe to kiss him. "And this is my best argument."

He surrendered himself to her kiss, his body curving around her, his mouth drinking her in. Violet felt the surge of heat through his body, the quickening of his breath, and she melted into him in response. Finally he tore his mouth from hers and stood, his head resting against hers, as he pulled himself back under control.

With a final hard kiss to her forehead, he took her hand and started up the path again. "Come. We are here to search the castle, remember?"

"I know." She fell in beside him, smiling. "But I can do more than one thing at a time. Cannot you?"

"I am a very single-minded man."

They took the path toward Baillannan, but long before they reached the looming gray house, Coll took another trail that twisted through the trees, emerging finally onto a well-worn walkway. At the end of the path was a barren rise of land, and atop it stood the stark remains of white stone walls, mostly tumbled down, sticking up here and there from the ground like the bleached bones of some great animal.

Violet sucked in a breath. "It's wonderful." She moved forward eagerly.

"You've got that look in your eye."

"What look?" She widened her eyes at him innocently.

"Like you're about to start digging."

She laughed. "Oh, no, this is much too recent for me. Still, it's fascinating." She strolled around the perimeter first, then moved in to study the pieces of walls remaining. "I don't see any markings, do you?"

"I wouldn't think there's much place on the surface for hiding a treasure." He glanced around the flat, barren land. "It's too exposed. If my grandmother hid anything here, it would be in the cellars."

He strode to the gaping hole at one end of the ruins, marked off with a wooden fence, and led her around the railing to the opposite end. "We've shored it up since Jack and Isobel found it. They tumbled off into the pit when the ground caved in on them."

"Were they hurt?"

"It'd take more than that to kill that Englishman. Kensington's got the devil's own luck. And he fell first, so he was there to catch Isobel when she came looking to rescue him."

"Life at Baillannan sounds . . . exciting."

He chuckled. "Yes. Though it's been quite dull lately. Here's the ladder we built into the cellars. Better let me go down first to make sure it's still sturdy." He swung over the edge.

"Hmph. You just want to watch me coming down the ladder."

He grinned up at her. "I'll admit, I'll enjoy the view."

Violet followed him, bunching up her skirts with one hand to keep from entangling her feet. Coll lit the lantern sitting beside the ladder, and they began their exploration. Light from above did not penetrate the far reaches of the cellars, making the lantern necessary as they moved away from the cave-in. Piles of rubble partially blocked some corridors. Arches of stone and brick still held up the vaulted stone ceilings, braced in several places by new wooden beams.

"When were these put in?" Violet patted one of the rough beams.

"Jack and I did it the past few months."

"You did a lot of work here."

"We wanted to make sure it was safe. So no one else would get caught in a collapse." He cast her a sheepish smile. "And we wanted to look for tunnels."

"Did you find any?"

"One or two, but they've both been blocked by a cave-in. Back here, the chambers are dug into the rock." Coll led her past a pile of rubble. As they ambled along, hand in hand, he said, "If we found the treasure, what would you do with the money?"

"I'm not sure." She glanced over at him, surprised. "I hadn't really thought past locating it. Would part of it be mine?"

"I don't know why not. Who else would it belong to? A French monarchy that no longer exists? A prince long ago defeated? It wasn't Malcolm Rose's money. It has naught to do with Mardoun. No, I think if you and I found it, it would be ours."

"Well . . . I wouldn't have to depend on a patron to excavate. I could do as I want, go where I wish. And I'd want to do something for the education of women, which is currently absent. Not for women like me —"

"Are there any other women like you?" Coll grinned wickedly.

She sent him a quelling look. "I mean, women whose parents can afford to educate them. We at least are taught to read and write, and we can turn to books to educate ourselves. But education for the poor is woefully lacking, for both boys and girls. There are those who want to establish village schools, available to all. Perhaps I'd do that."

"That seems a fine ambition."

"What about you? What would you do with the money?"

"It would be grand not having to earn my keep. To be able to do just as I pleased, to spend my time making things, carving — it's a heady thought. I'd want to do something for the crofters, too, though. I've thought of creating a place where they could own their strips of land and not be turned out on the whim of another. I imagine I could get Mardoun and Kensington to donate a bit of their properties as well."

"A new village — that sounds marvelous. And I shall set up a village school there."

Coll laughed. "Now all we need to do is find the treasure."

"Yes, that is a slight problem." Violet sighed and looked around. "I haven't seen any mark like the one on your knife. Or any carving at all, really."

"Nae."

"Do you think we've taken the wrong track? That the engraving on the sgian-dubh had nothing to do with the treasure? Or we're looking in the wrong place?"

"I don't know. I don't even know that there *is* a treasure. But not finding the sign here does not mean that it isn't the key. It could be any number of other places — the graveyard in Kinclannoch or maybe we missed it at the Munro graves. We dinna know about the sign when we looked before. It could be around Meg's cottage."

"Perhaps even somewhere among the standing stones."

"Aye, or at Baillannan itself." He took her hand. "Come now, lass, dinna be discouraged. We still have the subcellars to explore. That's where the secret room and the tunnel to the new house were."

He led her back toward the entrance and down a narrow stone staircase. The long room below was so low-ceilinged that Coll had to stoop to walk through it. New wooden beams braced the walls. Carvings were along one wall, a strip of small rosettes repeated endlessly. It was hushed and still, the sound of their footsteps muffled by the dirt floor.

"This is the secret room." He stopped before the wall at the end of the passage.

"Where?"

Coll reached into his pocket and pulled out a watch key. Holding the lantern up, he searched the strip of stone rosettes that decorated the wall close to the ceiling. To Violet's surprise, he stuck the key into the center of one of the rosettes and turned it firmly. The wall separated along a thin line, and Coll swung the concealed stone door outward.

Violet pulled in a sharp breath of excitement. "That's all it takes?"

"Aye. But you have to know about the key and which rosette to use. Those blasted flowers are all over the place at Baillannan; you could look till your eyes bleed and still miss the right one." He ducked through the low doorway.

The small chamber inside was furnished, a table and chairs, bed, and cabinet seemingly waiting for its occupants. Candlesticks stood in the center of the small table.

"The tunnel to Baillannan is beyond the far wall; there's another rosette to use. But it has collapsed halfway there."

"Surely someone did not live down here." Violet's voice was hushed. An eerie quality to the small room seemed to call for low voices.

"We think it was the room where Malcolm used to meet Faye in secret."

"Their trysting place." Violet shivered. "It seems a little foreboding."

"Maybe it was not back then, before

343

murder was done here. We think Malcolm hid here when he returned after Culloden. Certainly he was killed here." Coll pointed to the floor beside the table. "Jack and Isobel found the skeleton there, a dagger thrust in his back."

Violet gazed down at the floor. "That's a terrible price to pay for loving someone."

"Mm. I think it was more for his betrayal than his love."

"You're a hard man, Coll."

"He pledged himself to his wife, had children by her. And he broke that faith."

"You think he deserved to die for that?" She studied him.

"Nae. Not to die. But I understand why Lady Cordelia hated him for it. I canna think of him as a tragic hero. He was off seeking glory, raising rebellion and bringing back treasure, but it was the rest of them, his women, his children, who were left to deal with the British soldiers and the punishment, the hunger and loss of land, the sorrow. A better man would have stayed to shoulder the burden."

"You would have stayed." Violet took his hand in both of hers and went up on tiptoe to brush a kiss across his lips.

"Aye, well, I'm not romantic."

"Are you not? You seemed romantic

enough last night." She slanted a teasing glance up at him.

"Is that what you call it?" He cocked an eyebrow, his hands sliding around her waist and tugging her up flush against his body. "I'd have said I was desperate."

Violet stretched sensuously, arching up against him. "Desperate?"

"Aye." He bent to nuzzle her neck. "Hungry. Wild. Mad to have you. You always drive me to the brink. I can scarcely sit still of an evening, biding my time till I can come to your room, thinking about how it will be." His mouth moved over her neck and face, punctuating his words with soft, breathy kisses. "Thinking how you'll quiver beneath my hand and make those little moans, the way your eyes will close and that secret smile of yours when I enter you. Your face when you come all undone beneath me."

"Coll . . ." She twined her fingers through his hair. "You'll have me all undone right here."

He let out a noise that might have been smugness or frustration or both, and his arms tightened around her, grinding her into his hard body. He kissed her as if he would never have another chance, his mouth searing, demanding. Violet welcomed the heat and the hunger, giving it back in full measure. The shattering of Coll's control never failed to stir her, the passion that overrode his strength challenging and matching her own. Something wild was in him, barely leashed, and she ached to meet it, to tame him . . . and surrender herself.

"No." He pulled back, setting her away from him. "I will not take you like this. Not here. Not in haste and secrecy. And by God not in the cellars where Malcolm Rose was slain." Coll drew a long, shuddering breath. "I promised myself this day with you. No one to pry or see, no need to pretend we are nothing to each other. I told Mrs. Ferguson we would be here all day and not to hold supper for us. I am going to have you in my bed. In my home."

Violet looked up at him from beneath her lashes, her mouth sultry and reddened from his kisses. "Then take me there."

21

Violet scrambled up the ladder from the cellars, with Coll right behind her, his hand in a strategic place boosting her up over the edge.

"Coll!" She whipped around as she stepped out onto the ground, unsure whether she wanted more to scold him or to throw herself into his arms and pull him down on the ground with her.

"Yes, my dear?" He climbed out, the sack containing the food the cook had given them flung over his shoulder. Desire was stamped clear on his face, but a teasing twinkle accompanied the heat.

"I thought you wanted to go home to, um, 'properly' do this."

"I do." He grinned, hooking his arm around her waist and pulling her tight against him. He bent down to nip lightly at her earlobe. "But that does not mean I canna savor a few 'improper' liberties along the way."

"So you think you can have it both ways?" She cocked an eyebrow.

He chuckled and leaned in to whisper, "I'd like to have it every way I can with you."

Heat flooded her at his words, and she wrapped her arms around his neck, pressing her lips against the tender hollow of his throat.

Her name was a low rumble in his chest, and he dug his fingers into her buttocks, pressing her even more tightly against him. "Would you have us do it here? With Old Angus watching?"

"What!" Violet sprang back from him and whirled around, scanning the area. Behind her Coll laughed, and she gave him a black look.

"Well, he could be." Coll cast a glance all around. "Look at all the trees out there he could be hiding behind."

"Now I feel as if someone *is* watching us." Violet scowled at him. She could not help but remember the day when she had walked home from Meg's cottage and had along the way felt so strongly that someone had been hiding, watching. It gave her a little shiver to think about it.

"We could give him something to see." Coll's hand slipped beneath her cloak to glide over her body. "But I think that I would rather have you all to myself."

But they saw no one on their way to the dock, not even Old Angus. To Violet's surprise, Coll rowed the boat straight across the loch and tied up near Meg's cottage, taking the longer path around to the gatehouse. Avoiding Duncally sprang, she knew, from his desire to be apart and alone and freely together, and she wanted it as much as he.

Inside his house, Coll turned the lock, his face filled with both satisfaction and anticipation as he pulled her into his arms and kissed her. But now that they were here, he seemed in no hurry. He stripped off his jacket and stoked the fire, letting its warmth seep into their bones. Bracing his hands on the mantel, he gazed down at her for a long moment, then bent to kiss her. He touched her nowhere but her mouth, and somehow the separation of inches between them was as arousing as if his hands had played over her body.

He stepped back and dropped into the chair before the fire, stretching his long legs out in front of him. His voice came out in a rasp: "Undress for me."

Violet's eyes widened with surprise. "What?"

"I want to watch you."

His words coiled in her like a flame. Locking her gaze on his, she reached up and began to unfasten the small, round buttons. Her fingers moved with slow deliberation, and gradually the bodice sagged open, revealing a slice of white cotton chemise beneath. Violet slipped her arms from the dress and let it slide inch by inch down her body to pool at her feet on the floor.

Color flared along his cheekbones, and his chest rose and fell more rapidly. Violet untied her chemise and hooked her forefingers into the neckline, sliding them back and forth along her skin. The garment drooped lower and lower. She left it hanging, looped on her arms and barely covering the pink circles of her nipples, and reached down to undo the ties of her petticoats. The garments whispered down her legs, leaving her clad in only the flimsy covering of her pantalets and the chemise that barely clung to her breasts.

With a shrug, the chemise was gone, the full, round globes of her breasts freed. Coll sucked in his breath sharply, and her lips curved up at the sound. Violet's smile teased and promised, beckoned and tempted, as she lifted her hands to pull the pins from her hair. He swallowed, his eyes fixed on her hair as bit by bit the strands slipped from her fingers. Soft as silk, her thick, dark hair spilled over her breasts, parting over the thrusting points of her nipples.

Coll's fingers dug into the arms of his chair, his heavy lids drooping over the fire in his eyes. She stepped out of her shoes and braced her foot on the seat of the chair beside him, sliding her garter and stocking down her leg. Violet lowered the other stocking, and then, finally, untied the ribbon of her pantalets and let the last of her undergarments fall. Coll reached for her, but she evaded him nimbly.

"Oh, no. I'm not yet done."

Violet sank to her knees before him. Coll's breath hitched in his throat as she untied his heavy boots and pulled them off, her breasts swaying with every movement. Stretching up, she went to work on the buttons of his shirt, starting at his waist. He jerked at the touch of her hands, then stilled, his body taut as wire stretched to the snapping point.

Violet thrilled to the fire in his eyes, the fierce control that lay in his bunched muscles, the barely leashed hunger. She slid her hands down the open sides of his shirt, grazing his skin as she pulled his shirt free from the waistband and reached for the buttons of his breeches. The muscles of his stomach jumped, his skin washed with heat.

Suddenly he was on her, bearing her back onto the rug in front of the fire, his mouth ravaging hers, his body covering her. Coll plunged his fingers deep into her hair, and he slid down her, his mouth roaming over her neck and breasts. Shucking off his breeches, he parted her legs and thrust into her, hard and fast and deep. His breath was ragged in her ear, heat pouring from him in waves.

Violet curled around him, moving in instinctive rhythm with him, her hunger and fire at one with his. No thought was in her, no caution or reason, only a primitive, deep desire to join with him, to take this man inside her and lose herself in him. She clung to him, and together they rode the storm into a shattering ecstasy.

Coll's eyes opened. It was dark, and he lay cocooned in warmth. His arms were around Violet, her bottom fitted snugly against him in a delightful way. Her hair spilled across the pillow and flowed over his arm, silky and sweet smelling. He moved a little, bringing his hand up to curve around one of her breasts, and she nestled back against him. He smiled, drifting in contentment.

They had spent the rest of the day at the gatehouse, marooned in their private paradise. They had lain together in front of the fire, lazily talking and soaking up its warmth, then made love again, this time teasing and laughing until desire swept them away. They had eaten together, Violet wrapped in one of his shirts, her lower legs enticingly bare to his gaze and touch, and they had talked. Unsurprisingly, they had argued, and they had ended it in bed in a way that left him feeling as if his very bones had melted.

He had wanted, achingly, not to return to Duncally, but of course they had to. They had walked back down to the boat and taken it to the Duncally dock, climbing up from the garden. The deception ate at him; he hated pretense and had always prided himself on his truthful nature. It had to be done to keep Violet's reputation from being muddied. He would do far worse to shield her from harm. But it scored his soul, and he knew that had any other man acted as he did, Coll would have held him in contempt.

He had told himself that this night, at least, he would sleep alone in his room, his hunger sated by the hours with Violet. But in the end, when he climbed the stairs, he had gone to her chamber, unwilling to face the emptiness of his own bed. He had become too accustomed to holding her.

Now, before he slipped back down the dark hall to his room, he savored these last few minutes with his arms around her. He drew his hand down her side, curving over the swell of her hips, and considered waking her with kisses.

The door rattled, and Coll went still. When nothing else happened, he leaned across Violet and pushed back the enveloping bed curtain. The room was dim but no longer black. He let out a low curse and eased his arm from beneath Violet's head, turning to climb out the other side of the bed.

"Coll?" Violet murmured, opening her eyes and turning to him.

"I overslept," he whispered back. "I think the maid was at the door."

"It's all right. I locked it." She sat up, pushing back her hair, a distracting sight with the covers sliding down to her waist.

Coll firmly turned his eyes away. "Yes, but unfortunately, my door is not locked, and I am not there. When the maid comes in to light the fire, she'll see at a glance that I have not spent the night there."

"Oh." Violet slipped out of bed and donned her dressing gown.

Inwardly cursing his carelessness, Coll

pulled on his clothes as Violet went to the door and unlocked it, opening it a crack. He picked up his boots and joined her.

"She's dusting the table," Violet whispered. "All right, she is picking up the ash bucket and going down the hall again. Almost to your room. She's gone into your room."

"She'll be there awhile, cleaning out the ashes."

Violet opened the door wider and stuck her head out. "It's clear." She stepped back, and Coll slipped past her.

Moving on silent feet, he slipped down the hall and stairs to the landing, where the stairs turned. He sat down, yanking on his boots and hurriedly tying them. The maid would know he had spent his night in another's bed. But as long as she thought that bed had been out of the house, not down the hall, that was all that mattered. He could live with the servants gossiping about his libertine ways. Standing up, he trotted noisily up the stairs.

Striding into his bedroom, he stopped abruptly just inside the door. The maid popped up from the fireplace, her eyes bright with curiosity. She bobbed a quick curtsy. "Mr. Munro."

"Oh, sorry." It was not difficult for Coll to

355

act embarrassed. "Uh . . . I decided I'd stay at the gatehouse last night. It was — I mean —" He gave her a conspiratorial smile and took a few more steps into the room. "You willna tell *her,* will you?" He nodded down the hall. "Lady Violet. She wouldna like it that I left the house unprotected. Mrs. Ferguson, either."

"Oh, nae, sir, I willna say a word." She bobbed him another curtsy, picked up the bucket of ashes, and fled the room, no doubt eager to get downstairs and relay her news to the other servants.

Coll closed the door after her and sank down on the bed. Letting out a groan, he lay back and stared blackly at the ceiling. What the devil was he doing?

He could not continue this way. It should have been easier now. He could go to her any night he wanted. Touch her, kiss her. Have her. But still she occupied all his thoughts. Whenever anyone else was around, he felt as if he were on tenterhooks, afraid he would inadvertently give away what truly lay between them. Unable to say or do what he wanted. He, who had always prided himself on his honesty, his integrity, had become a deceiver — lying, sneaking about, hiding his intentions. It seemed scarcely a justification that he did so to keep from sullying the reputation of a lady, since the lady's reputation would not have been in danger if he had not given in to his passion for her.

Yesterday had been glorious. In the privacy of his home, there had been no need for pretense, no frustration, no guilt or prevarication. But much as he had reveled in it, the return to their customary behavior was now even more unbearable. It was like having a single day of freedom, only to return to a cage.

If he were a better man, he would give her up. If Violet were a different woman, he could woo her into marriage. But she was a woman who would follow her mind, not her heart. And he was a man whose heart was at war with his honor. The result was that he spent half his day wanting to put his fist through a wall. They could not go on like this. *He* could not go on like this. One way or another he must end it.

Violet was not surprised to find Coll absent at breakfast that morning. He had been chagrined at oversleeping and thereby putting her reputation at risk. She wished he would not worry so. She would not relish her name being bandied about the glen, but she was a grown woman and capable of handling whatever came.

She was relieved that afternoon when she returned from the excavation and found Coll waiting for her in the corridor in front of the library. He hurried forward and took her by the wrist, pulling her into the room. He shut the door behind him and turned to face her. His face was set and blank, his posture stiff, and the look in his eyes was both determined and wary.

Alarm prickled along her nerves. "Coll? What is it? Has something happened?"

"No. I just — I have something to say to you."

"All right." She waited.

He took a breath and squared his shoulders. "We have to marry."

22

His words were so unexpected that for a long moment all Violet could do was stare. "What?"

"I said, we must get married. We cannot continue like this. It's mad to think we can. Someone is bound to realize what we're doing; it was sheer luck this morning that I was able to leave your room without anyone seeing. The maid obviously knew I hadn't spent the night in my own bed; all I could do was pretend I had spent the night away from Duncally. God only knows what they'll all be speculating."

"It was one time!"

"How many more times can we escape? Even if we could, I canna bear . . . what we do. What we are."

"Oh." It suddenly hurt to draw a breath. "I see. I did not realize you found it so unsatisfactory."

"I don't like lying. I don't enjoy pretense.

Or watching everything I say or do. I'm an honest man, Violet. A simple one."

"I have not asked you to lie, have I? You are the one who insisted on secrecy. If you don't want to pretend we are not sharing a bed, don't. It's not as if someone is going to bar you from sleeping in my room."

"Do you think I would expose you to scorn like that? Openly occupy your bed as if I thought you unworthy of respect or honor? Your reputation would be in rags. I am not the kind of man who takes a woman's innocence and leaves her to face the consequences. I dinna shirk my responsibility. I talked to the minister at the kirk today. We can post the banns this coming Sunday, and in two weeks, we can have the ceremony."

"*You* 'dinna.' *You* decided. *You* talked to the minister. What about me? Do I have nothing to say about the matter?"

"Of course you do. This is *for* you! Can't you see? It is you whose name will be slandered. They will gossip about me, but I will not be labeled a —" He stopped, clenching his jaw.

"A what? A doxy? A whore? Is that what you think I am?"

"No! Of course not! But that is what others will say of you."

"Let them. I cannot stop them, but I do not have to care what they think."

"That's easy enough to say until you have to face it. But by the time you do know what it's like, it will be too late. You canna go back and change what's been done. Violet . . . be sensible."

"So now I'm not sensible? Because I am not willing to be ruled by others' opinions? Because I choose to live as I want to? I refuse to spend my days in fear of having my reputation damaged. I have no intention of marrying. Have you not listened to anything I've said?"

"Yes, I've listened. I understand how you feel. You dinna want to live under a man's thumb. But I will not try to rule you."

"Oh, will you not?" Her blood was throbbing in her temples, hot and furious and . . . *frightened.* She felt as if something were slipping away, sliding right out of her hands, and the harder she grasped, the faster it shot away. "What do you call it when you decide I should marry? You go to see the minister without even a word to me. How is that anything but laying out my life for me? It's exactly what my father would do."

"I am *not* your father!" He slammed his fist back against the door. "Nor am I that other fool who expected you to live in his shadow. I am trying to take care of you. What about children? Have you thought that even now you could be carrying my child? What would happen to him? I have no desire to limit you. I dinna expect you to be meek and subservient. Do you think I am unkind? That I would treat you harshly? That I would take your money or forbid you to pursue your interests?"

"No, I don't. But that is not the point. The point is that you *could.* And I would have no recourse. I would not even have my name. I would *belong* to you."

"And, of course, it would be a dreadful thing to belong to me." His voice rang with bitterness. "To be Mrs. Munro instead of Lady Thornhill. I know I am not a gentleman, not the man a lady would expect to marry."

"That's not fair. That has nothing to do with it!"

"No? And is it fair to demand that I live as *you* want to live? To let myself be branded a libertine and my children bastards? To live my life sneaking about, snatching a few minutes with you when no one is watching, leaving your bed every morning before dawn, playing the cad, the scoundrel? I cannot live like that. I will not."

"Then don't!" Violet shot back, stung by

the contempt in his voice. She realized it now: he wanted her, but hated that he did so. And to think she had let herself believe that he understood! Pain slashed through her, and behind it a cauterizing fury. "Go away and live your proper, pure life. Don't let me contaminate you with my wicked ways. Enjoy your sanctity and sleep in your own bed."

"I will!" Coll slammed open the door and strode out of the room.

Violet stared after him, shocked and numb, almost shaking under the flood of rage and loss and a hundred other emotions she couldn't name. The sound of the door's banging shut brought her out of her paralysis. She left the library, almost running up the stairs to her bedroom. She closed the door and locked it after her, as if that would somehow shelter her more.

She went across to the window to stare out. Dusk was falling, suiting her mood. In the distance, she could see Coll striding down the driveway toward his home. Obviously anger drove him, for he had already reached the edge of the trees. Well, apparently she would not have to worry about facing him at the dinner table in a few minutes. She swallowed hard, feeling as if she were choking. She leaned her head on the cold glass, closing her eyes against the tears that welled up in them.

How could she have been so foolish? Why had she let herself believe Coll understood her? Knew her? Liked her? He did not feel for her as she did for him, as if nothing the world thought mattered as long as they were together.

She shook her head, swiping at the tears on her cheeks, and began to pace the room, pulling up her anger and resentment to fill the emptiness inside her. It was so like a man to hold her at fault because he suddenly felt the burden of his conscience. To decide to assuage his guilt by making her his possession, turning her into something she was not, giving her a life she did not want.

She, apparently, was not expected to have a choice in the matter. No doubt she should simply be grateful that a man would give her the protection of his good name. Coll had not even bothered to cloak his decision in words of love. No, it had all been what other people would think and how it reflected on him. He refused to be a liar and a libertine, which left the obvious implication that she was both.

It should not have shocked her. The only

real surprise was that she had been so naïve as to believe he was different. That he accepted her without feeling the need to change her. She stopped before the window again, leaning her head against the cold glass and staring out sightlessly into the darkening evening. A shudder shook her as she thought of how he had looked at her with such bitterness, such anger and contempt.

It was foolish to have let herself feel so much for the man. She was not in love with him, and she did not expect him to love her, either. It had been far too short a time to have fallen in love. But she had thought he liked her, thought he cared. In the end, it was only physical attraction.

But, oh, what a strong attraction! Again the tears came. There was a hole inside her now, a cold and lonely ache. Violet knew, however little she liked to admit it, that she had felt much more for Coll than desire. She had been perilously close to falling in love with the man.

No doubt she was fortunate that it had ended before she took that fatal misstep. She only wished that being fortunate did not hurt so much.

Coll was not in the dining room when she

went down to supper. She had no desire for food and had almost sent a note to the kitchen, pleading illness. But in the end she would not allow herself to be such a coward. Coll might run away, but she would not.

She ignored the empty place across from her just as she ignored the curious sidelong glances of the footman. She hoped none of the servants had been able to distinguish their words, but she was certain they had not missed the loud and angry tone of their voices or the crashing of doors as Coll stormed out. They were bound to be curious.

The food could have been sawdust for all she tasted it. Violet pushed it around on her plate enough to give the appearance of eating and was relieved to find that Jamie removed and served the courses with good speed. Afterward, she went up to bed. There would be no more evenings spent researching the treasure, she supposed, any more than there would be tender nights in bed with Coll. Still, when she went to sleep, she left the door unlocked.

She awoke the next morning, unsurprisingly, in a cold and empty bed. At breakfast, no one was in the dining room but her and the footman.

"I presume Mr. Munro is not joining us

this morning," she remarked coolly, thinking that she should say something just to show his absence did not gnaw at her insides.

"Nae, I wouldna think sae, with the heid he'd have on him this morning." Jamie cast a wary glance at her.

So Coll had spent the evening drinking. He had probably walked straight to the tavern when he left her. Violet wondered bitterly if he had spent the evening with a serving wench as well as a bottle of whiskey. Was he drowning his disappointment because Violet had turned him down or celebrating his newfound freedom? Better not to think of that.

Bundling up, she made her way to the ruins, arriving before anyone else. There was a wind, and the cold was biting, but the gray day suited her mood. Grimly, she began to dig. Before long the other workers joined her. They seemed to have little inclination to talk, either, and the few times they said anything to one another, it disappointingly had nothing to do with Coll or how he had spent the evening before. The damp cold was more penetrating than usual, and even Angus McKay's visit did not liven things up.

It was a relief when the day ended. Climbing the hill to Duncally, she wondered if Coll would once again avoid the dining room. It occurred to her that he might have decided to move back to the gatehouse. Clearly, he did not want to be around her. He was not the sort of man who would take his revenge by sending her from Duncally and the work she loved. But he might conclude that since two weeks had passed without any further sign of the intruder, there was no longer any danger and therefore no need for his presence in the main house.

Her stomach squeezed at the thought of living in that great, silent house by herself, but she knew that it was less fear that pierced her than it was the thought of not seeing Coll anymore. She had made the choice long ago. She had always known that the life she wanted would be lonely; it was the price she would pay for being free. But she realized now how much easier that decision had been in the abstract than it was in reality. The prospect of night after cold night in her bed alone filled her with a bitter pain.

There was no sign of him when she entered the house. Violet went up the back stairs to her room, telling herself that it was closer, but inside she knew that she did so because she dreaded walking past Coll's chamber. She spent time on her appearance, brushing out her hair and re-pinning it, and choosing the most flattering of her dresses. It would all be for naught if Coll was not there, but if he was, she was determined to look her best. She would not let him see the turmoil his ultimatum had inspired in her.

Coll was, in fact, waiting in the dining room when she entered it. He stood, looking out the window, hands in his pockets, a stance so familiar that it hurt Violet's heart to see it. He turned toward her, his movements as stiff as the expression on his face. Any hopes she might have harbored that he had changed his mind died a quick death.

"Good evening, Coll." She was pleased to hear how calm her voice sounded. "I hope I have not kept you waiting long."

"No." His short reply was followed by an awkward silence.

"I was not sure whether you would be here." Violet saw little reason to tiptoe around the subject. It gave her a small measure of satisfaction to see his glance flicker uncomfortably over to the footman and back.

"Yes, of course."

"I was sorry to hear you were ill this morning."

Now the look Coll shot the footman held

369

more annoyance than unease. "I'm fine."

"I am glad to hear it."

Jamie seemed slower than usual at serving the food. Violet suspected he hoped to hear more conversation to provide grist for the gossip mill in the servants' hall. Coll, however, remained stubbornly silent, and Violet was not about to try to strike up a conversation.

For a long time, the only noise was the slice of a knife or stab of a fork against china. Violet kept her gaze on the table, though once she glanced up at Coll's face and found him watching her. He immediately looked away and pushed the food about on his plate. No doubt, she thought uncharitably, he was still queasy from all the whiskey he had drunk the night before.

But no. It was unhappiness that blanketed the man. However infuriating, however stubborn and wrongheaded she thought him, the truth was that the man was miserable. Violet's throat tightened.

"You need not stay in this house," she said quietly. She set down her fork and raised her gaze to meet his. "I am sure you would prefer to return to your home." Her voice had a maddening hoarseness.

"Is that what you think of me?" Coll set his jaw. "That I'm the sort of man who would just leave? That I would allow you to face danger alone just because I did not get what I wanted?"

"No. I think you are the sort of man who is entirely stubborn. It has been two weeks now and the intruder has not come back. You have frightened him away. Or he has realized that there is no treasure here. Or he got what he wanted the first time, and we just don't know what it was. In any case, there is no longer any danger here."

"Ah." He gave a short nod of his head. "I did not realize you could foretell the future."

Violet thought how satisfying it would be to fling her glass of wine in his face. "I am able to draw reasonable inferences from the evidence."

"I am not moving out," he said flatly.

Perversely, she wanted to argue with him, even though only an hour earlier she had been fearful he would do exactly what she was trying to persuade him to do now. "I am quite capable of taking care of myself."

"I am aware that you are sufficient unto yourself." Coll's voice dripped sarcasm. "However, there is the negligible matter that I have been entrusted with the care of this house and its contents, as well as the safety of those who live and work here."

"Of course. I would not presume to deflect

you from your *duty.*"

He snorted. "That is the only thing you would not presume to do."

Violet's eyes glinted. She felt buoyed by the antagonism rising in her. It was a much easier feeling than the sense of loss that had been sitting on her chest all day. "Pray forgive me for attempting to relieve you of your burden."

"What burden?"

"The burden of having to remain in the same house with me." She whipped her napkin down on the table and jumped up.

Coll came to his feet, leaning forward and bracing his fists on the table. "I think I am capable of handling one wee woman."

"I'd like to see you try."

His eyes lit. "Would you now?"

Fire swept along Violet's nerves like the rush of strong liquor. They faced each other, their bodies taut. Violet wanted nothing more than to launch herself at him and beat her fists against that broad, implacable chest — unless it was to wrap herself around him and kiss him until he broke and carried her to the ground with him. And feeling that, seeing that reflected in his eyes, she hung poised, breathless and furious and eager.

It was Coll who moved. Swinging away with a throaty, unintelligible growl and shoving his chair back so hard it crashed to the floor, he stormed out.

And that was that, Violet thought. It seemed they could not even sit in the same room with each other without flaring into rage. She sat down, her knees suddenly shaky. She heard a noise behind her, and for an instant her heart leapt, thinking he had returned. But it was only the footman, coming around the table to set the chair back in its place.

Violet rose to her feet. "I believe we are done now."

23

Coll did not eat at the breakfast table any longer but grabbed a scone and coffee and left early. He returned late, oftentimes staying to eat with one of the crofters, thus managing to avoid the evening meal at Duncally as well. When he was there at supper, he spent his time pushing the food about on his plate, exchanging a few stiff comments with Violet about her work at the ruins. After supper, he disappeared again, taking a long walk around the grounds and the house to secure it from intruders. Later he shut himself up in his bedroom, though now and then he loitered in the library, aimlessly searching through the stacks of books without choosing any.

Violet knew these things because she could not stop herself from keeping track of him. Her eyes turned toward his room each time she exited her own. She listened to the servants' chatter, carefully pretending not to hear. Now and then she even strolled down the drive toward the gatehouse, but by the time she reached the trees, she always turned back. And if by chance she went down to get a book and found Coll prowling through the library, she did not enter the room. He was obviously avoiding her company, so she refused to seek him out, no matter how much she missed seeing him, talking to him, being in his arms.

She also refrained from mentioning the shadows that had taken up residence beneath his eyes or the lines of weariness stamped on his face. One evening she noticed a blue bruise on one cheek, which was more difficult for her to keep silent about, but a glance at his stony expression told her she would not receive an answer. Coll had walled himself off from her. She had made her choice and he had made his.

Why was the man so insistent? So determined? It seemed odd that he was ruled by other people's opinions. He had, after all, been raised unconventionally. His mother had not married, and Coll loved and respected her, just as he did his sister, who had apparently had the same sort of life, at least until the Earl of Mardoun came along. It was one of the reasons Violet had hoped that he, of all men, would understand her determination to be a free woman.

The scars of his own illegitimacy must run deep. Did he feel a respectable woman would erase the shame he'd felt in his youth? Violet remembered his words about children. She had never thought much about children, though it made her smile to think of towheaded boys who looked like Coll, coltish young girls who would grow up tall and slender. Coll would want children, love them. And clearly he refused to make them live with the shadow on their birth that he had known.

He should have children. It was wrong of her to want Coll for herself. He deserved the kind of life he yearned for. Children and a virtuous wife, marriage. Respectability and honor. Family. Tradition. She could not be the woman he needed. Strangely, the pain that pierced her at the thought was not only for herself but also for Coll, because he had not found in her the woman he could love.

She should be content with only her work. After all, here she was with a ruin all her own, living the life she had always dreamed of. It should be enough for her. It *was* enough.

The excavation was exceeding anything she could have hoped for. They were proceeding at a good pace despite the cold and were making new discoveries almost daily, it seemed. They had uncovered the remains of the fourth wall, even finding a gap in it that marked what must have been a crude doorway. A jumble of rocks lay just outside the entrance. Curious, Violet had the men dig out from it, uncovering more stones.

"It's almost like a path," she mused to Angus one afternoon as they stood looking down on the trench.

"Mayhap." McKay eyed the scattered rocks doubtfully.

"And then it all ends." She pointed to where the men were now digging, wincing as one of the trowels clanked against stone. "Careful! What have you hit?"

Violet moved closer, dropping down on her knees above the trench where Dougal worked.

He squinted up at her. "I think it's another wall, miss."

"Another wall," she breathed. "Going off at a right angle. Oh!" She jumped to her feet. "It's a passageway!" She whirled toward Angus. "It collapsed."

"Wha' did?"

"A sort of tunnel, I think. Over the years, as the dirt built up above it, the weight grew to be too much, and it collapsed, just as the roof would have done back there." She gestured toward the first area of the dig. "But here most of the walls fell in, as well as the ceiling. Oh, this is marvelous." She reached out to clutch McKay's arm, startling him. "Look! The stones extend from the doorway, go down a few feet, and end right where a wall starts to one side. It's another doorway."

"Sae you're saying there's another hoose under here?" Angus gazed down to where Dougal knelt.

"I hope so. And a passageway in between!" Violet concluded triumphantly. "Low. They would have had to crawl along it, but think how useful it would have been to be able to move between the houses in the cold of winter or during raging storms. It shows a great deal of sophistication for something as early as I think these ruins are."

Violet left the dig early and hurried up the path to Duncally, buoyed by the excitement of the find. She could hardly wait to tell Coll what they had found. He would be happy for her, even with the strain between them. Indeed, perhaps sharing this with him would break the dreadful ice between them, make it possible for them to talk again, to be at ease with each other.

She climbed the stairs and crossed the vast expanse of the formal garden. Glancing up, she saw Coll standing at the top of the stairs to the upper levels, talking to a buxom blond woman. Dot Cromartie.

Violet stopped abruptly. Her heart hammered in her chest. Coll was facing Dot, who was talking with great vivacity. They stood sideways to Violet, so she could not read Coll's expression. It was easy enough to read Dot's intentions, though, in the way she lifted her face to his and swayed closer. In a seemingly casual movement of her arm, Dot shoved aside her cloak, exposing the white swell of her bosom above her neckline.

Violet glowered. A trifle cold, surely, for such an expanse of naked flesh.

Coll nodded to Dot, then turned and started along the path to the upper gardens. Violet let out her breath, pleased, but Dot whipped around and caught up with Coll, tucking her hand through his arm. They moved out of sight.

Violet lifted her skirts and ran to the stairs. She went up the steps as quietly as she could and started along the path the couple had taken. The walkway curled back on itself, and as she rounded the corner, suddenly there they were, not twenty feet in front of her. Violet jumped behind a tree and peered cautiously around it.

The pair had stopped beside a stone

bench. Dot was smiling, tugging Coll toward the seat. Annoyingly, Violet was able to make out no words, only the light (and grating, she had to say) trill of the other woman's laughter, followed by the familiar rumble of Coll's voice. Violet's heart squeezed within her chest at the sound.

Coll turned to look around, and Violet ducked her head back behind the tree, her pulse slamming in her throat. She heard the scrape of a shoe on a flagstone. Peeking out once more, she saw Coll and Dot climbing the steps at the far end.

When they disappeared into the trees at the top, Violet left her hiding place and darted to the set of stairs on the opposite side. She had become familiar with the gardens on her many trips from the ruins, and she knew that the various levels and stone stairs all led to the same central terrace below the house. She would be able to find them again without staying on their path.

The leafless trees and bushes of the winter landscape unfortunately offered less concealment for her so that she could not get close, but Violet was able to track them by Dot's giggle. How could Coll stand to listen to that nerve-shredding noise? Violet saw the flash of a blue dress through the tangle of the rose arbor and realized that she was closer to them than she had thought.

Violet eased along the arbor and slipped around a tree. They were only a few feet from her, separated by a high hedge. Now she could hear them, but see nothing but the tops of their heads. Violet stepped up onto a rock, curling her hand around a low branch of the tree for balance. What she saw gave her little joy. Dot was standing only inches from Coll, gazing up at him with an expression of wonder.

"How clever you are," she breathed. "I would never have thought of that." Dot edged closer, laying her hand on his arm.

"Aye, well . . ." Coll took a step back. "I'm sure it would have come to you in a bit."

"Nae, I dinna think so." Dot fluttered her eyelashes. "I'm just a silly girl."

"Well, um, I wouldn't say that." Coll cleared his throat.

Violet was certain that she would.

"I'm so glad I can turn to you for help." Dot stretched up on her tiptoes and murmured something.

Violet leaned forward, straining to hear. And suddenly she was overbalanced and falling. Violet flailed her arms, desperately grabbing at the branch above her. She crashed into the hedge.

"Violet!"

She lifted her head and saw Coll and Dot staring at her, wide-eyed. Coll started forward. Violet fought her way out of the hedge before he could reach her.

"What happened? Are you all right?" Coll took Violet's arm, his eyes running all over her. He picked a twig from her hair. "What were you doing?"

Violet jerked her arm away and stepped back, her face flooding with red. "I — um —"

"Spying on us!" Dot snapped. "That's what she was doing."

"Nonsense." Violet sent the other woman a withering glance. "I was — I was looking at a bird."

"A bird!" Coll gaped.

"Yes." Violet set her jaw. "In the tree. I saw a most unusual bird in the tree, and I was trying to get a better look at it. I got up on that stone, and, ah, somehow tipped over."

Dot snorted.

Violet whirled on her. "What exactly are you doing here at Duncally, Miss Cromartie?"

Dot fisted her hands on her hips. "Talking to Coll — until you barged in."

"I feel sure Coll has more important

things to do. Perhaps you should let him get back to work."

"Violet, there's no reason to . . ." Coll reached out to her, and Violet stopped him with a blazing look.

Dot stalked forward. "You dinna rule me. Or Coll. It's none of your business who he talks to."

Violet went still. Suddenly she could feel tears burning at her eyes. "No." Her voice was clipped. "You're right. Coll is none of my business." She whirled and started toward the house.

Behind her Dot began to babble and Coll answered her, short and sharp. His footsteps rang on the stone path. "Violet! Stop."

She whipped around to face him. Coll stopped a few feet from her, his face taut. Behind him, Dot was flouncing away, which gave Violet grim satisfaction.

"What the devil is the matter with you?"

"Nothing! Why should anything be the matter?" Violet strove for a cool tone, but was maddeningly aware that she was missing it. "If you want to spend your afternoon flirting in the garden with Miss Cromartie, it's none of my concern."

His jaw dropped. "Flirting! I wasna *flirting.*"

"Well, she certainly was, and I didn't see

you protesting. Apparently dallying with *her* doesn't offend your fine moral principles."

"Violet Thornhill!" His eyes narrowed. "You're jealous."

"Hah! Of that fluff-brained, little —" She broke off. "Don't be ridiculous."

"You *are* jealous." He let out a bark of laughter that was devoid of humor. "That's rich. You don't want me, but you don't want anyone else to have me either. Is that it?"

"Not want —" Violet's throat closed with tears. She would not, absolutely would not, reveal just how very much she wanted him. "That's absurd. Indeed, I wish you to be very happy with Miss Cromartie. I know how important it is to you to have a wife."

She turned and marched off. This time Coll did not follow her.

The following afternoon Violet was engrossed in digging at the ruins when the sound of horses made her glance up. A carriage rolled up the road toward her and stopped, and Isobel Kensington climbed out of it. The advent of another visitor seemed to be Angus McKay's impetus to leave, for he popped up from his seat on a nearby rock and bid Violet good-bye.

"I hope I did not chase Auld Angus away," Isobel said as she reached the ruins.

"I would not worry." Violet smiled wryly. "I think the company of two women is more than Mr. McKay can bear. I'm glad to see you."

Violet's feelings at seeing Isobel were more mixed than she let on. She liked Isobel and had enjoyed talking to her the other time Isobel had visited. But she was uncertain how Isobel felt about Violet in return. She was close to Coll. Had he told Isobel how angry he was at Violet, how stubborn and willful he found her? The thought sent a sharp stab of pain through her.

"I have been wondering about your progress," Isobel said, her smile holding neither disapproval nor curiosity. Violet began to relax. "Aunt Elizabeth wanted to come with me, but I fear the cold was too much for her today. I promised I would present her with a full and faithful report."

Violet cheerfully showed Isobel the walls they had uncovered. "We have made a lot of progress. You can see how far we've dug down here. I am more and more certain that this was a house."

"Really? It seems so small."

"I suspect the occupants were smaller, too. And their primary concern would have been shelter from the elements rather than comfort. But see these two layers of rock that jut out from the wall?" Violet pointed to the flat stones.

"Yes. They look a bit like shelves."

"Exactly!" Violet smiled. "That is what I thought."

"You think all these different pieces of walls were houses? That it was a village?"

"Possibly. It would have been, of course, a very small number of people, but the more I see of it, the more I think it was a whole community. And very, very old. Let me show you what we found yesterday."

Violet showed her the trench, explaining her theories about the collapsed passageway. Violet was surprised at how eager she was to talk to Isobel, to show her everything they'd done. With a start, Violet realized that, little as she knew her, Isobel was the closest thing Violet had to a friend here. Quite frankly, she was probably the closest thing Violet had to a friend anywhere.

"Would you like to come up to the house and see the other artifacts we've uncovered?" Violet asked, adding almost shyly, "If you like, we could have tea."

"Why, yes, that sounds delightful."

They took Isobel's waiting carriage to Duncally. As they passed through the gates, Isobel glanced toward the gatehouse. "Will Coll join us for tea?"

"Not likely." Violet's voice was flat and terse, and she saw Isobel's surprised glance.

"Is something the matter?" Isobel asked, her brow knitting.

"No. I am sure Coll is fine. He is gone . . ." To Violet's dismay, her throat suddenly clogged. She swallowed hard. "He is doubtlessly working on the estate. He is — he has a great deal to do." She could not hold Isobel's gaze, and she looked down, smoothing her gloves on her hands.

"Violet . . ." Isobel leaned forward, her voice filled with concern. "What is wrong?"

"Nothing. I assure you, Coll is in good health."

"I had heard a little differently," Isobel said softly, and Violet shot her an agonized glance. "But I did not really mean Coll. I meant what is wrong with you. I can see that you are . . . troubled."

"No. Really." Violet forced a smile. "I am quite well. I am rarely ill; I have a deplorably stout constitution, my mother always said." Dismayed, she felt her eyes suddenly fill with tears. She looked away, battling them back. Isobel reached across the carriage and took her hand. Violet drew a little hitching breath, embarrassed yet seemingly unable to control herself. "I'm sorry. This is foolish."

"Of course it's not." Isobel gave Violet's hand a soft squeeze of encouragement. "Tell me what is wrong."

"I cannot. You will hate me." Violet pulled her hand away and wiped the tears from her cheeks.

"No! Why would I?"

"Because I am not — I am not like you and Coll. I am not upright or proper and — I slept with him." The words were out before she could stop them. What an idiot she was — saying the very thing she dreaded Isobel knowing. But she could not seem to stem the tide of words. "And now he is so dreadfully angry with me. But I could not do it. I cannot."

There was a stunned silence. Violet could not stop her tears; they seeped from her eyes no matter how hard she willed them away. She was afraid that in a moment she would dissolve into sobs. The carriage rolled to a stop, and Violet flung open the door and jumped out. Thoroughly humiliated and gulping back her sobs, Violet rushed toward the house.

To her astonishment, Isobel followed her, catching up as Violet opened the door. Without a word, Isobel curled her arm around Violet and steered her into the drawing room, closing the door firmly after them.

"I'm sorry," Violet choked out, and began to cry in earnest. Isobel patted her soothingly as she led her to a sofa. When Isobel tugged her down onto the seat beside her, Violet gave up and let herself weep on Isobel's shoulder.

Finally Violet quieted and sat up, giving Isobel an apologetic smile. "I beg your pardon. Truly, I am not usually such a watering pot." She fumbled in her pocket and pulled out her handkerchief.

"I do not think you qualify as that at all." Isobel smiled and reached out to take Violet's hand. "Now, tell me, what has upset you so? I don't understand. Coll is . . . is pressing you to, um" — Isobel's face flushed with embarrassment — "to sleep with him and you do not wish to?" She could not quite hide the astonishment in her voice.

"No! Oh, no! I want to! I want to very much!" Violet's cheeks now matched Isobel's in color. "I'm sorry. You must think I am a terrible person."

"Not at all." Isobel smiled. "I know the feeling."

"Do you? Of course, how silly of me. You are married." Violet's expression turned a little wistful. "Happily, I think?"

"Yes, very much so. But what did you mean, then, about Coll, when you said you

389

could not do it?"

"He wants me to marry him."

Isobel absorbed this in silence for a moment. "You, I take it, do not feel that way about him?"

"No! I do! I —" Violet paused, trying to order her thoughts. "I mean . . . I feel a great deal for him. I've never — Coll is the only man I've ever . . . felt this way about." She focused her attention on her skirts, picking at a nearly invisible piece of lint and smoothing the material into pleats. "Indeed, I fear that I am, well, close to falling in love with him." Violet glanced at Isobel anxiously. "Please, you will not tell Coll what I said, will you?"

"Of course not, if you do not wish it. But I suspect Coll knows. Clearly he feels the same way about you."

"You think he loves me?" Violet could not help but smile, but then she shook her head. "No. I think not."

"He asked you to marry him."

"It doesn't mean he loves me. He *wants* me. He does not speak of love, you understand. Never. What he feels for me is merely attraction. Well, stronger than that — it is desire. Lust." Violet glanced at Isobel. "I'm sorry. I do not mean to shock you."

"It is a trifle odd to talk about such things

390

in regard to Coll, 'tis true. He is very like a brother to me. But I am not shocked by your words. He is a man, and I know how men are. I have no doubt that Coll is, um, attracted to you. But I find it hard to believe that Coll wants to marry you only because he lusts after you."

"No, there are other reasons as well. Children, you see, and my reputation, and responsibility. He is shamed by the way he feels. He struggles against it. He believes he *ought* to marry me. Coll is a very . . . good man."

"Yes, he is."

"He does not want others to think he is wicked. He is very bothered by gossip."

"I do not think Coll does things just because other people want him to."

"I did not mean that. But he hates to have people talking about him. He has a strong moral code. And he feels he is violating that code. He said . . ." Again Violet struggled against the hitch in her voice. "He said he could not continue the way we were." She sighed. "But I am not as good a person as Coll. He is shocked by my behavior; he wishes that I cared more what others think of me. I'm not saying that he did not enjoy my loose behavior, you understand, but it gave him qualms, as well. I am not indifferent to gossip; I don't want people to think that I am wicked. I've heard the servants whispering behind my back, and Mrs. Ferguson quite holds me in contempt. I don't like it, but it is not as important to me as . . . as being myself. Being my own woman. I don't want to give up my name. I don't want to be an appendage of a man." Violet glanced at Isobel. "I know most women don't feel that way."

"I think anyone would dislike giving up her freedom." Isobel frowned, feeling her way carefully. "But surely marriage doesn't have to mean a loss of freedom. I took Jack's name, but I didn't give up myself. He would not ask me to. I don't think Coll would ask it, either."

"No. I do not think he would. But, you see, he *could.*"

Isobel nodded. "I understand. It frightens you. You cannot help but think, what if you are wrong about him?"

"I could not bear it." Violet's voice was low and choked. "To find that Coll is not the man I think he is. To give my trust, my . . ."

"Your heart?"

"My *everything* into his keeping." Violet knotted her hands in her skirts.

Isobel reached out and curved her hand

over Violet's. "It is a little frightening. If I found out that Jack betrayed me, I would be crushed. But I know that he will not. I trust him with all my heart."

"I trust Coll. I do. I know he would never hurt me or force me to do anything I did not want." Surely she, like Isobel, could be happy in marriage. Looking at Isobel's glowing face, Violet wanted badly to believe it. She could go to Coll and tell him she had reconsidered. He would be happy; she would once again see his smile. She would know the warmth of his embrace, the sweetness of his kiss. It was not so much, surely, to say those few words. But even at the thought, she could feel the iron bars of ownership wrapping around her. "The thing is, he would think he knew what was best for me. He would want to protect me, help me, guide me. With the best of intentions, he would decide . . . my life."

"Coll is . . . well, rather certain he is right." Isobel smiled faintly. "He has tried to 'direct' me on more than one occasion. Meg, too. Older brothers tend to do that, I think. We squabbled a few times, but he didn't hold a grudge when he didn't get his way. And in time he accepted that Meg and I were grown and going to do what we wanted." Isobel paused. "Do you think that you would be unwilling to argue with his decisions? That you would give in to everything he wanted?"

Violet stared at her. "Good Lord, no. We fight like cats and dogs. I don't know which of us drives the other more insane." She sighed and shook her head. "I don't mind a good fight. But if we were married . . ." She shook her head. "I don't know. It makes me cold inside to think of it. I cannot give myself to another unreservedly. I haven't your ability to trust."

Violet did not add that she was prickly and hard and unfeminine, a woman who could not love as other women did. Isobel, thank goodness, was too kind to point that out, either.

"Marriage is a scary proposition." Isobel gently squeezed Violet's hand. "I was quite terrified at the prospect myself. But I know that you and Coll will find a way. I refuse to accept anything but happiness for both of you."

"I wish I had your confidence."

Isobel just smiled. "Just wait. You'll see."

The next day Violet plunged back into her work. She worked later and later despite the increasingly cold weather as November crept toward December. Woolen scarves and gloves, as well as an extra flannel petticoat or two, took care of most of the cold, and if she brought a lantern along, she could continue to work even after darkness fell.

Angus McKay sometimes stayed late with her. She supposed it must be a sign of how bleak her life had become that she welcomed his company. At least with Angus, she never wanted to burst into tears, as she felt sometimes under the sympathetic glances of Sally or the maids. Angus did not realize, as the women obviously did, how very much she had lost when Coll removed his affection.

Leaving the ruins late one evening, she heard a rustling behind her as she climbed up the hill to Duncally. She turned around, holding up her lantern to cast a light on the path behind her. Seeing nothing, she started forward again, telling herself that she was too on edge these days. But she had not taken two steps when after a rush of sound an arm wrapped around her from behind, knocking the lantern to the ground and clamping her arms to her body. Another hand came up to cover her mouth.

"Dinna scream, and I won't hurt you."

24

For an instant Violet was too stunned to act, but then she began to struggle, twisting and turning. She was unable to accomplish anything except for a kick backward with her heel. Her captor let out a grunt when her heel connected with his shin.

"Damn! Stop it!" His gloved hand clamped down tightly over her nose as well as her mouth, cutting off her air. "Stop fechting me or you're deid."

Violet continued instinctively to struggle, panicked, but as black dots began to dance before her eyes, rationality resurfaced, and she went limp. His hand moved back to her mouth, and Violet sucked in air.

"I want it," the voice growled. "If you want to live lang, you'll gie it tae me."

Violet tried to talk but could not because of his muffling hand.

"I'm gang to take my hand off, but if you scream, I'll snap your neck. You ken?"

She nodded her head decisively, and the hand lifted.

"I don't know what you're talking about," Violet hissed, though she had the sinking feeling that she did. "Give you what?"

"The treasure, you fool. What else?" He gave her a shake. "The French gold."

"I can't! I don't have it."

He shook her again, harder this time. "Dinna lie to me! You do."

"No! I don't. You know it's not in the house; you searched there." This had to be the intruder. Surely there could not be two villains running about attacking people.

"Nae, not then. But you've found it. You and Munro been sticking your nebs in everywhere."

"You *have* been watching me!" It had not been her imagination.

"Aye, I've seen you."

"Then you must know we haven't found anything."

"You hae! I saw you carrying it frae the auld castle."

"No, we —" She broke off as he shook her so hard her teeth clacked together.

"I saw you. That great oaf was carrying a sack. You found it."

"A sack?" For a moment Violet was baffled. "No! That was only our lunch! I tell

397

you, we do not have it. We have not found any treasure."

"Then you'd best get it. Elseways, you'll find yourself a world of trouble instead."

"Hey!" a voice shouted from behind them. "Let her gae!" She heard the sound of a person scrambling up the trail, and something hit the ground behind them.

Violet's attacker let out an oath and shoved her to the ground. Violet struggled to her feet, impeded by her skirts and cloak, and whirled around. Her attacker was no longer there, only the swaying branches in the dark to show where he had gone. A walking stick lay across the path where it had been thrown, and farther down the path Angus McKay was hurrying toward her as fast as his aged legs would carry him, cursing all the while.

"Angus!" Violet picked up the old man's walking stick and hurried to meet him.

Angus leaned over, bracing his hands on his thighs, and panted. "Stupid, bloody, useless legs!"

"Are you all right?" Violet bent down to peer into his face.

"Of course I am! I'm no' the ain he was grabbing! Gie me that." Angus jerked the staff from her hand and planted one end in the ground, using it to help him straighten up. "You shouldna be gang home sae late, you foolish lass."

"I wouldn't have if I'd realized people were going to be jumping out at me!" Her tone softened. "Thank you. I am very glad you came along."

"Och, fat lot of help I was tae you."

"You scared him off."

"Aye, weel, it was a guid thing I decided to gae home this way," Angus grumbled. "Where is himself then? All over the glen these days, but no' here when you need him."

"Coll?" Violet bristled. "I don't need Coll to protect me."

"Aye, weel, you need someone."

Violet did not bother to argue, just let the old man grumble and fuss until his anxiety had worn away. He insisted on walking up to the Duncally gardens with her before he turned aside to head toward his own cottage.

"Tell that lad to keep a better eye on you," he said as a parting shot and trudged off, muttering.

Violet turned toward the house. Whatever Old Angus thought, she had no intention of telling Coll about the attack. He would only harangue her and probably insist that she walk with one of the workers back and forth to the house. Besides, she refused to run to him for help. Not with the way things lay between them. It would make her insistence that she was an equal and competent to take care of herself look utterly foolish if, at the slightest sign of trouble, she sought protection from him.

Coll couldn't do anything about it, anyway. However much the attacker threatened, whatever he did, they did not have the treasure — not that she would give it to him if she did. Violet scowled. The last thing she intended to do was give in to that blackguard's threats.

She would simply take more care in the future. She had been unprepared for this attack, but no longer. She would get a sturdy walking stick like Angus's. And she would be more careful about looking around and being alert. She would even go back and forth to the ruins with her workers.

Perhaps she would start searching for the treasure again. On her own, of course; she would not ask for Coll's assistance. If he wanted to continue to sulk, let him. She would calmly, coolly go on about her business. She did not need Coll Munro.

Coll was certain he was living in hell. He had been doing so for ten days — every aching night burned into his brain. He hated the bed in which he slept because Violet was not there. He hated the chamber in which his bed lay because it did not carry the scent of roses that clung faintly to everything in her room. And he hated the whole bloody, pernicious house because he was trapped there for God only knew how long — the rest of his life, he was beginning to think — unwilling to leave Violet unprotected, determined not to touch her, his whole body continually thrumming with unsatisfied lust.

All he had to do was look at her and his nerves began to sizzle. But if he avoided the sight of her, he thought about her instead. It was, perhaps, even worse to think about her, for then he recalled the way she looked beneath him as he drove to his climax, the way she melted into ecstasy under his hands, the way she took his breath away with a smile.

Nor was it desire only — though that bubbled inside him like a volcano — but a host of other stings and burns, as well. The emptiness when he was alone. The cold that pierced him at Violet's aloof glance. The absence of laughter, of argument, of lively discussion. Her rejection of him was a constant gaping wound.

Of course, *she* was unaffected by it all.

The woman had a heart of stone. No word, no glance, betrayed anything but serene calm. Violet came down to supper every night, perfectly able to make meaningless chitchat all through the meal, with none of the tongue-tied awkwardness that blanketed him. She spent her evenings contentedly alone, usually puttering around in the library — unless he was there. More than once, even though his good sense had screamed that it was a foolish idea, Coll had gone to the library. He told himself that he went late so he could avoid Violet, but in truth he was there only because of the idiotic hope that she might come in, and that there, in that room where they had been so often together, he could somehow bridge the gulf between them. She never came.

The worst of it was that Coll knew that all he had to do to end his torment was to give in to her. To swallow all pride and return to her even though she had wanted nothing of him — not his name, his protection, his entire life — only what lay between his legs. She'd take that if he was willing to accept the pitiful scraps of a life she offered him. What sort of a weak imitation of a man would that make him? Coll wished Violet had never come to Duncally. Yet the thought of not knowing her cut him like a knife.

He threw himself into his work, hoping it would free him from thoughts of her. Hoping he would be tired and sore enough to sleep when he fell into his bed each night. It rarely worked. He had spent most of the previous day working on Tom Connery's farm, helping him repair a stone wall. Still, slumber had eluded Coll for hours. When he had finally fallen asleep, he had awakened before dawn, sweating and rock hard, from a lascivious dream that he could not remember. That had been the end of sleep.

Coll left the house early, stopping first in the kitchen for a cup of Sally's tea. She looked at him in that worried way and pressed him to eat, as if he were starving to death just because he had missed supper a time or two. How was a man to endure sitting at the table with Violet, pretending to eat when it all tasted of ashes, when all he could think about was the way each morsel of idle conversation fell from her soft, rosy lips?

He arrived at Connery's croft before the man had finished his own breakfast. Coll swallowed his comments about the man's laziness — he was well aware that his temper was quick these days, causing everyone to walk on eggshells around him — and went down to haul up the stones from the brae himself. They finished the wall by mid-afternoon and Coll left, wondering what he could find to do for the next few hours. He had hoped to avoid Violet's presence for another meal.

He almost accounted himself lucky when he came across the ewe that had blundered into a muddy ditch and gotten mired in it. His opinion changed when, splattered with mud and still unable to extract her, he had to walk back to Connery's croft to get a rope to pull her out.

He had managed to wrap the rope around her, with a great deal of struggling and curs-ing, when he heard the sound of a rider. He did not turn around until a cool masculine voice said, "Well. Wrestling with sheep now?"

Coll turned to look up at the man silhou-etted against the sun. "Jack. What the devil are you doing here?"

"I might ask you the same thing. Never thought I'd see you turn shepherd."

"Och, and you never will. The more I'm around the creatures, the less I can abide them. She's not even the bloody earl's animal, she's one of Dougal MacKenzie's, but she's well and truly stuck. I canna leave her like this." Coll lifted his hand to shield his eyes against the sun. "Don't just sit there, man, get down here and help me."

"In the mud?" Jack Kensington grimaced, but swung off his horse, leaving it placidly cropping grass.

"Just pull." Coll tossed him the end of the rope. "I'll shove her from this end. I'm already so covered in mud, it'll make no difference."

Jack shrugged and took the rope. Pulling it around behind him and leaning against it, he began to back up. Coll shoved the animal's hindquarters. With an audible squelch, the sheep's back legs came free, and the ewe scrambled up the side of the ditch. The sudden shift of momentum sent both men tumbling.

"How is it you get me into these situations?" Jack grumbled, pushing himself up onto his elbows.

"Me! It's you that's always pulling me into trouble. At least you're not the one sitting in the mud."

Jack looked down at Coll sprawled at the bottom of the ditch and began to laugh. "True. And glad of it."

Coll climbed out of the ditch, wiping his hands clean on the grass. Little enough, he thought ruefully, could be done with the rest of him. He unwound the rope from the sheep and flopped down on the grass beside Jack. "What brings you here? You passing by or did you track me down?"

"The latter. I went by Duncally and they told me you were at the Connery croft. I was on my way there when I saw you rolling about in the ditch."

"I'm guessing Isobel sent you." Coll looked away, idly plucking at the blades of grass.

"You know her well. She wants you to visit. We have not seen you in some time. I scarcely noticed myself, you understand, but Isobel misses you. You might bring Lady Violet along. Isobel and Aunt Elizabeth admire her."

"Mm."

"I'm even curious to hear about your treasure hunt."

Coll rolled his eyes. "Aye, well, that's as dead as everything else."

Jack glanced at him, then went on carefully, "The invitation, of course, is only my wife's excuse. Her real reason for sending me is to inquire into your state of mind."

"Pry, you mean."

"If you want to be blunt about it."

"You can tell Mrs. Kensington that I am fine and she has no need to worry about me."

"I will be sure to do so. But after that, she'll ask me if you look like you've been sleeping and eating. I, you understand, shall have to answer honestly that you've shadows the color of Loch Baille beneath your eyes and hollows in your cheeks."

"I dinna." Coll sent him a baleful glance. "And you are a traitor to males everywhere."

"I am a man who likes to sleep in my bed every night. After my wife has established the state of your health — or the lack thereof — next will come the inquisition as to whether it's true you have taken to frequenting the tavern in Kinclannoch."

"Once. I went there one time ten bloody days ago."

"I was told you were singing laments."

Coll winced. "Dinna remind me."

"Isobel holds that the laments are an ominous sign. But she is more concerned about the reports of a fistfight."

"Ronald Fraser would try the patience of a saint."

"Which we all know you are not. Then, in the end, Isobel will arrive at an accounting of the reason you have been working round the clock."

"Does everyone in the Highlands know every single thing that happens in my life?"

"I cannot say. However, I can assure you

that Isobel hears it within twelve hours."

Coll heaved a sigh. "I asked Violet to marry me."

Jack studied him. "You are, um, in love with the lady?"

"I dinna know. I've never been in love. But I have never wanted any woman as much as I want her. Violet is the most aggravating, combative female that walks this earth, and I am sure she would prove a constant trial to any husband." Coll blew out a long, weary breath. "But the only thing I want is to be with her."

"Lady Violet does not return the feeling?"

"I don't know what she feels," Coll said darkly. "If indeed she feels anything. All I know is, she does not want to marry me. I am, you see, a monster who would rule her and break her, take her money and possessions, and not allow her air to breathe or room to live. In short, I am like her father, a man she despises. Holy hell, Jack, what woman wishes never to marry? Did Isobel refuse you when you asked her? Did she act as if you'd thrust a dagger in her?"

"Well, actually . . ." A smile of reminiscence touched Jack's lips. " 'Twas Isobel who proposed to me."

"Of course it was." Coll rolled his eyes. "You don't even have to ask, women are so eager to have you."

"In fairness, I believe it was my house Isobel was eager to have. Fortunately she was willing to take me in the bargain."

Coll chuckled. "True enough. Perhaps if I had a handy ruin or two, Violet would be more amenable to my suit."

"I have heard she covets the barrow and standing stones."

"Aye. I should offer them in trade." The momentary humor faded from Coll's face. "I told her I could not keep on the way we were, lying and sneaking about. Now I've no peace at all. But if I did *not* care about her, if I were callous and irresponsible and selfish, I could be in her bed every night."

"There are a large number of men who would consider that attitude a great good fortune."

"I know. But I am the fool who wants to be bound to her."

"Why?" When Coll cast a sharp glance at him, Jack shrugged. "You just said you don't know if you love her. You want her; you can have her. Why not take what she offers?"

"I could. I did. And when we are alone, when I am in her bed, it's all I could want. Christ. It's all I *do* want, it seems. But I feel like a villain. If her reputation is not ruined already, it will be soon enough. She can say she does not care, but she doesn't know what it would be like for her. She will regret it when it is too late. I can do naught to shield her except lie and hide and pretend she is nothing to me and I nothing to her. And I *hate* it." Coll surged to his feet and began to pace. "I want her children to be *mine*. I swore . . . I swore my children would not be bastards."

Jack rose, too, frowning. "Is she with child?"

"No. At least, I dinna think so." Coll paused, then added bitterly, "If she was, she probably would not tell me. No doubt that would be all her business, too, and none of mine." He swung toward Jack. "Would you accept that? If it was Isobel, would you not care if she dinna have your name? Your protection? If she did not even *want* it?"

"No." Jack's face hardened. "I wouldn't like it."

"Nor do I." Coll jammed his hands in his pockets. "So . . . that is why I am in the state I'm in. You can assure Isobel that there is naught she can do for me. It will pass, no doubt. At some point, Violet will go back home. In the meantime, we are very civilized, Lady Violet and I. We exchange polite chitchat through dinner."

"And you work day and night to avoid her."

"Aye." Coll smiled ruefully. "At least there is ample opportunity for that." He bent to pick up the rope and coil it. "I'd best get this back to Connery. It'll soon be dark."

"Very well." Jack took the reins of his horse. "I got in a few bottles of brandy last week. You should come by one evening. We'll open one, and I'll take some of your money at whist."

"I may be a fool about women, but I'm not gudgeon enough to play cards with you. And Isobel will fuss over me."

"True." Jack swung up into the saddle. "But I find sometimes a woman's fussing helps. And you'll have three of them, for so will Elizabeth and my mother, who persists in believing that you saved my life."

"Thrice." Coll held up three fingers.

Jack laughed. "You might be right."

"I'll come one night." Coll nodded a good-bye and walked away.

By the time he returned the rope to Connery and trudged home, Coll had managed to miss another excruciating meal with Violet. He turned toward his gatehouse instead of the mansion. He was filthy after his tussle with MacKenzie's sheep, in dire need of a bath before he climbed between the clean sheets of his bed. He could have gone to Duncally, but he hated to put the servants to the trouble of hauling and heating water. It was easier to fill the tub in his own cottage, and besides, the thought of bathing only a few doors down the hall from Violet did troublesome things to his insides.

He filled up the tub and added steaming water from the kettle, then poured himself a whiskey and settled down to soak. The water was so hot it stung his skin, and that was glorious on his aching muscles. Leaning his head back against the high edge of the tub, he sipped his whiskey and relaxed. And thought of having Violet in the water with him — the water lapping at her breasts, washing up over the rounded flesh and falling to reveal the dark rose tips, her wet hair clinging to her neck and shoulders. He imagined, too, soaping down her body, his hand gliding over her slippery skin. He could picture her face going slack in sensual pleasure, her legs parting to allow his questing fingers to find her.

With an oath, he grabbed the bar of soap and roughly lathered his hair and body, pouring fresh cold water over himself to rinse the suds free. It was pointless to torture himself this way. He downed the rest of his whiskey in one gulp and stepped out to dry off. He should eat, he thought as he dressed and poured out the water, but nothing appealed to him. Perhaps later.

A knock sounded on his door, surprising him. With a sigh, he went to answer it. He was not eager to solve anyone's problems tonight. He gaped at the man on his doorstep. "What the devil are you doing here?"

Angus McKay glared back at him. "That's a fine way to answer your door, I maun say."

Coll snorted. "As if you ever greeted anyone politely." He stepped back. "Come in, then, it's bloody cold out."

"I know it. I've just been walking about in it, haven't I?"

Coll rolled his eyes and walked away. He would need another drink if he had to deal with Angus. He looked toward the old man. "Whiskey?"

"I wouldna say nae to a wee dram." Angus shuffled forward and sat, laying his walking stick on the table.

Coll took a seat across from him and waited as the old man tossed down the drink.

"Ahh. It's guid whiskey you hae. No' as guid as mine, you ken."

"Of course not. Why are you here, Angus?"

"Weel, it's about herself."

"Who? Violet?"

"Aye. It's been two days now, and I hae no' seen a sign you're doing anything about her."

Coll stared, wondering if the whiskey had affected him more than he'd realized.

"Dinna gawp at me, lad. Hae you no plan? I walked her home both nights, but the truth is, I am no' fast enough if she needed help. I thought it would be you bringing her and taking her back. But then —"

"What in the name of all that's holy are you talking about?" An icy dread stole through him, bringing him to his feet. "Why did you walk Violet home? Why would I be bringing her and where?"

Angus scowled. "To keep her safe! Are you daft?" He peered at Coll. "Did she no' tell you?"

"Tell me what?" Coll wanted to grab the man up and shake the words from him.

"About the man the other nicht. The one whae attacked her."

Coll went still as death. "Violet was attacked?"

"Aye. He dinna hurt her," Angus said quickly. "He grabbed her, and I saw it and yelled, and he ran away."

"When?"

"Two nights ago. Coming back frae the ruins."

"Two nights ago. And she did not tell me?" His face flooded red, his eyes blazing, as he roared, "She did not tell me!"

Coll whirled and charged out the door.

25

Violet was in the library, books spread out in front of her on the wide expanse of the table, when the sound of a door slamming shut reverberated through the house, followed by the rapid tromp of feet over the stone floor. Violet lifted her head from her book, everything in her tightening. She knew those footsteps. She rose and faced the door, holding the book tightly against her as if armoring herself. She had barely reached her feet before Coll filled the doorway.

"Bloody hell, woman! You dinna even bother to tell me!" He took another step into the room and slung the door shut behind him. "I have to find out from bloody Angus McKay that you were attacked!"

"Oh." She should have known, Violet thought, her heart hammering. Coll was bound to find out. But she had not been prepared for the strength of his anger. She

416

had never seen his eyes so blazing, his face so tight with fury. She refused to let her trepidation show. "For pity's sake. I wasn't hurt. I didn't tell you because I knew this is how you would react. I knew it would make you fly into a fury."

"*You* make me fly into a fury."

"Naturally it *would* be my fault." She kept her voice dry. "That's always the way it is, isn't it? It has been since Eve — I am at fault because you have no control."

"Damn it to hell! This is not about *me.* It's about you and your reckless, willful, foolish behavior. How am I supposed to protect you? How can I take care of you when you willna even tell me he threatened you? That he grabbed you and hurt you. That he put his hands on you." Coll took another long step toward her, his eyes murderous, hands clenching into fists at his side.

"I don't need you to take care of me."

"Am I so worthless in your eyes? So low, so incapable, that you would seek help from that crabbit auld man rather than come to me?"

"I did not seek help from Angus; he happened to be there."

"Of course he was. He is always hanging about, and that, apparently, is fine with you.

But I — I am ever held at a distance."

"Oh!" Anger surged in Violet at the injustice of that remark. "If that isn't just like you!" She threw the book she was holding down on the table beside her. "As if *I* am the one who puts distance between us. It is you who chooses to run and hide from me, not the other way round."

"I dinna run and hide!" he thundered. His entire body was taut, almost vibrating in its intensity. "Least of all from a wee slip of a lass."

"A wee slip of a lass who frightens you, apparently." Violet cocked one eyebrow at him, her tone laced with disdain.

He grabbed her arms, yanking her forward and up onto her toes. "You do not frighten me."

"No?" Violet was suddenly surging with power, reveling in the humming tension in Coll, the barely leashed control. With a slow smile, she reached up and began to unbutton her dress.

Coll's hands dropped away from her. He stood as if frozen to the spot, his face stark, his eyes fathomless and dark.

"I think this is what scares you, Coll. That you want me, and it is out of your control." Her fingers continued inexorably downward. The sides of her dress sagged open, exposing the delicate white chemise beneath, held together by a saucy pink bow. "That you hunger for something but you cannot rule it." Taking one end of the ribbon between her fingers, she pulled it out in a long, slow motion until the bow fell apart. "That you need me, but you cannot brand me as yours."

Coll's chest rose and fell in hard, fast breaths. Red burned along the wide ridges of his cheekbones. Still he did not move.

Violet began to pull the pins from her hair so that the long strands uncoiled and slithered down over her shoulders. "That I give myself to you freely and you cannot say, 'This is mine.' "

A low growl issued from Coll's throat, and he moved almost faster than she could see. His hands sank into her waist and jerked her to him. His mouth fastened on hers. Heat radiated from him, encompassing her as his arms went around her, lifting her up and into him. His mouth was bruising and desperate, and he did not break the kiss even as he stepped forward.

Hooking his heel around the leg of her chair, Coll sent it tumbling out of his way. He bent her back over the table, reaching down to sweep the books aside. Violet heard the thuds as the books, then his kicked-off shoes, hit the floor, but he filled her vision and she could see nothing but him as he laid her flat upon the table and covered her with his huge body.

He pulled her arms up over her head, his hands anchoring her wrists. His weight pinned her to the hard wood, almost taking away her breath, but Violet received his weight eagerly. He stared down into her face, his eyes shining with an unholy fire, his breath rasping in the utter silence of the room. "You *are* mine."

He kissed her mouth, her face, her neck, his hands releasing her arms to travel over her body. Violet made no move to lower her arms. Indeed, she felt so boneless and melting beneath the onslaught of his passion that she was not sure she *could* move. He yanked apart the sides of her chemise, the ribbons pulling through the aglets and ripping when they caught. Her breasts spilled forth, and he took the trembling flesh in his hands. His mouth joined his supple fingers on her breasts, and a primitive sound rumbled in his chest.

Coll shoved his hand up under her skirts, finding the heat that burned at her core. Impatiently he stripped away the flimsy cotton barrier of her pantalets and moved between her legs, his fingers fumbling at the buttons of his breeches.

Then he was thrusting deep inside her, so hard and huge and hungered-for that Violet let out a helpless cry of pleasure. Her arms clung to him, fingers digging into his back. She wrapped her legs around him as he pounded into her, days of repressed need surging too strongly for delicacy or restraint. He took her in a wild rush, and when he exploded within her, a groan torn from his throat, Violet shuddered under her own release, pleasure rippling out through her in a great wave.

Coll collapsed upon her. His skin was damp, his chest rising and falling like a bellows. She could feel the tremors running beneath his skin, like those of a hard-run horse. A primal satisfaction swelled in her at these remnants of the cataclysm that had taken him, sparking arousal in her even after the furious burst of pleasure she'd just experienced.

Until this moment, Violet thought, she had not realized how essential Coll was to her, how he filled her, and how empty she had been without him. She loved him. It was all she could do not to let the words spill out of her.

"Holy hell." Coll rolled onto his back, his hands going up to push across his face and into his hair. "Ah, Violet . . . I'm sorry. So sorry. I dinna mean — I wouldna hurt you for the world."

Violet turned on her side, propping herself up on her elbow to see his face. His hands were pressed against his skull, and the satisfaction that had just exploded within him mingled discordantly with misery. Regret and shame glittered in his eyes, and the sight of it pierced her heart.

"Coll . . . no, don't feel that way."

"How else should I feel? I come in here raving about protecting you, and then I — I fall on you like a savage. I force you. Take you without a thought to whether I hurt you. I should be taken out and whipped."

"Och, Coll." She rolled out the Scots intonation and reached up to caress his cheek. "Dinna fash yourself."

Rising onto her knees, she straddled him. His eyes widened, lips parting in surprise. Violet leaned over him and her hair spilled down like a curtain on either side of his face.

"You didn't hurt me. You didn't force me." She bent down and tenderly kissed his lips. "My sweet, kind, *good* man. You deserve a much better woman than I." She smoothed her thumbs across his cheekbones. "But I won't let her have you." She bent to brush her lips across the ridges she had just caressed. "You did not make me do anything. Did I struggle? Did I protest?"

"You hadn't the time. You haven't the strength."

"I knew I wasn't in any danger from you. If I had said no, you would have stopped, even though it cost you."

"I heard you cry out, and I dinna stop."

Violet sat up, leaning back on her heels. "I cried out because it felt so good, Coll."

His hips were snug between her legs, and Violet felt him stir beneath her. She smiled provocatively, settling into him. "I wanted you as much as you wanted me."

"Impossible," he murmured, a smile beginning in his eyes.

"It's true." Her hands went to the ties of Coll's shirt, unfastening them, and she spread the sides apart. "I will not hear any talk of whipping." She peeled his shirt back and down off his arms, then bent to press her lips to the center of his chest. "I would not want any cut to mar this lovely skin."

"Violet . . ." His eyes were lambent, his face soft. He let his hands fall back onto the table above his head, his entire body relaxing.

"It *is* true that you had your way with me." Violet reached down, grabbing her dress, still hanging about her hips, and tore it off over her head, followed by her chemise and petticoats. "And now . . ." She slid her hands up his arms and gripped his crossed wrists as if to hold him prisoner. "I intend to have my way with you."

She heard the quick, little intake of his breath. "Do you now?"

"Indeed." Violet glided her hands down his arms, bending to press her mouth to the tender skin inside his elbows, trailing her lips along his flesh. Her hair flowed over his face and onto his chest, and she felt him turn his head to catch her hair between his cheek and arm, rubbing against it like a cat.

Laying feathery kisses over his brow, his eyes, his cheeks and chin, she avoided his lips though he turned toward her, searching. "No," she breathed into his ear, and took the lobe between her teeth to worry it. "I will kiss you when and where I choose. It's my turn now."

She felt the heat flare in his skin. With the tip of her tongue she traced the whorls of his ear, and the rasp of his breath in his throat aroused her. She kissed the side of his neck, loving the leap of pulse beneath her lips, then moved to the other side, working her way up to his ear.

Violet slid her hands up his arms, so that her own arms lay aligned with his. Her lips hovered above his as she gazed down into his eyes. "You see, I am going to fall upon you like a savage now." Again she felt his flesh turn to flame under hers, and she smiled and kissed him.

In a long, delicious kiss she savored the taste of him, the feel of his lips and tongue on hers, the heat that poured from him. It was so delicious that when she pulled back from him, she tilted her head the other way and kissed him again.

"I shall force you," she whispered as she nuzzled into his neck. "I shall take you without a thought to whether I hurt you."

He chuffed out a little laugh. "I think you've passed that point."

Violet raised up to gaze down in his face. "Do you want me to stop your torment? Release you from my retaliation?"

"Nae." Passion etched his features. "I want to feel your revenge in full measure."

"Then I" — she kissed the point of his chin — "shall oblige."

Violet moved down him, caressing his naked chest with her hands and body and mouth, stopping to lay a soft, moist kiss on his navel. Coll groaned, reaching for her breasts.

"None of that." She caught his wrists and pressed a kiss to each one before pinning them to the table beside him. "Just for that, I think, I must pay special attention here." Her mouth lingered over the shallow well of his navel, then she worked her way across the soft flesh of his stomach, taking her time with it until she wrested another groan from him.

Violet slipped her hands beneath his back and down under his breeches. He jerked at her touch, his hands breaking free of her light hold.

Stroking her hair, he grabbed a handful of the silky mass and pressed it against his lips. Releasing the locks, he linked his hands behind his head, his gaze hot and slumberous, and smiled at her. "No doubt you shall add that transgression to my punishment."

"I shall." Her answering grin was wicked.

She stripped his breeches from his legs. Tossing them onto the floor, she cast a slow, appreciative eye over him. "You're a long, lovely sight of a man, Coll Munro."

Curling her hand under his knee, she moved exploringly up his leg and on to the tender skin of his inner thigh. He made a low, muffled noise, and she glanced up at his face as she traced a teasing pattern over his skin. His heavy lids drooped over his eyes, the fire in them enough to burn her. His face was flushed and slack with hunger;

his lips, lusciously reddened from their kisses, were parted as he labored for breath. He was the very image of a man in the throes of desire, and the sight of him made Violet's own hunger pulse within her. She wanted him, ached for him deep inside her — so much so that she could not bear to wait, but still she did, for she yearned even more to build their fever to the highest pitch.

Violet prowled up the table on all fours, seeing the fire leap in his eyes as he watched her. She bent to kiss the point of his shoulder, then sent her thumbnail sliding down his arm. "Turn onto your side."

"What?" He looked at her distractedly, his eyes vague with lust. "Why?"

"I want to see the rest of you."

He swallowed and let out a shuddering breath. "Are you trying to kill me, Violet?"

She smiled. "No. I do not want that." She stroked her hand over his chest. "But you see . . ." She ran a finger around his nipple, keeping her gaze locked on his as she toyed with him. "You are mine." Violet drifted lightly down his chest. "And I want to look at all of you."

He said nothing, just rolled onto his side. Violet let out a long sigh of appreciation. "You are a beautiful man. I've missed looking at you."

She caressed the breadth of his back, tracing the smooth lines of muscles and running her thumb down the knobby ridge of his spine. Lying down beside him, she began to kiss his back, her hand gliding up and down his side. She slid down, her hand going to the outcropping of his pelvic bone. She curved her palm over the thick muscles of his buttocks, delighting in the way they bunched beneath her touch.

Leaning on her elbow, she laid her lips against his sharp hip bone. Her hair cascaded over him as she kissed her way along the side of his hip and on to his thigh. Coll had a death grip on the edge of the table, his knuckles white. Violet's hand crept between his legs from behind, cupping him, and he jerked, his breath ragged.

"Enough," he growled, rolling back and pulling her to him. "I have to be inside you. Now."

Violet straddled him. His hands went to her hips, guiding her down onto him. She sank, taking him into her fully, and began to move. She took her pleasure slowly, greedily, gliding up and down, her eyes on his face. He looked like a man caught in torment or ecstasy. Perhaps it was both. His fingertips dug into the fleshy mounds of her buttocks, silently urging her on. He turned, pulling her beneath him, and drove into her, hard and fast and desperate. He cried out as passion took him, and Violet clung, convulsing with him.

They lay tangled together, awash in pleasure and too wrung out to move. Violet rested on his chest, her long, loose mane of hair spread out over them both. Coll's hand moved slowly, lightly over her, sifting through the silky strands, fingertips grazing her skin.

"I dinna lock the door," he said after a moment. "What if Mrs. Ferguson was to come in?"

Violet giggled. "She'd see a sight she wouldn't soon forget."

Coll's laugh rumbled in his chest. "Do you think they're clustered outside the door, listening?"

"I wouldn't be surprised. No doubt half the glen heard you storm in."

"Why did you not tell me, Violet?" She lifted her head to look at Coll, shocked by the thread of pain in his voice. It was in his eyes as well, despite the deep satisfaction. "Do I have so little place in your thoughts?"

"No! Oh, Coll, no." Violet cupped his face in her hands and laid gentle kisses all across him. "You have a very large place in my thoughts. Indeed, you occupy far too many of them for comfort. I did not tell you because I —" She sighed. "I was angry with you. I missed you. I wanted you. And it made me furious. I hated feeling so bereft. Powerless."

"Powerless? Don't be daft." Coll took her hand and pressed it to his lips. "You ruled my life the whole time I was apart from you; I could do nothing but think about you. Ache for you."

"Do you think I was any better off? That I did not lie in my bed missing you every night?"

"Did you?" A distinctly smug smile lit his face.

"Yes. You needn't get conceited about it, though." She drilled her finger into his side, but he only laughed and caught her hand, kissing it again.

"Then you were punishing me?" Oddly, the idea did not seem to displease him.

"I suppose I was." She looked abashed. "I didn't think so; I just . . . did not want you to have to rescue me. I hated the thought of being another of the many people you feel you must take care of."

"I like to take care of you."

"I don't like needing you." Violet sat up, turning away from him, and pulled up her knees, wrapping her arms around them.

Coll's fingers drifted over her back. "Do you think that you're the only one who needs?"

Violet looked at him over her shoulder. "I hope not." She turned and lay back down on his chest. "I am sorry, Coll. It was petty of me not to tell you. Perhaps I wanted to make you angry. But I didn't mean to hurt you." She pressed her lips to his skin. "I never want to hurt you."

His arms went around her, holding her to him. "Dinna trouble yourself. I am not feeling any hurt now."

"I'm glad." Violet smiled, tracing a pattern over his skin with her forefinger. "What shall we do now?"

Coll's eyes gleamed in response, but he said, "First, I am going to sneak into the kitchen and find something to eat. I'm starving." He kissed her soundly. "Then I'm going to get rid of the bastard who attacked you."

26

"How do you plan to find him?" Violet asked sometime later as they sat at the kitchen table with bread, slices of cold roast beef, cheese, and pickles spread out before them.

"I haven't decided." Coll dug into his food with obvious pleasure. "Tell me exactly what happened."

"I thought Old Angus told you." Violet kept her hand on his arm on the table, caressing it now and then, unwilling to completely break contact.

"I dinna wait for the details." Coll's eyes glinted.

"Mm. I'm sure you didn't." Violet recounted the incident, ending with the providential arrival of Angus McKay.

"So he thought we had the treasure because he was watching us that day at the castle?"

"And other times, I think. Several times

lately I've had an eerie feeling that someone was watching me. That day that we went to the Munro graves, as I was walking home, I thought there was someone else in the woods."

"Someone's been spying on you? Following you? And you dinna say anything?"

"What could I say? 'I keep getting an eerie feeling'? I never saw anyone. I decided I was imagining it."

"What about since the day he grabbed you? Has he tried again? Has he been watching you?"

"I have not seen him. He hasn't done anything. It's only been two days, Coll, and I have not been foolish, whatever you may think. In the mornings I wait to walk with the workers, and I come back with them or Angus."

"McKay is eighty if he's a day. He's not much use if someone attacks you."

"He frightened him off the other day. I think the man feared exposure. I imagine he is someone Angus would recognize."

"No doubt. He's bound to be from the glen."

"We could lure him out," Violet suggested. "I could walk back by myself, and —"

"Nae." Coll stopped her with a stony look. "Absolutely not."

"He won't hurt me. He wants the treasure, and I can hardly give it to him if he's killed me. I can arrange to give it to him, and you can be waiting to catch him when I do."

"He could do a great deal to convince you to help him without actually killing you. And if you think I am going to sit around while you lure some villain to attack you, you are even madder than I thought."

"What do you suggest? If you are guarding me every step of the way, he won't show himself. And do *not* suggest I stay inside Duncally until you catch him."

"I wasn't about to suggest that; I know how little cooperation I could hope for from you."

They glared at each other until Violet began to laugh. "There. Already we are at daggerpoint." She stroked her hand over his, and he opened it, lacing their fingers together. She lifted his hand to kiss his knuckles. "I know you are concerned for me. And I am glad of it. But you must see that I cannot stop living my life."

"Dinna worry. You're going back to your ruins as usual. Now that I know what he's doing, we can hoist him on his own petard."

"How?"

Coll smiled, a cold glitter to his eyes that Violet had never before seen. "We shall give your attacker something to steal."

Two days later, Violet stood at the ruins watching the men dig. Yesterday Isobel and her aunt had spent most of the afternoon at the ruins, accompanied by Isobel's husband, Jack. Violet had enjoyed the visit, but she had known that they were there because Coll had asked them to watch over her. Curiously, she found it amusing, even endearing. It was a trifle disconcerting to feel herself changing.

Today, however, there were no guests, just herself and the workers and, of course, Angus McKay, who had not missed a single day since he had frightened off her attacker. Violet glanced now and then toward the edge of the cliff. She was glad that the role she had to play today called for a show of anxiety and eagerness, for she did not think she could have managed to seem calm.

She heard Coll whistling before she saw him, followed by the chorus of a song. It would take a deaf man not to look as Coll came up the path from the beach. Coll carried a sack over his shoulder, obviously weighty. His clothes and face were smeared with dirt, but his smile was bright. Coll was either a better actor than Violet would have guessed or he was enjoying the prospect of a confrontation.

"Did you find it?" Violet ran to him.

"Aye, I did." Coll dropped the sack and picked her up to whirl her around.

"Coll! Put me down! You're filthy." But she laughed.

He set her down, and Violet tried to look annoyed as she brushed the dust from her cloak, but a grin broke through.

"Whisht, lad! What do you hae there?" Angus hurried toward them as fast as his aged legs would carry him. The workers had ceased digging and were leaning on their shovels, watching with great curiosity. Angus reached for the sack, but Coll whisked it away and again slung it over his back.

" 'Tis nothing."

"A michty heavy nothing." Old Angus set his hands on his hips and glared up at Coll. The old man, Violet thought, was enjoying this as much as Coll.

"I'm going back to the house," Violet said abruptly. "You men finish up here. Angus." She gave him a good-bye nod.

"You're leaving? Sae early?" Angus asked.

"I'm tired. Coll?" Violet turned toward him and he nodded.

Despite Angus's splutters of protest, Violet and Coll started off, Coll shortening his strides to match Violet's. Violet was on edge, listening, waiting. She fought her instinct to stay silent. They continued their performance.

"Was it difficult? Did you have much trouble?" She turned to look up at Coll, surreptitiously scanning the land around them.

"Nae. I found it easy enough. It was where the journal said, in an inner cave. I've passed it hundreds of times, but not gone in it. The entrance is low; you have to crawl through it."

"Was it much?"

"Oh, aye. Four bags, you ken. We'll live in style." He cast her a grin, and Violet knew he, too, was surveying the area.

They continued to talk about money and opportunities for spending it as they started up the rough, narrow path to Duncally. The trees were thicker here, with ample places for someone to hide. The problem was whether their quarry would have the nerve to stop Coll. It would have worked better with Violet alone, but Coll would never have allowed that. And frankly, Violet would not have relished plunging up this trail by herself.

If Coll's presence deterred him, there would be another opportunity tonight. With that in mind, Coll turned their talk to plans for stowing the sack in the butler's pantry tonight.

"I'll just be glad to get it in the bank tomorrow." Violet gave a shiver. "And I won't have to worry that that man will come after me again." She hoped they were not being too obvious.

Violet heard a snap among the trees, and she felt the subtle increase in the tension of Coll's body, but she carefully kept her eyes straight ahead and her face nonchalant. Ahead of them lay a sharp turn in the path, the most secluded part of the trail. Violet's nerves stretched tighter with every step she took. She went around the curve and took two steps, Coll right behind her.

"Stop!"

Violet froze, Coll doing the same. Slowly they turned around. A man stood on the path behind them. His hat was pulled low and a scarf was wrapped round his lower face. Violet scarcely took in his attire, however; her attention was riveted on the pistol in his hand.

"Will Ross." Coll's voice dripped scorn. "Do you think I dinna recognize you because of that stupid scarf? I've known you since you could walk, lad."

Violet's fingers curled into her hands. She knew Coll was delaying, but didn't he realize his contempt made the man more likely to shoot him?

"Is that supposed to make me flee?" Ross sneered. "Should I quake in my boots because the michty Coll Munro knows my name? Or maybe you think I will believe you are my friend."

"Nae. I would not claim friendship with you, Will. But you will be sorry if you try to take this from me."

The other man snorted in disgust. "You're the one whae will be sorry if you dinna hand over the gold. Gie it to me." He waggled his fingers in a summoning gesture.

Coll let out a sigh and lowered the sack. Taking a step forward, he tossed the sack on the ground at Ross's feet.

Will leaned down to grab the sack with one hand, keeping the pistol trained squarely on Coll. "Mayhap I'll shoot you anyway."

"No!" Violet cried, and started around Coll, but he pushed her behind him.

"Violet, stop."

Ross chuckled. "Don't like that, lassie? Maybe you'd like to bargain for him then. But I already hae all this money. What'll you offer for his sorry life?"

A pistol cocked loudly behind him, and Jack Kensington jammed the barrel of a pistol against Ross's skull. "Well, I will offer to not put this ball through your brain if you drop your gun. How does that bargain sound?"

Coll let out a long breath. "Christ, English, what took you so long?"

"So Will Ross is the man who broke into Duncally?" Aunt Elizabeth asked several hours later. She and Isobel had been waiting at Duncally, along with Jack's mother, and the three women had stayed with Violet while Coll and Jack escorted Will to gaol in Kinclannoch. Violet, unaccustomedly shaky, found it rather comforting to be fussed over.

Now the whole group was gathered around the dining table, and once they had satisfied the first sharp pangs of hunger, they settled down to discuss the events of the afternoon.

"Yes, I'm afraid the thief was Will." Coll shook his head. "I should not have let him get involved with that group."

"You cannot blame yourself for the way Will Ross turned out," Isobel told him.

"I suspect young Will would have found his way into thievery, clearances or no clearances," Jack agreed.

"You may be right."

"But I don't understand — how did you

noon?" Jack's mother asked.

"It was more hope than certainty, Mrs. Kensington," Coll replied. "We knew he had been spying on us, so we thought that if we put on a show of finding the treasure, he would see it and come after us. The tricky thing was getting him to seize it immediately."

"That's why we discussed putting it in the safe in the butler's pantry as soon as we got to Duncally," Violet explained.

"Even so, he might have decided it would be safer to sneak in and steal it at night from the pantry," Aunt Elizabeth pointed out.

"That's true." Coll smiled fondly at the older woman. "So we also talked about going to Baillannan this evening. Of course we wouldn't have. We would have been waiting for him when he broke in."

"And we discussed taking it tomorrow to the bank so he would know he had to strike very soon or it would be quite out of his reach."

"You are so clever!" Mrs. Kensington exclaimed admiringly. "I cannot imagine how you had the courage to carry on the pretense, Lady Violet. I would have fainted from fear."

Coll sent a laughing glance at Violet. "I

441

dinna think Lady Violet is given to fainting. Or fear."

"My main worry was that our exchange would sound too rehearsed and make him suspicious." Violet decided she would not share the terror that had risen up in her when she thought Ross might shoot Coll.

"Mine was that Will wouldn't have been on the watch today, and it would have all been for naught," Coll added.

"Fortunately he was there. And he took the bait." Jack sipped his wine. "Naturally, while Coll got to put on a grand show, my part was to spend the day crouched in the bushes, waiting."

"And an excellent job you did of it, too, my love." Isobel grinned as she patted his arm.

"You are all safe; that's the important thing. And you don't have to worry about him stealing the treasure," Mrs. Kensington said happily.

"The unfortunate thing is we still have no idea where the treasure is."

"I had hoped that the hiding place was marked with the sign on Coll's knife," Violet told them. "But we have not found the symbol anywhere. We've searched the old castle, which seems the likeliest place. I even examined the standing stones, thinking perhaps it had been carved on one of them."

"Coll's knife?" Aunt Elizabeth looked puzzled. "Why would your knife be a clue to the gold Papa brought back?"

"Because it was Sir Malcolm's knife — or so Meg believes."

"Oh, no, dear, it could not be Papa's knife. That was on him. Isobel and Jack found it with . . . his body." Tears glimmered in Elizabeth's eyes.

"Nae, not the long knife he carried on his belt. It was his sgian-dubh." Coll reached behind him and pulled out the small knife, holding it out to Elizabeth.

"Oh! Yes." Elizabeth studied it, nodding.

"Do you remember it, Auntie?" Isobel leaned forward hopefully.

"The sgian-dubh? No, I'm afraid I cannot remember what Papa's sgian-dubh looked like, though of course he wore one. But it seems likely this one was his, doesn't it? Since he and Faye were the guardians."

"The guardians?" Violet stiffened.

"Yes, dear, you know, the guardians of the tomb." Elizabeth pointed at the hilt of the knife. "That mark is the one that's on the barrow."

27

For a moment there was dead silence in the room. Elizabeth glanced around. "I don't understand. Why is everyone looking so odd?"

"Of course!" Violet let out a long breath. "The barrow!" She looked at Coll. "That must be what Faye meant. She was talking about their ancient ancestors — the ones who are buried in the barrow by the ring." Violet turned to Elizabeth, her excitement growing. "You called Sir Malcolm and Faye Munro the guardians?"

"Yes." Elizabeth, unsettled by everyone's reactions, was clearly relieved to be on more solid ground. "It is one of the legends about the loch. Part of the pact between the lairds of Baillannan and the goodwives of the Munros."

"The pact?"

"Not a formal one, of course. Just an ancient tradition. No one knows how or

444

when it began. The two families, the Munros and the Roses, were given the duty of protecting the old ones."

" 'Those who went before,' "Violet quoted Faye's journal.

"Exactly." Elizabeth nodded. "The Baillannan, of course, protected by force of arms. He was the landholder, the fighter. The Munros were more . . . the protectors of the spirit. The ones who preserved the traditions."

"That is what the symbol means." Violet pointed to the sgian-dubh, now lying on the table beside Coll. "The Norse rune meant protection. The Ogham letter was the sign of the yew tree — which stood for death and eternity."

"And rebirth," Elizabeth added. "That was the significance of the Long Night."

"The Long Night?" Mrs. Kensington looked around blankly.

"It's what they called the winter-solstice ceremony long ago," Isobel explained. "Wasn't it, Aunt Elizabeth?"

"Yes. It was celebrated by the Old Ones, or so they say."

"I am familiar with the idea that the ancients observed the solstices — the very people, perhaps, who lived in that village we are excavating." Violet's eyes glowed with enthusiasm. "It was a religion that centered on the land and the elements. They celebrated the planting of the crops in the spring and the growing of them in the summer, and so on. The winter solstice, coming in the darkest part of winter — the longest night, as you say, Lady Elizabeth — was vitally important for reaffirming their belief in the return of the spring, the crops. The death of winter, followed by a promise of rebirth and renewal."

"But they no longer actually practice that religion." Jack looked puzzled. "Do they? I mean, the people around here don't gather at the circle on the shortest day of the year."

"No. They moved past that a long time ago." Isobel smiled. "There's nothing done there now."

"Not by the public," Elizabeth hedged. "But that is what the legend is about — the protectors preserved the tradition of the Long Night."

Everyone stared at her. Finally Isobel said, "Are you saying that the laird and a Munro healer went to the standing stones on the winter solstice?"

"No, dear, of course not." Elizabeth smiled fondly at her niece. "They went to the tomb."

"Ma?" Coll's jaw dropped.

"Papa?" Isobel looked equally astounded.

"Oh, no, John and Janet no longer practiced the tradition," Elizabeth agreed. "Or, at least, they never told me if they did. But the tale is that such was the duty of the Munros and the Baillannan. They were also bound to keep all others from violating the barrow and the ring — as Meg saved the Troth Stone last summer, you remember." She turned toward Coll.

Coll seemed too stunned to answer, but Isobel said, "But what did they do at the tomb?"

"I've no idea." Elizabeth shrugged. "It was no longer done by the time Janet and John and I were of age. When my father died, my brother was just a boy, even younger than I, and of course Janet was a baby. There would have been only Janet's grandmother to continue it, and she was getting on in years. My brother and Coll's mother were modern-thinking people. I don't believe they took up the practice again. But Faye and Sir Malcolm might have done so."

Violet looked at Coll. "Do you think that is what Faye meant? That she hid it somewhere around the tomb?"

"Aye." He gazed back at her. "Or in it."

"Inside? But how could she have gotten inside? The entrance is blocked by rubble."

"Ah." Coll grinned at Violet. "Now *that* is one of the Munro secrets. I know another way in."

"Do you really know how to get into the barrow?" Violet asked a few hours later as she sat at her vanity table, brushing out her hair.

Coll lay on her bed, arms linked behind his head, gazing at her with a lazy heat in his eyes. He had waited to come to her room until he was sure the servants had retired for the night. Though he had returned to Violet's bed, he still did his utmost to keep her reputation safe.

Watching her take down her hair was one of his favorite occupations, Violet knew. More than once he had taken the brush from her hand and brushed her hair himself. Then he had sunk his fingers into her hair and massaged her scalp with his fingertips, which had melted her right down to her toes. Now that she thought about it, Coll's watching her brush out her hair was one of her favorite things, as well.

"In theory, I do," Coll replied. "I've never actually gone inside. But there are two stones above the entrance that can be moved. It's a drop down, so you have to take a rope and secure it to climb in and out."

Violet shivered. "It's a little frightening, isn't it? To think of going down into that tomb in the dark."

"Aye, a bit."

"Not knowing what will be inside. Or even if the structure is still safe." She paused, contemplating the idea. "It's exciting as well."

He laughed. "I'm not surprised to hear you say that."

"Do you think your mother continued the tradition? That she went into the tomb on the solstice?"

"No. Ma was a practical sort who believed in the here and now. She knew the old stories, the old ways, well enough, and she used to tell us stories that would make our hair stand on end." He smiled reminiscently. "But she dinna believe them. My great-grandmother was a bitter old woman; looking back on it, I think she mourned Faye all her life. I suspect she raised my mother differently; she scorned the old ways with Ma — after all, they hadn't saved her daughter. Inside, though, Gran was still bound to them; she was the one who told me about the Long Night and the way into the barrow."

"And you never tried to go in there?" Violet swung around on the stool to face him, setting her brush aside.

"I did not. There *are* those of us who are reluctant to disturb the dead."

Violet made a face and crossed to the bed to sit beside Coll. "Still, I find it difficult to believe that you didn't want to explore it when you were sixteen."

"I thought about it once or twice." He toyed with the sash of her dressing gown, idly untying it, and grinned at her. "But I never had a wicked companion to urge me to sin . . . until now."

Freed from the sash, her robe sagged open, but Violet chose to ignore it. It was more difficult to ignore Coll's thumbnail dragging along her thigh. "Did she tell you what this Long Night ceremony entailed?"

He shook his head. "Not really. They may have had to spend the night there."

"With all the remains?" Even Violet was daunted by that prospect.

"I don't know. Perhaps it was a test of their resolve." His reply was distracted. His eyes were on his fingers, busily bunching the material of her nightgown in small increments, shortening it bit by bit. "The main thing was to be there when the light came in."

"Why? What light?"

"The sunrise." Violet's legs were exposed now up to her thigh, and Coll slipped his fingers beneath the hem of the gown.

She giggled and lightly slapped his hand. "Coll, stop it. Tell me what happens at dawn."

"You're a hard woman." He heaved a dramatic sigh and stopped the movement of his hand, leaving it there, warm and firm against her skin. "Very well. The story is that inside the barrow at dawn on the winter solstice, the sunlight shines in and strikes the altar. It only happens on that one day at that exact time."

"Coll . . ." Violet's eyes glowed. "What a thing to see. It would have seemed a visible proof of rebirth."

"Not to mention substantiating the words of their holy men. A grand way to assure everyone that their faith is justified."

"You're a cynical man."

Coll's agile fingers moved upward again, teasing across her sensitive flesh. Violet closed her eyes as she leaned back, bracing her hands on the bed.

"Nae, not cynical. Just a man who seeks a different sort of truth. Ah . . . there, I think I have found it." He watched her as her face softened in pleasure under his teasing fingers.

Violet let out a noise very like a purr. "I believe you have."

"Good. I always like to attain my goal."

Violet moved her legs a little farther apart, and she heard the telling uptick in Coll's breathing. "And what is your goal?"

"Why, 'tis only to please you, my lady."

"Only me?"

"Well, perhaps I derive a certain enjoyment from it myself." His fingers continued their skillful movements, gliding over her slick, aching nub of flesh and sending shivers of need through her. "I enjoy hearing you moan." His grin was almost feral. "Yes, just like that. I love the scent of your arousal. Most of all" — he pressed hard and fast — "I like to watch your face as you melt."

Violet could not hold back the deep groan rising in her throat as she shuddered under the force of the ecstasy he brought her. After a long moment, she opened her eyes. He was right, she thought. She felt as if she had melted. At the same time her whole body hummed with eagerness. She looked at Coll. He was lying back against the pillows, one arm still tucked beneath his head and his other hand curled around her knee. Heat radiated from his large body and glowed in his eyes. His mouth was curved into a smile that bordered on smug.

"Two can play at that game." Her voice was low and husky. She saw a swift response flare in his eyes.

"Good," Coll said as Violet slid up his body and kissed him thoroughly, deeply. When she pulled back, he sank his hands into her hair. "Show me."

And so she did. Methodically Violet undressed him, taking her time and pausing to kiss and caress each part of him she revealed. She lingered on his chest, using her lips and teeth and tongue to arouse the tightening buds of his nipples. Tracing the pattern of the hair on his chest downward, she pulled his breeches down and off, then took him into her hands.

Coll pulled in his breath sharply. Violet looked up at him. His strong face was loose and vulnerable, his eyes closed, shadows of his lashes cast across his cheeks. She could not resist going to his lips again, drawn by their kiss-bruised color. She took his lower lip between her teeth, worrying it gently as her hand returned to the hard, silken shaft, pulsing with desire. Caressing and stroking, she drove him higher, teasing him in such small, tender increments that he hovered on the brink for what seemed an age of pleasurable ache.

Finally, with a low growl, he turned and pulled her beneath him, driving into her with a fierce hunger, his entire being focused solely on this passion-drenched moment. He shuddered against her, pouring his seed into her with a cry that seemed torn from the bottom of his soul, and Violet followed him into that sweet release.

Violet was not sure what awakened her, but she was aware instantly of the absence of Coll's long, warm body beside her in the bed. She turned, opening her eyes, and saw him at the window. He had shoved the draperies aside and stood looking out, buttoning his shirt. The square of the window cast a faint light upon his face, and her heart clenched inside her at the sadness that tinged his features.

"Coll . . ." She rose on her elbow, reaching out to him. He turned and smiled, the unhappiness banished from his features though the shadow of it remained in his eyes.

"I'm sorry. I dinna mean to wake you." He took her hand and raised it to his lips. "I must leave. It's near dawn."

"You do not have to go."

"Aye, I do." He stroked his fingers down her cheek. "I will see you at breakfast."

Coll kissed her again, then went to the door and, after a cautious check, slipped out. Violet sighed and lay back, aware of an ache in her chest. She wished that Coll would stay with her. That she did not feel empty when he left. Most of all, she wished she could erase the sorrow she had glimpsed on his face. Coll had come back to her, but it caused him pain.

It hurt her to the core to see him unhappy — far worse, knowing that she was at the root of it. Not for the first time, she thought about giving in to him. Giving up. Coll would never set out to hurt her. He would always do what was right. What he thought was right. What he thought was best.

Her throat tightened with the familiar fear, and with a groan, Violet buried her face in her pillow. After a long moment, she pulled herself out of bed and began to dress. Accept what you have, she told herself. It was far more than she had ever hoped for.

She arrived at the dining room before him, as was often the case. Coll, despite his early rising, usually took a walk around the house, inside and out, to make sure everything was as it should be. Now that they had caught Will Ross, it was no longer necessary, of course. In fact, Coll had no need to live here in the house anymore. Violet hastily pushed that thought to the back of her mind.

Violet's heart lifted, as it always did, when Coll came through the door. He smiled at her, and she wished that she could kiss him in greeting, but that was unthinkable when at any moment a servant might walk in.

Instead she said, "When can we start on the barrow?"

"Do you plan to dig out the entrance? You could take a break from the ruins and set the men to that."

"It seems a shame to interrupt their work at the ruins. We have come so far."

"Ah, but do you think you can possess yourself in patience until you're finished there?" Coll raised a doubtful eyebrow.

"No. But you know another way into the barrow."

"A possible way in. We canna be sure."

"Until we try it."

"Until we try it." He grinned. "I got a rope and a lantern from the shed. But I'd suggest a hearty breakfast first."

"You were already planning on going."

"I know you."

This simple, even offhand, statement struck Violet hard. Coll knew her. In every

456

way that mattered, Coll knew her. And even so, he chose to be with her. She turned away, a trifle flustered, and began to fill her plate.

After breakfast, they walked to the ring of stones and climbed the grassy slope of the barrow. On the sides the tomb rose gradually. The front, however, had two distinct levels. Above the rubble-filled entrance to the tomb was a small level surface, a terrace above which the barrow rose sharply to the top. Lying flush against the barrow at the back of the flat area were two stone blocks. Both were inscribed with wavy lines and swirls around the edges, and in the middle of each, clear though worn and rough, was engraved the symbol on Coll's sgian-dubh.

A shiver ran through Violet, and she looked over at Coll. She could see in his eyes the same anticipation mingled with awe. They stood on the edge of a discovery. The blocks were not light, but Coll was able to push both of them aside. Lifting the lantern, they peered down into the darkness. The passageway was narrow, but widened out at the bottom, and they could see several feet of the earthen floor. Coll went back down to the barrow's entrance to tie the rope around one of the large slabs of rock there. Returning, he tied the lantern on the other end of the rope and lowered it carefully into the opening until it settled on the floor.

Hands around the rope, Coll edged backward into the hole and climbed down, then held the rope as Violet followed him. Her stomach took flight for an instant as she dangled half in and half out of the hole, but then she wrapped her legs around the rope and slid down, her hands protected by thick leather gloves. She joined Coll in the center of the narrow passageway. On either side rose slabs of stone, forming a corridor. Behind them, the lantern revealed a jumble of rocks that Violet knew must be the entrance. In front of them, the stone hallway stretched into darkness.

Lantern in hand, they started down the hall. It was eerily silent among the stones, the sounds of their movement loud in the ancient stillness. As they moved forward, the ground rose, the slope so gradual that it seemed as if it were the stone slabs above their heads that grew lower and lower, giving the corridor a stifling, ominous appearance. Before long Coll had to lower his head to avoid hitting it on the rocks.

He held the lantern up as they walked, revealing the careful placement of stone slabs above them across the pathway. The horizontal stones rested on the tall, vertical rocks on either side, forming a sort of doorway and buttressing the stone roof. Most of the slabs that made up the walls stood with their narrow sides in, but now and then one of them was turned to face the corridor. On these latter stones were carved more swirls and wavy lines, as well as other symbols.

Abruptly the corridor flared out into a large, round chamber, and the roof of stone slabs disappeared. With Coll holding up the lantern as high as he could, they could see that the walls of the chamber were built of more slabs in an intricate pattern of horizontal and vertical rocks. They tilted their heads back to gaze up at the amazing height of the walls, so tall that the roof lay beyond the yellow pool of lantern light. On either side of the roughly circular room was a doorway, and both doors were covered by large, flat stones that would require several men to move. These, too, were decorated with symbols and swirls.

"I imagine those are the burial chambers," Violet said in a hushed voice, somehow reluctant to break the silence of the tomb. "What a marvelous creation! Can you imagine a primitive people constructing this? To have so tall a ceiling — to brace and buttress all these stones so that it is sturdy and strong — and all without mortar."

"Think of the years it must have taken them to build it."

"I have never seen anything like it."

For several minutes all they could do was turn around, studying the chamber, but finally Coll shook his head, almost as if dispelling the mood of admiration and astonishment, and turned to Violet. "Where's the altar?"

He moved forward into the middle of the circle, and his lantern lit the wall opposite them. Unlike the other walls, this one was built with a multitude of smaller rocks, much like the construction of the ruins they were excavating — and of many modern boundary walls throughout the glen. The stacked rocks were buttressed at regular intervals by larger, vertical slabs that served as columns. Long, horizontal stones stretched across these column-like stones and supported yet more rows of small rocks. The pattern repeated as far up as they could see.

"I don't know. I don't see an altar." Violet followed him to the far wall.

"Makes one wonder about the legend. If there was no altar, what exactly did this light illuminate?"

"Any shaft of light piercing this darkness would have been impressive. However, my guess would be that this stone is what the light struck." She pointed to a spot directly across from the corridor through which they had entered. Three feet square, the stone rested on top of one of the long, horizontal supporting stones, facing outward. In the center of the stone was a large carved spiral similar to the other swirls that decorated much of the tomb.

"That does seem to be a place of importance. If light could strike anywhere, it would be directly across from the hallway." Coll cast another long look around the chamber. "But where would she have hidden the sacks of gold? Obviously she could not have moved any of these rocks."

"I suppose she could have dug a hole in the floor somewhere."

Coll looked doubtfully at the ground. "That's a great deal of area to just begin digging randomly. Let's look for the symbol again. If we could find it inscribed on one of the rocks, it would at least give us an approximate place to start digging."

They began around the chamber, searching the walls for another marking that resembled the one on the outside. Taking their time, they made a full circuit of the high-ceilinged chamber as well as the walls of the passageway. It took hours, and they were tired, hungry, and thirsty by the time they finished, but they had not found the mark they sought.

They left the barrow in reverse of the way they had entered, Coll holding the rope while Violet scrambled up it, then Coll following, pulling up the lantern. He shoved the rocks back into place, and the two of them flopped down, leaning back against them.

"I am beginning to think that my grandmother hid those bags too well."

"Or someone else already found them."

"If someone had found them, there would have had to be at least rumors of it. Anyone coming into a large amount of money in the glen would have been noticed. And how could a stranger have stumbled over something so well hidden?"

"Perhaps we were wrong about the tomb."

"It's the only place where we've found the symbol."

"True. But perhaps I am wrong about the symbol being significant. Maybe we misunderstood the clues Faye left." Violet sighed. "Frankly, I cannot really envision a pregnant woman getting in and out of that barrow, carrying bags of gold."

"She would have been stronger than you think. She was no fine lady; she worked hard."

"But climbing up and down a rope?"

"She would have tossed the bags in, then climbed down. They were accustomed to coming here at least once a year, if we are correct in our assumptions, so perhaps they had developed an easier way to go up and down. Perhaps they had a rope ladder — or had even hidden a wooden ladder nearby. Faye was used to clambering around on the rocks near the sea and in the caves; Meg does it all the time, gathering plants for her remedies. Or she might have known of another way in — a back entrance, say."

"I suppose she could have done it. She would have had to bring down a shovel, too, and dig a hole."

"She was determined."

"I can't help but think we're missing something." Violet raised her legs, resting her crossed arms on her knees and leaning her head upon them. She thought about the young woman that day long ago, starting out to complete her task. "Do you suppose she went down there all by herself at night? Or waited till dawn and —"

"That's it!" Coll stiffened beside her, his

eyes suddenly bright. "That's the key. She hid it at dawn. On a particular day!"

28

Violet stared at him, her thoughts suddenly racing. "Yes. Of course."

"In the Long Night ceremony, the light illuminates a certain spot at dawn. But we think Faye hid the gold on the date she noted in her journal, not on the solstice."

"December sixth," Violet agreed.

"And on December sixth the light would fall on a different spot. Where it falls on that day is where she buried the treasure."

"That's it!" Violet jumped up, suddenly charged with excitement. "The date *is* the key. And the symbol, too."

"Aye, that entry in the journal tells us when and where." Coll, too, stood up.

They went straight to Faye's journal when they returned to Duncally and checked the date of Faye's entry. It was, as Coll remembered, December 6. It seemed flimsy enough evidence, and Violet worried that they were building their plans on a paper chain of guesses and ambiguous hints. Still, it was the best chance they had.

The days passed incredibly slowly. Though Violet did her best to keep her attention focused on the excavation of the ruins, her mind was often somewhere else. If she was not thinking of the upcoming exploration of the tomb, she was thinking about Coll. Happy as she was to have his affection again, something was missing. When she caught him watching her unawares, she often saw that same trace of sadness in his eyes — or perhaps it was regret. He wanted something more from her. And she could not banish the nagging feeling that perhaps she wanted something more as well.

They were awake long before dawn on the day they would go to the barrow. Violet was too jittery and anxious to sleep. She got up before dawn, leaving Coll sprawled across the bed, and went to huddle in front of the fire, stirring it into life. Before long Coll awakened and joined her by the fire.

It took only minutes to dress in their warmest clothes. They had gathered their supplies the night before and set them by the front door, and now they left the house in the blackness before dawn. Coll carried a coiled rope, a shovel resting on his shoulder, and Violet held the lantern that lit their way down the twisting path.

They talked little as they went, for the dark hush of the night discouraged speech, and the anticipation bubbling in Violet left little room for any thought save that of the adventure before them. They climbed the side of the barrow, and Coll lowered the lantern again, following it down into the tomb. Violet crouched by the opening, watching him, and it seemed suddenly cold and lonely here in the dark by herself. Coll looked up and smiled, beckoning to her, and Violet swung down to join him.

The lantern created eerie shadows and pools of light along the corridor, but at least it was warmer here than crouched above on the barrow. They settled down to wait. After a time, Coll turned down the lantern to its dimmest glow, the shields covering every side but one, so that the sunlight — if it came — would show clearly.

The dark was almost palpable, deep and brooding in the utter silence. It grew paler so gradually that it was hardly noticeable, but suddenly Violet realized that the far end of the corridor was no longer black.

"Coll?"

"Aye, I see it. Dawn's come." They walked closer to the entrance. The light came in bit by bit, a wide, pale band that ended before the corridor widened out into the large chamber.

"Well, I was expecting something a bit more dramatic." Violet frowned. Within minutes the light began to recede, the clear demarcation on the wall fading. Soon there would be only the general paler darkness that had lain in the barrow the first time they entered it.

"Perhaps it looks grander on the solstice. The angle and direction will change slightly every day." Coll took the shovel and drew a line across the floor. "Here is approximately where it ended. I hoped it would be a bit more definitive, but I'll start in the center on the theory that symmetry is a natural tendency." He raised the shields on the lantern, giving the scene more light, and plunged the shovel into the ground.

"I would not think it would be buried far beneath the surface. She was pregnant and in something of a hurry."

"I agree. I'll work my way out all around this point."

Not many inches down, the shovel struck rock. Coll shifted to a spot a few inches away. Time passed with little said, only the slice of the shovel and the clank when time after time it struck rock. The search area spread out methodically until finally Coll had exposed a large square of earth between the two stone walls.

He rested his forearms on the shovel and regarded the floor in disgust. "There is nothing here. I think we were wrong."

"Once again." Violet sat down on the floor. She had been growing increasingly certain of the same thing. "Oh, Coll . . . I was so sure we had figured it out."

"My grandmother was too clever by half." Coll set aside the shovel and squatted down beside her.

"Or we are not clever enough."

He gave her a wry grin. "Or that." He glanced around them. "I could dig up the entire floor."

"It seems a great deal of work, and it's not as if we're sure the gold is buried here. Really, when you think about it, shouldn't the ground be disturbed if she had dug a hole? I realize it's been sixty years, but the place was sealed up. The elements would not have been at work inside here."

"She would have smoothed it over, but still . . . I would think there would be some difference." Coll considered the matter. "We're on top of solid rock. The soil is very shallow. If something were buried here, there should be a hump. Yet it's level. I don't know how large the bags were, but . . ."

"You're right. I fear it's not in the barrow at all."

"It seems a very good hiding place." He glanced around. "I doubt anyone's been inside here in all that time."

"I hate to give it up as a possibility."

"But you think we should?"

Violet sighed. "I don't know where it could be. The stones lie flush against one another. There are no spaces between them wide enough to hide a sack, even a small one. No one person could have moved those stones covering the burial chambers, much less a pregnant woman. Where else is there to hide it except the floor? And after today, that looks less and less likely."

He curved his hand over her cheek. "I'm sorry. I wish I could find it for you. I'm not sure where else to look."

"Neither am I." Violet felt unaccustomedly discouraged. "I think I shall set the matter aside, at least for the moment."

"You still have your ruins," he said encouragingly.

"Yes. And they are wonderful ruins." Violet smiled at him and kissed his cheek, curling her arms around his neck. "You are a kind man, Coll."

"I dinna know if it's kindness." He looked

seriously into her eyes. "I want you to be happy."

"I want the same for you."

"Then you need not worry. How could I not be happy when I'm with you?"

Violet tightened her arms around him, squeezing him to her, and buried her face in his neck. She wished with all her heart that she believed him.

Coll rubbed the fine sandpaper over the wood, then smoothed his thumb across the piece, testing for roughness. He traced the line of the figure's cheeks and jaw, the curve of her lips. It didn't do her justice, of course; he could not recreate the exact set of her jaw or the look in her eyes. It was a fair representation of her physically, but the beauty came across too soft, without Violet's characteristic strength.

He set the wooden head back on the table, absently stroking it as he gazed across the room. He wondered where Violet was right now. Probably in the library, her head bent over a book. The last few days she had left the ruins early and spent the remainder of the afternoons in the library, searching for a clue they had overlooked in Faye's journal. Violet did not admit defeat easily.

A smile touched his lips. He could picture

her, her head propped on her hand, her eyes intent on the page before her, oblivious of all else. A strand of her hair was bound to have come loose by now and trailed down over her neck. He wished she were sitting with him in his house, where he could glance over at her as he worked and enjoy the picture she made. Where he could know she was here and safe and his.

Coll sighed and shoved to his feet. Violet would doubtless treat him to a scorching lecture if she heard him say that. She belonged to no man. He understood that . . . in a way. As for the rest of what he felt, well, it was better all around just to leave it alone. He was not about to return to those hellish days when he had separated himself from her, even if it meant concealing how her refusal to marry him still ate at him.

He went to the window and stared out at the gray day. He had never dreamed he would be caught like this. He had assumed he would eventually find the right woman, that he would live out his days in love and contentment. He would marry her and be a devoted husband and father. But for him he had been sure there would be none of the emotional fires that had afflicted others — the jealousy and fear and raging lust that drove a man mad. Not for him his father's impulsive, careless life nor the shattering heights and depths that had marked Damon's courtship of Meg. He would never know the searing terror he had seen in Isobel's eyes when she thought Jack was about to die nor the stark despair when Jack thought himself betrayed by the woman he loved.

No. He was a steady man. A careful man. Responsible. Yet here he was, his heart like an open wound, aching for a woman who would not be his. Coll Munro, who'd never feared much of anything, and now his heart quailed inside him at the thought that one day Violet would finish her work here and be gone, leaving him behind. He could not give himself to her or have her for his in any way other than physically. God knew, he seemed scarcely able to live without having her in that way. But he yearned for the rest of it, as well.

Coll ground his teeth. Reaching up, he yanked down his coat from the hook and pulled it on as he left the house. Without conscious thought, his feet turned toward the road to the village. Head down, he walked to a small, white-washed house in Kinclannoch.

He paused outside it a moment, gazing at the door. He didn't know what he was doing here. Still, he'd come all this way, and it seemed even more foolish to turn and leave now. He rapped sharply on the door, and at his father's answering call, he stepped inside.

Alan McGee was in the middle of the cottage, a pile of clothes in his hands, and glanced over at his visitor, his eyebrows soaring up. "Son! Weel, I dinna expect to see you today."

Coll took in the open valise on his father's chair and the stack of shirts in his hands. "I see you're leaving again."

"Aye. Near yuletide there's ayeways a job to be had fiddling in Edinburgh." Alan set the clothes in the bag and hauled it off the chair. "Come, sit doon, and I'll gie you a cup o' tea." He cast a questioning look at Coll. "Or a wee dram, perhaps?"

"Aye. Whiskey would be good." Coll saw the surprise, quickly hidden, on his father's face. "Am I such a stickler, then, that you dinna think I'd take a dram?" Coll flopped down on the chair and folded his arms, knowing he sounded surly, but somehow unable to keep from it.

"Och, nae, the surprise is you taking one with me." Alan pulled a jug out of a cabinet and poured a healthy splash into each of two glasses.

"You talk as though I never see you."

"Oh, nae, we see each ither at a dance or if I gae up to Duncally to visit you." Alan's blue eyes danced.

Coll scowled. "I dinna ken why I came here."

"That makes the both of us. But it doesna matter, does it?" Alan gave him the winsome smile that had sweetened many a temper and won hearts the width and breadth of the country. "You are here now, and we'll drink to that." Alan lifted his glass in a salute.

Coll sighed and drank, watching as his father poured two more shots into the glasses. "I never was in this house much." It was as much apology as explanation. "Gran wasna . . ."

"Welcoming?" Again Alan's eyes twinkled. Coll had never understood how his father could find the world so amusing. "Nae, my mither was not an easy person. She dinna like Janet overmuch." Coll snorted, and Alan dipped his head in acknowledgment. "True, she dinna like anyone overmuch. But she hardened her heart to my Jan — mithers are like that. Hard to blame them for wanting their lads to be happy."

"Were you not happy?"

"With your mither?" This time, sorrow

was in his father's smile. "Och, that was when I was the happiest, with Janet. She was a bonny, bonny lass, your ma. And not just the way she looked, you ken; she was bonny in every way. Sometimes still I can hear her laugh, and it makes me smile. I should hae said, my mither wanted me to hae what *she* counted as happiness. It wasna ever my idea of it."

"If you loved Ma so, why did you always leave?" The words were out before Coll knew it, and he glanced away, chagrined.

"I never left *her,* Son." Surprise colored Alan's voice. "You canna think I dinna want to be with Jan. Or you and Meg. I would hae taken you with me, wherever I went, but your ma was tied to this place. She couldna leave any more than I could stay here ayeways. Meg's the same, though not as much so." Alan's brow wrinkled, and he swirled the whiskey in his glass, staring into it. "I hope your sister's man understands that."

Coll grunted. "That one will stay or go as Meg pleases. You dinna need to worry. Mardoun's a bloody arrogant Sassenach, but Meg's his center. He'll not leave her, any more than —" Coll broke off and drained his glass. This time it was he who picked up the jug and poured again.

"Good, then. You'd understand that better than I. The not leaving, I mean."

Coll shrugged and downed the whiskey.

"What is it, Coll?" His father watched him. "What's troubling you?"

"How did you do it?" Coll's voice came out quiet but fierce, and he leaned forward, setting the glass down hard on the table. "How did you stand to be with her and not really have her? If you loved her, how could you not want to marry her?"

"Whoever said I dinna want to marry Janet?" Alan asked reasonably. "Surely you dinna think I was the one who wouldna take the vows?"

"No. I know. But did it not eat you up inside? Knowing she would not let you —" Coll shook his head, unable to find the words, and curled his fingers into his palm.

"I take it this is about the lady with the ruins. The one with the lovely name and the eyes like a doe." Coll shot him a sullen glance, and Alan hid a smile. "Och, weel, Son, there are some women you canna own."

"I do not want to own her. Why do you assume that? Why does she? Am I such a monster? Am I so overbearing, so dictatorial?"

"Dinna play the fool, Coll. You know no

one thinks you're a monster. But you are the sort of man who — who fills up a room. Who does things. Fixes things. Takes charge. You want people to be . . . better than they are."

"I dinna ask her to change. I certainly would not demand it. And she's no shy flower, despite her name. She'll argue you into the ground over whether some bloody rock should be up or down. She has no fear of me or any man." Coll jumped to his feet as if unable to sit still and began to pace the small room. "She knows I would never hurt her."

"Of course you wouldna."

"Or force her."

"Clearly."

"Or push her to do anything."

"Weel, now, there I dinna think you can say you would not push if you thought it for the best."

Coll swung around to glare at him. "As if she would not do the same! She is the pushiest woman I have ever met. She *likes* to argue. She *likes* to poke and prod at me until I want to —" He broke off and plopped back into the chair. "Well, you know what I want to do."

"I've a fair idea," Alan agreed wryly. He chuckled. "Ah, she sounds like a grand woman, Coll."

"She is. I just want . . ."

"Yes? What is it you want of her?"

"I want to *be* with her. I want to marry her. I want to give her my name. I want her to bear my children. I want to see her hold them and cuddle them and scold them. I want a life with her." Coll sighed, bracing his elbows on the table, and dropped his head into his hands, fingers pushing into his skull. "And she does not." He looked up at his father, his eyes desolate. "She does not love me."

"She told you this?"

"No." Coll grimaced.

"Then how do you know?"

"It's clear, is it not? She will not marry me."

"So you believe your mither did not love me because she wouldna marry me? That she lied when she told me she did?"

"Nae! Ma did not lie. Everyone knew she loved you."

"However foolish that was of her."

"I dinna say that."

"Weel, I suppose I should be thankful for that." Alan sat back, studying Coll, folding his arms across his chest in a mirror image of his son, which anyone other than the two of them would have recognized. "But this woman, your Violet, is the sort of woman who *would* lie about it?"

"No! Not at all. She's damnably blunt. She never said she loved me; she never pretended to."

"She must hae given you some encouragement for you to ask for her hand."

Coll shrugged.

"Och . . . getting words out of you is a miserable business. Does the woman hae no interest in you? No interest in men? Does she want nothing to do with you?"

"Oh, no, she's fine with that! Bedding down is perfectly acceptable to her." Coll stopped, looking abashed. "No, I should not have said that. I dinna mean — you must not think — Violet is not loose. She's not known any man but me — oh, bloody hell!" Coll jumped to his feet again. "I canna talk to you about that."

"I'd just as well you not." Alan paused, frowning. "But I dinna understand. I thought you said you could not be with her. But now you're saying she would be happy to have the . . . um, sort of life that Janet and —"

"Yes!" Coll flung out his hands. "Yes. She, apparently, would like that. She does not care that I canna take her hand or that I have to mind how I look at her in front of

Mardoun's servants. It doesna bother her that I have to sneak into her bed at night and out again before the maids get up. Indeed, she said why worry about it, as if that would not make her a scandal on the tongue of everyone in the glen. I dinna want to have to pummel every man who makes a remark about her — and I canna do so with the women. But I will not have her scorned. I will not be the sort of man who exposes her to their gossip."

"The sort of man I was." Alan rose to face him.

"I dinna say that." Coll looked away.

"You dinna hae to. Do you think I dinna ken what you think of me? What I'm sure others think of me?"

"This isn't about you or Ma."

"Is it not?" Alan swung away. "I was not the father you wanted. Or needed. I admit that. I love my music; I canna stay anywhere long; I dinna know how to be an upright man or a guid father."

"Da . . . no . . . do not . . ."

"Hsst." Alan raised his hand in a stopping gesture. "You listen to me this once. Whatever I am or however I hae lived my life, I loved your mother. I never touched another woman from the time I first kissed her. I gave Janet everything she asked of me, every

481

part of me she would take. Mayhap she dinna love me as much as I loved her. Or mayhap it was that she wanted something else as much as she wanted me. But I loved her enough, I was man enough, to let her love me as she wanted. To let her live the life she needed no matter what others might think of me for doing so."

Coll turned to him, frowning. "Da, I'm sor—"

"Nae. I'm done with it. I am as I am. You are as you are. And no doubt you'd be a far better husband and father than I ever was. But I want to give you one bit of fatherly advice. In all your thinking about what you want of her, what you want to do or be or what other people think of you, have you considered what *she* wants of you? Do you love this woman enough to give her what she needs?"

Coll had no answer for him.

It was a long walk back to Duncally, and Coll took it slowly. As he walked through the gates, he heard Violet calling his name. His head snapped up. She ran down the drive toward him, her face lit from within.

"Coll! Coll! I have it! I figured it out!"

29

He opened his arms and Violet leaped into them. "What are you talking about? What do you have?"

"The answer!" She kissed him hard, then raised her head. "At least, I think it's the answer."

"You aren't making any sense. Here." He set her back down on the ground. "Take a few breaths." He led her into the gatehouse and sat her down at the table. "Now, what is this all about?"

"The treasure. I realized where I went wrong about the treasure. We were looking for it on the wrong day!"

"It wasn't the date Faye wrote in her journal?"

"No, it was on that date." His eyebrows shot up, and Violet hastened to add, "Wait, just listen." She drew a deep breath. "It was the day *she* knew as December sixth. But it is not the date we know as December sixth.

They changed the calendar."

Coll dropped down onto the chair beside her. "I beg your pardon?"

"In 1750, they changed the calendar!"

"Who changed the calendar?"

"England. It had been changing all over Europe for some time, but they didn't do it in Britain until an act of Parliament in 1750. I should have realized this before."

"Explain this to me. How could the calendar change?"

"For years everyone followed the Julian calendar, which established a year of twelve months and 365 days."

"Aye. Like now."

"Yes, except for the way they accounted for leap years. You have to add an extra day every so often to keep in tune with the actual cycle of the earth, you see."

"I understand that. Leap year."

"Well, the Julian calendar added that extra day too often. The result was that over years and years and years, the real seasonal equinoxes were falling on dates that were too early. It would throw church holidays like Easter into the wrong season. So during the sixteenth century, the Gregorian calendar came into use. For a while both were in use in different countries. England did not adopt the new calendar until an act of Parliament in 1750."

"All right. What does that mean about the treasure?"

"By the time they adopted the new calendar, they were eleven days off. So suddenly the calendars jumped forward eleven days. They also changed the month when the year was considered to begin, but that doesn't matter here. What is important is that in 1747, the date Faye hid the treasure was December sixth. But if it had been under the calendar we use now, it would have been eleven days past that. December seventeenth."

"Oh." Light dawned in Coll's eyes. "It might not matter about a number of other things what date was attributed to something, but it matters very much if you are talking about the position of the sun."

"Exactly. It's the time dawn arrived on the day Faye hid the treasure that is important, not what number has been given to that day." Violet sat back, her face flushed with excitement. "In 1747, the winter solstice would have been on December tenth. Today it is on December twenty-first."

"And on December seventeenth, the sunlight will fall in the barrow on the same spot that it fell when Faye put it there on

December sixth."

"So we were not wrong in the theory; we were simply wrong about the date. Instead of last week, we need to dig for it the day after tomorrow."

Coll grinned. "Good thing you didn't think of this in January."

They waited again in the darkness. Violet's nerves danced, and she laced her fingers through Coll's, clutching his hand to steady her. Everything was always much easier with Coll beside her. The thought of his not being there was enough to send cold chills through her. Not, she realized, because she would have been frightened or could not have done it without him, but simply because everything without him would be wrong.

She glanced up at Coll. Like her, he was watching the corridor, waiting for dawn, but feeling her gaze on him, Coll turned and smiled at her. Violet could see him only dimly in the light. His eyes were shadows. Just looking at him made her heart turn over. It occurred to her that whether she married him or not, she was under his control. He already owned her heart.

The thought took her breath away, and she turned her head. An arrow of light flashed into existence, bright and pointed, spearing into the darkness of the room.

"Coll . . ." she breathed, staring.

"I see." He tightened his hand around hers.

The ray of light moved forward. It was not the diffuse glow they had witnessed eleven days earlier, but an intense shaft of light, focused into a point. As they watched, it touched the ground at the end of the corridor. Behind the bright spear, light fanned out in a narrow triangle of a paler glow.

As if it were a living creature, the beam flowed across the floor. When it reached the wall, it inched upward, halting just below the large stone bearing the whorl symbol. It remained there, unmoving.

"Impressive." Coll's voice was hushed, almost reverent.

"Yes. Can you imagine how that must have appeared to a primitive people? Like a miracle, a sign from the universe."

"I know how it appeared to me." Coll studied the finger of light. "Do you think it's buried at the bottom of that wall?"

"I'm not sure. Look, now it's moving down. Receding. I think it's that specific stone."

"So do I, but how — I mean, the rock is part of the wall."

"Yes, but it lies right beneath that cross-beam. The heavy stones above it are actually supported by the long rock, which in turn is supported by the vertical slabs of stone."

"True. That stone doesn't actually bear any weight."

As the light inched backward, Coll crossed to the rock in question, Violet beside him. Grasping the edges of the rock, he wiggled it. Stone scraped against stone as he pulled the rock toward him. It slid out, and he set the stone carefully on the floor. He looked at Violet, the two of them barely daring to breathe. Holding up the lantern, he lifted its shield so that the light filled the hole where the rock had been. On one side was the tall, upright support column of a long stone. Below and beside the empty space were rocks twice as long as the one he had pulled out.

In the empty space behind the stone he had removed lay three leather bags. Violet let out a long, wordless breath.

"The French gold." Coll reached in and pulled out the bags.

They were heavy. He set them on the floor side by side, and for a moment they simply looked at them. Then Violet knelt and untied one. Her fingers trembled as she pulled the bag open. Reaching in, she picked up a single coin and examined it.

"Louis d'or," she murmured.

Coll thrust his hand inside, lifting out a palmful of gold coins and letting them sift back into the sack.

"I can hardly believe it." Violet turned a tremulous smile on Coll. "There is your model crofters' village."

"Aye. And your school." He lowered his head to kiss her. "Whatever you want to do. Wherever you want to go."

Strangely, pain pierced Violet at that thought. She turned away quickly and opened the other bags. One was as full of gold coins as the first. The third was half-full of louis d'or pieces, but the remainder was filled with precious gems. Violet wrapped her arms around Coll's neck and pressed herself against him. Emotions swept through her, and she could do nothing but cling to him, teetering perilously on the edge of tears. His arms wrapped around her like iron bands, and he lowered his mouth to hers.

It was several minutes later before they released each other, though Coll snatched her back for one brief, hard kiss before he stood up. The light had receded into the corridor again. A moment later it was gone.

Coll carefully replaced the stone that had concealed the treasure, and picking up the lantern, they carried the sacks back to the entryway. Coll had had the foresight today to store a wooden ladder near the entrance, so it was easier to climb out. Violet went first. She stopped near the top of the ladder and Coll handed the bags up to her one by one. She set them down on the ground just outside the entrance hole, then scrambled up the last few rungs and out onto the ground. On her hands and knees, she started to rise.

Someone grabbed her around the waist, jerking her up and back against him. Violet let out a startled cry and began to struggle, but something hard and round jabbed into her temple. It was unmistakably the barrel of a pistol. She went still.

"Violet?" Coll's voice came from below, and she heard the sound of his feet rushing up the ladder.

"Coll, no!"

"Shut up!" a male voice barked in her ear. He went on, "Come on up, Coll, and join us."

Coll's head and shoulders emerged from the opening. It was too small a hole and at too much of an angle for him to exit it in a rush. "Donald MacRae. You bloody bastard."

Coll crawled the rest of the way out and stood up. The look in his eyes would have made an intelligent man shiver, Violet thought, but the man holding her let out a high, excited laugh.

"Aye. It's me. And I'm going to be a rich man."

"So it *was* you. You were in on it with Will Ross. Is that where you stayed after you left the village?" Coll took a step toward them.

"No closer!" MacRae cocked the pistol. Coll stopped, raising his hands in a peacemaking gesture. "Yes, I had to live in that miserable hovel because of you. But I wasn't 'in on it' with that peasant. Will Ross worked for me."

"Did he now?"

"Yes, he began to bring me things when I moved to Inverness, items he stole, and I sold them for him. But I was able to see a grander scheme. So I set him to looking for the treasure."

Coll grinned. "You thought he would turn the treasure over to you when he stole it? You were always a stupid man, MacRae."

"I'd be careful of calling me stupid when you're the one giving me that gold. I'd say the intelligent man is the one who lets others do his work for him. Now hand over those bags."

Coll bent to pick up one of the bags and started forward.

"No!" MacRae screeched. "Just toss it." When Coll swung his arm back, MacRae snapped, "Gently."

"Aye, I'll be gentle." Coll tossed the bag softly to the ground in front of Violet.

The gunman let go of Violet's waist and poked her in the back. "Pick it up."

"I won't."

"What?" MacRae's voice rose.

"Violet, no . . ." Coll tensed.

"I said, I won't." Violet turned her head toward her captor, which drew a strangled sound from Coll and a curse from MacRae, but he did not fire.

"You will if you bloody well want to stay alive! Now pick it up."

"Or what, you will shoot me?" Violet gazed at him coolly. "Surely you realize how nonsensical that is. If you shoot me, you will have thrown away your bargaining power over Coll. Moreover, you will have used your one bullet, which was the only advantage you had. Coll will therefore attack you, and being far taller, heavier, and stronger than you, not to mention in a rage, he will overcome you easily. If you are lucky, he won't beat you to death, only cause you a great deal of pain. Then you will be arrested for murder as well as theft."

MacRae's face flooded with fury. "Shut up!" The pistol trembled in his hand. "Pick up the damned gold."

"Are you deaf as well as stupid?" Violet crossed her arms over her chest. "I said no."

"You will do as I say!" MacRae roared, gesturing wildly with the pistol.

Coll flung himself forward, pushing Violet aside as he rammed into MacRae's stomach. She flung herself to the ground. The pistol went off, the ball shooting harmlessly up into the air.

The air went out of MacRae in a whoosh as Coll slammed him into the ground. MacRae flailed his arms and legs, gasping for breath until Coll knocked him out with a blow to the point of his chin. Shoving the man aside, Coll scrambled over to Violet.

"Are you all right?" He ran his hands over her, checking for injuries. "Did he hurt you?"

Violet flung her arms around his neck. "Coll! Yes, I'm fine. It's all right. Really, I'm not hurt."

He sat down on the ground, cradling her to him and pressing his lips to her head in a flurry of kisses. "Lord save me, Violet! You scared the devil out of me, taking him on like that. What in hell possessed you?"

"I knew if I made him angry enough, it would distract him, and you could take him by surprise. I'm not big enough to fight him, but I am very good at infuriating people."

Coll began to laugh. "Ah, lass, that you are." He tilted up her chin and kissed her thoroughly. "I always knew you could argue a man into the ground."

Coll bound MacRae's hands and feet and left him at the barrow, then took Violet and the treasure home. After locking the gold away securely in the safe in the butler's pantry — Violet had the feeling Coll would dearly have liked to lock her away there, too — he went back to march MacRae into town.

Violet waited for Coll in the library. She spent most of the time pacing about the room, too surging with thoughts and emotions to sit still. When at last she heard Coll's tread in the hallway outside, she ran to the door. "Coll!"

He was walking down the hall, hands in his pockets, obviously in a deep study. He lifted his head, and his face was so sober and grim that Violet felt suddenly uncertain, even shy. "Coll. Are you all right?"

"Of course." He gave her a faint smile that did little to strengthen his words. "MacRae is locked up."

"Who was that man? I've never seen him."

"Probably the last person I expected to see. He used to be Mardoun's steward, the filthy scum. Mardoun sent him packing when he found out what sort of man he was and how ill he had treated the earl's crofters. I thought him long gone from here. Everyone did. But apparently he's been hiding in the hills, biding his time and cozying up to fellows like Will Ross. They used to be on opposite sides, but when it came down to it, they found common ground in thievery."

"You look very tired." Violet had her speech all prepared, but looking at Coll, she thought it was not the best time to bring up the matter. "Would you like some tea? Whiskey?"

He shook his head. "Nae. I — I want to talk to you, Violet. I need to talk to you."

His words stirred her uneasiness even more. "Coll . . ."

"You have money now. You can do what you want. Go where you want."

"Coll, why are you saying this?" Violet's heart thudded, her stomach turning to ice. "What do you mean?"

"I want to know . . . do you plan to leave?"

"Leave here?" She gaped at him.

"Aye." He raised his head, his face taut, shoulders braced. "Leave me."

"No!" Violet stared at him. "No, why would you think that?" She hesitated. "Are you — do you want me to leave?"

"God, no! Are you mad?"

She relaxed at his stunned expression. "I don't know. I thought perhaps I was going mad. The last I'd heard, you wanted to marry me."

"No." He held up his hand. "Dinna worry. I am not asking you to marry me."

"You're not?"

"No. But I — I want to be with you."

"I want to be with you, too. Coll, I've been thinking . . ."

"No, I'm nae finished." He drew in a breath. "I dinna want to . . . to bully you or browbeat you into doing something you don't want to." He paused, then added candidly, "Though I probably would if I thought it would work."

Violet smiled and reached out to take his hands in hers. "I am glad you realize that it won't. But you are welcome to try, if you wish."

"You will want to finish the ruins, I suppose."

"Yes. And the barrow."

"And the barrow. But eventually, you will be done here. You will want to leave. And when you do, I want to go with you."

"Really?" Violet's eyes widened in surprise, and a knot unwound in her chest. "You would not mind leaving the Highlands?"

"No. I would like to come back, from time to time. But I would like to see other places. It would be . . . freeing, I think, not to have to . . . deal with everyone."

"You mean, not to have to solve everyone's problems."

"Maybe." A smile twitched at the corner of his mouth. "But that is not the point. The thing is, I want to be with you."

"I want to be with you, too." Violet moved closer, bringing their linked hands up to her chest and cradling them to her.

"I'm glad." His blue eyes warmed. "I know you dinna want to marry me."

"Coll, I —"

"No, wait, let me finish. I'm not asking you to. But I want . . . more than this. I want to be with you in every way. To live with you. I want to sleep with you in the same bed and wake up with you in the morning. I know you dinna belong to me. But I need to belong to you."

"Coll!" She drew in a sharp breath, and tears glimmered in her eyes.

Seeing them, Coll rushed on. "I have no interest in ruling you. I dinna want to own you or have rights over you. But I do want — I want very badly — to have the right to be with you. I hope that I can give you what you want, be what you want in a man. But I must be what I can respect as well. I love you. I love you more than anyone or anything in this world. I want to say so before the world. I want to pledge myself to you, to commit myself to you and to our children, to give you my vow that I will be with you always, loving no one but you. I want to join my life to yours."

She squeezed his hands, swallowing hard, love rushing up in her so fast and strong she could hardly breathe.

"And I'm asking you to pledge yourself to me, as well. I want to know if you feel the same. If you will give yourself to me as I give myself to you. Not for the law or other people or the church or anything else. Just for the two of us."

Tears ran down Violet's cheeks. She was so filled with emotion that she could not talk, could not think, could only let the tears spill over in crystal drops.

"Nae, love, please . . . dinna cry." Coll

smoothed his thumbs across her cheeks. "I dinna want to make you sad."

"I'm not. I'm not sad. Really. Oh, Coll, I cannot speak!"

"Now there's a wonder." He smiled and pressed his lips to her forehead. "There is a ceremony they used to do here: a handfast."

"I know." Violet nodded. "We talked about it once, when I first saw the stones."

"That is what I am asking you to do. To pledge ourselves to each other at the Troth Stone, as they used to."

"Oh, Coll." Violet pressed her fingers against her lips. She began to cry in earnest.

"I've upset you. Dinna fear." He brushed his hand over her hair, his face etched in sorrow. "I will not push you."

"No! Oh, no, Coll, I am not crying because I don't want to do it. I'm — I'm just so very happy!" Violet threw her arms around him and clung to him.

"Happy?" His arms curved around her, and he leaned his head down to hers. "I don't understand."

"I don't either!" She sniffed, wiping at her cheeks, and smiled, going up on tiptoe to kiss him. "I love you." She smattered kisses all over his face as she rattled on breathlessly. "There in the tomb, when you held me, I knew that none of those things mattered. All that mattered was that I love you. I can't separate myself from you; you have my heart. I am yours. I want to be yours. And you are mine," she added fiercely. "All the time you were gone, I was working out what to say, how to tell you I would marry you. In a church or at the Troth Stone, I don't care. Whatever you want."

"Oh, Violet, my love, my love." Coll laughed and squeezed her to him. "All I want is your love."

"That you already have. I pledge myself to you, forever and always."

"And I to you." He bent to kiss her. "Forever and always."

EPILOGUE

They were joined the next month at the Troth Stone, when Coll's sister and the earl had returned to Duncally. With Isobel and Jack on one side and Meg and Damon on the other, Violet and Coll stood and clasped hands through the ancient stone and spoke their vows in sure, firm tones.

People came from all over the glen for a celebration afterward at Duncally, to join in the dancing and laughter and joy. Alan Mc-Gee played for them, and Coll was persuaded to sing a song to his bride. For that he earned a kiss from Violet. Old Angus insisted on a dance with her.

Meg, glowing and more beautiful than ever, stood with Coll and watched as the crusty old man circled the floor with Violet.

"Who would have thought it would happen like this?" Meg sent her brother a sparkling glance. "That I, the wicked woman of the glen who vowed never to marry, would marry my love all prim and proper in a church — and you would be the one to live handfast."

"Och, I've always been the wild one, Meg." Coll grinned, his eyes going back to Violet. "It just took the right woman to let me be what I am."

The party was still in full swing when Coll took Violet's hand and whisked her unnoticed out a side door.

"Coll . . . we cannot just leave," Violet protested, laughing. "Surely we should say good-bye."

"Nae, it's the only way. Otherwise, they'll carry us over to the house and plague us to death. You dinna want to see it." He curled his arm around her shoulders, and they strolled to the gatehouse, too happy, too full of love, to mind the cold.

At the door, Coll swept Violet up in his arms and carried her over the threshold. "There's our luck for life." He closed the door and lowered the bar. "And that will hold them all at bay."

"And now?" Violet smiled up at him, linking her arms around his neck.

"Ah, now . . . now we have each other. It's all I want." He bent to kiss her. *"Mo cuishle."*